THE ITALIAN RENAISSANCE READER

EDITED BY
JULIA CONAWAY BONDANELLA
AND MARK MUSA

A reader that spans two centuries of important writing in Italian art, literature, and the political and social sciences, this volume also includes the following outstanding features:

- a general critical Introduction by Julia Conaway Bondanella
- introductions to and biographical information on each author
- helpful commentaries on each work
- individual bibliographies
- new translations that modernize punctuation and vocabulary for readability
- a list of suggested further readings

JULIA CONAWAY BONDANELLA is Associate Professor and Associate Director of the Honors Division at Indiana University. She is the author of *Petrarch's Visions and Their Renaissance Analogues* and is co-editor of the *Dictionary of Italian Literature*.

MARK MUSA, a former Fulbright and Guggenheim Fellow, is the co-translator of the highly acclaimed Mentor edition of Boccaccio's *Decameron*, as well as Dante's *Divine Comedy*.

D0964823

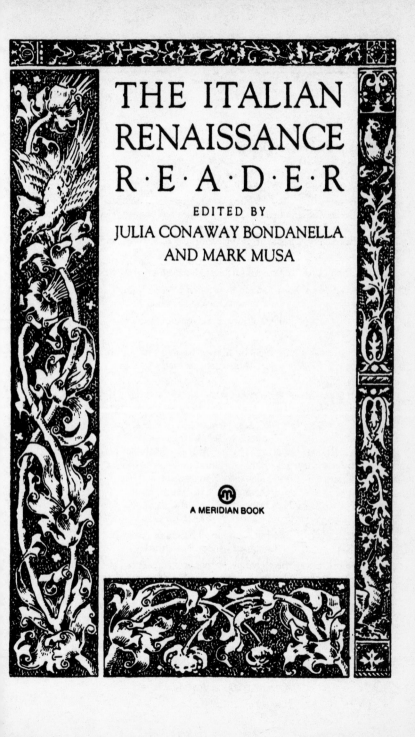

THE ITALIAN
RENAISSANCE
R·E·A·D·E·R

EDITED BY

JULIA CONAWAY BONDANELLA
AND MARK MUSA

A MERIDIAN BOOK

FOR PETER

MERIDIAN
Published by the Penguin Group
Penguin Books USA Inc., 375 Hudson Street,
New York, New York 10014, U.S.A.
Penguin Books Ltd, 27 Wrights Lane, London W8 5TZ, England
Penguin Books Australia Ltd, Ringwood, Victoria, Australia
Penguin Books Canada Ltd, 10 Alcorn Avenue, Toronto, Ontario, Canada,
M4V 3B2
Penguin Books (N.Z.) Ltd, 182–190 Wairau Road, Auckland 10, New
Zealand

Penguin Books Ltd, Registered Offices: Harmondsworth, Middlesex, England

Published by Meridian, an imprint of Dutton Signet, a division of
Penguin Books USA Inc.

First Printing, November, 1987
24 25 23

Copyright © 1987 by Mark Musa and Julia Bondanella
All rights reserved

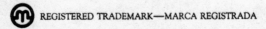 REGISTERED TRADEMARK—MARCA REGISTRADA

LIBRARY OF CONGRESS CATALOGING IN PUBLICATION DATA:
The Italian Renaissance reader.
1. Italian literature—15th century.   2. Italian literature—
16th century.   3. Italy—Civilization—1268-1559.   4. Italy—
Civilization—1559-1789.   5. Renaissance—Italy.   I. Bondanella,
Julia Conaway.   II. Musa, Mark.
PQ4204.A3183   1987   850'.8   87-15354
ISBN 0-452-01013-6

Printed in the United States of America
Designed by Barbara Huntley

CONTENTS

· ❦ ·

PREFACE

· ❧ ·

The Italian Renaissance Reader provides within a single volume an intro-
duction to some major Italian writers of the Renaissance, poets, political
and social thinkers, and artists, for students in a number of disciplines.
Selections were made on the basis of two criteria: their importance
within the Italian Renaissance, and their relevance to other national
cultures of the period. The selections are arranged in chronological order,
and each is preceded by a brief introductory commentary, which, along
with the other annotations, is intended to assist the readers in under-
standing the context and content of the works.

Selections from Giovanni Boccaccio are taken from *The Decameron*,
eds. and trans. Mark Musa and Peter Bondanella (New York: New
American Library, 1982); some of those from Petrarch originally ap-
peared in Francesco Petrarca, *Selections from the Canzoniere and Other
Writings*, ed. and trans. Mark Musa (Oxford: Oxford University Press,
1985), while a number of Petrarch's lyric poems were freshly translated
for this anthology by Mark Musa. The translation of Machiavelli's *Prince*
reprinted here originally appeared in *The Prince*, ed. Peter Bondanella
and trans. and ed. Peter Bondanella and Mark Musa (Oxford: Oxford
University Press, 1984), which was itself a revised version of an earlier
edition first published in *The Portable Machiavelli*, eds. and trans. Peter
Bondanella and Mark Musa (New York: Penguin, 1979).

The passages from Alberti, Pico, Leonardo, Castiglione, Guicciardini,
and Cellini are fresh translations done especially for this anthology by
Julia Conaway Bondanella and Mark Musa. The translations from Mi-
chelangelo and Vasari are new translations done by Julia Conaway
Bondanella.

The editorial apparatus (introduction, introductory commentaries,
bibliographies, and the notes not previously published in earlier editions)
was prepared by Julia Conaway Bondanella.

Our debt to Peter Bondanella for his significant contributions to
different stages of this project is incalculable.

I also offer special thanks to Deborah Hoskins for able proofreading,
to Bruce Cole and Adelheid Gealt for valuable suggestions, and, most
particularly, to Chandler Beall and Walter King for enduring inspiration.

J. C. B.

INTRODUCTION

———————— · ❦ · ————————

The Italian Renaissance gave rise to a robust and exuberant vision of human life, but over the centuries its dimensions have escaped exact definition and engendered controversy. The Renaissance in Italy spaned the period roughly from Petrarch's lifetime (1303–73) to the mid-sixteenth century. Much debate has arisen over what this Renaissance was like and how it differed from the Middle Ages. Jacob Burckhardt, the famous nineteenth-century Swiss historian, claimed that the Italian Renaissance came to constitute the foundations of the modern world.* More recent historians have argued that, in economic terms, the Renaissance was actually a period of decline, which began with the catastrophic Black Death. Drawing a distinction between the political, social, and cultural character of the Renaissance and the Middle Ages can be misleading, but there was a perceptible shift in vision that caused even thinkers of the time to conceive of a rebirth. Certain crucial changes in the way people lived and thought produced a transition from the medieval orientation to that typical of the modern world.

AFTER THE EMPIRE

As the land of the ancient Romans and the birthplace of many great artists, writers, statesmen, and popes, Italy has always exercised a special power over the Western imagination. Separated from the rest of the continent by Europe's greatest mountain ranges, the boot-shaped peninsula stretches for six hundred miles southward toward Africa and is nowhere more than eighty miles wide. Its remarkable light, magnificent mountain chains, and clear coastal waters tend to obscure the essential harshness of the terrain, the ruggedness of the hillsides, the sparseness of the vegetation, and its inhospitable marshes.

*See his *Civilization of the Renaissance in Italy*, 2 vols. (New York: Harper & Row, 1958).

INTRODUCTION

Within the peninsula, the awesome ranges of the Apennines raise natural barriers between the habitable places that came to harbor the great city-states of the Renaissance—Florence, Venice, Rome, Milan—as well as the Kingdom of Naples. South of the Alps and Dolomites, which divide Italy from the rest of Europe, lie the great and fertile Po valley and the provinces of Lombardy, the Veneto, and Emilia Romagna, with the cities of Milan, Venice, Ferrara, Mantua, Padua, and Bologna. Beyond the northwestern ridges of the Apennines, which bifurcate the peninsula from east to west and north to south, is Tuscany and the valley of the Arno, with its cities of Florence, Pisa, Siena, and Arezzo. Over the central Apennines to the southeast are the Marches with the small hilltop town of Urbino, immortalized in Castiglione's *Book of the Courtier*. Farther south, Rome is situated in another relatively level area that leads into the rugged mountainous interior, still part of the central Apennine chain, and toward Naples. The southern Apennines reach far into the toe of the boot. Finally, to the west, Mount Etna rises over the coastal cities of Sicily, whose medieval monarch, King Frederick II, was a great patron of the arts, a worthy heir to the Greeks and Romans among whose monuments he lived.

Italy's geography was not the only impediment to political unity, which came only late in the nineteenth century. After the abdication of the Emperor Romulus Augustulus in 476 A.D., the result of constant struggles for power among various Germanic tribes including the Ostrogoths, Franks, and Visigoths, there was a continual fragmentation of power. The early Germanic invaders established kingdoms after the Roman model, but the fusion of Roman political, legal, and cultural traditions with Christian views and Germanic customs gave rise to feudal institutions, which flourished in various degrees from around 850 to 1300. As the Empire disintegrated, the early popes attempted to fill the vacuum, but they proved too weak to enforce their will against powerful bishops, local lords, and resourceful families.

Eventually, Pope Leo III enlisted an ally in Charlemagne, whom he illegally crowned Holy Roman Emperor on Christmas Day in 800 in order to shore up the power of the papacy. This gave the northern Europeans a foothold in Italy to which they clung long past the Renaissance. From a historical point of view, considerations of the Renaissance in Italy must take into account the impact of the continual struggles between the pope, the Holy Roman Emperor, and other foreign invaders (especially those from France), the increasingly powerful city-states with their new political and social structures, and small armies of mercenary soldiers marauding throughout the peninsula.

INTRODUCTION

In Italy, the decline of the feudal system and the Holy Roman Empire gave rise to autonomous city-states with a secular orientation and diverse forms of government, professional armies, increasingly sophisticated forms of diplomacy, and the practice of keeping permanent civic records, all of which resembled ancient practices much more than the medieval. The late medieval and Renaissance Italian cities were not only geographically isolated, but they erected fortifications to protect themselves from invaders. Many of these walls can still be seen today in cities from Milan to Rome. Even individual cities within naturally defined regions, despite their similarities in customs and appearances, often found allies at a distance to protect their private concerns from encroaching neighbors. If anything, the competition between the cities of a region was all the more fierce for their proximity. Florence, for example, was constantly at war with Pisa and Siena, and they in turn formed alliances with such distant powers as Milan; Emilia Romagna was allied with the Church and Rome rather than with Milan or Venice; and Milan, Venice, and the Church states bargained with the Holy Roman Emperor and the French against each other.

From the eleventh to the thirteenth centuries, the economy recovered from the decline of Rome and the barbarian invasions, although there were setbacks in the fourteenth century with an agricultural crisis and a financial crisis following the Black Death. The rugged landscape and a tenacious and sometimes provincial civic patriotism constantly mitigated against communication and cooperation, but at the same time Italy had important advantages of location and heritage that inspired her impressive cultural and economic contributions. Lying at the heart of southern Europe with a commanding position in the Mediterranean, Italy was ideally situated to serve as Europe's gateway to the world just when the medieval West was experiencing an economic, political, and cultural recovery. Italy's great seafaring cities, Venice and Genoa, controlled trade from Asia, Africa, and the Middle East, bringing into Europe new goods, peoples, and ideas, from the precious spices of the Orient to the scientific knowledge that flourished in the Middle East after the fall of the Roman Empire.

Despite intense internecine rivalries, inhabitants of individual cities thought of themselves as Italians. Early poets and writers, inspired by their common ancient Roman heritage, conceived of a nation named Italy and wrote impassioned pleas for Italian unification, including Petrarch's famous *canzone* "Italia mia" and Machiavelli's *Prince*, a book that eloquently analyzes the Italian predicament and gives practical advice to a prince capable of taking advantage of a unique opportunity to unite his country. No doubt the inhabitants of the peninsula shared a common source of inspiration in their belief that they were the descendants of the ancient Romans as well as the guardians of Christianity, some of whose holiest places were in the Eternal City. Indeed, Italy has always been united more by its language, culture, and religion than by its political institutions.

RENAISSANCE ITALIAN SOCIETY

After the millennium, medieval Western civilization experienced momentous transformations—population increased, commerce and foreign trade flourished, new lands came under cultivation, frontiers were pushed back, urban areas were revitalized, and higher culture once again thrived. Governments and institutions were reorganized and stabilized; new political and social structures developed. Even the Christian Church and its theology were examined and reformed. Artists became active in the service of the church and eventually turned to wealthy secular patrons. The magnitude of these changes and their impact on every sphere of Western life laid the foundations for the Italian Renaissance, which set Western culture on a new course.

The feudal organization in Italy, which arose out of the disorders following the disintegration of the Roman Empire, yielded power to the cities. Classical civic traditions survived in many places, and power came to rest in the hands of the communes. The traditional medieval view of social organization, with its emphasis on hierarchy, assumed that humans functioned in specific roles in the social order. Each person was expected to carry out the task that fell to him or her, with the good of the individual subordinated to that of the whole. However, from the eleventh to the thirteenth centuries, the economy recovered from the decline of Rome and the barbarian invasions. A newly emerging urban, mercantile economy capable of producing wealth unknown since Roman times created the possibility of civic participation and gracious living, and it soon became apparent that earthly existence might be shaped by talented individuals to produce the fullest personal satisfactions.

The growth and commercial success of the Italian city-states of the Renaissance and the particular configuration of the urban family stimulated and encouraged cultural and intellectual pursuits and artistic production.* In order to enjoy the benefits of the new economy and to

*For an excellent analysis of social change during the Italian Renaissance, see David Herlihy and Christiane Klapisch-Zuber, *Tuscans and Their Families: A Study of the Florentine Catasto of 1427* (New Haven: Yale University Press, 1985).

establish themselves financially, men married later in life. Thus, in the cities, older men tended to marry younger women. Since husbands discouraged their wives from remarrying after their deaths, the urban population failed to increase at the same rate as the population of the countryside. To increase their labor force, cities encouraged immigration from the country, and provided opportunities for skilled and talented immigrants such as Giovanni Boccaccio and Leonardo da Vinci.

The increasing complexity and expansion of commercial activities forced people to educate themselves, and as they did, they developed more refined and elevated tastes. Even girls were often given some education, since literacy was necessary for the wives of shopkeepers, merchants, and aristocrats who had to manage households and businesses. Women, who took most of the responsibility for the education of children, influenced the revival of arts and letters. The domestic concerns of the age also inspired such books as Leon Battista Alberti's *Book of the Family*, in which he explained how wives should be chosen, children raised, domestic matters managed, and friends cultivated. Many other treatises were devoted to educational reform and the development of humanistic education.

The vigorous, competitive, and volatile nature of Italian society also brought members of Italian families to seek civilized ways of governing their relationships with others. The period produced many essays on manners, the most famous and widely read of which was probably Baldassare Castiglione's *Book of the Courtier*, which served Europeans as a guidebook to the proper comportment of gentlemen and ladies not simply at court but in polite society everywhere. All of Europe emulated his courtiers.

The instability of urban life was also exacerbated by the high mortality rate in the fourteenth and fifteenth centuries throughout Europe. The Black Death, described in Boccaccio's *Decameron*, afflicted young adults. Hence, few lived to old age, and the rapid turnover of leaders gave room to young, dynamic, creative types in every field. The tempo of cultural change was not slowed by an older generation clinging to tradition. With little of the generational strife typical of more recent times, the Renaissance in Italy was an age of opportunity for men of energy and talent, especially in business and artistic endeavors, in which skill rather than birth contributed most to success. Despite limited modes of communication, new generations were much more able to impose radical changes than in our own society, but they had to do so quickly because of the mortality rate. The pace of development and change was fast and exciting.

INTRODUCTION
THE CULTURAL REBIRTH

The Renaissance was in the best sense a vast educational process, and Italy was the teacher of Europe. The early brilliance of Italian achievements in arts, sciences, letters, and manners cannot fully be explained; the causes for its eventual fading in the late seventeenth century are equally complex. In the nineteenth century, a French historian named Jules Michelet first employed the term Renaissance to refer to this period.* He used it to describe an artistic rebirth inspired by the rediscovery of antiquity. This conception of rebirth was defined in greater detail by Jacob Burckhardt in *The Civilization of the Renaissance in Italy* (1860), the greatest and most influential single book ever devoted to this period. Burckhardt argued that the Italian Renaissance rediscovered the world and man. And he believed that the change in men's attitudes towards themselves and worldly existence in the fourteenth and fifteenth century in Italy marked the beginning of the modern world, when life was once again valued for the rewards it could bring, just as it had been in classical antiquity.

In education, the influence of medieval universities was undermined by the humanist schools that trained most of the important rulers and power brokers of the Renaissance. The university curriculum, which stressed the scholastic disciplines of logic, natural philosophy, metaphysics, and theology, came into competition with the *studia humanitatis*—the humanists' program of education in rhetoric or antique literature, grammar, history, and moral philosophy, based at first on classical Latin writers and, from the time of Manuel Chrysoloras' appearance in Italy in 1396, upon Greek authors as well. These curricula responded to the needs of the new mercantile class and produced different outlooks and values. The increased attention to human achievement in the world marked a new stage in the development of Western culture.

Unlike other periods, there was a conscious awareness during the years between 1350 and 1550 that new ways in which men thought about themselves, their lives, and their creations had been formulated. Unlike John of Salisbury, who saw the men of his time as dwarfs standing upon the shoulders of giants, the thinkers of the Italian Renaissance saw themselves living in a new era, an age in which human potential was at least as great as it had been in classical antiquity. The poet and humanist Francesco Petrarca, known in English as Petrarch, saw himself as a man standing between two worlds, the past and the future. He was one of the first to understand antiquity as a separate historical epoch.

*Michelet used the term in this way in his *History of France* (1855).

INTRODUCTION

Giovanni Boccaccio, Petrarch's friend and fellow humanist, was already conscious of the changes taking place in the plastic arts when he wrote in *The Decameron* of how Giotto "had revived that art of painting which had been buried for many centuries under the errors of various artists who painted more to delight the eyes of the ignorant rather than to please the intellect of wise men."* The concept of progress in the arts was popularized by Giorgio Vasari, who was the first to conceive of a *rinascità* or "rebirth" in his *Lives of the Artists.* Vasari blamed early Christianity for the decay of classical art and credited the new interest in the classics with reviving an art that first rivaled that of antiquity and then surpassed it in the supreme skill of Michelangelo.

The heroes of the Italian Renaissance were no longer the great warriors in service of church and emperor. Petrarch's life and works had made a heroic figure of the scholar and intellectual. Boccaccio's *Decameron* did much the same for the courageous and innovative merchant trader. By the time the Renaissance drew to a close in the sixteenth century, Alberti had depicted the model family; Machiavelli had culled from examples both ancient and modern the superlative political ruler; Castiglione had eulogized the perfect courtier; and a new heroic individual had arisen to capture the Western imagination—the artist, celebrated in Vasari's *Lives of the Artists,* Cellini's *Autobiography,* and by the almost superhuman figures of Leonardo da Vinci and Michelangelo.

The revival of classical learning was in many ways the key to the Italian Renaissance. Early Italians who strove to improve and renew their medieval heritage by annexing the legacy of the classical world hoped even to surpass the achievements of antiquity. Their central goal was to guide the new literatures written in vernacular languages to greater depth and maturity by recovering the art and wisdom of the ancients. This ambitious project came to be known as humanism, an Italian invention, and those involved in it as humanists. Humanism is synonymous with critical thinking, for which an alert and discriminating intelligence had to be joined to a critical spirit; the humanists thus learned languages, taught grammar and rhetoric, and studied both modern and ancient literature in order to cull the best from both traditions. In other words, the central ideal and justification for humanism was the importance of studying great works of literature in the broad sense—that is, the humanities. Emulation of the art of classical writers that permeated Italian culture brought the moderns into contact with their ideas, especially

*Giovanni Boccaccio, *The Decameron,* trans. Mark Musa and Peter Bondanella (New York: New American Library, 1982), p. 392.

those of writers like Cicero, Petrarch's favorite classical author, many of whose writings are devoted to living a good and happy life through public activities, strong friendships, and private contemplation of the good.

Petrarch was the central figure in the rise of Italian humanism. Despite his spiritual qualms about earthly pursuits, he taught the Renaissance about antiquity and how to retrieve classical learning. Petrarch was an intrepid collector of classical works and traveled widely to develop his own library. He became an editor and showed future humanist scholars how to read a classical work with his edition of Livy. While reading the works of classical authors, Petrarch discovered how nearly he resembled them and how much he had in common with them. He viewed their works as the means of becoming acquainted with human beings from another time. For example, having discovered some letters of Cicero in a library in Verona, Italy, he was disappointed that Cicero the high-minded philosopher could also be petty and venal. From then on, Petrarch saw books not as the embodiment of an abstract and impersonal truth but as the expression of an individual personality. He found the ancient writers so appealing that he wrote a series of letters to them, suggesting to his contemporaries that they could be approached as fellow human beings. This was a startling revelation.

Petrarch himself provided his age with an example of what it meant to be human in his life and his writings. He showed them that an individual life was significant and that a person could play many roles in the world. He lived fully as a nature-lover, a solitary, a gardener, a dog owner, a lover, a scholar, a poet-laureate, a public figure, and a friend. He was never limited to one rank or place, and he showed all of Europe how full and rich one life could be. Petrarch achieved a freedom that sometimes troubled him, but that to others represented his greatness. He is the prototype of the Renaissance ideal of the universal man. Because of his introspective qualities, self-awareness, and skill as a writer, we know more about him than we do about any other individual before him. Petrarch was an event in European cultural history and is sometimes referred to as the "first modern man."

The humanists, following Petrarch's example, rediscovered the ancient world of letters. This rebirth of interest in classical history, culture, and literature was paralleled by a similar reawakening of interest in the art and architecture of the ancient past. The modern science of archaeology arose to study the remains of Rome's magnificent artistic heritage, and by the mid-fifteenth century, Italian artists, sculptors, and architects had completed a revolution in the arts that dominated Western culture until the end of the nineteenth century and the rise of non-representational forms of artistic expression.

The Italian Renaissance was a period of real diversity and change that can conveniently be divided into two phases. The earlier, or ascending, phase progressed from Petrarch's sometimes anxious orientation toward life in this world and the complex but accepting view of humanity in Boccaccio toward the highly optimistic view of human possibilities expressed in Pico della Mirandola's *Oration*. This period was characterized by a basic optimism about human beings, social idealism, enthusiasm over the recovery of classical culture, and the belief that it would be fully harmonized with the Christian view of the world and the institutions inherited from the Middle Ages. Works of the early Renaissance offered positive visions of life founded upon the assumptions that reasonable human beings are educable, society capable of improvement, and the writer's and reformer's tasks possible. In the plastic arts, this enthusiasm for the lessons learned from the Roman past and the renewed value of the individual were embodied in the new geometric forms of Giotto's frescos, the light and sprightly sculpture of Donatello, and the studies of perspective typical of Piero della Francesca.

The later, or descending, phase of the Renaissance arose from the slow erosion of the medieval world view and from the realization that human limitations and the very nature of the world stand in the way of earthly perfection. This period was characterized by the anxiety experienced by the citizens of any age in crisis when old values are clearly giving way to the new. Machiavelli's optimistic message about imitation of the past was tempered with a highly critical view of flawed human possibilities. While Guicciardini began to doubt even the possibility of learning from the past, Leonardo elevated practical experience over book learning and erudition.

The crisis in values typical of the late Renaissance of the sixteenth century, so clearly reflected in the works of Machiavelli, Guicciardini, or Cellini, perhaps found its most dramatic expression in the evolution of the period's most brilliant individual, Michelangelo. At the dawn of the sixteenth century, Michelangelo's statue of *David* (1501–04) provided a celebration of the human form that served as the symbol of a free, self-governing city-state in Florence. Later (1508–12), the Sistine Chapel ceiling with its moving centerpiece, the famous fresco depicting God's creation of Adam, continued Michelangelo's celebration of man as the measure of all things. By the end of his life, however, Michelangelo was profoundly troubled by spiritual questions, as his poetry makes clear. This less optimistic and more tragic view of human nature, so vividly depicted in one of his latest works—the fresco of the *Last Judgment* on the Sistine Chapel altar wall (1534–41)—came to permeate Italian life.

The Italian Renaissance evolved in several stages. At first, a social Renaissance produced the economic and political changes in medieval Italian life that would eventually give rise to a cultural flowering in letters, science, and the arts. The innovations of the high culture took their rise from the restless commercial genius and civic ideals of the thirteenth-century communes and the early, bold efforts of geniuses such as Dante, Petrarch, and Boccaccio. The idealistic optimism of the early Italian Renaissance soon gave way to questioning, doubts, and philosophical perplexities—all of which were made more serious by the fact that Italy after 1496 had become the battlefield of Europe and was constantly invaded by less cultured but militarily far superior foreign "barbarians." By the mid-sixteenth century, Michelangelo's spiritual anxieties and his doubts that art or culture could satisfy man's fundamental aspirations came to be shared by many other Italians.

Besides this crisis of confidence in the intellect, which was probably an inevitable product of Renaissance introspection, there was an additional change in intellectual climate. With the Counter-Reformation and the Council of Trent (1563), intellectual conformity became more acceptable and much more politic. Institutions such as the Inquisition and especially the Index of Prohibited Books stunted inquiry and innovation. In fact, the books placed on the Index between 1554 and 1596 included most of the great works of the Renaissance: a number of Petrarch's sonnets; Boccaccio's *Decameron* (unless expurgated); Castiglione's *Book of the Courtier* (unless expurgated); Guicciardini's *History of Italy* (unless expurgated); and all of Machiavelli's writings.

Once freedom of inquiry and the powers of the imagination were limited by church censorship, political repression, and social conformity, the golden age of the Italian Renaissance gave rise to an entirely different kind of culture than the one reflected in the various selections in this anthology.

JULIA CONAWAY BONDANELLA
Indiana University

FRANCESCO PETRARCA
1304–74

ITALY'S GREATEST HUMANIST AND MOST INFLUENTIAL AND LASTING LYRIC POET, Francesco Petrarca, or Petrarch, as he is known in English, was born in Arezzo, a small town in central Italy. He spent much of his youth in Provence, where his father, a Florentine notary, was living in exile in the city of Avignon, then the temporary location of the papacy. He studied law first at Montpellier and then at Bologna, returning to Avignon after his father's death in 1326. It was on Good Friday of 1327 in a church in Avignon that he claimed to have seen for the first time his beloved Laura, the inspiration for his *Canzoniere*, a collection of 366 lyric poems of various subjects and metrical forms (sonnets, madrigals, *canzoni* or songs, sestinas).

Soon afterward, Petrarch entered the service of the powerful Colonna family, and by 1341 his reputation as a classical scholar was so great that he received two separate invitations to be crowned poet laureate from the city of Rome and the University of Paris. He accepted the first invitation—thus symbolically asserting for future generations of Renaissance humanists who followed his model the primacy of Rome and the Latin classics over the theological speculations associated with the Scholasticism of the French university—and received the poet's crown from the Roman Senate on April 8, 1341. From that point on, Petrarch became a major force in European culture, traveling all over Italy and Europe and writing a number of major Latin works, including the epic poem *Africa*, numerous personal and literary letters, and various philosophical and moral works. He died in Arquà, a small town near Padua, on the night of July 18–19, 1374, after having achieved the goal he had set years earlier for himself—universal fame as a scholar and poet.

Petrarch's reputation rests upon two very different, though related, bodies of work. His Latin writings (two brief selections of which are included here) reflect his interest in the revival of classical antiquity, his tireless efforts to locate and edit the major texts surviving from the ancient period, and his desire to leave his mark on European culture.

Not only was he a brilliant intellectual, but he also understood quite well the role of the individual human being and the place of fame in society. His "Letter to Posterity" shows us the self-portrait of a man who wished to be remembered as a student, scholar, poet, and humanist. "The Ascent of Mount Ventoux," describing his climb of the 6,273-foot-high mountain near Avignon in 1336, reveals another characteristic quality of his thought which would color all of the Renaissance culture—his introspection, his interest in nature, and his unique blend of Christian values with the best of the learning from classical antiquity.

Petrarch claimed to prefer his Latin works to his vernacular poems. Yet his *Canzoniere* became the model for stylish, elegant, and eloquent love poetry not only in Italy but also throughout all of Western Europe from his own day until the seventeenth century. It inspired a major tradition in Western lyric poetry, known as Petrarchism, and it was a major and determinant influence upon Chaucer, Spenser, Shakespeare, Milton, Ronsard, Donne, and countless other late-medieval and Renaissance poets and playwrights, who often employed Petrarchan language or conceits in their dramatic works. Laura—the beautiful but enigmatic muse who inspired these lyrics—apparently died during the Black Plague of 1348 (the same pestilence eloquently described in Boccaccio's *Decameron*), and Petrarch's *Canzoniere* ("Songbook") recorded the various changes in his thoughts and emotions between his first vision of Laura until and after her death. Like all of the truly great love poetry of the Western lyric tradition, a major portion of which Petrarch did so much to establish, the *Canzoniere* actually concentrated more upon the psychology of the poet in love than upon the beloved.

Petrarch's humanism, incorporating the ideas of newly rediscovered classical texts, might be said to have given the European Renaissance its direction. More than any other man, he helped to establish what it meant to be a learned, cultured individual, and the humanist movement in Italy and later throughout all of Europe was to follow his example. In his lyric poetry (written in Italian rather than Latin), Petrarch invented what became a universal poetic language, providing a model for centuries of poets who found his *Canzoniere* a veritable gold mine of conceits, metaphors, and attitudes toward literature which they would incorporate into their own personal expression.

BIBLIOGRAPHY

Petrarch, *Selections from the Canzoniere and Other Works*, ed. and trans. Mark Musa (Oxford: Oxford University Press, 1985); Thomas G.

FRANCESCO PETRARCA

Bergin, *Petrarch* (New York: Twayne, 1970); Julia Conaway Bondanella, *Petrarch's Visions and Their Renaissance Analogues* (Madrid: Studia Humanitatis, 1978); Julia Conaway Bondanella and Mark Musa, "Petrarch," in William T. H. Jackson, ed., *European Writers: The Middle Ages and the Renaissance* (New York: Scribner's, 1983); Nicholas Mann, *Petrarch* (Oxford: Oxford University Press, 1984); Charles Trinkaus, *The Poet as Philosopher* (New Haven: Yale University Press, 1979); E. H. Wilkins, *The Life of Petrarch* (Chicago: University of Chicago Press, 1961).

LETTER TO POSTERITY*

·❦·

You may, perhaps, have heard tell of me, though even this is doubtful, since a poor and insignificant name like mine will hardly have traveled far in space or time. If, however, you have heard of me, you may wish to know the kind of man I was or about the fruit of my labors, especially those you may have heard of or, at any rate, of those whose titles at least may have reached you.[1]

To begin with myself, then, what men say about me will differ widely, since in passing judgment almost everyone is influenced not so much by truth as by whim; there is no measure for praise and blame. I was, in truth, one of your own, a poor mortal, neither of high origin, nor, on the other hand, of too humble birth, but belonging, as Augustus Caesar says of himself, to an old family.[2] As for my disposition, I am not by nature evil or wanting in modesty except as contagious custom may have infected me. My youth was gone before I realized it; young manhood carried me away; but a maturer age brought me to my senses and taught me by experience the truth I had read in books long before: that youth and pleasure are vain—the lesson of that Author of all times and ages, Who permits wretched mortals, puffed with emptiness, to wander for a time until at last, becoming mindful of their sins, they learn to know themselves. In my youth I was blessed with an agile, active body, though not particularly strong; and while I cannot boast of being very handsome, I was good-looking enough in my younger days. I had a clear complexion, between light and dark, lively eyes, and for many years sharp vision, which, however, unexpectedly deserted me when I passed

*This and most of the other selections from Petrarch come from Petrarch, *Selections from the Canzoniere and Other Works*, trans. and ed. Mark Musa (Oxford: Oxford University Press, 1985), although some poems from the *Canzoniere* were newly translated for this volume by Mark Musa. Additional explanatory notes have been added to those previously published in *Selections from the Canzoniere and Other Works* by Julia Conaway Bondanella.

my sixtieth birthday, and forced me, reluctantly, to resort to the use of glasses. Although I had always been perfectly healthy, old age assailed me with its usual array of discomforts.

My parents were good people, Florentine in origin, and not too well off; in fact, I may as well admit it, they were on the edge of poverty. Since they had been expelled from their native city,[3] I was born to exile, at Arezzo, in the year 1304 of the age beginning with Christ's birth, July the twentieth, on a Monday, at dawn. I have always had great contempt for money; not that I wouldn't like to be rich, but because I hate the work and care which are invariably associated with wealth. I never liked to give great feasts; on the contrary, I have led a happier life with a plain diet and ordinary foods than all the followers of Apicius,[4] with their elaborate dinners. So-called banquets, those vulgar bouts, hostile to sobriety and good manners, I have always found to be repugnant. I have always thought it tiresome and useless to invite others to such affairs, and no less so to be invited to them myself by others. On the other hand, to dine with one's friends I find most pleasant, and nothing has ever given me more delight than the unannounced arrival of a friend—nor have I ever willingly sat down to table without a friend. And nothing annoys me more than display, not only because it is bad in itself, and opposed to humility, but because it is disturbing and distracting.

In my younger days I struggled constantly with an overwhelming but pure love affair—my only one, and I would have struggled with it longer had not premature death, bitter but salutary for me, extinguished the cooling flames.[5] I certainly wish I could say that I have always been entirely free from desires of the flesh, but I would be lying if I did. I can, however, surely say this: that, while I was being carried away by the ardor of my youth and by my temperament, I always detested such sins from the depths of my soul. When I was near the age of forty, and my vigor and passions were still strong, I renounced abruptly not only those bad habits, but even the very recollection of them—as if I had never looked at a woman. This I consider to be among my greatest blessings, and I thank God, who freed me while I was still sound and vigorous from that vile slavery which I always found hateful. But let us turn to other matters now.[6]

I have taken pride in others but never in myself, and insignificant as I was, I have always considered myself to be even more so. As for anger, it very often did harm to me but never to others. I have always been most desirous of honorable friendships, and have cherished them faithfully. And I boast without fear, since I know I speak sincerely, that while I am prone to take offense, I am equally quick to forget offenses and have a good memory for benefits received. I had the good fortune of associating with kings and princes, and having the friendship of nobles to the point of exciting envy. But it is the cruel fate of the elderly that sooner or later they must weep for friends who have passed away. Some of the greatest kings of this age have loved me and cultivated my friendship. They may know why; I certainly do not. I was on such terms with some of them that in a certain sense they seemed to be more my guests than I theirs; their eminence in no way made me uncomfortable; on the contrary, it brought with it many advantages. I kept aloof, however, from many of whom I was very fond; such was my innate spirit for freedom that I carefully avoided those whose high standing seemed to threaten the freedom I loved so much

I had a well-balanced mind rather than a keen one, one adapted to all kinds of good and wholesome study, but especially inclined to moral philosophy and poetry. In the course of time I neglected the latter and found pleasure in sacred literature, finding in it a hidden sweetness which I had previously taken lightly, and I came to regard the works of the poets as mere amenities. Though I was interested in many subjects, I devoted myself especially to the study of antiquity, for I always disliked our own age—so much so, that had it not been for the love of those dear to me, I would have preferred to have been born in any other time than our own. In order to forget my own times, I have always tried to place myself mentally in another age; thus I delighted in history—though I was troubled by the conflicting statements, but when in doubt I accepted what appeared to me most probable, or else yielded to the authority of the writer.

Many people have said that my style is clear and compelling; but to me it seems weak and obscure. In fact, in ordinary conversation with friends, or acquaintances, I never worried about my language, and I have always marveled at the fact that Augustus Caesar took such pains in this respect.[7] When, however, the subject matter or the circumstances or the listener seemed to demand otherwise, I have given some attention to style, with what success, however, I cannot say. Let those to whom I spoke be the judges. If only I have lived well, I care little how well I spoke. Mere elegance of language can result at best in an empty reputation.

My life up to now has, through circumstances or my own choice, been disposed as follows. Some of my first year was spent at Arezzo, where I first saw the light of day; the following six years were, since my mother had by this time been recalled from exile, spent at my father's estate at Ancisa, about fourteen miles above Florence. My eighth year was spent at Pisa, the ninth and later years in Transalpine Gaul, at

Avignon, on the left bank of the Rhone, where the Roman Pontiff holds and has long held the Church of Christ in shameful exile,[8] though a few years ago it seemed as if Urban V was on the point of restoring the church to its ancient seat. But clearly nothing is coming of this effort and, what is worst of all, the Pope, while he was still living, seemed to repent of his good deed. If he had lived a little longer, he certainly would have learned what I thought of his return.[9] My pen was in my hand when suddenly he gave up both his exalted office and his life. Unhappy man! To think he could have died before St. Peter's altar and in his own home! Had his successors remained in their capital he would have been looked upon as the cause of this fortunate change or, had they left Rome, his virtue would have been all the more conspicuous as their fault, in contrast, would have been the more evident. But such lamentations here stray too far from my subject.

So then, on the windy banks of the river Rhone I spent my boyhood, under the care of my parents, and then, my entire youth under the direction of my own vanities. There were, however, long intervals spent elsewhere, for at that time I spent four full years in the little town of Carpentras, a little to the east of Avignon. In these two places I learned as much grammar, logic, and rhetoric as my age permitted, or rather, as much as is usually taught in school, and how little that is, dear reader, you well know. Then I went to Montpellier to study law, and spent four years there, and then to Bologna for three years where I attended lectures on civil law, and many thought I would have done very well had I continued my studies. But I gave up the subject altogether as soon as it was no longer necessary to follow the wishes of my parents. It was not because I disliked the power and authority of the law, which is undoubtedly very great, or because of the endless references it contains to Roman antiquity, which I admired so, but rather because I felt it was being continuously degraded by those who practice it. I hated the idea of learning an art which I would not practice dishonestly, and could hardly hope to practice otherwise. Had I made the latter attempt, my scrupulousness would undoubtedly have been ascribed to incompetence.

So at the age of twenty-two I returned home.[10] Since habit has nearly the force of nature, I call home my Avignon exile for I had lived there since childhood. I was already beginning to become known there, and my friendship was sought out by prominent men. Why, I do not know. I must confess that this is a source of surprise to me now, although it seemed natural enough at an age when we are used to considering ourselves as worthy of the highest respect. I was courted first and foremost by that eminent and noble Colonna family which at that period adorned the Roman Curia with their presence. While I might be now, at that time I was certainly unworthy of the esteem in which the family held me. I was especially welcomed and taken to Gascony by the incomparable Giacomo Colonna, then Bishop of Lombez,[11] the like of whom I doubt that I have ever seen or ever shall see. There in the shade of the Pyrenees I spent a heavenly summer in delightful conversation with my master and the members of our company, and never do I recall the experience without a sigh of regret.[12]

Returning, I spent many years in the house of Giacomo's brother, Cardinal Giovanni Colonna, not as if I were a servant and he my lord but rather as if he were my father, or better, a most affectionate brother. It was as though I were in my very own home.[13] About this time, youthful curiosity impelled me to visit France and Germany. And while I invented other reasons to gain the approval of my elders for the journey, the real reason was burning desire for new sights. First I visited Paris, as I was anxious to discover what was true and what fictitious in the accounts I had heard of that city. After my return from this journey I went to Rome, which I had ardently desired to visit since I was a child. There I soon came to be a great admirer of Stefano, the noble head of the Colonna family, who was an ancient hero, and I was in turn so welcomed by him in every respect that it was as though I were his son. The affection and good will which this excellent man showed me persisted until the end of his life, and it lives with me still, and never will it fade, not until I myself cease to be.

Having returned I experienced the innate repugnance I have always felt for city life, and especially for that disgusting city of Avignon which I truly abhorred. Seeking some means of escape, I fortunately discovered a delightful valley, narrow and secluded, called Vaucluse, about fifteen miles from Avignon, where the Sorgue, the prince of streams, has its source. Captured by the charms of the place, I transferred myself and my books there. If I were to tell you what I did there during those many years, it would prove to be a long story. Indeed, almost every bit of writing I did was either done or begun or at least conceived there, and my undertakings were so numerous that even to the present day they keep me busy and weary. My mind, like my body, is more agile than strong, so that while it was easy for me to conceive of many projects, I would drop them because they were too difficult to execute. The aspect of my surroundings suggested my undertaking the composition of a sylvan or bucolic song, my *Bucolicum carmen*. I also composed a work in two books on *the Life of Solitude (De vita solitaria)*, which I dedicated to Philip, now exalted to the Cardinal and Bishop of Sibina. He was always a great man, but at the time of which I speak, he was only the humble Bishop of Cavaillon.[14] He is the only one of my friends who is still left, and he has always loved and treated me not episcopally, as Ambrose did Augustine, but as a brother.

One Friday in Holy Week while I was wandering in those mountains I had the strong urge to write an epic poem about Scipio Africanus the Great, whose name had been dear to me since childhood. While I began the project with great enthusiasm, I soon, owing to a variety of distractions, put it aside. The poem was called *Africa*, after its hero, and by some fate, whether the book's or my own, it did not fail to arouse the interest of many even before its publication.[15]

While leading a leisurely existence there, on one and the same day, remarkable as it may seem, I received letters from both the Roman Senate and the Chancellor at the University of Paris, summoning me to appear in Rome and Paris, respectively, to receive the poet's laurel crown.[16] In my youthful elation I convinced myself that I was quite worthy of this honor and recognition which came from such eminent judges, and I measured my own merit by the judgment of others. But I hesitated for a time over which invitation I should accept, and sent a letter to the Cardinal Giovanni Colonna, of whom I have already spoken, asking his opinion. He was so nearby that, having written to him late in the day, I had his reply before nine the next morning. I followed his advice, and recognized the claims of Rome as superior to all others (I still have the two letters I wrote to him on that occasion showing that I took his advice). So I set off for Rome. And although, as is the way of youth, I was a most indulgent judge of my own work, I was still uneasy about accepting my own estimation of myself as well as the verdict even of such men as those who summoned me, despite the fact that they would certainly not have honored me with such an offer, if they had not believed me worthy.

So I decided to visit Naples first, and there I went to see that celebrated king and philosopher Robert,[17] who was as illustrious a ruler as he was a man of letters. He was, in truth, the only monarch of our times who was both a friend of learning and of virtue, and I asked him to examine me in such things as he found to criticize in my work. The warmth of his reception and judgment remains to this day a source of astonishment to me, and undoubtedly also to the reader who happens to know something of the matter. When he learned the reason for my coming, the king seemed very pleased. He was gratified by my youthful faith in him, and felt, perhaps, that he shared in a way the glory of my coronation, since I had chosen him above all men as my qualified critic.

After talking over a great many things, I showed him my *Africa*, which pleased him so much that he asked me as a great favor to dedicate it to him. This was a request I certainly could not refuse, nor, in fact, would I have wished to refuse, even had it been in my power. He then set a day during which he would consider the object of my visit. He kept me busy from noon until evening, and since the time proved too short, with one discussion leading to another, we spent the two following days in the same way. Thus, having tested my ignorance for three days, the king finally pronounced me worthy of the laurel. He wanted to bestow that honor upon me at Naples, and urged me to agree to this, but my love for Rome was stronger than the insistence of even so great a monarch as Robert. At length, finding me inflexible in my purpose, he sent me on my way with royal escorts and letters to the Roman Senate in which he enthusiastically expressed his flattering opinion of me. This royal judgment was in accord with that of many others, and especially with my own, but today I cannot accept either of those verdicts. In his case, there was more affection and encouragement of youth than devotion to truth.

So then, I went to Rome, and continuing in spite of my unworthiness to rely upon the judgment of so eminent a critic, I who had been merely a simple student received the laurel crown to the great joy of the Romans who attended the ceremony.[18] This occasion is described elsewhere in my letters, both in prose and verse. The laurel, however, in no way gave me more wisdom, though it did arouse some envy—but that is a tale too long to be told here.

Leaving Rome, I went to Parma, and spent some time with the members of the Correggio family, who were very good men and most generous to me but much at odds with each other. They gave Parma such a good government as it had never before had within the memory of man, and such as it is not likely ever to enjoy again.

I was most conscious of the honor I had just received, and worried for fear that I might seem to be unworthy of the distinction; consequently, as I was walking one day in the mountains and happened to cross the river Enza in the region of Reggio Selvapiana, I was struck by the beauty of the spot and began to write again the *Africa*, which I had put aside. In my enthusiasm, which had appeared to be dead, I wrote some lines that very day, and some more each day that followed until I returned to Parma. Here I happened to find a quiet and secluded house (which I later bought, and which is still my own), and I continued my task with such ardor and completed the work in so short a time that the fact I did so still amazes me to this day. I was already thirty-four years old when I returned to the fountain of the Sorgue, and to my transalpine solitude. I had stayed long both in Parma and Verona,[19] and I am thankful to say that everywhere I went I was treated with much greater esteem than I merited.

Some time after this, my growing reputation attracted the kindness of Giacomo the Younger of Carrara, a very fine man whose equal, I doubt, cannot be found among the rulers of this time. For years, when I was beyond the Alps, or whenever I happened to be in Italy, he constantly sent messengers and letters, and with his petitions he urged me to accept his friendship. At last, though I expected little satisfaction from the venture, I made up my mind to go to him and see what this insistence on the part of so eminent a person, and one who was a stranger to me, was all about. Then, after some time I went to Padua, where I was received by that man of illustrious memory not as a mere mortal might be received, but as the blessed are received in heaven— with such joy and such unbelievable affection and respect that I cannot adequately describe it in words and must, therefore, be silent. Among other things, when he learned that I had been a cleric from boyhood, he had me made a canon of Padua in order to bind me closer to himself and to his city. In short, if his life had been longer, that would have put an end to all my wanderings. But alas! nothing mortal is enduring, and there is nothing sweet which sooner or later does not become bitter. He had scarcely given two years to me, to his country, and to the world before God, Who had given him to us, took him away.[20] And it is not my blind love for him that makes me feel that neither I, nor his country, nor the world was worthy of him. Although the son, who succeeded him, was a very sensible and distinguished man, who like his father was always very cordial and respectful to me, I could stay no longer after the death of this man to whom I was so closely linked (even by the similarity of our ages) and I returned to France, not so much from desire to see again what I had already seen a thousand times, as from hope of getting rid of my misfortunes (the way a sick man does) with a change of scene. . . .[21]

NOTES

· ❧ ·

1. This letter was intended to conclude the *Epistolae Seniles*, one of Petrarch's two main collections of letters, and to reveal to succeeding generations a structured account of his life. In his vast correspondence, Petrarch was inspired by the letters written by classical writers, such as Cicero, some of whose letters to Atticus he had discovered in Verona. These letters showed him that earthly undertakings and the life of an individual, even one of modest birth, could be of interest to posterity.

2. See Suetonius, *Life of Augustus*, 2.

3. Petrarch's father was exiled in 1301 as a result of fighting among the Guelph factions in Florence.

4. Apicius was a Roman chef of considerable sophistication who lived in the time of Tiberius and wrote a famous cookbook.

5. This reference to a love affair suggests Petrarch's attachment ended at the woman's death. Yet in the poetry and other works, Petrarch's preoccupation with Laura is lifelong.

6. Petrarch had taken minor orders in the Church and had two natural children whom he legitimatized: Giovanni, born in 1337; and Francesca, in 1343.

7. Suetonius, *Life of Augustus*, 87.

8. In 1309, Clement V, the French Pope, (1305–14), had moved the papal court to Rome.

9. Urban V (1362–70) took the papal court back to Rome in 1367 but returned to Avignon in 1370. In several metrical epistles to Urban's predecessors, Petrarch urged them to return to Rome.

10. After his mother's death around 1320, Petrarch and his brother Gherardo went to Bologna and studied law. They left Bologna in 1326 when their father died.

11. Lombez is thirty miles southwest of Toulouse in France. Giacomo was bishop from 1328 until his death in 1341.

12. During the summer of 1330, Petrarch also met Ludwig van Kempen (his friend "Socrates") and Lello di Pietro Stefano dei Tosetti ("Laelius"), to whom he addressed many letters.

13. Petrarch served as household chaplain on the staff of Cardinal Giovanni Colonna (d. 1348) for about fifteen years, between 1330 and 1348.

14. Philippe de Cabassoles (d. 1372) shared Petrarch's love of learning and the rural life. His diocese included Vaucluse. He became a cardinal in 1368.

15. Petrarch began his Latin epic in 1338 or 1339; it was never completed and was published only after his death in 1396. Petrarch never seemed fond of this work.

16. Through his own persistent efforts, Petrarch received these invitations to become poet laureate on his thirty-sixth birthday, September 6, 1340. Little of his work had been written or published by that time.

17. Petrarch set out for Naples on February 16, 1341. The grandson of Charles of Anjou (the brother of Saint Louis), King Robert, was also Count of Provence. Hence, Avignon belonged to him, and he resided there between 1318 and 1324.

18. The coronation held on Easter Sunday, April 8, 1341, was adapted from the medieval academic graduation ceremony.

19. He went to Vaucluse in 1342, returning to Parma the next year.

20. Petrarch accepted his canonry on April 18, 1349. Giacomo was assassinated by his nephew in December 1350 and was succeeded by his son Francesco.

21. Petrarch returned to France in June 1351. The letter breaks off at this point with no explanation.

THE ASCENT OF MOUNT VENTOUX

———————— · ❦ · ————————

To Dionisio da Borgo San Sepolcro[1]

Today I climbed the highest mountain in this region, which is not improperly called Ventosum (Windy).[2] The only motive for my ascent was the wish to see what so great a height had to offer. I had had the project in mind for many years, for, as you know, I have lived in these parts from childhood on, having been cast there by the fate which determines human affairs. And so the mountain, which is visible from a great distance, was always before my eyes, and for a long time I planned on doing what I have finally done today. The impulse to make the climb actually took hold of me while I was reading Livy's *History of Rome* yesterday, and I happened upon the place where Philip of Macedon, the one who waged the war against the Romans, climbed Mount Haemus in Thessaly.[3] From its summit, it was reported that he was able to see two seas, the Adriatic and the Euxine. Whether this is true or false I do not know, for the mountain is too far away, and there is disagreement among the commentators. Pomponius Mela, the cosmographer—not to mention the many others who have talked about this occurrence—accepts the truth of this statement without hesitation, while Livy, on the other hand, thinks it false. I, certainly, would not have left the question long in doubt if that mountain had been as easy to explore as this one. But let us drop the matter and return to my mountain here: I thought it proper for a young man in private life to attempt what no one would criticize in an aged king.

When I thought about looking for a companion for the ascent I realized, strangely enough, that hardly any of my friends were suitable—so rarely does one find, even among those most dear to one, the perfect combination of character and purpose. One was too phlegmatic, another too anxious; one too slow, another too hasty; one too sad, another too happy; one too simple, another more sagacious than I would like. I was frightened by the fact that one never spoke while another talked too much; the heavy deliberation of some repelled me as much as the lean incapacity of others. I rejected some for their cold lack of interest and

[14]

others for their excessive enthusiasm. Such defects as these, however grave, are tolerable enough at home (for charity suffers all things, and friendship rejects no burden), but it is another matter on a journey, where such weaknesses become more serious. So, with only my own pleasure in mind, with great care I looked about weighing the various characteristics of my friends against one another without committing any breach of friendship and silently condemning any trait which might prove to be disagreeable on my journey. And would you believe it? I finally turned to my own family for help and proposed the ascent to my younger brother, the only one I have, and whom you know well.[4] He was delighted beyond measure and gratified by the thought of acting at the same time as a friend as well as a brother.

On the appointed day we left the house and by evening reached Malaucène, which lies at the foot of the mountain on the north side. We rested there a day and finally this morning made the ascent with no one except two servants. And it is a most difficult task indeed, for the mountain is a very steep and almost inaccessible mass of rocky terrain. But, as a poet once put it well: "Persistent labor conquers all."[5] The day was long and the air invigorating, our spirits were high and our agile bodies strong, and everything else necessary for such an undertaking helped us on our way. The only difficulty we had to face was the nature of the place itself. We found an old shepherd among the mountain's ridges who tried at great length to discourage us from the ascent, saying that some fifty years before he had, in the same ardor of youth, climbed to the summit and had got nothing from it except fatigue and repentance and torn clothes and scratches from the rocks and briars. Never, according to what he or his friends knew, had anyone ever tried the ascent before or after him. But his counsels merely increased our eagerness to go on, as a young man's mind is usually suspicious of warnings. So the old man, finding his efforts were useless, went along with us a little way and pointed out a steep path among the rocks, continuing to cry out admonitions even after we had left him behind. Having left him with those garments and anything else we thought might prove burdensome to us, we made ready for the ascent and started to climb at a good pace. But, as often happens, fatigue soon followed upon our strenuous effort, and before long we had to rest on some rock. Then we started on again, but more slowly, I especially taking the rocky path at a more modest pace. My brother chose the steepest course straight up the ridge, while I weakly took an easier one which turned along the slopes. And when he called me back showing me the shorter way, I replied that I hoped to find an easier way up on the other side, and that I did not mind taking a longer course if it was not so steep. But this was merely an excuse for my laziness; and when the others had already reached a considerable height I was still wandering in the hollows, and having failed to find an easier means of ascent, I had only lengthened the journey and increased the difficulty of the ascent. Finally I became disgusted with the tedious way I had chosen, and decided to climb straight up. By the time I reached my brother, who had managed to have a good rest while waiting for me, I was tired and irritated. We walked along together for a while, but hardly had we left that rise when I forgot all about the circuitous route I had just taken and again tended to take a lower one. Thus, once again I found myself taking the easy way, the roundabout path of winding hollows, only to find myself soon back in my old difficulty. I was simply putting off the trouble of climbing; but no man's wit can alter the nature of things, and there is no way to reach the heights by going downward. In short, I tell you that I made this same mistake three or more times within a few hours, much to my brother's amusement and my anger.[6]

After being misled in this way a number of times, I finally sat down in a hollow and my thoughts quickly turned from material things to the spiritual, and I said to myself more or less what follows: "What you have experienced so often today in the ascent of this mountain, certainly happens to you as it does to many others in their journey toward the blessed life. But this is not so easily perceived by men, for the movements of the body are out in the open while those of the soul are invisible and hidden. The life we call blessed is to be sought on a high level, and straight is the way that leads to it.[7] Many, also, are the hills that stand in the way that leads to it, and we must ascend from virtue to virtue up glorious steps. At the summit is both the end of our struggles and the goal of our journey's climb. Everyone wishes to reach this goal, but, as Ovid says: 'To wish is not enough; you must yearn with ardent eagerness to gain your end.'[8] And you certainly both wish and ardently yearn, unless you are deceiving yourself in this matter, as you so often do. What, then, is holding you back? Nothing, surely, except that you take a path which seems at first sight easier leading through low and worldly pleasures. Nevertheless in the end, after long wanderings, you will either have to climb up the steeper path under the burden of labors long deferred to its blessed culmination, or lie down in the valley of your sins; and—I shudder to think of it!—if the shadow of death finds you there, you still spend an eternal night in constant torment." These thoughts stimulated my body and mind to a remarkable degree and made me face up to the difficulties which still remained. Oh, that my soul might follow that other road for which I long day and night, even as today I conquered material obstacles by bodily force! And why should it not be far easier: after all, the agile, immortal soul can reach its goal in the twinkling of an eye without intermediate space, while progress today had to be slow because my feeble body was burdened by its heavy members.

One mountain peak, the highest of all, the country people call Filiolus ("Sonny"); why, I do not know, unless by antiphrasis, as is sometimes the case, for the peak in question seems to be the father of all the surrounding ones. At its top is a little level place, and it was there that we could, at last, rest our weary bodies.

My good father, since you have listened to the troubles mounting in the heart of a man who ascends, listen now to the rest of the story, and devote one hour, I pray you, to reviewing the events of my day. At first, because I was not accustomed to the quality of the air and the effect of the wide expanse of view spread out before me, I stood there like a dazed person. I could see the clouds under our feet, and the tales I had read of Athos and Olympus seemed less incredible as I myself was witnessing the very same things from a less famous mountain. I turned my eyes toward Italy, the place to which my heart was most inclined. The great and snowcapped Alps seemed to rise close by, though they were far away—those same Alps through which that fierce enemy of the Roman name once made his way, splitting the rocks, if we can believe the story, by means of vinegar. I sighed, I must admit, for Italian skies which I beheld more with my thought than with my eyes, and an inexpressible longing came over me to see once more my friend and my country,[9] though at the same time I reproached myself for this double weakness which came from a soul not yet up to manly resistance—and yet there were excuses for both my desires, and several excellent authorities could be cited to support me.

Then a new idea came to me, and I started thinking in terms of time rather than space. I thought: "Today marks ten years since you completed your youthful studies and left Bologna. Oh, eternal God! Oh, immutable wisdom! Think of all the changes in your character these intervening years have seen! I suppress a great deal, for I have not yet reached a safe harbor where I can calmly recall past storms. The time, perhaps, will come when I can review all the experiences of the past in their order saying with the words of your St. Augustine: 'I wish to recall my foul past and the carnal corruption of my soul, not that I love them, but that I may the more love you, O my God.'[10] Much that is dubious and evil still clings to me, but what I once loved, I love no longer. Come now, what am I saying? I still love it, but more moderately. No, not so, but with more shame, with more heaviness of heart. Now, at last, I have told the truth. The fact is I love, but I love what I long not to love, what I would like to hate. Though I hate to do so, though constrained, though sad and sorrowing, I love none the less, and I feel in my miserable self the meaning of the well-known words: 'I will hate if I can; if not, I will love against my will!'[11] Not three years have passed since that perverse and wicked desire which had me in tight hold and held undisputed sway in my heart began to discover a rebellious opponent who was no longer willing to yield in obedience. These two adversaries have joined in close combat for supremacy, and for a long time now a grueling war, the outcome of which is still doubtful, has been waging in the field of my mind."

Thus my thoughts turned back over the last ten years, and then with concentrated thought on the future, I asked myself: "If you should, by chance, prolong this uncertain life of yours for another ten years, advancing toward virtue in proportion to the distance from which you departed from your original infatuation during the past two years since the new longing first encountered the old, could you not face death on reaching forty years of age, if not with complete assurance at least with hopefulness, calmly dismissing from your thoughts the residuum of life that fades into old age?"

Such thoughts as these, father, occurred to me. I rejoiced in my progress, mourned for my weaknesses, and took pity on the universal inconstancy of human conduct. I had by this time forgotten where I was and why we had come; then, dismissing my anxieties to a more appropriate occasion, I decided to look about me and see what we had come to see. The sun was sinking and the shadows of the mountain were already lengthening below, warning us that the time for us to go was near at hand. As if suddenly roused from sleep, I turned to gaze at the west. I could not see the tops of the Pyrenees, which form the barrier between France and Spain, not because of any intervening obstacle that I know of but simply because of the inadequacy of mortal vision. But off to the right I could see most clearly the mountains of the region around Lyons and to the left the bay of Marseilles and the sea that beats against the shores of Aigues-Mortes, though all these places were at a distance requiring a journey of several days to reach them. The Rhône was flowing under our very eyes.

While my thoughts were divided thus, now turning my attention to thoughts of some worldly object before me, now uplifting my soul, as I had done my body, to higher planes, it occurred to me to look at Augustine's *Confessions*, a gift of your love that I always keep with me in memory of the author and the giver. I opened the little volume, small in size but infinitely sweet, with the intention of reading whatever came to hand, for what else could I happen upon if not edifying and devout words. Now I happened by chance to open it to the tenth book. My brother stood attentively waiting to hear what St. Augustine would say from my lips. As God is my witness and my brother too, the first words my eyes fell upon were: "And men go about admiring the high mountains and the mighty waves of the sea and the wide sweep of rivers and the sound of the ocean and the movement of the stars, but they themselves they abandon."[12] I was ashamed, and asking my brother, who was anxious to hear more, not to bother me, I closed the book, angry with myself for continuing to admire the things of this world when I should have learned a long time ago from the pagan philosophers themselves that nothing is admirable but the soul beside whose greatness nothing can be as great. Then, having seen enough of the mountain I turned an inward eye upon myself, and from that moment on not a syllable passed my lips until we reached the bottom. The words I had read had given me enough food for thought and I could not believe that I happened to turn to them by mere chance. I believed that what I had read there was written for me and no one else, and I remembered that St. Augustine had once thought the same thing in his own case, as he himself tells us when opening the book of the Apostle, the first words he saw were: "Not in rioting and drunkenness, not in chambering and wantonness, not in strife and envy, but put ye on the Lord Jesus Christ, and make not provision for the flesh in its concupiscences."[13] The same thing happened earlier to St. Anthony, as he listened to the Gospel where it is written, "If thou wilt be perfect, go and sell what thou hast, and give to the poor, and thou shalt have treasure in heaven; and come follow me."[14] He believed this scripture to have been spoken specifically for him, and by means of it he guided himself to the Kingdom of Heaven, as the biographer Athanasius tells us.[15] And as Anthony on hearing these words asked for nothing more, and as Augustine after reading the Apostle's admonition sought no farther, so did I conclude my reading after the few words which I have recorded. I thought in silence of the vanity in us mortals who neglect what is noblest in ourselves in a vain show only because we look around ourselves for what can be found only within us. I wondered at the natural nobility of that human soul which unless degenerate has deserted its original state and turned to dishonor what God has given it for its honor. How many times I turned back that day to look at the mountain top which seemed scarcely more than a cubit high compared with the height of human contemplation, unless it is immersed in the foulness of earth? As I descended I asked myself: "If we were willing to endure so much sweat and labor in order to raise our bodies a little closer to heaven, how can a soul struggling toward God, up the steps of human pride and mortal destiny, fear any cross or prison or sting of fortune?" How few, I thought, are they who are not diverted from this path for fear of hardship or the love of ease! And how happy those few, if any such there be! It is they, I feel, the poet had in mind when he wrote:

> Blessed the man who is skilled to understand
> The hidden cause of things; who beneath his feet
> All fear casts, and death's relentless doom,
> And the howlings of greedy Acheron.[16]

How earnestly should we strive to trample beneath our feet not mountain tops but the appetites which spring from earthly impulses!

In the middle of the night, unaware of the difficulties of the way back and amid the preoccupations which I have so frankly revealed, we came by the friendly light of a full moon to the little inn which we had left that morning before daybreak. Then, while the servants were busy preparing our supper, I spent my time in a secluded part of the house, hurriedly and extemporaneously writing all this down, fearing that if I were to put off the task, my mood would change on leaving the place, and I would lose interest in writing to you.

You see, dearest father, that I wish to conceal nothing of myself from you. I describe to you not only the course of my life but even my individual thoughts. And I ask for your prayers that these vague and wandering thoughts of mine may some day become coherent and, having been so vainly cast in all directions, that they may direct themselves at last to the one, true, certain, and never-ending good.

MALAUCÈNE
26 April

NOTES

—————————— • 🎐 • ——————————

1. One of the *Epistolae Familiares* (*Letters on Familiar Matters* IV.1), this letter may have been written in 1336 or as late as the 1350s. It is addressed to an Augustinian monk, once Petrarch's confessor, who was a professor of philosophy and theory at the University of Paris. Petrarch probably met him in Paris in 1333. He had given Petrarch the copy of St. Augustine's *Confessions* mentioned later in this letter which Petrarch always carried with him.

2. Mount Ventoux is in southern France near Malaucène, from which Petrarch and his brother began their climb with two servants. Before the nineteenth and twentieth centuries, mountain-climbing was a rather uncommon pastime. People tended to protect themselves from nature.

3. Petrarch implicitly compares himself to Philip of Macedon, who according to Livy made a climb of Mount Haemus (Mount Balkan in Bulgaria), which is in Thrace, not Thessaly.

4. Petrarch's brother Gherardo joined him in law school in Bologna and chose the monastic life in 1342. Petrarch was always troubled by his inability to devote his own life exclusively to God.

5. Virgil, *Georgics* I. 145–46. This often-cited line comes from Virgil's poem on farming, which explores the beauties of nature and the dignity of man who understands the natural world through hard work.

6. Dante's *Divine Comedy* begins with the protagonist's efforts to climb a hill covered by a dark wood.

7. Petrarch alludes to Matthew 7 and 14.

8. *Epistulae ex Ponto* (*Letters from the Black Sea* III.i.35).

9. Giacomo Colonna, the friend, had been in Rome since 1333.

10. *Confessions* II.1.1. Augustine was an important influence on Petrarch's writings.

11. The quotation is from Ovid (*Amores* III.xi.35). The problem of the divided will is in St. Paul (Romans 7:14–25) and St. Augustine (*Confessions* VIII.5.10).

12. *Confessions* X.8.15. On the date Petrarch claims to have made the climb, he was thirty-two years old, the same age as Augustine at his conversion.

13. St. Paul (Romans 13:13–14) is quoted in *Confessions* VIII.12.29.

14. Matthew 19:21.

15. Augustine cites the *Life of St. Anthony* II in the *Confessions* (VIII.12.29).

16. Virgil, *Georgics* II. 1490–93.

[21]

SELECTED POEMS FROM THE
CANZONIERE

· ❦ ·

1[1]

O You who hear within these scattered verses[2]
the sound of sighs with which I fed my heart
in my first errant youthful days when I
in part was not the man I am today;

for all the ways in which I weep and speak
between vain hopes, between vain suffering,
in anyone who knows love through its trials,
in them, may I find pity and forgiveness.

For now I see, since I've become the talk
so long a time of people all around
(it often makes me feel so full of shame),

that from my vanities comes fruit of shame
and my repentance and the clearest knowledge
that worldly joy is a quick passing dream.

· ❦ ·

3

It was the day the sun's ray[3] had turned pale
with pity for the suffering of his Maker
when I was caught, and I put up no fight,
my lady, for your lovely eyes had bound me.

It seemed no time to be on guard against
Love's blows; therefore, I went my way
secure and fearless—so, all my misfortunes
began in midst of universal woe.

Love found me all disarmed and found the way
was clear to reach my heart down through the eyes
which have become the halls and doors of tears.

It seems to me it did him little honor
to wound me with his arrow in my state
and to you, armed, not show his bow at all.

· ❦ ·

16

The old man takes his leave, white-haired and pale,
of the sweet place where he filled out his age
and leaves his little family, bewildered,
beholding its dear father disappear;

and then, dragging along his ancient limbs
throughout the very last days of his life,
helping himself with good will all he can,
broken by years, and wearied by the road,

he comes to Rome, pursuing his desire,
to look upon the likeness of the One[4]
he hopes to see again up there in heaven.

Just so, alas, sometimes I go, my lady,
searching as much as possible in others
for your true, your desirable form.

· ❦ ·

22[5]

For any animal that lives on earth,
except for but those few that hate the sun,
the time to toil is while it is still day;
but then when heaven lights up all its stars

some go back home while some nest in the wood
to find some rest at least until the dawn.

And I, from the first signs of lovely dawn,
shaking the shadows from around the earth
awakening the beasts in every wood,
can never cease to sigh while there is sun;
then when I see the flaring of the stars
I start to weep and long for the gone day.

When night drives out the clarity of day
and our darkness brings out another's dawn.
I gaze all full of care at the cruel stars
that once created me of sentient earth,
and I curse the first day I saw the sun
which makes me seem a man raised in the wood.

I think there never grazed in any wood
so cruel a beast, whether by night or day,
as she for whom I weep in shade and sun,
from which I am not stopped by sleep or dawn;
for though I am a body of this earth,
my firm desire is born from the stars.

Before returning to you, shining stars,
or sinking back into the amorous wood[6]
leaving my body turned to powdered earth,
could I see pity in her, for one day
can restore many years, and before dawn
enrich me from the setting of the sun!

Could I be with her at the fading sun
and seen by no one, only by the stars,
for just one night, to never see the dawn,
and she not be transformed into green wood[7]
escaping from my arms as on the day
Apollo had pursued her here on earth!

But I'll be under earth in a dry wood
and day will be full of tiny stars
before so sweet a dawn will see the sun.

· ❦ ·

23[8]

                In the sweet springtime of my early years
which saw the birth and the still tender green
of the fierce passion which grew up against me,
since singing can unripen bitter pain,
I'll sing of how I lived in liberty
while love had not been welcomed in my home;
                then I'll go on to tell how this offended him
too deeply, and what happened to me then
that I became a lesson for the many,
even though my harsh undoing
has been recorded elsewhere, exhausting
a thousand pens by now, and every valley
is echoing with the sound of my grave sighs,
attesting to a painful way of life.
If now memory is no help to me
as once it was, let pain be my excuse
and that thought which alone inflicts such anguish,
it makes me turn my back on any other
and forces me to lose all sense of self—
it owns my insides, I merely the shell.
                I tell you that from the day Love first thrust
his blow at me many a year had passed
and I was giving up my youthful looks;
around my heart the frozen thoughts had formed
a kind of adamantine toughness there,
which never let my hard decision out;
                no tear until this time had bathed my breast
nor broke my sleep, and what was not in me
appeared miraculously so in others.
O, what am I? What was I?
The end lauds life, the night what day has brought;
because that savage one of whom I speak,
aware that until now his arrow's blow
had not pierced me beyond the clothes I wore,
took as his patroness a mighty lady
against whom wit or force or begging pardon

did serve me just as little then as now;
both of them changed me into what I am:
from living man they turned me to green laurel
that does not lose its leaves in the cold season.
        The way I felt when I became aware
of the transfiguration of my body
and saw my hair turning into those leaves
I once had hoped to make into my crown,
and both the feet I stood on, moved and ran
(as every limb responds to the soul's power)
        turning into two roots above the waves
not of Peneus but a prouder river,[9]
and both my arms transformed into two branches!
Nor do I feel less fear
all covered in white feathers later on
when struck by lightning and by death my hope,
presuming to ascend too high, had fallen;[10]
for since I did not know just when or where
I would recover it, alone, in tears,
I would go searching night and day that place
where I had lost it, near and in the waters;
and never from then on was my tongue silent
while I could speak about that evil fall,
and with the swan's song I took on its color.
        And so I went along the shores I loved,
and wanting to express myself, I sang
with a strange voice, constantly begging mercy;
but I could never make my amorous cries
resound in tones so sweet or soft enough
to bring her harsh, cruel heart to condescension.
        What I felt then, if thinking back, still burns!
But much more than what I have told about
that sweet yet bitter enemy of mine
I feel I must reveal,
although she is beyond what words can say.
This one, who with glance can steal a heart,
opened my breast and took my heart in hand,
saying to me: "Say not a word about this."
Then I saw her alone in other garb
and did not know her, oh, who understands!
And full of fear I told her what the truth was,

and she resuming her accustomed form
quite quickly turned me into, (oh, my grief)
a hardly living, baffled piece of stone.[11]
        She spoke with so much anger on her face,
it made me tremble in that stone to hear
"Perhaps I am not what you think I am."
I told myself: "If she were to unrock me,
no life could be as sad or hard as this;
come back and make me weep again, my lord.
        I know not how, but I got out of there
blaming no one but my own self that day
I walked away half living and half dead.
But since my time is short,
my pen cannot keep up with my goodwill,
so, many things recorded in my mind
I pass them by and tell only of those
that stun the mind of anyone who listens.
Death had now wrapped itself around my heart,
and silence could not take it from her hands;
to use my spoken voice had been denied me
and so I shouted out with pen and paper;
"I'm not mine, no! If I die, it's your fault."
        I thought by doing this that I, unworthy,
would in her eyes be worthy of her mercy,
and in such hope I found boldness to try;
but sometimes meekness will put out disdain,
sometimes inflame it—this I found out later,
        for with my prayers my light had disappeared,
and I, who found nowhere, nowhere the slightest
trace of herself, not even of her feet,
just like the tired traveler,
collapsed weary upon the grass one day.
And there, accusing her fugitive ray,
to desperate tears of mine I gave free rein
and let them fall whenever they decided.
Snow never disappeared beneath the snow
as I felt myself melt entirely
and turn to fountain where the beech tree grows.
For a long time I traveled the wet road.
Who ever heard of man turned into fountain?[12]
And yet I speak of clear and well-known things.

The soul that God alone created noble—
for grace like this could come from no one else—
is similar to her own Creator's state;
therefore, she never stops forgiving one
who with humility in heart and face,
though he offended countless times, begs mercy.
    And if, unlike herself, she is insistent
on one's insistent prayer, she mirrors Him
in order that the sinning be more feared;
for one about to sin
again does not repent well of his sin.
After my lady, who was moved by pity,
agreed to look at me, and knew and saw
that punishment was equal to the sin,
she graciously restored my old condition.
But wise men count on nothing in this world:
for when I begged again, my bones and nerves
she turned to hardest stone,[13] and I was left
a voice shaken from its old, heavy self,
calling for Death and only her by name.
    A mournful wandering spirit (I remember)
through unfamiliar and deserted caves,
I wept for many years my unleashed boldness,
and still again from that ill I found freedom
and I assumed once more my living form
to suffer greater pain therein, I think.
    And my desire I pursued so far
that one day, hunting as I often would,
I came upon that cruel and lovely beast
naked within a fountain
when the sun strikes the hottest time of day.
I, since no other sight can please me more,
stood gazing at her, but she felt ashamed
and to revenge herself or else to hide
she splashed some water up into my face.
I'll tell the truth, though it may seem a lie!
I felt myself ripped from my very image
and quickly turn into a solitary,
wandering stag that moves from wood to wood,
and still I flee the rage of my own hounds.[14]

Canzone, I was never that gold cloud
that once descended in a precious rain
so as to quench in part Jove's burning flame;[15]
but surely I was flame lit by love's glance,
I was the bird[16] that rises through highest air
raising the one whom in my words I honor;
and no strange shape could ever make me leave
the first laurel, for still its lovely shade
clears every lesser pleasure from my heart.

34

Apollo, if the lovely wish still lives
that made you burn on the Thessalian wave,
and if those blond and cherished locks of hers
you have not with the passing years forgotten,[17]

from lazy frost and weather harsh and cruel
which lasts as long as your face is concealed,
now come defend the honored, sacred leaf
by which you first and then I, too, was snared;

and then by virtue of the amorous hope
that kept you going through your bitter life
make clear the atmosphere of such impression;

then we shall see together wondrously
our lady sitting there upon the grass,
her arms casting their shade around herself.

35

Alone and deep in thought I measure out
the most deserted fields, with slow, dark steps,

with eyes intent to flee whatever sign
of human footprint left within the sand.

I find no other shield for my protection
against the knowing glances of mankind,
for in my bearing all bereft of joy
one sees from outside how I burn within.

So now, I think, only the plains and mountains,
the rivers and the forests know the kind
of life I lead, the one concealed from all.[18]

And still, I never seem to find a path
too harsh, too wild for Love[19] to always join
me and to speak to me, and I to him!

— · ❦ · —

50

It is the time the rapid heavens bend
toward the West, the time our own day flees
to some expectant race beyond, perhaps,[20]
the time an old and weary pilgrim-woman
feeling the loneliness of foreign lands,
doubles her pace, hastening more and more;
      and then at her day's end,
though she is all alone,
at least she is consoled
by resting and forgetting for awhile
the labor and the pain of her past road.
But, oh, whatever pain the day brings me
grows more and more the moment
the eternal light begins to fade from us.

     When the sun's burning wheels begin to turn,
renouncing their place to the night, and shadows
are now cast deeper by the highest mountains,
the avid workman packs away his tools
and with the words of mountain songs he clears

the weight of that day's labor from his chest;
            and then he spreads his table
all full of meager food
like acorns of whose praises
all the world sings and manages to shun.[21]
But let who will find joy from time to time,
for I've not had, I will not say a happy,
but just one restful hour,
for all the turning of the sky and stars.

            And when the shepherd sees the great sphere's rays
are falling toward the nest in which it dwells
and in the east the country turning dark,
he stands up straight and with his trusty crook,
he leaves the grass and springs and beech's shade,
quietly moving his flock on its way;
            then far away from people
a hut or kind of cave
he weaves out of green leaves,
and there without a care he lies and sleeps.
But, ah, cruel Love, you drive me on to chase
the voice, the steps, the prints of a wild beast
who is destroying me;
you do not catch her: she couches and she flees.

            And sailors on their ship when sun is set
in some protected cove let their limbs drop
on the hard boards and sleep beneath coarse canvas.
But I, though sun may dive into the waves
and leave behind his back all that is Spain,
Granada and Morocco and the Pillars,
            and though all men and women,
animals and the world
may come to calm their ills—
but I cannot end my insistent anguish;
it pains me that each day augments my grief,
for here I am still growing in this love
for nearly ten years now,
wondering who will ever set me free.

And (to relieve my pain a bit by talking)
I see at evening oxen coming home,
freed from the fields and furrows they have plowed—
why, then, must I not be free of my sighs
at least sometimes? Why not my heavy yoke?
Why day and night must my eyes still be wet?
    Oh what I did that time
when I fixed them upon
the beauty of her face
to carve it in my heart's imagination
whence neither by coercion nor by art
could it be moved—not till I am the prey
of him who all does part![22]
And could he even then I am not sure.

    My song, if being with me
from morning until night
has made you join my party,
you will not show yourself in any place
and will care little to be praised by others—
it will suffice to think from hill to hill[23]
how I have been consumed
by fire of the living stone[24] I cling to.

————————— · 🐦 · —————————

52[25]

Diana never pleased her lover more[26]
when just by chance all of her naked body
he saw bathing within the chilly waters,

than did the simple mountain shepherdess
please me, the while she bathed the pretty veil
that holds her lovely blond hair in the breeze.

so that even now in hot sunlight she makes me
tremble all over with the chill of love.

61

Oh blessed be the day, the month, the year,
the season and the time, the hour, the instant,
the gracious countryside, the place where I
was struck by those two lovely eyes that bound me;

and blessed be the first sweet agony
I felt when I found myself bound to Love,
the bow and all the arrows that have pierced me,
the wounds that reach the bottom of my heart.

And blessed be all the poetry
I scattered, calling out my lady's name,
and all the sighs, and tears, and the desire;

blessed be all the paper upon which
I earn her fame, and every thought of mine,
only of her, and shared with no one else.[27]

81

I am so weary under the ancient burden
Of my sins and evil ways,
That I fear I shall faint beside the road
And fall into the hands of my enemy.

Indeed, a great Friend came to save me
In His exquisite and ineffable courtesy;
Then soared out of my sight,
so that in vain I try to look on Him.

But his voice still resounds here below:
"O ye that labor, this is the way;
Come unto me, if no one bars your path."

What grace, what love, what divine decree,
Will give me wings like a dove
To rise from earth and find rest.[28]

(TRANSLATED BY CHANDLER B. BEALL)

90

She'd let her gold hair flow free in the breeze[29]
that whirled it into thousands of sweet knots,
and lovely light would burn beyond all measure
in those fair eyes whose light is dimmer now.

Her face would turn the color pity wears,
a pity true or false I do not know,
and I with all love's tinder in my breast—
it's no surprise I quickly caught on fire.

The way she walked was not the way of mortals
but of angelic forms, and when she spoke
more than an earthly voice it was that sang:

a godly spirit and a living sun
was what I saw, and if she is not now,
my wound still bleeds, although the bow's unbent.[30]

122

Seventeen years the heavens have revolved[31]
since I first burned with fire that rages still;
when I think of the state that I am in
I feel a chill within those flames of mine.

How true the saying is: we lose our hair
before our vices, and though senses slacken

the human passions are no less intense—
the bitter shadow of our heavy veil.[32]

Ah grief! how long before I see the day
when, gazing at the flight my years have taken,
I step out of my grievous trial by fire?

Will that day ever come when the sweet air
about her lovely visage pleases these eyes
no more than I would wish and as is fitting?

· ❧ ·

126

Clear, cool, sweet, running waters[33]
where she, for me the only
woman, would rest her lovely body,
        kind branch on which it pleased her
(I sigh to think of it)
to make a column for her lovely side,
        and grass and flowers which her gown
richly flowing covered
with its angelic folds,
sacred air serene
where Love with those fair eyes opened my heart:
listen all of you together
to these my mournful, my last words.

        If it, indeed, must be my fate,
and Heaven works its ways,
that Love close up these eyes while they still weep,
        let grace see my poor body
be buried there among you
and let my soul return to its home naked;
        then death would be less harsh
if I could bear this hope
unto that fearful crossing,
because the weary soul
could never in a more secluded port,

in a more tranquil grave
flee from my poor belabored flesh and bones.

       And there will come a time, perhaps,
that to the well-known place
the lovely animal returns, and tamed,
       and there where she first saw me
that day which now is blessed
she turns her eyes with hope and happiness
       in search of me, and—ah, the pity—
to see me there as dust
among the stones, Love will
inspire her and she will sigh
so sweetly she will win for me some mercy
and force open the heavens
drying her eyes there with her lovely veil.

       Falling from gracious boughs,
I sweetly call to mind,
were flowers in a rain upon her bosom,
       and she was sitting there
humble in such glory
now covered in a shower of love's blooms:
       a flower falling on her lap,
some on her golden curls,
like pearls set into gold
they seemed to me that day;
some fell to rest on ground, some on the water,
and some in lovelike wandering
were circling down and saying, "Here Love reigns."

       How often I would say
at that time, full of awe,
"She certainly was born up there in Heaven!"
       And her divine behavior,
her face and words and her sweet smile
so filled me with forgetfulness
       and so divided me
from the true image
that I would sigh and say:
"How and when I did I come here?"—

thinking I was in Heaven, not where I was;
and since then I have loved
this bank of grass and find peace nowhere else.

If you had all the beauty you desired,
you could with boldness leave
the wood and make your way among mankind. [34]

· 🐝 ·

129

From thought to thought, mountain to mountain top
love leads me on; and every trodden path
I find unsuited to a peaceful life.
If on a lonely slope a brook or spring
or a dark vale between two peaks exist,
that is the place my frightened soul takes refuge.
And with Love urging it
it laughs or weeps, now fears and now takes heart,
and my face, following the soul's direction,
clouds up and clears again
never remaining long in one condition:
at such a sight the man who knows such fate
would say, "He burns and his state is uncertain."

In the high mountains and harsh woods I find
some peace; and every habitable place
is for my eyes a mortal enemy.
With every step I take comes a new thought
about my lady which often will turn
to pleasure torment that I bear for her.
And on the verge of changing
the bittersweetness of this life of mine
I say, "Perhaps it is Love saving you
for better days; perhaps,
you're loathsome to yourself but dear to her."
Then to another thought I pass and sigh:
"Now could this be the truth? But how? But when?"

Whenever pine or mountain casts its shade
I sometimes stop, and on the first stone seen
with all my mind I etch her lovely face;
            returning to reality I find
my breast softened with pity, and I cry:
"What have you come to? How far from her you are!"
            But for as long as I
can hold my wandering mind on the first thought
and look at her and not think of myself,
I feel Love so close by,
my soul is satisfied by its own error;
in many places I see her, so lovely
that all I ask is that my error last.

            I've seen her many times—now who'll believe me?—
in the clear water and above green grass,
alive, and in the trunk of a beech tree,
            and in a cloud of white so shaped that Leda[35]
would certainly have said her daughter's beauty
fades like a star in sunlight next to it.
            The wilder the place is,
the more barren the shore where I may be,
the more lovely do my thoughts depict her image;
but when the truth dispels
that sweet mistake, right then and there I sit
down cold as dead stone set on living rock,
a statue that can think and weep and write.

            Up to that mountain which no mountain shades,
up to the highest and the freest peak,
I feel my whole desire being drawn.
            Then I begin to measure with my eyes
my losses, and while weeping I unburden
the painful cloud that gathers in my heart
            to see and think how much
air separates me from her lovely face
always so near but yet so far from me.
Then softly to myself:
"How do you know, poor fool? Perhaps out there,
somewhere, someone is sighing for your absence."
And with this thought my soul begins to breathe.

My song, beyond these Alps
where skies are more serene and happier,
you'll see me by a running brook once more[36]
where you can sense the aura
distilling from the fresh and fragrant laurel:[37]
there is my heart and there is one who steals it;
what you see here is but the ghost of me.

· ❦ ·

132

If it's not love, then what is it I feel?[38]
But if it's love, by God, what is this thing?
If good, why then the bitter mortal sting?
If bad, then why is every torment sweet?

If I burn willingly, why weep and grieve?
And if against my will, what good lamenting?
O living death, O pleasurable harm,[39]
how can you rule me if I not consent?

And if I do consent, it's wrong to grieve.
Caught in contrasting winds in a frail boat
on the high seas I am without a helm,

so light of wisdom, so laden of error,
that I myself do not know what I want,
and shiver in midsummer, burn in winter.

· ❦ ·

134

I find no peace, and I am not at war,[40]
I fear and hope, and burn and I am ice;
I fly above the heavens, and lie on earth,
and I grasp nothing and embrace the world.

One keeps me jailed who neither locks nor opens,
nor keeps me for her own nor frees the noose;
Love does not kill, nor does he loose my chains;
he wants me lifeless but won't loosen me.

I see with no eyes, shout without a tongue;
I yearn to perish, and I beg for help;
I hate myself and love somebody else.

I thrive on pain and laugh with all my tears;
I dislike death as much as I do life:
because of you, lady, I am this way.

156

I saw on earth angelic qualities
and heavenly beauties unique in the world,
and to recall them pains and pleases me,
for all I see seems shadow, smoke, and dreams.

And I saw weeping those two lovely lights
both envied by the sun a thousand times,
and I heard words pronounced amid deep sighing
that would make mountains move and rivers stop.

Love, wisdom and worth, pity and sorrow
made out of tears a sweeter symphony
than any other heard throughout the world;

the heavens were so entranced by harmony
that not a leaf upon its branch dare move,
so full of sweetness was the air and wind.

· ❦ ·

159

From what part of the Heavens, from what Idea
did Nature take the model[41] to derive
that lovely face of charm by which she chose
to show down here her power up above?

What fountain nymph, what woodland goddess ever
let such fine hair of gold flow in the breeze?
How did a heart collect so many virtues
the sum of which is guilty of my death?

Who seeks for divine beauty seeks in vain,
if he has not yet looked upon those eyes
and seen how tenderly she makes them move;

he does not know how love can heal and kill,
who does not know the sweetness of her sighs,
the sweetness of her speech, how sweet her smile.

· ❦ ·

161

O useless steps, O thoughts charming and quick,
O solid memory, O burning love,
O powerful desire, O failing heart,
O my eyes (eyes no more, but fountains),

O leafy bough, honor of famous brows,
O single symbol for those dual values,
O weary life of mine, O my sweet error
which forces me to search the shores and hills,

O lovely face where Love has put together
both spurs and rein with which he pricks and turns me
as pleases him, and kicking back is useless,

O loving souls who love in graciousness,
if there are any, all you shades and dust,
ah, stay awhile and see what pain is mine.[42]

———————————— · 🐦 · ————————————

189

My ship[43] full of forgetful cargo sails
through rough seas at the midnight of a winter
between Charybdis and the Scylla reef,[44]
my master, no, my foe, is at the helm;

at each oar sits a quick and insane thought
that seems to scorn the storm and what it brings;
the sail, by wet eternal winds of sighs,
of hopes and of desires blowing breaks;

a rain of tears, a mist of my disdain
washes and frees those all too weary ropes
made up of wrong, entwined with ignorance.

Hidden are those two trusty signs of mine;
dead in the waves is reason as is skill,
and I despair of ever reaching port.

———————————— · 🐦 · ————————————

248

Who seeks to see the best Nature and Heaven
can do among us, come and gaze on her,
sole sun, and not for just my eyes alone
but for the blind world which cares not for virtue;

come quickly now, because Death steals away
the best ones first and leaves for the last the worst:
this one, awaited in the kingdom of the gods,
this lovely, mortal thing will pass, not last.

He shall see, if he comes in time, all virtue,
all loveliness, all regal-mannered ways
joined in one body, tempered marvelously;

then he will say that all my verse is dumb,
my talent overcome by too much light.
But if he waits too long, he'll weep forever.

264

I'm always thinking, and I'm caught in thought
by such abundant pity for myself
that often I am led
to weeping for a different kind of grief:
for seeing every day the end come closer,
a thousand times I begged God for those wings
with which our intellect
can soar to Heaven from this mortal jail.[45]
But until now I have received no help,
no matter how I plead or sigh or weep,
and it is only just that it be so—
if he who can walk straight chooses to fall,
then he deserves to lie upon the ground.
Those arms stretched out in mercy[46]
in which I trust are open to me still,
but I still fear to think
how others ended, and I dread my state
and am spurred on, and it could be too late.

A thought speaks to the mind and it declares:
"You're longing still? What help do you expect?
You poor thing, don't you see
with what dishonor time is passing by?
Make up your mind now, wisely, and decide
to pull out of your heart every last root
of pleasure that can never
bring happiness, nor will it let you breathe.
Since you have long been tired and disgusted

by that false sweetness of a fleeting good,
a gift the treacherous world bestows on some,
why do you still place hope in such a thing
devoid of all peace and stability?
While life is in your body
you have the rein of all thoughts in your hands.
Hold tight now while you can,
for, as you know, delay is dangerous,
and now is not too early to begin.

How well you know the great amount of sweetness
your eyes have taken from the sight of her,
the one I wish now were
still to be born, that we may have more peace.
You certainly remember, as you must,
the image of her rushing down into
your heart, there where, perhaps,
the flame of other torches could not enter.
She set it burning, and if the false flame
has lasted many years waiting the day
that for our own salvation never comes,
now raise yourself to a more blessed hope,
by gazing on the heavens whirling round you,
beautiful and immortal:
if here desire, happy in its ills,
achieves its satisfaction
by a mere glance, a word or two, a song,
what will that joy be like, if this is great?"

There is another thought that's bittersweet
with difficult and yet delightful weight
sitting within my soul
which fills my heart with need and feeds it hope;
only for love of glorious, kindly fame
it does not feel the times I freeze or burn
or if I'm pale or thin;
and killing it makes it grow back the stronger.
This,[47] from the day I slept in baby clothes,
has been growing with me all of my days,
and I fear both of us will share one grave;

for when my soul is naked of its body,
glory's desire cannot accompany it.
If Latin or Greek tongues[48]
praise me when I am dead, it is all wind;
and since I fear to be
always hoarding what in a moment scatters,
I would embrace the truth,[49] and leave the lies.

But then that other passion filling me
seems to block out all others born around it;
meanwhile time flies while I
with no concern for self write for another;
the radiance of those lovely eyes melting me
mellifluously in warmth of clarity
has hold of me with reins
against which neither wit nor might avails.
So then what good is it for me to oil
my boat when it is caught upon a reef
and still tied up so tight by those two knots?[50]
You,[51] who from other knots that bind the world
in different ways have liberated me,
my Lord, why do you not,
once and for all, wipe from my face this shame?
For like a man who dreams
I seem to see Death standing there before me,
and I would fight for life, and have no weapons.

I know myself, and I am not deceived
by a mistaken truth; I'm forced by Love
who blocks the path of honor
for anyone who trusts too much in him;
I feel enter my heart from time to time
a virtuous disdain, harsh and severe,
which pulls all hidden thoughts
up to my brow for everyone to see.
To love a mortal thing with such great faith,
the kind that should be placed in God alone,
is less becoming the more one looks for honor.
And this[52] in a loud voice also calls back
my reason which went wandering with the senses;
but though it hears and means

to come back home, bad habit drives it further
and paints before my eyes
the one born only so that I may die
because she pleased me, and herself, too much.

Nor do I know how much space Heaven gave me
when I was newly brought upon the earth
to suffer that harsh war
that I managed to start against myself;
nor can I through my body's veil foresee
the day that must arrive to close my life;
but I see my hair changing
and within me all of my desires aging.
Now that I feel the time for my departure
approaches—it cannot be far away—
as he whose loss makes him wary and wise,
I think back to the point it was I left
the right road leading to the port of good:
on one side[53] I am pierced
by shame and sorrow, and they turn me back:
the other[54] will not free me
from pleasure which through time has grown so strong
that it dares bargain now with Death itself.

Song, this is how I live and my heart is
colder with fear than snow that's turned to ice,
feeling for certain that I am perishing;
in trying to decide I've wound the spool
by now with a good length of my short thread;[55]
never was there a weight
heavier than the one I carry now,
for with Death at my side
I seek new rules by which to lead my life,
and see the best, but still cling to the worst.

271

The burning knot which hour after hour
bound me for twenty-one entire years[56]
Death has untied; I never felt such grief,
nor do I think that man can die of sorrow.

Love, not yet willing to let go of me,
had set another snare within the grass
and with new tinder lit another fire
making it very hard for me to flee.

And if it had not been for long experience
of my first labors, I'd be caught and burned
and all the more for being less green wood.

Death has delivered me another time—
broken the knot, stamped out the scattered fire—
against whom neither force nor wit avails.

272

Life runs away and never rests a moment
and death runs after it with mighty stride,
and present things and things back from the past
and from the future, too, wage war on me:

anticipation, memory weigh down
my heart on either side so that, in truth,
if I did not take pity on myself,[57]
I would, by now, be free of all such thoughts.

What little sweetness my sad heart once felt
comes back to me; but from the other side
I see turbulent winds blowing my sails;

I see a storm, in port, and weary now
my helmsman,[58] and my masts and lines destroyed,
and the fair stars I loved to look at, dead.

298

When I turn back to look upon those years
that flying by have scattered all my thoughts
and quenched the fire in which I, freezing, burned
and ended my repose so full of woes,

broken the faith of amorous deceptions
and made two separate parts of all my good—
one in Heaven, the other in the ground—
and lost the profits of my painful gains,

I'm startled and I feel so very naked
that I envy the gravest of misfortunes,
so much I fear and suffer for myself.

O Star of mine, O Chance. O Fate, O Death,
O Day [59] always so sweet yet cruel to me,
to what low state you have reduced me now!

310

Zephyr[60] comes back and brings with him fair weather
and his sweet family of grass and flowers,
and crying Philomel and chirping Procne,[61]
and Springtime all in whiteness and vermilion;

the meadows smile, the skies turn clear again,
and Jove takes joy in gazing at his daughter;[62]
the waters, earth, and air are full of love
and every living thing is bent on loving.

But there comes back to me only the gravest
of sighs that from the bottom of my heart
are drawn by her who took its keys to Heaven;

the song of birds, the flowering of meadows,
the noble graciousness of lovely ladies
for me are deserts now, wild savage beasts.

· ❦ ·

319

My days, swifter than any fawn, have fled
like shadows, and for me no good has lasted
more than a wink, and few are those calm hours
whose bittersweetness I keep in my mind.

O wretched world, changing and arrogant,
a man who puts his hope in you is blind:
from you my heart was torn and now is held
by one whose flesh and bones are turned to dust.

But her best form,[63] which still continues living
and will forever live high in the heavens,
makes me fall more in love with all her beauty;

and as my hair is changing I think only
what she is like today and where she dwells,
what it was like to see her lovely veil.[64]

· ❦ ·

323

One day while at my window all alone,[65]
where I could see so many strange things happen
that merely looking at them made me weary,
a beast I saw appear on my right side
with human face to make Jove flare with love

pursued by two swift hounds,[66] one black one white,
    who dug their teeth so deep
into both sides of such a noble beast
that in no time they forced her to the pass
where, trapped within the stone,
untimely death now vanquished such great beauty,
and I sighed from the sight of her harsh fate.

    Then out on the deep sea I saw a ship[67]
with silken ropes and sails made out of gold
all wrought with ivory and ebony;
    the sea was calm, the breeze was gently blowing,
and there was not a cloud to veil the sky;
with rich and precious cargo she was laden.
    And then a sudden storm[68]
out of the east so shook the air and waters,
the boat was shattered up against the rocks.
O what oppressing grief:
in short time crushed, and little space now hides,
tall riches that are second to no others!

    Within a youthful grove were flowering
the boughs of a young, slender laurel tree
that seemed to have been grown in Paradise;
    and from her shade there came so sweet a sound
of different birds and so much other joy
that it had cut me off from the real world.
    And as I stared at her
the sky around her changed, and turning black
it struck with lightning, and then by the roots
that happy plant was torn
up suddenly, and now my life is sorrow,
for shade like hers can never be regained.

    Inside that very grove a sparkling fountain
sprang from a rock, and its fresh, loving waters
it poured forth with a gentle murmuring.
    To that secluded place so fair and shady
no shepherds and no boors would come, but only
muses and nymphs singing to that clear flow.
    I sat down there, and while

I took more sweetness from such harmony
and from that sight, I saw a chasm open
and sweep it all away,
fountain and place, and I am still left grieving,
and just the thought of it fills me with fear.

A marvelous phoenix[69] with both of its wings
adorned in purple and its head in gold,
I saw there in the woods, proud and alone.
 At first I thought it was a holy thing,
immortal, till it reached the torn-out laurel
and came upon the spring stolen away.
 All things rush to their end;
for, seeing all the leaves strewn on the ground,
the trunk broken, those living waters dry,
against herself she turned
her beak, as if in scorn, and quickly vanished—
pity and love then set my heart aflame.

 At last I saw through grass and flowers walking
in thought a lady fair, so full of joy—
to think of it sets me aflame and shaking—
 humble within herself, haughty to Love;
and she had on a gown so very white,
so woven that it seemed of snow and gold,
 but all the upper part
of her was shrouded in a mist of dark.
Then stung upon her heel by a small snake,[70]
as a cut flower withers,
she left in joy and more than confident:
ah, nothing but our tears last in this world!

 My song, you well may say:
"These six visions just given to my lord
have given him a sweet desire to die."

333

Go now, my grieving verse, to the hard stone
that hides my precious treasure in the earth;
and there call her, who will respond from Heaven
although her mortal part be darkly buried,

and tell her I am weary now of living,
of sailing through the horrors of this sea,
but that, by gathering up her scattered leaves,[71]
I follow her this way, step after step,

speaking of her alone, alive and dead
(rather, alive, and now immortalized),
so that the world may know and love her more.

Let her watch for the day I pass away
(It is not far from now), let her meet me,
call me, draw me to what she is in Heaven.

346

The chosen angels and the blessed souls
of Heaven's citizens, on the first day
my lady passed away, surrounded her,
all full of wonder and of reverence.

"What light is this, and what unusual beauty,"
they said to one another, "for so lovely
a soul in all this time has never risen
out of the erring world to this high home."

She, happy to have changed her dwelling,
is equal to the most perfected souls,
meanwhile, from time to time, she turns to see

if I am following her, and seems to wait;
so all my thoughts and wishes strain to Heaven—
I hear her praying that I hurry up.

———————————— · ❦ · ————————————

353

O lovely little bird singing away
in tone of grief for all the time gone by,
you see the night and winter hastening,
the day and all those happy months behind;

aware as you are of your grievous troubles
could you be so of my plight like your own,
you would fly to the bosom of this wretch
to share with him some of his painful grief.

I cannot say our portions would be equal,
since she you weep for may still have her life
which Death and Heaven in my case were stingy;

but the forbidding season and the hour,
the memory of sweet years and bitter ones,
invites me to discuss with you my pity.

———————————— · ❦ · ————————————

365

I go my way regretting those past times
I spent in loving something which was mortal
instead of soaring high, since I had wings
that might have taken me to higher levels.

You who see all my shameful, wicked errors,
King of all heaven, invisible, immortal,
help this frail soul of mine for she has strayed,
and all her emptiness fill up with grace,

so that, having once lived in storms, at war,
I may now die in peace, in port; and if my stay
was vain, at least let my departure count.

Over that little life that still remains to me,
and at my death, deign that your head be present:
You know You are the only hope I have.

NOTES

·❦·

1. This first poem, like 316 other verse compositions in the *Canzoniere*, is a Petrarchan sonnet. The sonnet form was developed in the thirteenth century by poets of the Sicilian School, writing at the court of Frederick II. Giacomo da Lentini is usually considered its inventor, although Petrarch made it popular throughout all of Western literature. The Petrarchan sonnet is a lyric poem, generally of fourteen hendecasyllabic lines, which is divided into an octave (rhyme scheme *ababab*) and a sestet (the rhyme scheme is usually *cdecde* but it may also be *cdcdcd* or *ccdccd*, for instance). In English literature, in addition to the Petrarchan sonnet, the Shakespearean and the Spenserian sonnet variants exist. In the Shakespearean sonnet, there are usually four divisions rather than two: three quatrains (usually rhymed *abab cdcd efef*) and a rhymed couplet (*gg*), which provides a more epigrammatic conclusion than is typical of the Petrarchan sonnet. The Spenserian sonnet has three quatrains and a couplet but employs linking rhymes between the quatrains (*abab bcbc cdcd ee*).

2. Toward the end of his life, Petrarch referred to his collection of poems as "trifles," and he never actually assigned a specific title to them. The book is often called the *Rime sparse* ("Scattered Verses") after Petrarch's description of them in the first line of his first poem. It is often also called the *Canzoniere* ("Songbook"). Petrarch's apparent nonchalance about these lyrics was really only a ruse, since he spent his entire life composing and revising them carefully.

3. The anniversary of Christ's crucifixion. According to poem 211, Petrarch first saw Laura on April 6, 1327.

4. This is a reference to the Veronica, the legendary kerchief with which St. Veronica wiped Christ's brow on the way to Calvary. The Veronica is believed to have retained the features of Christ's face and is preserved in St. Peter's in Rome.

5. Poem 22 is a sestina, a six-stanza poem, each stanza of which is made up of six hendecasyllabic lines plus a closing three-line *tornada*. Each stanza uses six different words in end-rhyme position, and these same six words are repeated in a different end position in all six stanzas: *abcdef/ faebdc/ cfdabe/ ecbfad/ deacfb/ bdfeca*. Each successive stanza repeats the end-word of the preceding stanza in the order of the lines 615243.

6. According to Virgil (*Aeneid* VI, 442ff.), the "amorous wood" is the place in the Underworld assigned to those who die for love.

[55]

7. Apollo's pursuit of Daphne was "vain," because she was transformed into a laurel when she prayed to her father, god of the river Peneus in Thessaly, to preserve her virginity. The laurel became sacred to Apollo, god of truth, and it is identified with Petrarch's Laura throughout the *Canzoniere*. Petrarch's desire to be with Laura is, like Apollo's, a physical one.

8. Poem 23 is a *canzone*, a lyric "song" consisting of a varying number of equal stanzas and a shorter envoy. Petrarch's usual practice was to employ five or six stanzas with a brief envoy, or closing stanza.

9. Either the Rhône or the Durance rivers in Provence.

10. In Ovid's *Metamorphoses*, Phaeton drove his father the sun god's chariot and was unable to control the horses. As they raced off course, the earth was set ablaze and Jupiter destroyed Phaeton with a thunderbolt. He fell near the river Po, where his sisters mourned him by weeping until they were transformed into poplars, and Cygnus, his friend and relative, turned into a swan out of grief.

11. In Ovid's myth, when Battus revealed Mercury's theft of Apollo's oxen, Mercury turned him into a stone.

12. Ovid's myth of Byblis tells of how her brother rejected her love and she was changed into a fountain.

13. According to Ovid, Echo helped conceal Jupiter's infidelity from Juno, who punished her by making it impossible for her to speak except by echoing the voices of others. Her body wasted away and turned to stone when Narcissus rejected her love, and she became a disembodied voice.

14. Ovid's myth of Actaeon tells of how he was punished for accidentally seeing the goddess Diana at her bath. She turned him into a stag, and he was pursued and torn to pieces by his own hounds, who could not recognize him.

15. Jupiter visited Danae, a mortal maiden, in a golden rain when her father tried to conceal her from the god by locking her in a tower. He also fell in love with another mortal woman, Semele, the daughter of Cadmus. At the jealous Juno's behest, he appeared to his beloved in the form of lightning and thunder, which consumed her.

16. Jupiter, in the form of an eagle, took the Trojan Ganymede to Olympus to serve the gods as a cupbearer.

17. A reference to Apollo's love for Daphne and her transformation into a laurel on the banks of the river Peneus in Thessaly.

18. This sonnet, considered one of the outstanding poems in the *Canzoniere*, reflects Petrarch's search for solace in nature, and this tercet provides an example of the "pathetic fallacy," a practice common to many poets of nature, who credit nature with human feelings.

19. The conceit externalizing Petrarch's inner feelings as Amor or Cupid was often imitated in the Renaissance.

20. The time is the mysterious and sleepy hour near sunset.

21. An allusion to the Golden Age. The world may praise the simple life, but is not willing to live it.

22. A reference to death.

23. See the beginning of *canzone* 129.

24. Laura is as cold and hard as a stone, but a stone that can also light the fires of passion.

25. This poem is a madrigal, a short poem composed of from eight to eleven lines (usually of eleven syllables or a mixture of eleven and seven syllables). It was frequently set to music.

26. Another reference to the myth of Diana and Actaeon. See *canzone* 23 and note 14.

27. The hymnlike atmosphere of this sonnet echoes the beatitudes in Luke 6:17, 20–23 in the rhetorical device of anaphora. The repetition gives the impression of Petrarch's monotonous suffering but is also a quiet exaltation of Laura and his own thoughts and works.

28. This sonnet, one of Petrarch's most original, contains a host of Biblical allusions, especially to Psalms 38 and 55, as well as to Christ's words in Matthew 11:28.

29. The description of Laura in lines 1 and 9–11 is an allusion to Virgil's description of Venus (*Aeneid* I. 314–20, 327–28, 402–405).

30. Although Laura has aged, the poet still feels the pain of his love, described as a wound—yet another allusion to Virgil's *Aeneid*, where Dido constantly describes her love for Aeneas as a wound.

31. Another anniversary poem.

32. The "heavy veil" refers to the human body.

33. The waters of the Sorgue, the river near Vaucluse, Petrarch's home in southern France. This is perhaps the most famous *canzone* in the *Canzoniere*. It focuses upon the changes time works in our lives and moves back and forth from past to present to future. The theme of memory is important here and throughout the *Canzoniere*.

34. This *congedo* ("leavetaking"), a particular form the *envoi* (envoy, or ending) may take in a *canzone*, is addressed to the poem itself. The tradition of the poet addressing his own poem began with the troubadours of Provence, the inventors of the modern European love lyric in the twelfth and thirteenth centuries, and Petrarch is very much aware of their literary traditions.

35. Zeus visited Leda, wife of Tyndareus, King of Sparta, in the form of a swan. In most myths, Clytemnestra is her child by Tyndareus; Helen of Troy, Castor, and Polydeuces are her children by Zeus.

36. The Sorgue.

37. Petrarch frequently puns on the name of Laura, as he does here.

38. This poem was the source of Chaucer's "Canticus Troili."

39. This line falls among a series of several rhetorical questions, each of which embodies a contrast; it sums up in four words the paradox of Petrarchan love.

40. A series of antitheses or oxymora depicts the lover's psychological state in this sonnet, which was the most popular poem in the European Renaissance.

41. An allusion to Platonic forms and Laura's perfections.

42. This sonnet is an example of the use of the rhetorical device of anaphora.

43. The ship is a frequent metaphor in Renaissance poetry. Here it embodies the lover's mental state.

44. Charybdis and Scylla were the two mythical monsters symbolizing the two dangerous sides (the whirlpool and the reef) of the Strait of Messina between Sicily and Italy.

45. Although this poem was probably written in 1348 while Laura was still alive, Petrarch places it at the beginning of the poems on Laura's death.

46. The arms of Christ upon the cross.

47. "This" refers to the thought described in the preceding stanza.

48. Latin and Greek were considered the most noble languages by Renaissance humanists. Although the study of Latin was widespread, Greek was hardly known in Petrarch's day.

49. A reference to God.

50. The "two knots" are Petrarch's love for Laura and his desire for worldly fame, which keep him from devoting his entire life to God. He debates his "two chains" with St. Augustine in the *Secretum*.

51. The poet addresses God directly until the end of the stanza.

52. "This" refers back to "virtuous disdain" in line 96.

53. The side of reason is afflicted.

54. This "other" is the side of the appetite or passion.

55. Metaphors for a man's life.

56. Another anniversary poem.

57. If it were not for Petrarch's fear of eternal damnation, he would, by this time, have killed himself.

58. The "helmsman" is reason.

59. The day Petrarch first saw Laura coincides with the day of her death. Both were on April 6.

60. The Zephyr is the west wind that blows in the spring. This is a traditional *départ printanier* or "spring opening" often employed by the troubadours and poets such as Petrarch who use the conventions they invented, but, in this poem, it is followed by thoughts not of love but of death, which have ruined the beauties of that season, the season of love.

61. In Ovid's *Metamorphoses*, Philomela was raped by her sister Procne's husband, and he cut out her tongue so that she could not report the crime. But she wove a tapestry telling her story to her sister. Procne then avenged Tereus' crime by killing their son Itys and feeding him to her husband in a meal. When Tereus tried to kill Philomela and Procne, he was changed into a hoopoe, while Philomela and Procne were turned into a nightingale and a swallow.

62. Jove and his daughter are the planets Jupiter and Venus, which are aligned favorably at this time of year.

63. A reference to Laura's soul.

64. The veil is the mortal body.

65. In this poem, which derived from the visionary tradition and inspired a family of sonnets by such major European poets as Du Bellay and Spenser, Petrarch reflects on Laura's death and what it meant to him. The six metaphors

of her death (the beast, ship, laurel tree, fountain, phoenix, and fair lady) are images seen elsewhere in the *Canzoniere*. To the witness of each calamity, death is final and always unexpected, even though it is depicted as an integral part of the nature of earthly things, including the most beautiful and admirable.

66. The two hounds probably represent day and night.

67. Compare this use of the image of the ship with that in sonnet 189.

68. The storm refers to the Black Plague of 1348 which killed Laura.

69. A mythical bird of incredible beauty which died after five hundred to six hundred years consumed by fire, arising from the ashes to live another long life. It is usually a symbol of immortality.

70. Eurydice, trying to flee from an unwanted suitor, was bitten when she trod upon a serpent. Orpheus tried unsuccessfully to recover her from the Underworld.

71. The poet is gathering together all the poetry he has written in praise of Laura.

GIOVANNI BOCCACCIO
1313–75

BORN EITHER IN FLORENCE OR IN THE NEARBY VILLAGE OF CERTALDO, Giovanni Boccaccio was the illegitimate son of a successful merchant associated with the powerful Bardi Bank of Florence. In 1327, his father (who had by then recognized him as his son) took him to Naples, where Boccaccio learned the banking trade. Drawn more to letters than to business, however, Boccaccio stayed in Naples until 1340, where he spent most of his time studying the classics and associating with other scholars and members of the Neapolitan court. A number of his works in the vernacular during this period were to be very influential upon the course of European literature—especially the *Filostrato* (1335–36), a poem which introduced the Troilus and Cressida story into Western literature and would later be important sources for both Chaucer and Shakespeare.

The economic crisis of that time and the failure of the Bardi Bank forced Boccaccio to return to Florence at the end of 1340. There he wrote a number of other Italian poetic works and shortly after the Black Plague struck the city (1349–50), he completed his masterpiece, the *Decameron*. Soon thereafter (1350), Boccaccio met Petrarch, and from that time on he became more and more interested in classical scholarship, completing a number of Latin works which were to have a wide European readership among humanist scholars and intellectuals. During the later part of his life, Boccaccio enjoyed international fame as a poet and humanist, also serving the Florentine government on a number of diplomatic missions. He died only a year after his great friend and mentor, Petrarch, had passed away.

Boccaccio's *Decameron* is a collection of one hundred short stories, or *novelle*, told by a group of seven young ladies and three young men during a retreat from the city of Florence in order to escape the plague of 1348. It constituted the greatest single work of imaginative fiction in European literature until that time and continued to serve as a model of prose fiction for the entire European Renaissance. Its stories were used by a number of major dramatists and poets (including Shakespeare), and the

Decameron may fairly be said to have given birth to the modern tradition of short fiction.

The selections reprinted in this anthology represent a number of the important themes typical of Boccaccio's work—the concern with the dialectic between appearance and reality; the place of religion in society and a critique of the church's human failings; the acceptance of a hearty sensuality; the admiration for wit and intelligence; and the role of women in Renaissance culture. Boccaccio's *Decameron* is the first great collection of fiction which grants to ordinary men and women a dominant role as protagonists. It takes the "business logic" of the prosperous Florentine merchant class and turns this mercantile wisdom into a philosophy for everyday living. All of the multifaceted and colorful atmosphere of Renaissance Italy is given inimitable artistic expression by Boccaccio in what has often been described as a "human comedy."

BIBLIOGRAPHY

Giovanni Boccaccio, *The Decameron*, trans, Mark Musa and Peter Bondanella (New York: New American Library, 1982); Teodolinda Barolini, "Giovanni Boccaccio," in William T. H. Jackson, ed., *European Writers: The Middle Ages and the Renaissance* (New York: Scribner's, 1983); Thomas G. Bergin, *Boccaccio* (New York: Viking, 1981); Vittore Branca, *Boccaccio: The Man and His Works* (New York: New York University Press, 1976); Robert Dombroski, ed., *Critical Perspectives on the "Decameron"* (New York: Barnes & Noble, 1976); Millicent Marcus, *An Allegory of Form: Literary Self-Consciousness in the "Decameron"* (Saratoga: Anma Libri, 1979); Giuseppe Mazzotta, *The World at Play in Boccaccio's "Decameron"* (Princeton: Princeton University Press, 1986); Joy H. Potter, *Five Frames for the "Decameron"* (Princeton: Princeton University Press, 1982).

STORIES FROM
THE DECAMERON[*]

— · 🕊 · —

Preface

Here begins the book called The Decameron,[1] also known as Prince Galeotto,[2] in which one hundred tales are contained, told in ten days by seven ladies and three young men.

To have compassion for those who suffer is a human quality which everyone should possess, especially those who have required comfort themselves in the past and have managed to find it in others. Now, if any man ever had need of compassion and appreciated it or derived comfort from it, I am that person; for from my earliest youth until the present time I have been aflame beyond all measure with a most exalted and noble love, perhaps too much so for my lowly station, if I were to tell about it. And even though those judicious people who knew about my love praised me and held me in high regard because of it, it was, nevertheless, still extremely difficult to bear: certainly not because of the cruelty of the lady I loved but rather because of the overwhelming passion kindled in my mind by my unrestrained desire, which, since it would not allow me to rest content with any acceptable goal, often caused me to suffer more pain than was necessary. In my suffering, the pleasant conversation and the admirable consolation of a friend on a number of occasions gave me much relief, and I am firmly convinced I should now be dead if it had not been for that. But since He who is infinite had been pleased to decree by immutable law that all earthly things should come to an end, my love, more fervent than any other, a love which no resolution, counsel, public shame, or danger that might result from it could break or bend, diminished by itself in the course of time, and at present it has left in my mind only that pleasure which it usually retains for those who do not venture too far out on its deep, dark

[*]The following selections and notes are from Giovanni Boccaccio, *The Decameron*, trans. Mark Musa and Peter Bondanella (New York: New American Library, 1982).

waters; and thus where there once used to be a source of suffering, now that all torment has been removed, there remains only a sense of delight.

But while the pain has ceased, I have not lost the memory of favors already received from those who were touched by my heavy burdens; nor, I believe, will this memory ever pass, except with my death. And because it is my feeling that gratitude is the most praiseworthy of all qualities, and that its opposite the most worthy of reproach, in order not to appear ungrateful, I have promised myself to use my limited talents in doing whatever possible (now that I am able to say I am free of love) in exchange for what I have received—if not to repay with consolation those who helped me (since their intelligence and their good fortune will perhaps make this unneccessary), then, at least, to assist those who may be in need of it. And however slight my support or, if you prefer, comfort may be to those in need, nevertheless I believe it should still be available where the need is greatest, for there it will be the most useful and the most appreciated.

And who will deny that such comfort, no matter how insufficient, is more fittingly bestowed on charming ladies than on men? For they, in fear and shame, conceal the hidden flames of love within their delicate breasts, a love far stronger than one which is openly expressed, as those who have felt and suffered this know; and furthermore, restricted by the wishes, whims, and commands of fathers, mothers, brothers, and husbands, they remain most of the time limited to the narrow confines of their bedrooms, where they sit in apparent idleness, now wishing one thing and now wishing another, turning over in their minds a number of thoughts which cannot always be pleasant ones. And because of these thoughts, if there should arise within their minds a sense of melancholy brought on by burning desire, these ladies will be forced to suffer this terrible pain unless it is replaced by new interests. Furthermore, they are less able than men to bear these discomforts; this does not happen to a man who is in love, as we can plainly see. If men are afflicted by melancholy or ponderous thoughts, they have many ways of alleviating or forgetting them: if they wish, they can take a walk and listen to or look at many different things; they can go hawking, hunting, or fishing; they can ride, gamble, or attend to business. Each of these pursuits has the power, either completely or in part, to occupy a man's mind and to remove from it a painful thought, even if only for a brief moment; and so, in one way or another, either consolation follows or the pain becomes less. Therefore, I wish to make up in part for the wrong done by Fortune, who is less generous with her support where there is less strength, as we witness in the case of our delicate ladies. As support and diversion for those ladies in love (to those others who are not I leave the needle, spindle, and wool winder), I intend to tell one hundred stories, or fables, or parables, or histories, or whatever you wish to call them, as they were told in ten days (as will become quite evident) by a worthy group of seven ladies and three young men who came together during the time of the plague (which just recently took so many lives), and I shall also include several songs sung for their delight by these same ladies. These stories will contain a number of different cases of love, both bitter and sweet, as well as other exciting adventures taken from modern and ancient times. And in reading them, the ladies just mentioned will, perhaps, derive from the delightful things that happen in these tales both pleasure and useful counsel, inasmuch as they will recognize what should be avoided and what should be sought after. This, I believe, can only result in putting an end to their melancholy. And should this happen (and may God grant that it does), let them thank Love for it, who, in freeing me from his bonds, has given me the power to attend to their pleasure.

------------------------ • ❦ • ------------------------

Introduction

Here begins the first day of The Decameron, *in which, after the author has explained why certain people (soon to be introduced) have gathered together to tell stories, they speak, under the direction of Pampinea, on any subject that pleases them most.*

Whenever, most gracious ladies, I consider how compassionate you are by nature, I realize that in your judgment the present work will seem to have had a serious and painful beginning, for it recalls in its opening the unhappy memory of the deadly plague just passed, dreadful and pitiful to all those who saw or heard about it. But I do not wish to frighten you away from reading any further, by giving you the impression that all you are going to do is spend your time sighing and weeping while you read. This horrible beginning will be like the ascent of a steep and rough mountainside, beyond which there lies a most beautiful and delightful plain, and the degree of pleasure derived by the climbers will be in proportion to the difficulty of the climb and the descent. And just as pain is the extreme limit of pleasure, so, then, misery ends with unanticipated happiness. This brief pain (I say brief since it contains few words) will be quickly followed by the sweetness and the delight which I promised you before, and which, had I not promised, might not be expected from such a beginning. To tell the truth, if I could have conveniently led you by any other way than this, which I know is a bitter one, I would have gladly done so; but since it is otherwise impossible to demonstrate how the stories you are about to read come to be told, I am obliged, as it were, by necessity to write about it this way.

Let me say, then, that thirteen hundred and forty-eight years[3] had already passed after the fruitful Incarnation of the Son of God when into the distinguished city of Florence, more noble than any other Italian city, there came a deadly pestilence. Either because of the influence of heavenly bodies or because of God's just wrath as a punishment to mortals for our wicked deeds, the pestilence, originating some years earlier in the East, killed an infinite number of people as it spread relentlessly from one place to another until finally it had stretched its miserable length all over the West. And against this pestilence no human wisdom or foresight was of any avail; quantities of filth were removed from the city by officials charged with the task; the entry of any sick person into the city was prohibited; and many directives were issued concerning the maintenance of good health. Nor were the humble supplications rendered not once but many times by the pious to God, through public processions or by other means, in any way efficacious; for almost at the beginning of springtime of the year in question the plague began to show its sorrowful effects in an extraordinary manner. It did not assume the form it had in the East, where bleeding from the nose was a manifest sign of inevitable death, but rather it showed its first signs in men and women alike by means of swellings either in the groin or under the armpits, some of which grew to the size of an ordinary apple and others to the size of an egg (more or less), and the people called them *gavoccioli*.[4] And from the two parts of the body already mentioned, in very little time, the said deadly *gavoccioli* began to spread indiscriminately over every part of the body; then, after this, the symptoms of the illness changed to black or livid spots appearing on the arms and thighs, and on every part of the body—sometimes there were large ones and other times a number of little ones scattered all around. And just as the *gavoccioli* were originally, and still are, a very definite indication of impending death, in like manner these spots came to mean the same thing for whoever contracted them. Neither a doctor's advice nor the strength of medicine could do anything to cure this illness; on the contrary, either the nature of the illness was such that it afforded no cure, or else the doctors were so ignorant that they did not recognize its cause and, as a result, could not prescribe the proper remedy (in fact, the number of doctors, other than the well-trained, was increased by a large number of men and women who had never had any medical training); at any rate, few of the sick were ever cured, and almost all died after the third day of the appearance of the previously described symptoms (some sooner, others later), and most of them died without fever or any other side effects.

This pestilence was so powerful that it was transmitted to the healthy by contact with the sick, the way a fire close to dry or oily things will set them aflame. And the evil of the plague went even further: not only did talking or being around the sick bring infection and a common death, but also touching the clothes of the sick or anything touched or used by them seemed to communicate this very disease to the person involved. What I am about to say is incredible to hear, and if I and others had not witnessed it with our own eyes, I should not dare believe it (let alone write about it), no matter how trustworthy a person I might have heard it from. Let me say, then, that the plague described here was of such virulence in spreading from one person to another that not only did it pass from one man to the next, but, what's more, it was often transmitted from the garments of a sick or dead man to animals that not only became contaminated by the disease but also died within a brief period of time. My own eyes, as I said earlier, were witness to such a thing one day: when the rags of a poor man who died of this disease were thrown into the public street, two pigs came upon them, and, as they are wont to do, first with their snouts and then with their teeth they took the rags and shook them around; and within a short time, after a number of convulsions, both pigs fell dead upon the ill-fated rags, as if they had been poisoned. From these and many similar or worse occurrences there came about such fear and such fantastic notions among those who remained alive that almost all of them took a very cruel attitude in the matter; that is, they completely avoided the sick and their possessions, and in so doing, each one believed that he was protecting his own good health.

There were some people who thought that living moderately and avoiding any excess might help a great deal in resisting this disease, and so they gathered in small groups and lived entirely apart from everyone else. They shut themselves up in those houses where there were no sick people and where one could live well by eating the most delicate of foods and drinking the finest of wines (doing so always in moderation), allowing no one to speak about or listen to anything said about the sick and the dead outside; these people lived, entertaining themselves with music and other pleasures that they could arrange. Others thought the opposite: they believed that drinking excessively, enjoying life, going about singing and celebrating, satisfying in every way the appetites as best one could, laughing, and making light of everything that happened was the best medicine for such a disease; so they practiced to the fullest what they believed by going from one tavern to another all day and night, drinking to excess; and they would often make merry in private homes, doing everything that pleased or amused them the most. This they were able to do easily, for everyone felt he was doomed to die and, as a result, abandoned his property, so that most of the houses had become common property, and any stranger who came upon them used them as if he were their rightful owner. In addition to this bestial behavior, they always managed to avoid the sick as best they could. And in this great affliction and misery of our city the revered authority of the laws, both divine and human, had fallen and almost completely disappeared, for, like other men, the ministers and executors of the laws were either dead or sick or so short of help that it was impossible for them to fulfill their duties; as a result, everybody was free to do as he pleased.

Many others adopted a middle course between the two attitudes just described: neither did they restrict their food or drink so much as the first group nor did they call into such dissoluteness and drunkenness as the second; rather, they satisfied their appetites to a moderate degree. They did not shut themselves up, but went around carrying in their hands flowers, or sweet-smelling herbs, or various kinds of spices; and they would often put these things to their noses, believing that such smells were a wonderful means of purifying the brain, for all the air seemed infected with the stench of dead bodies, sickness, and medicines.

Others were of a crueler opinion (though it was, perhaps, a safer one): they maintained that there was no better medicine against the plague than to flee from it; convinced of this reasoning and caring only about themselves, men and women in great numbers abandoned their city, their houses, their farms, their relatives, and their possessions and sought other places, going at least as far away as the Florentine countryside—as if the wrath of God could not pursue them with this pestilence wherever they went but would only strike those it found within the walls of the city! Or perhaps they thought that Florence's last hour had come and that no one in the city would remain alive.

And not all those who adopted these diverse opinions died, nor did they all escape with their lives; on the contrary, many of those who thought this way were falling sick everywhere, and since they had given, when they were healthy, the bad example of avoiding the sick, they in turn were abandoned and left to languish away without any care. The fact was that one citizen avoided another, that almost no one cared for his neighbor, and that relatives rarely or hardly ever visited each other—they stayed far apart. This disaster had struck such fear into the hearts of men and women that brother abandoned brother, uncle abandoned nephew, sister left brother, and very often wife abandoned husband, and—even worse, almost unbelievable—fathers and mothers neglected to tend and care for their children as if they were not their own.

Thus, for the countless multitude of men and women who fell sick, there remained no support except the charity of their friends (and these were few) or the greed of servants, who worked for inflated salaries without regard to the service they performed and who, in spite of this, were few and far between; and those few were men or women of little wit (most of them not trained for such service) who did little else but hand different things to the sick when requested to do so or watch over them while they died, and in this service, they very often lost their own lives and their profits. And since the sick were abandoned by their neighbors, their parents, and their friends and there was a scarcity of servants, a practice that was previously almost unheard of spread through the city: when a woman fell sick, no matter how attractive or beautiful or noble she might be, she did not mind having a manservant (whoever he might be, no matter how young or old he was), and she had no shame whatsoever in revealing any part of her body to him—the way she would have done to a woman—when necessity of her sickness required her to do so. This practice was, perhaps, in the days that followed the pestilence, the cause of looser morals in the women who survived the plague. And so, many people died who, by chance, might have survived if they had been attended to. Between the lack of competent attendants that the sick were unable to obtain and the violence of the pestilence itself, so many, many people died in the city both day and night that it was incredible just to hear this described, not to mention seeing it! Therefore, out of sheer necessity, there arose among those who remained alive customs which were contrary to the established practices of the time.

It was the custom, as it is again today, for the women relatives and neighbors to gather together in the house of a dead person and there to mourn with the women who had been dearest to him; on the other hand, in front of the deceased's home, his male relatives would gather together with his male neighbors and other citizens, and the clergy also came, many of them or sometimes just a few, depending upon the social class of the dead man. Then, upon the shoulders of his equals, he was carried to the church chosen by him before death with the funeral pomp of candles and chants. With the fury of the pestilence increasing, this custom, for the most part, died out and other practices took its place. And so not only did people die without having a number of women around them, but there were many who passed away without having even a single witness present, and very few were granted the piteous laments and bitter tears of their relatives; on the contrary, most relatives were somewhere else, laughing, joking, and amusing themselves; even the women learned this practice too well, having put aside, for the most part, their womanly compassion for their own safety. Very few were the dead whose bodies were accompanied to the church by more than ten or twelve of their neighbors, and these dead bodies were not even carried on the shoulders of honored and reputable citizens but rather by gravediggers from the lower classes that were called *becchini*. Working for pay, they would pick up the bier and hurry it off, not to the church the dead man had chosen before his death but, in most cases, to the church closest by, accompanied by four or six churchmen with just a few candles, and often none at all. With the help of these *becchini*, the churchmen would place the body as fast as they could in whatever unoccupied grave they could find without going to the trouble of saying long or solemn burial services.

The plight of the lower class and, perhaps, a large part of the middle class was even more pathetic: most of them stayed in their homes or neighborhoods either because of their poverty or because of their hopes for remaining safe, and every day they fell sick by the thousands; and not having servants or attendants of any kind, they almost always died. Many ended their lives in the public streets, during the day or at night, while many others who died in their homes were discovered dead by their neighbors only by the smell of their decomposing bodies. The city was full of corpses. The dead were usually given the same treatment by their neighbors, who were moved more by the fear that the decomposing corpses would contaminate them than by any charity they might have felt toward the deceased: either by themselves or with the assistance of porters (when they were available), they would drag the corpse out of the home and place it in front of the doorstep, where, usually in the morning, quantities of dead bodies could be seen by any passerby; then they were laid out in biers, or for lack of biers, on a plank. Nor did a bier carry only one corpse; sometimes it was used for two or three at a time. More than once, a single bier would serve for a wife and husband, two or three brothers, a father or son, or other relatives, all at the same time. And very often it happened that two priests, each with a cross, would be on their way to bury someone, when porters carrying three or four biers would just follow along behind them; and whereas these priests thought they had just one dead man to bury, they had, in fact, six or eight and sometimes more. Moreover, the dead were honored with no tears or candles or funeral mourners; in fact, things had reached such a point that the people who died were cared for as we care for goats today. Thus it became quite obvious that the very thing which in normal times wise men had not been able to resign themselves to, even though then it struck seldom and less harshly, became as a result of this colossal misfortune a matter of indifference to even the most simpleminded people.

So many corpses would arrive in front of a church every day and at every hour that the amount of holy ground for burials was certainly insufficient for the ancient custom of giving each body its individual place; when all the graves were full, huge trenches were dug in all of the cemeteries of the churches and into them the new arrivals were dumped by the hundreds; and they were packed in there with dirt, one on top of another, like a ship's cargo, until the trench was filled.

But instead of going over every detail of the past miseries which befell our city, let me say that the hostile winds blowing there did not, however, spare the surrounding countryside any evil; there, not to speak of the towns which, on a smaller scale, were like the city, in the scattered villages and in the fields the poor, miserable peasants and their families, without any medical assistance or aid of servants, died on the roads and in their fields and in their homes, as many by day as by night, and they died not like men but more like animals. Because of this they, like the city dwellers, became careless in their ways and did not look after their possessions or their businesses; furthermore, when they saw that death was upon them, completely neglecting the future fruits of their past labors, their livestock, their property, they did their best to consume what they had already had at hand. So it came about that oxen, donkeys, sheep, pigs, chickens, and even dogs, man's most faithful companion, were driven from their homes into the fields, where the wheat was left not only unharvested but also unreaped, and they were allowed to roam where they wished; and many of these animals, almost as if they were rational beings, returned at night to their homes without any guidance from a shepherd, full after a good day's meal.

Leaving the countryside and returning to the city, what more can one say except that so great was the cruelty of Heaven, and, perhaps, also that of man, that from March to July of the same year, between the fury of the pestiferous sickness and the fact that many of the sick were badly treated or abandoned in need because of the fear that the healthy had, more than one hundred thousand human beings are believed to have lost their lives for certain inside the walls of the city of Florence—

whereas before the deadly plague, one would not even have estimated there were actually that many people dwelling in the city.

Oh, how many great palaces, beautiful homes, and noble dwellings, once filled with families, gentlemen, and ladies, were now emptied, down to the last servant! How many notable families, vast domains, and famous fortunes remained without legitimate heir! How many valiant men, beautiful women, and charming young boys, who might have been pronounced very healthy by Galen, Hippocrates, and Aesculapius (not to mention lesser physicians), ate breakfast in the morning with their relatives, companions, and friends and then in the evening dined with their ancestors in the other world!

Reflecting upon so many miseries makes me very sad; therefore, since I wish to pass over as many as I can, let me say that as our city was in this condition, almost emptied of inhabitants, it happened (as I heard it later from a person worthy of trust) that one Tuesday morning in the venerable church of Santa Maria Novella there was hardly anyone there to hear the holy services except seven young ladies, all dressed in garments of mourning as the times demanded, each of whom was a friend, a neighbor, or relative of the other, and none of whom had passed her twenty-eighth year, nor was any of them younger than eighteen; all were intelligent and of noble birth and beautiful to look at, well-mannered and gracefully modest. I would tell you their real names, if I did not have a good reason for not doing so, which is this: I do not wish any of them to be embarrassed in the future because of what they said and what they listened to—all of which I shall later recount. Today the laws relating to pleasure are rather strict, more so than at that time, when they were very lax (for the reasons mentioned above), not only for ladies of their age but even for older women; nor would I wish to give an opportunity to the envious, who are always ready to attack every praise-worthy life, to diminish in any way with their indecent talk the dignity of these worthy ladies. But so that you may understand clearly what each of them had to say, I intend to give them names which are either completely or in part appropriate to their personalities. We shall call the first and the oldest Pampinea and the second Fiammetta, the third Filomena, and the fourth Emilia, and we shall name the fifth Lauretta and the sixth Neifile, and the last, not without reason, we shall call Elissa.[5] Not by any previous agreement, but purely by chance, they gathered together in one part of the church and were seated almost in a circle, saying their prayers; after many sighs, they began to discuss among themselves various matters concerning the nature of the times, and after a while, when the others were silent, Pampinea began to speak in this manner:

"My dear ladies, you have often heard, as I have, how proper use of reason can do harm to no one. It is only natural for everyone born on this earth to sustain, preserve, and defend his own life to the best of his ability; this is a right so taken for granted that it has, at times, permitted men to kill each other without blame in order to defend their own lives. And if the laws dealing with the welfare of every human being permit such a thing, how wrong or offensive could it be for us, or anyone else, to take all possible precautions to preserve our own lives? When I consider what we have been doing this morning and in the past days and what we have spoken about, I understand, and you must understand too, that each one of us is afraid for her life; nor does this surprise me in the least—rather I am greatly amazed that since each of us has the natural feelings of a woman, we do not find some remedy for ourselves to cure what each one of us dreads. We live in the city, in my opinion, for no other reason than to bear witness to the number of dead bodies that are carried to burial, or to hear whether or not the friars (whose number has been reduced to almost nothing) chant their offices at the prescribed hours, or to demonstrate to anyone who comes here the quality and the quantity of our miseries by the clothes we wear. And if we leave the church, either we see dead or sick bodies being carried all about, or we see those who were once condemned to exile for their crimes by the authority of the public laws making sport of these laws, running about wildly through the city, because they know that those who enforce these laws are either dead or dying; or we see the scum of our city, excited with the scent of our blood, who call themselves *becchini* and who ride all over the place on horseback, mocking everything, and with their disgusting songs adding insult to our injuries. Nor do we hear anything but 'So-and-so, is dead,' and 'So-and-so is dying'; and if there were anyone left to mourn, we should hear nothing but piteous laments everywhere. I do not know if what happens to me also happens to you in your homes, but when I go home I find no one there except my maid, and I become so afraid that my hair stands on end, and wherever I go or sit in my house, I seem to see the shadows of those who have passed away, not with the faces that I remember, but with horrible expressions that terrify me. For these reasons, I am uncomfortable here in church, outside, and in my home, and the more so since it appears that no one like ourselves, who has the financial means and some other place to go, has remained here except us. And if there are any who remain, according to what I hear and see, they do whatever their hearts desire, making no distinction between what is proper and what is not, whether they are alone or with others, by day or by night; and not only laymen but also those who are cloistered in convents have broken their vows of obedience and have given themselves over to pleasures of the flesh, for they have made themselves believe that these things are permissible for them and are improper for others, and thinking that they will escape with their lives in this fashion, they have become wanton and dissolute.

"If this is the case, and plainly it is, what are we doing here? What are we waiting for? What are we dreaming about? Why are we slower to protect our health than all the rest of the citizens? Do we hold ourselves less dear than all the others do? Or do we believe that our own lives are tied to our bodies with stronger chains than others have and, therefore, that we need not worry about anything which might have the power to harm them? We are mistaken and deceived, and we are mad if we believe this. To have clear proof of this we need only call to mind how many young men and ladies have been struck down by this cruel pestilence. I do not know if you agree with me, but I believe that in order not to fall prey, out of reluctance or indifference, to what we could well avoid, it might be a good idea for all of us to leave this city, just as many others before us have done and are still doing. Let us avoid like death itself the ugly example of others, and go to live in a more dignified fashion in our country houses (of which we all have several), and there let us take what enjoyment, what happiness, and what pleasure we can, without in any way going beyond the bounds of reason. There we can hear the birds sing, and we can see the hills and the pastures turning green, the wheat fields moving like the sea, and a thousand kinds of trees; and we shall be able to see the heavens more clearly, the heavens which, though they still may be cruel, nonetheless will not deny to us their eternal beauties and which are much more pleasing to look at than the deserted walls of our city. Besides all this, in the country the air is much fresher, and the necessities for living in such times as these are plentiful, and there are just fewer troubles in general; though the peasants are dying there even as the townspeople here, the displeasure is the less in that there are fewer houses and inhabitants than in the city. Here, on the other hand, if I judge correctly, we would not be abandoning anyone; on the contrary, we can honestly say it is we ourselves that have been abandoned, for our loved ones are either dead or have fled and have left us on our own in the midst of such affliction as though we were no part of them. No reproach, therefore, can come to us if we follow this course of action, whereas sorrow, worry, and perhaps even death can come if we do not follow such a course. So, whenever you please, I think we would do well to take our servants, have everything we need sent after us, and go from one place one day to another the next, enjoying what happiness and merriment these times permit; let us live in this manner (unless we are overtaken first by death) until we see what end Heaven has in store for these horrible times. And remember that it is no less proper for us to leave blamelessly than it is for most other women to remain here dishonorably."

When they had listened to what Pampinea had said, the other ladies not only praised her advice but were so anxious to follow it that they had already been discussing among themselves the details, as if they were going to leave that very instant. But Filomena, who was most discerning, said:

"Ladies, regardless of how convincing Pampinea's arguments are, that is no reason to rush into things, as you seem to wish to do. Remember that we are all women, and any young girl can tell you that women do not know how to reason in a group when they are without the guidance of some man who knows how to control them. We are fickle, quarrelsome, suspicious, timid, and fearful, because of which I suspect that this company will soon break up without honor to any of us if we do not take a guide other than ourselves. We would do well to resolve this matter before we depart."

Then Elissa said:

"Men are truly the leaders of women, and without their guidance, our actions rarely end successfully. But how are we to find these men? We all know that the majority of our relatives are dead and those who remain alive are scattered here and there in various groups and have no idea of where we are (they, too, are fleeing precisely what we seek to avoid), and since taking up with strangers would be unbecoming to us, we must, if we wish to leave for the sake of our health, find a means of arranging it so that while going for our own pleasure and repose, no trouble or scandal follow us."

While the ladies were discussing this, three young men came into the church, none of whom was less than twenty-five years of age. Neither the perversity of the times nor the loss of friends or parents nor fear for their own lives had been able to cool, much less extinguish, the love they bore in their hearts. One of them was called Panfilo, another Filostrato, and the last Dioneo,[6] each one very charming and well-bred; and in those turbulent times they sought their greatest consolation in the sight of the ladies they loved, all three of whom happened to be among the seven ladies previously mentioned, while the others were close relatives of one or the other of the three men. No sooner had they sighted the ladies than they were seen by them, whereupon Pampinea smiled and said:

"See how Fortune favors our plans and has provided us with these judicious and virtuous young men, who would gladly be our guides and servants if we do not hesitate to accept them for such service."

Then Neifile blushed out of embarrassment, for she was one of those who was loved by one of the young men, and she said:

"Pampinea, for the love of God, be careful what you say! I realize very well that nothing but good can be said of any of them, and I believe that they are capable of doing much more than that task and, likewise, that their good and worthy company would be fitting not only for us but for ladies much more beautiful and attractive than we are, but it is quite obvious that some of them are in love with some of us who are here present, and I fear that if we take them with us, disgrace and disapproval will follow, through no fault of ours or of theirs."

Then Filomena said:

"That does not matter at all; as long as I live with dignity and have no remorse of conscience about anything, let anyone who wishes say what he likes to the contrary: God and Truth will take up arms in my defense. Now, if they were only willing to come with us, as Pampinea says, we could truly say that Fortune was favorable to our departure."

When the others heard her speak in such a manner, the argument was ended, and they all agreed that the young men should be called over, told about their intentions, and asked if they would be so kind as to accompany the ladies on such a journey. Without further discussion, then, Pampinea, who was related to one of the men, rose to her feet and made her way to where they stood gazing at the ladies, and she greeted them with a cheerful expression, outlined their plan to them, and begged them in everyone's name, to keep them company in the spirit of pure and brotherly affection.

At first the young men thought they were being mocked, but when they saw that the lady was speaking seriously, they gladly consented; and in order to start without delay and put the plan into action, before leaving the church they agreed upon what preparations had to be made for their departure. And when everything had been arranged and word had been sent on to the place they intended to go, the following morning (that is, Wednesday) at the break of dawn, the ladies with some of their servants and the three young men with three of their servants left the city and set out on their way; they had traveled no further than two short miles when they arrived at the first stop they had agreed upon.

The place was somewhere on a little mountain, at some distance from the road, full of different kinds of shrubs and plants with rich, green foliage—most pleasant to look at; at the top of this hill there was a country mansion with a beautiful large inner courtyard containing loggias, halls, and bedrooms, all of them beautifully proportioned and decorated with gay and interesting paintings; it was surrounded by meadows and marvelous gardens, with wells of cool water and cellars full of the most precious wines, the likes of which were more suitable for expert drinkers than for dignified and respectable ladies. And the group discovered, to their no little delight, that the entire palace had been cleaned, all the beds had been made, fresh flowers were everywhere, and the floors had been strewn with rushes. Soon after they arrived and were resting, Dioneo, who was more attractive and wittier than either of the other young men, said:

"Ladies, more than our preparations, it was your intelligence that guided us here. I do not know what you intend to do with your troubled thoughts, but I left mine inside the city walls when I passed through them in your company a little while ago; and so you must either make up your minds to enjoy yourselves and laugh and sing with me (as much, let me say, as your dignity permits), or you must give me leave to return to my worries and to remain in our troubled city."

To this Pampinea, who had driven away her sad thoughts in the same way, replied happily:

"Dioneo, what you say is very true: let us live happily, for after all it was unhappiness that made us flee the city. But when things lack order they cannot long endure, and since it was I who began the discussions which brought this fine company together, and since I desire the continuation of our happiness, I think we should choose a leader from among us, whom we shall honor and obey as our superior and whose only thought shall be to keep us happily entertained. And in order that each one of us may feel the burden of this responsibility together with the pleasure of its authority, so that no one of us who has not experienced it can envy the others, let me say that both the burden and the honor should be granted to each one of us in turn for a day; the first will be elected by all of us; then, as the hour of vespers approaches, it will be the duty of the one who rules for that day to choose his or her successor; this ruler, as long as his reign endures, will prescribe the place and the manner in which we shall spend our time."

These words greatly pleased everyone, and they unanimously elected Pampinea Queen for the first day; Filomena quickly ran to a laurel bush, whose leaves she had always heard were worthy of praise and bestowed great honor upon those crowned with them; she plucked several branches from it and wove them into a handsome garland of honor, which whenever it was placed upon the head of any of them was to be to all in the group a definite symbol of royal rule and authority over the rest of them for as long as their company stayed together.

After she had been chosen Queen, Pampinea ordered everyone to refrain from talking; then she sent for the four servants of the ladies and for those of the three young men, and as they stood before her in silence, she said:

"So that I may set the first example for all of you which may be bettered and thus allow our company to live an orderly and pleasurable existence without any shame for as long as we wish, I first appoint Parmeno, Dioneo's servant, as my steward, and I commit to his care and management all our household and everything which pertains to the services of the dining hall. I want Sirisco, Panfilo's servant, to act as our buyer and treasurer and to follow Parmeno's orders. Tindaro, who is in the service of Filostrato, shall wait on Filostrato and Dioneo and Panfilo in their bedchambers when the other two are occupied with their other duties and cannot do so. Misia, my servant, and Licisca, Filomena's, will be occupied in the kitchen and will prepare those dishes which are ordered by Parmeno. Chimera, Lauretta's servant, and Stratilia, Fiammetta's servant, will take care of the bedchambers of the ladies and the cleaning of those places we use. And in general, we desire and command each of you, if you value our favor and good graces, to be sure—no matter where you go or come from, no matter what you hear or see—to bring us back nothing but good news."

And once these orders, announced so summarily and praised by all present, were delivered, Pampinea rose happily to her feet and said:

"Here there are gardens and meadows and many other delightful places, which all of us can wander about in and enjoy as we like; but at the hour of tierce let everyone be here so that we can eat in the cool of the morning."

After the merry group had been given the new Queen's permission, the young men, together with the beautiful ladies, set off slowly through a garden, discussing pleasant matters, weaving themselves lovely garlands of various leaves and singing love songs. After the time granted them by the Queen had elapsed, they returned home and found Parmeno busy carrying out the duties of his task; for as they entered a hall on the ground floor, they saw the tables set with the whitest of linens and with glasses that shone like silver and everything decorated with broom blossom; then they washed their hands and, at the Queen's command, they all sat down in the places assigned them by Parmeno. The delicately cooked foods were brought in and fine wines were ready to be poured; then, without a word, the three servants began to serve the tables. Everyone was delighted to see everything so beautiful and well arranged, and the meal was accompanied by merriment and pleasant conversation. Since all the ladies and young men knew how to dance (and some of them even knew how to play music and sing very well), when the tables had been cleared, the Queen ordered that instruments be brought, and on her command, Dioneo picked up a lute and Fiammetta a viola, and they began softly playing a dance tune. After the Queen had sent the servants off to eat, she began to dance a *carola*[7] with the other ladies and two of the young men; and when that was over, they all began to sing gay and carefree songs. In this manner they continued until the Queen felt that it was time to retire; therefore, at the Queen's request, the three young men went off to their chambers (which were separate from those of the ladies), where they found their beds prepared and the rooms as full of flowers as the halls; the ladies, too, discovered their chambers decorated in like fashion. Then they all undressed and lay down to rest.

Not long after the hour of nones, the Queen arose and had the other ladies and young men awakened, stating that too much sleep in the daytime was harmful; then they went out into a meadow whose tall, green grass was protected from the sun; and there, with a gentle breeze caressing them, they all sat in a circle upon the green grass, as was the wish of their Queen. She then spoke to them in this manner:

"As you see, the sun is high, the heat is great, and nothing can be heard except the cicadas in the olive groves; therefore, to wander about at this hour would indeed be foolish. Here it is cool and fresh, and, as you can see, there are games and chessboards with which all of you can amuse yourselves to your liking. But if you take my advice in this matter, I suggest we spend this hot part of the day not playing games (a pastime which of necessity disturbs the player who loses without providing much pleasure either for his opponents or for those who watch) but rather telling stories, for this way one person, by telling a story, can provide amusement for the entire company. In the time it takes for the sun to set and the heat to become less oppressive, you will each have told a little story, and then we can go wherever we like to amuse ourselves; so, if what I say pleases you (and in this I am willing to follow your pleasure), then, let us do it; if not, then let everyone do as he or she pleases until the hour of vespers."

The entire group of young men and young ladies liked the idea of telling stories.

"Then," said the Queen, "if this is your wish, for this first day I wish for each of you to be free to tell a story treating any subject which most pleases you."

And turning to Panfilo, who sat on her right, she ordered him in a gracious manner to begin with one of his stories; whereupon, hearing her command, Panfilo, with everyone listening, began at once as follows:

· ·

First Day, First Story

Ser Cepparello tricks a holy friar with a false confession and dies; although he was a very evil man during his lifetime, he is after death reputed to be a saint and is called Saint Ciappelletto.

Dearest ladies, it is fitting that everything done by man should begin with the marvelous and holy name of Him who was the Creator of all things; therefore, since I am to be the first to begin our storytelling, I intend to start with one of His marvelous deeds so that when we have heard about it, our faith in Him will remain as firm as ever and His name be ever praised by us.

It is clear that since earthly things are all transitory and mortal, they are in themselves full of worries, anguish, and toil, and are subject to countless dangers which we, who live with them and are part of them, could neither endure nor defend ourselves from if strength and foresight were not granted to us through God's special grace. Nor should we believe that such special grace descends upon us and within us through any merit of our own, but rather it is sent by His own kindness and by the prayers of those who, like ourselves, were mortal and who have now become eternal and blessed with Him, for they followed His will while they were alive. To these saints, as to advocates who from experience are aware of our weakness, we ourselves offer our prayers concerning those matters we deem desirable, because we are not brave enough to offer them to so great a judge directly. And yet in Him we discern His generous mercy toward us, and since the human eye cannot penetrate the secrets of the divine mind in any way, it sometimes happens that, deceived by popular opinion, we choose as an advocate before His majesty one who is sentenced by Him to eternal exile; nevertheless He, to whom nothing is hidden, pays more attention to the purity of the one who prays than to his ignorance or the damnation of his intercessor and answers those who pray to Him just as if these advocates were blessed in

His presence. All this will become most evident in the tale I am about to tell: I say evident, in accordance with the judgment of men and not that of God.

Now, there was a very rich man named Musciatto Franzesi who was a famous merchant in France and had become a knight; he was obliged to come to Tuscany with Lord Charles Landless, the brother of the King of France, who had been sent for and encouraged to come by Pope Boniface.[8] Musciatto found that his affairs, like those of most merchants, were so entangled in every which way that he could not easily or quickly liquidate them, so he decided to entrust them to a number of different people, and he found a means of disposing of everything—only one difficult thing remained to be done, to find a person capable of recovering certain loans made to several people in Burgundy. The reason for this hesitation was that he had been told the Burgundians were a quarrelsome lot, of evil disposition, and disloyal; and he could not think of an equally evil man (in whom he could place his trust) who might be able to match their wickedness with his own. After thinking about this matter for a long time, he remembered a certain Ser[9] Cepparello from Prato, who had often been a guest in his home in Paris. This person was short and he dressed with an affected kind of elegance; and the French, who did not know the meaning of the word "Cepparello" (believing it meant *cappello*, in their tongue "garland"), used to call him not Ciappello but Ciappelletto, since he was short; and as Ciappelletto he was known to everyone, and few knew him as Ser Cepparello.

Ciappelletto was, by profession, a notary; he was very much ashamed when any of his legal documents (of which he drew up many) was discovered to be anything but fraudulent. He would have drawn up, free of charge, as many false ones as were requested of him, and more willingly than another man might have done for a large sum of money. He gave false testimony with the greatest of pleasure, whether he was asked to give it or not; and since in those days in France great faith was placed on sworn oaths, and since he did not object to taking a false oath, he won a great many lawsuits through his wickedness every time he was called on to swear upon his faith to tell the truth. He took special pleasure and went to a great deal of trouble to stir up scandal, mischief, and enmities between friends, relatives, and anyone else, and the more evil that resulted from it, the happier he was. If he was asked to be a witness at a murder or at any other criminal affair, he would attend very willingly, never refusing, and he frequently found himself happily wounding or killing men with his very own hands. He was a great blasphemer of God and the saints, losing his temper at the slightest pretext, as if he were the most irascible man alive. He never went to church, and he made fun of all the church's sacraments, using abominable language to revile them; on the other hand, he frequented taverns and other dens of iniquity with great pleasure. He was as fond of women as dogs are of a beating with a stick; he was, in fact, more fond of men, more so than any other degenerate. He could rob and steal with a conscience as clean as a holy man making an offering. He was such a great glutton and big drinker that he often suffered the filthy price of his overindulgence; he was a gambler who frequently used loaded dice. But why am I wasting so many words on him? He was probably the worst man that ever lived! His cunning, for a long time, had served the wealth and the authority of Messer Musciatto, on whose behalf he was many times spared both by private individuals, whom he often abused, and by the courts, which he always abused.

When this Ser Cepparello came to the mind of Messer Musciatto, who was well acquainted with his way of life, he decided that this was just the man to deal with the evil nature of the Burgundians; and summoning him, he spoke as follows:

"Ser Ciappelletto, as you know, I am about to leave here for good, and since, among others, I have to deal with these tricky Burgundians, I know of no one more qualified than yourself to recover my money from them; and since you are doing nothing else at the moment, if you look after this matter for me, I shall gain the favor of the court for you and I shall give you a just portion of what you manage to recover."

Ser Ciappelletto, then unemployed and in short supply of worldly goods, saw refuge and support about to depart, and without further delay, constrained, as it were, by necessity, made up his mind and announced that he would be happy to go. After they had made their agreement, and Ser Ciappelletto had received the power of attorney and necessary letters of recommendation from the King, Messer Musciatto departed and Ciappelletto went to Burgundy, where hardly a soul knew him: and there, in a kind and gentle manner, unlike his nature, he began to collect the debts and to do what he had been sent to do—it was almost as though he were saving all his anger for the conclusion of his visit. And while he was doing this, he was lodged in the home of two Florentine brothers who lent money at usurious rates and who showed him great respect (out of their love for Messer Musciatto); during this time he fell ill. The two brothers had doctors and nurses brought in immediately to care for him, and they provided everything necessary to restore his health. But all help was useless, for the good man (according to what the doctors said) was already old and had lived a disordered life, and every day his condition went from bad to worse, like someone with a fatal illness. The brothers were most concerned about this, and one day, standing rather close to the bedchamber where Ser Ciappelletto lay ill, they began talking to each other:

"What are we going to do with him?" said one to the other. "We're in a fine fix on his account! Throwing him out of our house, as sick as he is, would surely earn us reproaches and would obviously make little sense, since people have seen how we received him at first, and then how we had him cared for and treated so well; and now what would they say if they see him, at the point of death, being thrown out of our house all of a sudden without having done anything to displease us? On the other hand, he has been such a wicked man that he does not wish to confess himself or to receive any of the church's sacraments; and if he dies without confession, no church will wish to receive his body, and he will be thrown into a ditch just like a dead dog. And suppose he does confess? His sins are so many and so horrible that the same thing will happen, since neither friar nor priest will be willing or able to absolve him, and so, without absolution, he will be thrown into a ditch just the same. And if this happens, the people of this city, who already speak badly of us because of our profession (which they consider iniquitous) and who wish to rob us, will rise up in a mob when they see this and cry out: 'These Lombard dogs are not accepted by the church; we won't put up with them any longer!' They will run to our house and rob us not only of our property but of our lives as well. In any case, we are in trouble if he dies."

Ser Ciappelletto, who as we said was lying near the place where they were talking, had sharp ears, as is often the case with the sick, and he heard what they said about him. He had them summoned and told them:

"I don't want you to worry on my account or be afraid that you will suffer because of me; I heard what you said about me, and I am very sure that things would, indeed, happen as you say they would if everything went as you think it might; but things will turn out differently. Since I have committed so many offenses against God during my lifetime, committing one more against Him now will make no difference. So find me the most holy and worthy priest that you can (if such a one exists), and leave everything to me, for I guarantee you that I shall set both your affairs and mine in order in a way that will satisfy you."

Although the two brothers did not feel very hopeful about this, they went, nevertheless, to a monastery of friars and asked for some holy and wise priest to hear the confession of a Lombard who had fallen ill in their home; and they were given an old friar who was a good and holy man, an expert in the Scriptures, and a most venerable man, for whom all the citizens had a very great and special devotion; and they took him with them. When the friar reached the bedchamber where Ser Ciappelletto was lying, he sat down at his side; first, he began to comfort him kindly, and then he asked him how long it had been since his last confession. To this question, Ser Ciappelletto, who had never in his life made a confession, replied:

"Father, I usually confess myself at least once a week, but there were many weeks that I confessed more often; and the truth is that since I have been ill—almost eight days now—I have not been to confession, so grave has been my illness."

Then the friar said:

"My son, you have done well, and you must continue to do so; but I see that since you have confessed so often, there will be little for me to ask or listen to."

Ser Ciappelletto replied:

"Father, don't say that; I have never confessed so many times or so often that I have not always wished to confess again all the sins I can remember from the day of my birth to the moment I am confessing; therefore, I beg you, my good father, that you ask me point by point about everything, as if I had never confessed before, and do not let my illness stand in your way, for I prefer to mortify this flesh of mine rather than, in treating it gently, do something which might lead to the perdition of my soul, which our Savior has redeemed with His precious blood."

These words pleased the holy man very much, and they seemed to him to be the sign of a well-disposed mind; and after he had commended Ser Ciappelletto highly for his practice, he began by asking him if he had ever sinned in lust with any woman. To this Ser Ciappelletto replied with a sigh:

"Father, on this account I am ashamed to tell the truth for fear of sinning from pride."

To this the friar answered:

"Speak freely, for the truth was never a sin either in confession or elsewhere."

Then Ser Ciapelletto said:

"Since you assure me that this is the case, I shall tell you: I am as virgin today as when I came from my mother's womb."

"Oh, you are blessed by God!" said the friar. "How well you have done! And in so doing, you merit even more praise, for you have enjoyed more freedom to do the opposite than we and others who are bound by religious rules enjoy."

Then, he asked if he had displeased God through the sin of gluttony. To this, breathing a heavy sigh, Ser Ciappelletto replied that he had, and many times; for in addition to the periods of fasting which are observed during the year by the devout, he fasted every week for at least three days on bread and water, but he had drunk the water with the same delight and appetite as any great drinker of wine would—especially after he had worn himself out in prayer or in going on a pilgrimage; and he had often longed for one of those little salads made of wild herbs—the kind women make out in the country—and on occasion eating had seemed better to him than it should have seemed to someone like himself who fasted out of religious devotion. To this the friar replied:

"My son, these sins are natural ones and are very minor; therefore, I do not want you to burden your conscience with them more than necessary. No matter how very holy he may be, every man thinks that eating after a long fast and drinking after hard work is good."

"Oh, father," said Ser Ciappelletto, "don't say this just to console me; as you well know, things done in God's service should be done completely and without any hesitation; anyone who does otherwise sins."

The friar, who was most pleased to hear this, said:

"I am happy that you feel this way, and your pure and good conscience pleases me very much. But tell me, have you ever committed the sin of avarice by coveting more than was proper or by keeping what you should not have kept?"

To this Ser Ciappelletto answered:

"Father, do not suspect me of this because I am in the home of these usurers. I have nothing whatsoever to do with their profession; on the contrary, I came here to admonish and chastise them and to save them from this abominable kind of profit-taking, and I believe that I might have accomplished this if God had not struck me down in this manner. But you should know that my father left me a rich man, and when he died, I gave the larger part of his possessions to charity; then, to sustain my life and to enable me to aid Christ's poor, I carried on my little business deals, and while in my work I did wish to make a profit, I always divided these profits with God's poor, giving one half to them and keeping the other half for my own needs; and my Creator has aided me so well in this regard that my business affairs have always prospered."

"Well done!" replied the friar. "But, now, how many times have you lost your temper?"

"Oh," said Ser Ciappelletto, "I certainly have, and very often. And who could keep himself from doing so, seeing all around me, every day, men doing evil deeds, disobeying God's commandments, and not fearing His judgments? Many times there have been days I would have rather been dead than live to see young men chasing after the vanities of this world and to hear them swear and perjure themselves, to see them going to taverns, not going to church, and pursuing the ways of the world rather than those of God."

Then the friar said:

"My son, this is righteous anger, and I can impose no penance upon you for that. But, by any chance, did your wrath ever lead you to commit murder or to abuse anyone or to do any other kind of injury?"

To this Ser Ciappelletto answered:

"Alas, father! How could you say such things and be a man of God? If I had even so much as thought about doing any of those things you mentioned, do you believe that God would have done so much for me? These things are for criminals and evil men, and every time I met such a man, I always said: 'Begone! And may God convert you!' "

Then the friar said:

"May God bless you, my son! Have you ever given false testimony against anyone, or spoken ill of anyone, or taken their property against their will?"

"Yes, indeed," answered Ser Ciappelletto, "I have spoken ill of others, for I once had a neighbor who did nothing but beat his wife unjustly, and one time I spoke badly about him to his wife's relatives, such was the pity I had for that poor creature; only God can tell you how he beat her every time he drank too much."

Then the friar said:

"Now then, you tell me you have been a merchant. Have you ever tricked anyone, as merchants are wont to do?"

"Of course," replied Ser Ciappelletto, "but I do not know who he was; all I know is that he was a man who brought me money which he owed me for some cloth I sold him, and I put it in my strongbox without counting it; a month later I discovered that he had given me four pieces more than he owed me, and since I saved the money for more than a year in order to return it to him but did not see him again, I finally donated it to charity."

"That was a small matter," said the friar, "and you did well in doing what you did with it."

And besides this, the holy friar asked him about many other matters, always receiving from him similar replies. And as he was about to give him absolution, Ser Ciappelletto said:

"Father, there is another sin which I have not mentioned."

The friar asked him what it was, and he answered:

"I recall that one Saturday after the hour of nones, I had my servant sweep the house and did, therefore, not show the proper reverence for the Holy Sabbath."

"Oh," said the friar, "that is a minor matter, my son."

"No," replied Ser Ciappelletto, "don't call it a minor matter. Sunday can never be honored too much, for on that day our Savior rose from the dead."

Then the friar asked:

"What else have you done?"

"Father," replied Ser Ciappelletto, "one time without thinking I spat in the house of God."

The friar began to smile and said:

"My son, that is nothing to worry about; we priests, who are religious men, spit there all day long."

Then Ser Ciappelletto said:

"Then you do great harm, for no place should be kept as clean as a holy temple in which we give sacrifice to God."

And, in brief, he told the friar many things of this sort; and finally he began to sigh and then to weep loudly, which he was very good at doing whenever he wished. The holy friar asked:

"My son, what's the matter?"

Ser Ciappelletto replied:

"Alas, father, there is one remaining sin which I shall never confess, such is the shame I have of mentioning it, and every time it comes to mind, I cry as you see me doing now, and I feel sure that God will never have mercy on me because of such a sin."

Then the holy man said:

"There now, my son, what's this you're saying? If all the sins which were ever committed by all men, or which will ever be committed as long as the world lasts, were all in one man, and he was as penitent and contrite as I see you are, the kindness and mercy of God is so great that if he were to confess, God would freely forgive him of all those sins. Therefore, speak without fear."

Still crying loudly, Ser Ciappelletto said:

"Alas, father, mine is too great a sin, and I can hardly believe that God will forgive me unless your prayers are forthcoming."

To this the friar replied:

"Speak freely, for I promise to pray to God for you."

But Ser Ciappelletto kept on crying without speaking, while the friar continued urging him to speak. But after Ser Ciappelletto had kept the friar in suspense with his prolonged weeping, he heaved a great sigh and said:

"Father, since you promise to pray to God on my behalf, I shall tell you: when I was just a little boy, I cursed my mother one time."

And having said this, he began crying loudly again. The friar answered:

"Now there, my son, does this seem like such a great sin to you? Oh! Men curse God all day, and He gladly forgives those who repent for having blasphemed against Him; do you not believe that he will forgive you as well? Do not cry; take comfort, for He will surely forgive you with the contrition I see in you—even if you were one of those who placed Him upon the cross."

Then Ser Ciappelletto said:

"Alas, father! What are you saying? My sweet mother, who carried me in her womb nine months, day and night, and who took me in her arms more than a hundred times! Cursing her was too evil, and the sin was too great; and if you do not pray to God on my behalf, He will not forgive me."

When the friar saw that Ser Ciappelletto had nothing more to say, he absolved him and gave him his blessing, thinking him to be a most holy man, just as he fully believed everything Ser Ciappelletto had told him. And who would not have believed it, seeing a man at the point of death confess in such a way? And then, after all this, he said to him:

"Ser Ciappelletto, with the help of God you will soon be well; but if it happens that God calls your blessed and well-disposed soul to Himself, would you like to have your body buried in our monastery?"

To this Ser Ciappelletto answered:

"Yes, sir, I would. Nor would I want to be anywhere else, since you have promised to pray to God for me; moreover, I have always been especially devoted to your order. Therefore, when you return to your monastery, I beg you to send me that most true body of Christ which you consecrate each morning upon the altar—although I am not worthy of it—so that I may, with your permission, partake of it, and afterward may I receive Holy Extreme Unction, for if I have lived as a sinner, at least I shall die as a Christian."

The holy man said that he would be pleased to do this and that he had spoken well and that he would arrange it so that the Sacrament should be brought to him immediately, which it was. The two brothers, who had strongly suspected that Ser Ciappelletto would trick them, had placed themselves near a partition which divided the bedchamber where

Ser Ciappelletto was lying from another room, and as they listened, they could easily overhear and understand everything Ser Ciappelletto said to the friar; and at times they had such a desire to break out laughing that they would from time to time say to each other:

"What kind of man is this? Neither old age nor illness, nor fear of death (which is so close), nor fear of God (before whose judgment he must soon stand), has been able to turn him from his wickedness, or make him wish to die differently from the manner in which he has lived!"

But when they heard it announced that he would be received for burial in the church, they did not worry about anything else. Shortly afterward, Ser Ciappelletto took Communion, and growing worse, without remedy, he received Extreme Unction; and just after vespers on the same day during which he had made his good confession, he died. Whereupon the two brothers, using his own money, took all the necessary measures to bury him honorably, and they sent word to the friars' monastery for them to watch over the body during the evening, according to custom, and to come for it in the morning. The holy friar that had confessed him, hearing that he had passed away, went with the Prior of the monastery and had the assembly bell rung, and to the assembled friars he described what a holy man Ser Ciappelletto had been, according to what he had been able to learn from his confession; and hoping that God might perform many miracles through him, he convinced his brothers that they ought to receive his body with the greatest reverence and devotion. The Prior and the other friars—all of them gullible—agreed to this, and in the evening, when they went to where the body of Ser Ciappelletto was lying, they held a great and solemn vigil over it, and the following morning, chanting and all dressed in their vestments with their prayer books in hand, and preceded by their crosses, they went to get his body, and with the greatest ceremony and solemnity they carried it to their church, followed by almost every person in the city, men and women alike; once the body had been placed in the church, the holy friar who had confessed him mounted the pulpit and began to preach marvelous things about him and his life, his fastings, his virginity, his simplicity, innocence, and holiness, recounting, among other things, what Ser Ciappelletto had tearfully confessed to him as his greatest sin, and describing to them how he was scarcely able to convince him God might forgive him for it; from this he turned to reprove the people who were listening, and he said:

"And you, God's wretched sinners, blaspheme against Him, His

Mother, and all the saints in Paradise when a little blade of straw is caught under your feet!"

And besides this, he said a good deal more about his loyalty and his purity; in short, with his words, which were taken by the people of the countryside as absolute truth, he fixed Ser Ciappelletto so firmly in the minds and the devotions of all those who were present there that after the service was over, everyone pressed forward to kiss the hands and feet of the deceased, and all his garments were torn off his corpse, since anyone who could get hold of a piece of them considered himself blessed. And it was necessary to keep his body there the entire day, so that all those who wanted to were able to look upon him. Then, the following night, he was honorably buried in a chapel within a marble tomb, and immediately the next morning, people began going there to light candles and to worship him and to make vows to him and to hang wax images as *ex votos*. And meanwhile, the fame of his sanctity and the devotion in which he was held grew so much that no other saint received as many vows as he did from every poor person who found himself in difficulty; and they called him and still continue to call him Saint Ciappelletto, and they claim that God has performed many miracles through him and continues to perform them to this day for anyone who seeks his intercession.

It was in this manner, then, that Ser Cepparello of Prato lived and died and became a saint, just as you have heard; nor do I wish to deny that it might be possible for him to be in the blessed presence of God, since although his life was evil and sinful, he could have become so truly sorry at his last breath that God might well have had pity on him and received him into His kingdom; this is hidden from us, but from what is clear to us, I believe that he is, instead, in the hands of the Devil in Hell rather than in Paradise. And if this is the case, we can recognize the greatness of God's mercy toward us, which pays more attention to the purity of our faith than to our errors by granting our prayers in spite of the fact that we choose His enemy as our intercessor—fulfilling our requests to Him just as if we had chosen a true saint as intermediary for His grace. And so, that we may be kept healthy and safe through the present adversity and in this joyful company by His grace, praising the name of Him who began our storytelling, let us hold Him in reverence and commend ourselves to Him when we are in need, being most certain that we shall be heard.

And here Panfilo fell silent.

· ❧ ·

First Day, Second Story

A Jew named Abraham, encouraged by Giannotto di Civignì, goes to the court of Rome, and after observing the wickedness of the clergy, he returns to Paris and becomes a Christian.

Panfilo's story was praised in its entirety by the ladies, and parts of it moved them to laughter; after all had listened carefully and it had come to an end, the Queen ordered Neifile, who was sitting next to Panfilo, to continue with a story of her own the order of the entertainment thus begun. Neifile, who was endowed no less with courtly manners than with beauty, answered that she would gladly do so, and she began in this manner:

Panfilo has shown us in his storytelling that God's mercy overlooks our errors when they result from matters that we cannot fathom; in my own tale, I intend to show you how this same mercy patiently endures the faults of those who with their words and deeds ought to bear witness to this mercy and yet do the contrary; I shall show how it makes these things an argument of His infallible truth, so that with firmer conviction we may practice what we believe.

I have heard it told, gracious ladies, that in Paris there once lived a great merchant and a good man by the name of Giannotto di Civignì, a most honest and upright man, who had a flourishing business in cloth; and he had a very close friend who was a rich Jew named Abraham, also a merchant and a straightforward, trustworthy person. Giannotto, recognizing his friend's honesty and upright qualities, began to feel deep regret that the soul of such a valiant, wise, and good man through lack of faith would have to be lost to Hell. Because of this he began to plead with him in a friendly fashion to abandon the errors of the Jewish faith and to turn to the Christian truth, which, as he said, his friend could see prospering and increasing continuously, for it was holy and good, while in contrast, he could observe his own Judaism growing weak and coming to nothing. The Jew replied that he believed no faith was holy or good except the Jewish faith and that since he had been born into it, he intended to live and die within it; nor could anything cause him to turn away from it. Giannotto did not, however, abstain on this account from addressing similar words to him some days later and from indicating to him in a clumsy way, as most merchants are wont to do, the reasons why our faith is better than the Jewish one. Although the Jew was a great master of Jewish Law he nonetheless, moved by the great friendship he had for Giannotto, or perhaps by the words which the Holy Spirit sometimes places in the mouth of an ignorant man, began to find Giannotto's arguments very entertaining; but he still remained fixed in his own beliefs and would not let himself be converted. And the more stubborn he remained, the more Giannotto continued to entreat him, until the Jew, won over by such continuous insistence, declared:

"Now see here, Giannotto, you want me to become a Christian. Well, I am willing to do so on one condition: first I want to go to Rome to observe the man you say is God's vicar on earth; I want to observe his ways and customs and also those of his brother cardinals; and if they seem to me to be such men that, between your words and their actions, I am able to comprehend that your faith is better than my own, just as you have worked to demonstrate it to me, I shall do what I told you; but if this is not the case, I shall remain the Jew that I am now."

When Giannotto heard this, he was extremely sad and he said to himself:

"I have wasted my time which I thought I had employed so well, believing that I might convert him, but if he goes to the court of Rome and sees the wicked and filthy lives of the clergy, not only will he not change from a Jew to a Christian, but if he had already become a Christian before, he would, without a doubt, return to being a Jew."

So, turning to Abraham, he said:

"Listen, my friend, why do you want to go to all that trouble and expense traveling from here to Rome? Not to mention the fact that for a rich man like yourself the trip is full of dangers both by land and by sea. Don't you think you can find someone to baptize you right here? And should you have any doubts concerning the faith that I have explained to you, where would you find better teachers and wiser men capable of clarifying anything you want to know than right here? For these reasons, in my opinion, your journey is unnecessary. Remember that the priests there are just like those we have here, except for the fact that they are better insofar as they are nearer to the Head of the Flock; therefore, you can save this journey for another time, for a pilgrimage to forgive your sins, and I may, perhaps, accompany you."

To this the Jew replied:

"I am convinced, Giannotto, that things are the way you say they are, but to be brief about it, if you want me to do what you have begged me so often to do, I am determined to go there—otherwise I shall do nothing about the matter."

When Giannotto saw his friend's determination he said: "Go, then, with my blessing!"—and he thought to himself that he would never become a Christian once he saw the Court of Rome; but since it would make little difference one way or the other, he stopped insisting. The Jew got on his horse and set out as quickly as he could for the Court of Rome, and upon his arrival, he was received with honor by his Jewish friends. While he was living there, without telling anyone why he had come, the Jew began carefully to observe the behavior of the Pope, the cardinals, and the other prelates and courtiers; and from what he heard and saw for himself—he was a very perceptive man—from the highest to the lowest of them, they all shamelessly participated in the sin of lust, not only the natural kind of lust but also the sodomitic variety, without the least bit of remorse or shame. And this they did to the extent that the influence of whores and young boys was of no little importance in obtaining great favors. Besides this, he observed that all of them were open gluttons, drinkers, and sots, and that after their lechery, just like animals, they were more servants of their bellies than of anything else; the more closely he observed them, the more he saw that they were all avaricious and greedy for money and that they were just as likely to buy and sell human (even Christian) blood as they were to sell religious objects pertaining to the sacraments or connected to benefices, and in these commercial ventures they carried on more trade and had more brokers than there were engaged in the textile or any other business in Paris; they called their blatant simony "mediation" and their gluttony "maintenance," as if God did not know the intention of these wicked minds (not to mention the meaning of their words) and might allow Himself to be fooled like men by the mere names of things. These, along with many other matters best left unmentioned, so displeased the Jew (for he was a sober and upright man) that he felt he had seen enough and decided to return to Paris—and so he did. When Giannotto learned that he had returned, the last thing he thought about was his conversion, and he went to his friend and together they celebrated his return; then, when he had rested for a few days, Giannotto asked his friend what he thought of the Holy Father and the cardinals and the other courtiers. To his question the Jew promptly replied:

"I don't like them a bit, and may God condemn them all; and I tell you this because as far as I was able to determine, I saw there no holiness, no devotion, no good work or exemplary life, or anything else among the clergy; instead, lust, avarice, gluttony, fraud, envy, pride, and the like and even worse (if worse than this is possible) were so completely in charge there that I believe that city is more of a forge for the

Devil's work than for God's: in my opinion, that Shepherd of yours and, as a result, all of the others as well are trying as quickly as possible and with all the talent and skill they have to reduce the Christian religion to nothing and to drive it from the face of the earth when they really should act as its support and foundation. And since I have observed that in spite of all this, they do not succeed but, on the contrary, that your religion continuously grows and becomes brighter and more illustrious, I am justly of the opinion that it has the Holy Spirit as its foundation and support, and that it is truer and holier than any other religion; therefore, although I once was adamant and unheeding to your pleas and did not want to become a Christian, now I tell you most frankly that I would allow nothing to prevent me from becoming a Christian. So, let us go to church, and there, according to the custom of your holy faith, I shall be baptized."

Giannotto, who had expected his friend to say exactly the opposite, was the happiest man there ever was when he heard the Jew speak as he did; so he accompanied him to Notre Dame, and asked the priests there to baptize Abraham. At his request, they did so immediately, and Giannotto raised him from the baptismal font and renamed him Giovanni, and immediately afterward he had him thoroughly instructed in our faith by the most distinguished teachers. He learned quickly and became a good and worthy man who lived a holy life.

First Day, Third Story

Melchisedech, a Jew, by means of a short story about three rings, escapes from a trap set for him by Saladin.

Neifile's tale was praised by all, and when she had finished talking, Filomena, at the Queen's command, began to speak in this fashion:

The tale that Neifile told brings back to my memory a dangerous incident that once happened to a Jew; and since God and the truth of our faith have already been well dealt with by us, from now on nothing should prevent us from descending to the acts of men. Now, I shall tell you this story, and when you have heard it, perhaps you will become more cautious when you reply to questions put to you.

You should know, my dear companions, that just as stupidity can often remove one from a state of happiness and place him in the greatest misery, so, too, intelligence can rescue the wise man from the gravest of dangers and restore him to his secure state. The fact that stupidity leads one from a state of happiness to one of misery is shown by many examples which, at present, I do not intend to relate, since thousands of clear illustrations of this appear every day; but, as I promised, I shall demonstrate briefly with a little story how intelligence may be the cause of some consolation.

Saladin,[10] whose worth was such that from humble beginnings he became Sultan of Babylon and won many victories over Christian and Saracen kings, one day discovered on an occasion in which he needed a large amount of money that he had consumed all his wealth fighting many wars and displaying his grandiose magnificence. Not being able to envision a means of obtaining what he needed in a short time, he happened to recall a rich Jew, whose name was Melchisedech, who loaned money at usurious rates in Alexandria, and he thought that this man might be able to assist him, if only he would agree to do so. But this Jew was so avaricious that he would not agree of his own free will, and the Sultan did not wish to have recourse to force; therefore, as his need was pressing, he thought of nothing but finding a means of getting the Jew to help him, and he decided to use some colorful pretext to accomplish this. He had him summoned, and after welcoming him in a friendly manner, he had him sit beside him and said to him:

"Worthy man, I have heard from many people that you are very wise and most versed in the affairs of God; because of this, I would like you to tell me which of the three Laws you believe to be the true one: the Jewish, the Saracen, or the Christian."

The Jew, who really was a wise man, realized all too well that Saladin was trying to trap him with his words in order to pick an argument with him, and so he understood he could not praise any of the three Laws more than the other without Saladin's achieving his goal; therefore, like one who seems to be searching for an answer in order not to be entrapped, he sharpened his wits, knowing full well already what he had to say, and declared:

"My lord, the question which you have put to me is a good one, and in order to give you an answer, I shall have to tell you a little story which you shall now hear. If I am not mistaken, I remember having heard many times that there once was a great and wealthy man who had a most beautiful and precious ring among the many fine jewels in his treasury. Because of its worth and its beauty, he wanted to honor it by bequeathing it to his descendants forever, and he ordered that whichever of his sons would be found in possession of this ring, which he would have left him, should be honored and revered as his true heir and head of the family by all the others. The man to whom he left the ring did the same as his predecessor had, having left behind the same instructions to his descendants; in short, this ring went from hand to hand through many generations, and finally it came into the possession of a man who had three handsome and virtuous sons, all of whom were obedient to their father, and for this reason, all three were equally loved by him. Since the father was growing old and they knew about the tradition of the ring, each of the three men was anxious to be the most honored among his sons, and each one, as best he knew how, begged the father to leave the ring to him when he died. The worthy man, who loved them all equally, did not know himself to which of the three he would choose to leave the ring, and since he had promised it to each of them, he decided to try to satisfy all three: he had a good jeweler secretly make two more rings which were so much like the first one that he himself, who had had them made, could hardly tell which was the real one. When the father was dying, he gave a ring to each of his sons in secret, and after he died each son claimed the inheritance and position, and one son denied the claims of the other, each bringing forth his ring to prove his case, and when they discovered the rings were so much alike that they could not recognize the true one, they put aside the question of who the true heir was and left it undecided, as it is to this day.

"And let me say the same thing to you, my lord, concerning the three Laws given to three peoples by God our Father which are the subject of the question you put to me: each believes itself to be the true heir, to possess the true law, and to follow the true commandments, but whoever is right, just as in the case of the rings, is still undecided."

Saladin realized how the man had most cleverly avoided the trap which he had set to snare him, and for that reason he decided to make his needs known openly to him and to see if he might wish to help him; and he did so, revealing to him what he had had in mind to do if the Jew had not replied to his question as discreetly as he had. The Jew willingly gave Saladin as much money as he desired, and Saladin later repaid him in full; in fact, he more than repaid him: he gave him great gifts and always esteemed him as his friend and kept him near him at court in a grand and honorable fashion.

· ❧ ·

First Day, Fourth Story

A monk, having committed a sin deserving of the most severe punishment, saves himself by accusing his Abbot of the same sin and escapes punishment.

Having completed her story, Filomena fell silent and Dioneo, who was sitting close to her, without awaiting any further order from the Queen (for he realized by the order already begun that he was the next to speak), started speaking in the following manner:

Lovely ladies, if I have understood your intention correctly, we are here in order to amuse ourselves by telling stories, and therefore, as long as we do nothing contrary to this, I think that each one of us ought to be permitted (and just a moment ago our Queen said that we might) to tell whatever story he thinks is likely to be the most amusing. Therefore, having heard how the good advice of Giannotto di Civignì saved Abraham's soul and how Melchisedech defended his riches against the schemes of Saladin, I am going to tell you briefly, without fear of disapproval, how cleverly a monk saved his body from a most severe punishment.

In Lunigiana, a town not too far from here, there was a monastery (once more saintly and full of monks than it now is), in which there lived a young monk whose virility and youth could not be diminished by fasts or by vigils. One day around noon while the other monks were sleeping, he happened to be taking a solitary walk around the church—which was somewhat isolated—when he spotted a very beautiful young girl (perhaps the daughter of one of the local workers) who was going through the fields gathering various kinds of herbs. The moment he saw her, he was passionately attacked by carnal desire.

He went up to her and began a conversation. One subject led to another, and finally, they came to an understanding; he took the girl to his cell without anyone's noticing them. His excessive desire got the better of him while he was playing with the girl, and it happened that the Abbot, who had just got up from his nap, was passing quietly by the monk's cell when he heard the commotion the pair was making. So that he might better recognize the voices, he silently edged up to the entrance of the cell to listen, and it was clear to him that there was a woman inside. At first he was tempted to have them open the door, but then he thought of using a different tactic; so he returned to his room and waited for the monk to come out.

Although the monk was, to his great pleasure and delight, quite occupied with this young lady, he nevertheless suspected something, for he thought he had heard some footsteps in the corridor. In fact, he had peeked out a small opening and had clearly seen the Abbot standing there and listening: he was well aware the Abbot must have realized that the young girl was in his cell, and knowing that he would be severely punished, he was very worried; but without revealing his anxiety to the girl, he immediately began to think of a number of alternative plans, in an attempt to come up with one which might save him. But then he thought of an original scheme which would achieve the exact end he had in mind, and pretending that he felt they had stayed together long enough, he said to the girl:

"I have to go and find a way for you to leave without being seen, so stay here until I come back."

Having left his cell and locked it with his key, he went immediately to the Abbot's room (as every monk must do before leaving the monastery) and with a straight face he said:

"Sir, this morning I could not bring in all of the firewood that was cut for me; with your permission, I should like to go to the forest to have it carried in."

The Abbot, thinking that the monk did not know he had been observed by him, was happy at this turn of events, and since this offered him the opportunity to get more firsthand information on the sin committed by the monk, he gladly took the monk's key and gave him permission to leave. And when he saw him go off, he began to plan what he would do first: either to open the monk's cell in the presence of all the monks in order to have them see what the sin was—and in doing so prevent any grumbling when he punished the monk—or to hear first from the girl how the affair had started. But then thinking that she might very well be the wife or the daughter of some person of importance and not wanting to shame such a person in front of all his monks, he decided first to see who the girl was and then to make his decision. And so he quietly went to the cell, opened it, entered the room, and closed the door.

When the young girl saw the Abbot come in, she became frightened and began to cry out of shame. Master Abbot gave her a quick look and found her to be beautiful and fresh, and although he was old, he immediately felt the warm desires of the flesh, which were no less demanding than those the young monk had felt, and he thought to himself:

"Well, now! Why shouldn't I have a little fun when I can get it?

Troubles and worries I can get every day! This is a pretty young girl, and no one knows she's here. If I can persuade her to serve my pleasure, I don't see any reason why I shouldn't! Who will be the wiser? No one will ever know, and a sin that's hidden is half forgiven! This opportunity may never prevent itself again. I believe it is a sign of great wisdom for a man to profit from what God sends others."

Having thought all this and having completely changed the purpose of his visit, he drew nearer to the girl and gently began to comfort her, begging her not to cry; and, as one thing will lead to another, he eventually explained to her what he wanted.

The young girl, who was by no means as hard as iron or diamond, most willingly agreed to the Abbot's wishes. He took her in his arms and kissed her many times, then lay down on the monk's bed. And perhaps out of concern for the heavy weight of his dignified person and the tender age of the young girl (or perhaps just because he was afraid to lay too much weight on her) he did not lie on top of her but rather placed her on top of him, and there he amused himself with her for quite a while.

Meanwhile, pretending to have gone into the woods, the monk had concealed himself in the dormitory; when he saw the Abbot enter his cell alone, he was reassured that his plan would be successful. And when he saw the Abbot lock himself inside, he knew it for certain. Leaving his hiding place, he quietly crept up to an opening through which he could see and hear everything the Abbot did and said.

When the Abbot decided that he had stayed long enough with the girl, he locked her in the cell and returned to his own room. And after a while, having heard the monk return and believing that he had come back from the woods, he decided that it was time to give him a sound talking to—he would have him locked up in prison in order to enjoy by himself the spoils they had both gained. He had him summoned, and he reprimanded him very severely, and with a stern face he ordered that he be put into prison.

The monk promptly replied:

"But sir, I have not been a member of the Order of Saint Benedict long enough to have had the opportunity to learn every detail of the order's rules. And up until just a moment ago, you never showed me how monks were supposed to support the weight of women a well as fasts and vigils. But now that you have shown me how, I promise you that if you forgive me this time, I shall sin no more in this respect; on the contrary, I shall always behave as I have seen you behave."

The Abbot, who was a clever man, realized immediately that the monk had outsmarted him: he had been witness to what he had done; because of this, and feeling remorse for his own sin, he was ashamed of inflicting upon the monk the same punishment that he himself deserved. And so he pardoned him and made him promise never to reveal what he had seen. They quickly got the young girl out of the monastery, and as one might well imagine, they often had her brought back in again.

* · ❦ · *

Second Day, Fifth Story

Andreuccio from Perugia goes to Naples to buy horses, is caught up in three unfortunate adventures in one night, escapes from them all, and returns home with a ruby.

The precious stones found by Landolfo—said Fiammetta, whose turn it was to tell the next tale—remind me of a story no less full of dangers than the one recounted by Lauretta, but it differs from hers in that these dangers all occur within the space of a single night, as you are about to hear, whereas in her story they happened over a period of several years.

There once lived in Perugia, according to what I have been told, a young man whose name was Andreuccio di Pietro, a dealer in horses who, when he heard that in Naples horses were being sold at a low price, put five hundred gold florins in his purse and, though he had never been outside of his own town before, set out for Naples with some other merchants and arrived there on Sunday evening around vespers, and at the advice of his landlord the following morning he went to the market-place, where he saw many horses, a good number of which he liked, but he was not able to strike a bargain no matter how hard he tried; in fact, to show that he was really ready to do business, being the crass and incautious fool that he was, more than once he pulled out his purse full of florins in front of everyone who passed by. While he was in the midst of these dealings, with his purse on full display, a young and very beautiful Sicilian lady—one who, for a small price, would be happy to please any man—passed close to him, and without being seen by him, she caught a glimpse of his purse and immediately said to herself:

"Who would be better off than I if that money were mine?"—and she walked past.

With this young lady there was an old woman, also Sicilian, who, when she saw Andreuccio, let her young companion walk ahead while she ran up to him and embraced him affectionately; when the young girl saw this, she said nothing, and waited nearby for her companion. Andreuccio turned around, recognized the old woman, and greeted her with a great deal of pleasure, and after she promised to visit him at his inn, they said no more and parted company, and Andreuccio returned to his bargaining; but he bought nothing that morning.

The young woman who had first seen Andreuccio's purse as well as his familiarity with her older companion cautiously began to ask who that man was and where he came from and what he was doing there and how her friend knew him, in order to see if she could find a way of getting that money of his—if not all of it, at least a part. The old woman told her everything about Andreuccio almost as well as he himself might have told it, for she had lived a long time in Sicily and then in Perugia with Andreuccio's father; she also told her where he was staying and why he had come. Once the young woman felt herself well enough informed about his relatives and their names, she devised a cunning trick, based on what she had learned, to satisfy her desires. As soon as she returned home, she sent the old woman on errands for the entire day so that she would not be able to return to Andreuccio; then, around vespers, she sent one of her young servant girls, whom she had well trained for such missions, to the inn where Andreuccio was staying. Arriving there, the servant girl found Andreuccio by chance alone at the door, and she asked him where Andreuccio was. When he told her he was standing right before her, drawing him aside, she said:

"Sir, a genteel lady who lives in this city would like to speak to you at your leisure."

When Andreuccio heard this, he immediately assumed, for he considered himself a handsome young man, that such a woman as that must be in love with him (as if there were no man in all of Naples as handsome as he), and he immediately replied that he was ready and asked her where and when this lady wished to speak to him. To this, the young servant girl answered:

"Sir, whenever you wish to come, she awaits you at her home."

Quickly, and without mentioning anything to anyone at the inn, Andreuccio replied:

"Let's go, then, you lead the way; I'll follow you."

Whereupon the servant girl led him to her house, which was in a district called the Malpertugio, which was as respectable a district as its very name implies.[11] But Andreuccio knew or suspected nothing, believing he was going to a most respectable place and to the house of a respectable lady, and so he calmly followed the servant girl into the house. Climbing up the stairs, the servant girl called to her mistress: "Here's Andreuccio!" and he saw her appear at the head of the stairs to greet him.

She was still very young, tall, with a very beautiful face, and elegantly dressed and adorned. Andreuccio started toward her, and she descended three steps to greet him with open arms, and throwing her arms around his neck, she remained in that position for a while without saying a word—as if some overpowering emotion had stolen her words—then she started crying and kissing his forehead, and in a broken voice she said:

"Oh my Andreuccio, how happy I am to see you!"

Andreuccio, amazed at such tender greetings, and completely astonished, replied:

"My lady, the pleasure is mine!"

Then she took his hand and led him through her sitting room, and from there, without saying a word, into her bedroom, which was all scented with roses, orange blossoms, and other fragrances; there he saw a very beautiful curtained bed, and many dresses hanging on pegs (as was the custom there), and other very beautiful and expensive things. And since all those lovely things were new to him, Andreuccio was convinced that she had to be nothing less than a great lady. They sat together on a chest at the foot of her bed, and she began speaking to him:

"Andreuccio, I am quite sure that you are amazed at my tears and caresses, for perhaps you do not know me or do not remember hearing of me; but you are about to hear something that will amaze you even more: I am your sister! And now that God has granted me the favor of seeing one of my brothers before I die (oh, how I wish I could see them all!), I assure you I shall pass away content. Since you know nothing about this, I shall tell you, Pietro, your father and mine, as I think you probably know, resided for a long time in Palermo, and because of his kindness and friendliness, he was dearly loved and still is loved by those who knew him; but among those who loved him very much, my mother, who was a lady of noble birth and then a widow, was the one who loved him the most, so much so that she put aside the fear of her father and brothers and her own honor and lived with him in so intimate a way that I was born, and here I am right before your eyes. Then when Pietro had to leave Palermo and return to Perugia, he left me, a tiny child, with my mother, and as far as I know, he never thought of me or my mother again. If he were not my father, I would criticize him severely for his ingratitude toward my mother (to say nothing of the love he owed me, his daughter, not born from any servant girl or from some woman of low birth), who had put herself as well as her possessions into his hands, moved by a true love for a man she did not really know.

"But what does it matter? Things done badly in the past are more easily criticized than amended—that's how it all ended. He abandoned me as a little girl in Palermo, where, grown up almost as much as I am now, my mother, who was a rich lady, gave me as a wife to a rich man of noble birth from Agrigento who, out of his love for me and my mother, came to live in Palermo; and there, as he was an avid supporter of the Guelfs,[12] he began to carry on some kind of intrigue with our King Charles. But King Frederick discovered the plot before it could be put into effect, and this was the cause of our fleeing from Sicily—and just when I was about to become the greatest lady that island ever knew. Taking with us those few things we could (I say "few" as compared to the many things we owned), we abandoned our lands and palaces and took refuge in this land, where we found King Charles so grateful to us that he restored in part the losses which we had suffered on his account, and he gave us property and houses; and he continues to provide my husband, your brother-in-law, with a good salary, as you can see for yourself; and so, my sweet brother, here I am, and with no thanks to you but rather through the mercy of God I have come to meet you."

And having said all this, she embraced him once more, and continuing to weep tenderly, she kissed his forehead. Hearing this fable so carefully and skillfully told by the young lady, who never hesitated over a word or fumbled in any way, Andreuccio recalled it was indeed true that his father had been in Palermo, and since he himself knew the ways of young men who easily fall in love when they are young and since he had just witnessed the piteous tears, the embraces, and the pure kisses of this young lady, he took everything she said to be the absolute truth; and when she had finished speaking, he said:

"My lady, it should not surprise you to see me amazed, for to tell the truth, either my father never spoke of you and your mother, or, if he did, I never heard a word about it, for I had no more knowledge of you than if you never existed; but I am all the more delighted to have found a sister, for I am completely alone here, and I never hoped for such a thing and, truly, I don't know of any man of whatever rank or station to whom you would not be very dear, not to mention an insignificant merchant like me. But I beg you to clarify one thing for me: how did you know I was here?"

To this she answered:

"I was told about it this morning by a poor woman whom I often see, and according to her story, she was with our father for a long time both in Palermo and in Perugia; and if it were not for the fact that it seemed to me more proper for you to come to my house than for me to visit you in a stranger's house, I would have come to see you much sooner."

Then she began to ask about all his relatives individually by name, and Andreuccio replied to all her questions about them, and her questions made him believe even more of what he should not have believed at all. They talked for a long time, and since it was so hot that day, she had Greek wine and confections served to Andreuccio; then it was suppertime, and Andreuccio got up to leave, but the lady would not hear of this, and pretending to get angry, she said as she embraced him:

"Alas, poor me! How clearly I see that you care very little for me! How is it possible? Here you are with a sister of yours that you have never seen before, and she is in her own house, where you ought to be staying, and you want to leave her, to eat at some inn? You shall certainly dine with me, and though my husband is not here (a fact which displeases me a great deal) I shall honor you as best a woman can."

Not knowing what to say to this, Andreuccio replied:

"I hold you as dear as one can hold a sister, but if I don't leave, they'll wait all evening for me to come to supper, and I'll make a bad impression."

And she said:

"God be praised! As if I did not have anyone to send to tell them not to wait for you! But you would do me an even greater courtesy by inviting all of your companions to have supper here, and then, if you still wished to leave, you could all leave together."

Andreuccio replied that he did not want to be with his companions that evening, and that he would stay as she wished. Then she pretended to send someone to notify the inn that he should not be expected for supper; and, after much conversation, they finally sat down and were served a number of splendid courses, and she cleverly prolonged the supper until night came; then, when they got up from the table and Andreuccio decided it was time to leave, she said that under no circumstances would she permit it, for Naples was not the kind of town in which to wander around at night, especially if you were a stranger, and furthermore, she said that when she had sent the message telling them not to expect him for supper, she had also told them not to expect him back that night. Since he believed everything she said and enjoyed being with her, because of his false belief, he decided to stay with her. After supper, and not without her reasons, she kept him engaged in a lengthy conversation; and when a good part of the night had passed, she left

Andreuccio in her bedroom in the company of a young boy who would assist him if he wanted anything, and she withdrew into another bedroom with her chambermaids.

The heat of the night was intense, and because of this and since he was alone, Andreuccio quickly stripped to his waist and took off his pants, placing them at the head of the bed; and then the natural need of having to deposit the superfluous load in his stomach beckoned him, so he asked the boy servant where he should do it, and the boy pointed to a place in one corner of the bedroom and said: "Go in there."

Andreuccio innocently entered the place and as he did, by chance he happened to step on a plank which was not nailed to the beam it rested on; this overturned the plank, and he with the plank plunged down through the floor. But by the love of God he was spared from hurting himself in the fall, in spite of the height from which he fell; he was, however, completely covered by the filth that filled the place. In order for you to understand better just what took place and what was going to take place, I shall now describe to you the kind of place it was. Andreuccio was in a narrow alley like the kind we often see between two houses; some planks had been nailed on two beams placed between one house and the other, and there was a place to sit down; and the plank which plunged with him to the bottom was precisely one of these two supporting planks.

Andreuccio, finding himself down there in the alley, to his great discomfort, began calling the boy, but as soon as the boy heard Andreuccio fall, he ran to tell the lady, and she rushed to Andreuccio's bedroom and quickly checked to see if his clothes were still there. She found his clothes and in them his money, which he stupidly always carried with him, for he did not trust anyone; and when this woman of Palermo, pretending to be the sister of a Perugian, had gotten what she had set her trap for, she quickly locked the exit he had gone through when he fell, and she no longer was concerned about him.

When the boy did not answer, Andreuccio began to call him more loudly, but that did not help either; then he became suspicious, and began to realize (only too late) that he had been tricked. He climbed over a small wall which closed that alley from the street and ran to the door of the house, which he recognized all too well, and there he shouted and shook and pounded on the door for a long time, but all in vain. Then, as one who sees clearly his misfortune, he began to sob, saying:

"Alas, poor me! I have lost five hundred florins and a sister, and in so short a time!"

And after many such laments, he began all over again to beat on the door and to scream; and he kept this up for so long that many of the neighbors were awakened and forced out of bed by the disturbance; one of the lady's servants, pretending to be sleepy, came to the window and said in a complaining tone of voice: "Who's that knocking down there?"

"Oh," said Andreuccio, "don't you recognize me? I am Andreuccio, brother to Madam Fiordaliso."

To this the servant replied:

"My good man, if you've drunk too much, go sleep it off and come back in the morning; I don't know what Andreuccio you are talking about or any other nonsense. Off with you, and let us sleep, if you please!"

"What," said Andreuccio, "you don't know what I'm talking about? You've got to know; but if this is what it is like to be related in Sicily—that you forget your ties so quickly—then at least give me back the clothes I left up there, and in God's name I'll gladly be off!"

To this, in a laughing voice the woman replied:

"You must be dreaming, my good man!"

No sooner had she said this than she shut the window. Andreuccio, now most certain of his loss, was so vexed that his anger was turning to rage, and he decided to get back by force what he could not get back with words: he picked up a large stone and began all over again—but with harder blows this time—to beat furiously at the door, and many of the neighbors who had been aroused from their beds not long before thought that he was some sort of pest who had invented all this to bother that good lady, and so they took offense at the racket he was making. They appeared at their windows, and began to shout in a way not unlike all the dogs in a neighborhood who bark at a stray:

"It's an outrage to come at this hour to a decent lady's house and shout such foul things. In God's name leave, good man; let us sleep, if you don't mind; if you have any business with her, come back tomorrow and don't bother us anymore tonight."

The good woman's pimp, who was inside the house and whom Andreuccio had neither seen nor heard, taking courage from his neighbors' words, exclaimed in a horrible, ferocious, roaring voice:

"Who's down there?"

Andreuccio raised his head at the sound of that voice and saw someone who, as far as he could tell, looked like some sort of big shot; he had a thick black beard and was yawning and rubbing his eyes as if he had just been awakened from a sound sleep. Andreuccio, not without fear, replied:

"I am the brother of the lady who lives here . . ."

But the man did not wait for Andreuccio to finish what he had to say; with a voice more menacing than the first time, he howled:

"I don't know what's keeping me from coming down there and beating the shit out of you, you dumb ass, you drunken sot—you're not going to let anybody get any sleep tonight, are you?"

He turned inside and banged the window shut. Some of the neighbors, who knew this man for what he was, said to Andreuccio in a kindly way:

"For God's sake, man, get out of here quick before you witness your own murder tonight! For your own good, leave!"

Frightened by the voice and face of the man at the window and persuaded by the advice of the neighbors, who seemed kindly disposed toward him, Andreuccio, as sorrowful as anyone ever could be and despairing over the loss of his money, and not knowing which way to go, started moving in the direction that the servant girl had led him that day, as he tried to find his way back to the inn. Even *he* found the stench he was giving off disgusting; so, turning to the left, he took a street called Catalan Street and headed for the sea in order to wash himself off; but he was heading toward the upper part of town, and in so doing, he happened to see two men with lanterns in their hands coming in his direction, and fearing that they might be the police or other men who could do him harm, he cautiously took shelter in a hut he saw nearby. But the two men were headed for the very same spot and they, too, entered the hut; once inside, one of them put down the iron tools he was carrying and began examining them and discussing them with the other. All of a sudden, one of them remarked:

"What's going on here? That's the worst stink I've ever smelled!"

As he said this, he tilted his lantern up a bit and saw Andreuccio, the poor devil. Amazed, he asked:

"Who's there?"

Andreuccio did not utter a word; the two men drew closer with the light, and one of them asked him how he had gotten so filthy; Andreuccio told them everything that had happened to him. Having guessed where all this must have taken place, they said to each other:

"This guy really knows the head of the Mafia—he's been to Spitfire's place!"[13]

Turning to Andreuccio, one of them said:

"My good man, you might have lost your money, but you still have God to thank for not going back into the house after you fell; if you had not fallen, you can be sure that before you fell asleep, you would have been murdered and, along with your money, you would have lost your life. You have as much chance of getting a penny of your money back as you do of plucking a star from the sky! You could even get killed if that guy finds out you ever said a word about it!"

After telling him this, he consulted with his companion for a while, then said:

"Look, we've taken pity on you, so if you want to come with us and do what we plan to do, we're sure that your share of what we all get will be more than what you've lost."

Andreuccio was so desperate that he said he was willing to go along. That day an Archbishop of Naples named Messer Filippo Minutolo had been buried, and with him the richest of vestments and a ruby on his finger which was worth more than five hundred gold florins; this is what they were out to get, and they let Andreuccio in on their plan. More avaricious than wise, he set off with them, and as they made their way toward the cathedral, Andreuccio stank so badly that one of them said:

"Can't we find some way for this guy to wash up a little, so that he doesn't stink so bad?"

The other answered:

"All right. We're near a well that should have a pulley and a large bucket; let's go give him a quick washing up."

When they reached the well, they discovered that the rope was there but the bucket had been removed, so they decided between themselves that they would tie Andreuccio to the rope and lower him into the well, and he could wash himself down there; then, when he was washed, he could tug on the rope and they would pull him up. And this is what they did. It happened that no sooner had they lowered him into the well than some police watchmen, who had been chasing someone else and were thirsty because of the heat, came to the well for a drink; when the two men saw the police heading for the well, they quickly fled without being seen.

Andreuccio, who had just cleaned himself up at the bottom of the well, gave a pull on the rope. The thirsty night watchmen had just laid down their shields, arms, and other gear and were beginning to pull up the rope, thinking that a bucket full of water was at the other end. When Andreuccio saw himself nearing the rim of the well, he dropped the rope and grabbed the edge with his two hands; when the night watchmen saw him, they were terrified, and dropping the rope without wasting a word, they began to run away as fast as they could. Andreuccio was very surprised at all this, and if he had not held on tightly, he would have fallen back to the bottom of the well and perhaps have hurt himself seriously or even killed himself; when he climbed out and discovered the weapons, which he knew his companions had not brought with them, he became even more puzzled. Afraid, not understanding a thing, and lamenting his misfortune, he decided to leave that spot without touching a thing; and off he went, not knowing where he was going.

But on his way, he ran into his two companions, who were on their way back to pull him out of the well, and when they saw him, they were amazed and asked him who had pulled him out of the well. Andreuccio replied that he did not know, and then he told them exactly what had happened and what he had discovered near the well. They then realized what had actually taken place and, laughing, they told him why they had run away and who the people were who had pulled him up. Without any further conversation (for it was already midnight), they went to the cathedral and managed to get in without any trouble at all; they went up to the tomb, which was very large and made of marble; with their iron bars, they raised up the heavy cover just as much as was necessary for a man to get inside, and then they propped it up. And when this was done, one of them said:

"Who'll go inside?"

To this, the other replied:

"Not me!"

"Not me either," answered the other. "You go, Andreuccio."

"Not me," said Andreuccio.

Both of them turned toward Andreuccio and said:

"What do you mean, you won't go in? By God, if you don't, we'll beat your head in with one of these iron bars till you drop dead!"

This frightened Andreuccio, so he climbed in, and as he entered the tomb, he thought to himself:

"These guys are making me go into the tomb to cheat me: as soon as I give them everything that's inside and I am trying to get out of the tomb, they will take off with the goods and leave me with nothing!"

And so he thought about protecting his own share from the start: he remembered the two men had talked about an expensive ring, so as soon as he had climbed into the tomb, he took the ring from the Archbishop's finger and placed it on his own; then he handed out the Archbishop's staff, his miter, and his gloves, and stripping him down to his shirt, he handed over everything to them, announcing, finally, that there was nothing left, but they insisted that the ring must be there and told him to look all over for it; but Andreuccio answered that he could not find it, and he kept them waiting there for some time while he pretended to search for it. The other two, on the other hand, were just as tricky as

Andreuccio was trying to be, and at the right moment they pulled away the prop that held up the cover and fled, leaving Andreuccio trapped inside the tomb.

When Andreuccio heard this, you can imagine how he felt. He tried time and again, with both his head and his shoulders, to raise the cover, but he labored in vain; overcome with despair, he fainted and fell upon the dead body of the Archbishop; and anyone seeing the two of them there together would have had a hard time telling which one of them was really dead: he or the Archbishop. Regaining consciousness, he began to sob bitterly, realizing that being where he was, without any doubt one of two kinds of death awaited him: either he would die in the tomb from hunger and from the stench of the maggots on the dead body (that is, if no one came to open the tomb); or, if someone came and found him in the tomb, he would be hanged as a thief.

With this terrible thought in his head, and filled with grief, he heard people walking and talking in the church; they were people, it seemed to him, who had come to do what he and his companions had already done—this terrified him all the more! As soon as these people raised the cover of the tomb and propped it up, they began arguing about who should go in, and no one wanted to do so; then, after a long discussion, a priest said:

"Why are you afraid? Do you think he is going to eat you? The dead don't eat the living! I'll go inside myself."

After saying this, he leaned his chest against the rim of the tomb, then swung around and put his legs inside, and he was about to climb down when Andreuccio saw him and rose to his feet, grabbing the priest by one of his legs and pretending to pull him down. When the priest felt this, he let out a terrible scream and instantly jumped out of the tomb. This terrified all the others, who, leaving the tomb open, began to flee as if a hundred thousand devils were chasing them.

Andreuccio, happy beyond his wildest dreams, jumped out of the tomb and left the church by the way he had come in. It was almost dawn, and he started wandering about with the ring on his finger until finally he reached the waterfront and stumbled upon his inn, where he found that the innkeeper and his companions had been up all night worried about him.

He told them the story of what had happened to him, and the innkeeper advised him to leave Naples immediately; he did so at once and returned to Perugia, having invested his money in a ring when he had set out to buy horses.

· ❧ ·

Third Day, Ninth Story

Giletta of Narbonne cures the King of France of a fistula; in reward she requests Beltramo di Rossiglione for her husband, who after marrying her against his will, goes to Florence out of indignation; there he courts a young woman whom Giletta impersonates and in this way sleeps with him in her place and bears him two children; as a result, he finally holds her most dear and accepts her as his wife.

When Lauretta's tale was finished, there remained only the Queen to speak, for she did not wish to deny Dioneo his privilege; and so, without waiting for any of her companions to urge her on, she began to speak in a most charming manner as follows:

After hearing Lauretta's story, who will ever be able to tell a story as good as that? It was certainly fortunate for us that her story was not the first. Otherwise, few of the others that followed hers would have pleased us, which is what I fear will happen to those tales still to be told this day. But be that as it may, I shall go on and tell you the story I have chosen to illustrate our proposed topic.

In the Kingdom of France, there was once a nobleman whose name was Isnardo, the Count of Rossiglione, who, because of his poor health, always kept by his side a physician named Master Gerardo of Narbonne. This Count had only one small son, who was most handsome and charming, named Beltramo, who was brought up with other children of his age, among whom was a daughter of the physician, named Giletta, and she felt for this Beltramo a boundless love, one which was far more passionate than was suitable for her tender age. When his father died and he was entrusted to the care of the King, Beltramo found that he had to go to Paris, and this plunged the young girl into the deepest despair; not long afterward her own father died, and had she been able to find a reasonable excuse, she would have gladly gone to visit Beltramo in Paris, but now that she was left alone in the world and was a wealthy girl, she was closely watched and could not see any plausible means of doing so. Even when she reached marriageable age, she never was able to forget Beltramo, and without giving any explanation she turned down many a man that her relatives wanted her to marry.

Now, while she burned more than ever with her love for Beltramo, having learned he had turned into a most handsome young man, the news happened to reach her that the King of France, because of a tumor on his chest which had been badly treated, had a fistula which caused him the greatest pain and anguish. Although he had tried many physicians, none of them had been able to cure him—on the contrary, all of them had made him worse; as a result, the King was driven to despair and no longer would consult with or seek assistance from any of them. The young girl was overjoyed with the news, for she realized that not only did it give her a legitimate reason to go to Paris, but if the illness was what she thought it was, she would easily be able to have Beltramo as her husband in marriage. Then, using the many things she had learned from her father in the past, she made a powder from certain herbs that were helpful in treating the illness she believed the King suffered from, and she took to her horse and left for Paris. The first thing she did was to devise a means of seeing Beltramo; then, after obtaining an audience with the King, she asked him if he would favor her by showing her his malady. Since she was such a young and pretty woman, the King could not refuse her, and he showed it to her.

As soon as the young girl saw it, she immediately felt confident that she knew how to cure him and said:

"My lord, whenever you please and without any pain or exertion on your part, I hope, with God's help, to have you cured of this illness in eight days."

The King scoffed at her words, saying to himself:

"How can a young woman like this know how to do what the best doctors in the world couldn't?" So, he thanked her for her goodwill and told her that he had promised himself never again to follow a doctor's advice.

To this the young lady said:

"My lord, you despise my art because I am young and a woman, but let me remind you that I practice medicine not only with my own knowledge but also with the help of God and with the knowledge of Master Gerardo of Narbonne, who was my father and a famous physician in his day."

The King thought to himself:

"Perhaps God has sent me this girl; why not find out what she knows how to do, since she claims she can cure me in a short time without any pain on my part?" And deciding to put her to the test, he said:

"Young lady, if you cannot cure us, thereby forcing us to break our resolution, what do you agree should be the penalty?"

"My Lord," replied the young lady, "keep me under guard, and if I do not cure you within eight days, have me burned; but if I do cure you, what shall be my reward?"

To this the King answered:

"It seems that you are still without a husband; if you succeed, we shall provide you with a proper and noble husband."

To this the young woman said:

"My lord, it would truly please me if you were to provide me with a husband, but I desire as a husband only the man I shall now request of you, excluding, of course, any of your sons or the members of the royal family."

The King immediately gave her his promise. The young woman began her cure, and shortly thereafter, and with time to spare, she restored him to health; feeling himself cured, the King declared:

"Young woman, you have certainly earned a husband."

To this she replied:

"If that is the case, my lord, I have earned Beltramo di Rossiglione, whom I began loving as a child, and whom I have loved most passionately ever since."

The King felt that giving him to her was a serious matter, but he had given his promise, and not wishing to break it, he had Beltramo summoned to him and spoke to him in this manner:

"Beltramo, you are now full grown and have been educated; we wish for you to return and govern your lands and that you take with you a young woman whom we have chosen as your wife."

Beltramo inquired:

"And who is the young woman, my lord?"

To this question, the King replied:

"She is the young woman who, with her cures, has restored our health."

Beltramo knew her and had seen her, but no matter how beautiful she appeared to him, he knew her not to be of a lineage which adequately matched his own nobility, and he said in a most indignant manner:

"My lord, do you therefore wish to give me a woman doctor as a wife? God forbid that I should ever take such a female!"

To this the King said:

"Do you therefore wish us to break the promise we made the young woman who asked for you as her husband in reward for restoring our health?"

"My lord," said Beltramo, "you can take whatever I possess and give me over to anyone you please, for I am your vassal, but I assure you that I shall never remain content with such a marriage match."

"Yes, you will," answered the King, "for the young woman is beautiful and wise and loves you very much; we are, therefore, hoping that you will have a much happier life with her than you would have with a lady of higher lineage."

Beltramo fell silent, and the King had great preparations made for the wedding feast; when the appointed day arrived, Beltramo did, however unwillingly, in the King's presence, marry the young woman who loved him more than herself. Having already decided what he had to do, after the wedding he announced that he wished to return to his lands to consummate the marriage there, and so he asked the King for his leave, and mounting his horse, he rode off not to his estates but rather to Tuscany. And as he knew that the Florentines were waging war against the Sienese, he decided to support them; whereupon he was cheerfully received and was honorably made captain of a number of men, and since they paid him a good wage, he remained in their service for a long while.

The new bride, little pleased with such an outcome but hoping that through her good administration of his estates he would be drawn back to them, came to Rossiglione, where she was received by everyone as their mistress. Since for so long a period of time the place had been without its count, when she arrived there she found everything in ruin and chaos, and being an intelligent woman, she reorganized everything with great diligence and care, thus making her subjects very happy indeed. They held her most dear and felt a great love for her, while they most strongly criticized the count for not being satisfied with her.

After completely setting in order the Count's domain, she notified him of this fact by way of two knights, begging him to tell her that if it was because of her that he was not returning to his lands, he should inform her of this, and to please him she would leave the place. To these emissaries, the Count replied harshly:

"She can do as she pleases; for my part, I shall return to live with her the day she wears this ring on her finger and holds a son of mine in her arms." He held his ring most dear, nor did he ever take it off, because of some power that he had been told it possessed. The knights realized how harsh were the conditions imposed by these two almost impossible demands, but seeing that their words were unable to dissuade him from his resolution, they returned to their lady and reported his answer to her.

She was filled with sorrow, but after much thought she decided to try to see if these two conditions might possibly be fulfilled. Having decided what she must do in order to regain her husband, she called together a number of the most eminent and distinguished men in her domain, told them in great detail and with piteous words all that she had done out of love for the Count, and pointed out what had come of it; finally, she told them that she had no intention of staying there any longer if this meant the Count's perpetual exile and that, on the contrary, she meant to spend the rest of her life on pilgrimages and in doing charitable works for the salvation of her soul; and she begged them to undertake the protection and government of her lands and to inform the Count that she had left him his possessions free and clear and had departed with the intention of never returning to Rossiglione. As she spoke, many tears were shed by these worthy men, who begged her many times over to change her mind and stay; but all this was of no avail.

Having commended them to God, accompanied by a cousin of hers and one of her chambermaids and dressed in pilgrim's garb, she took a large sum of money and precious jewels, and without letting anyone know where she was going she set out on the road, not stopping until she reached Florence; there she happened by chance to find a small inn, which a kindly widow kept, and she remained there living modestly in the guise of a poor pilgrim, hoping to hear news about her lord. It so happened that on the following day, she saw Beltramo pass by the inn on horseback with his troops, and although she certainly recognized him, she nevertheless asked the good woman of the inn who he might be.

To her question the innkeeper replied:

"He is a foreign nobleman called Count Beltramo, an affable and courtly man who is much beloved in this city, and he is passionately in love with one of our neighbors, who is a noblewoman but poor. To tell the truth, she is a most virtuous young lady, and it is because of her poverty that she is not yet married but lives with her mother, who is the most wise and goodly woman; if her mother were not present, perhaps by now she would have already done the Count's pleasure."

The Countess listened to every word and weighed them carefully; after examining the situation in more detail, looking at every particular to be certain that she clearly understood everything, she decided on a course of action: having learned the name and address of the lady and her daughter whom the Count loved, one day dressed in her pilgrim's garb she quietly went there. She found the lady and her daughter poverty-stricken, and after greeting them, she asked the lady if she could speak to her at her convenience.

The noble lady, rising to her feet, said that she was ready to hear her and led her into another room, where the two of them alone sat down, and the Countess began:

"Madam, it seems to me that you are just as much an enemy of Fortune as I am: but, if you wish, you may perhaps be able to improve the conditions of both yourself and me."

The lady replied that she desired nothing more than to improve her condition by honest means.

The Countess continued: "I must have your trust, on which I shall rely, and if you deceive me, you shall spoil both your prospects and my own."

"You may tell me with confidence anything you wish," said the noble lady, "for you shall never find yourself deceived by me."

Then the Countess, beginning from the first moment she fell in love, told her who she was and what had happened to her up until that very day, and she told her story in such a moving way that the noble lady, who had already heard parts of it from other people, was convinced by what she said and began to take pity on her. And the Countess, after telling of her misfortunes, continued:

"You may have heard, then, that among my other troubles there are two things I must possess if I am to regain my husband; I know of no person who could assist me in obtaining them other than you, if what I hear is true—that is, that the Count, my husband, is passionately in love with your daughter."

To this the noble lady said:

"Madam, I do not know if the Count loves my daughter, but he certainly acts as if he does; but what could I do to assist you in this matter?"

"Madam," replied the Countess, "I shall tell you, but first I want you to know what I intend for you to gain from all this, should you do me this favor. I see that your daughter is beautiful and old enough for a husband, and from what I have heard from what I have seen for myself, the fact that you lack wealth to marry her forces you to keep her at home. In exchange for the service you will perform for me, I intend immediately to provide her, from my own resources, the dowry that you yourself estimate would be suitable to marry her honorably."

As the lady was in need, the offer was welcome, but still, since she had a proud spirit, she said:

"Madam, tell me what I can do for you, and if it is an honorable thing for me to do, I shall gladly do it, and then you may reward me in whatever way you please."

The Countess said:

"I want you, through some person whom you trust, to tell the Count, my husband, that your daughter is prepared to fulfill his every desire whenever she may be assured that he loves her as much as he claims; this she will never believe unless he sends her the ring which he wears on his hand and which she has heard he is so fond of; if he sends this to her, you will give it to me. And then you will send someone to say that your daughter is prepared to fulfill his desires, and you will have him come here in secret and let him lie, unsuspectingly, with me who will be disguised as your daughter. Perhaps God will grant me the grace of becoming pregnant, and later, having his ring on my finger and the son engendered by him in my arms, I shall have him back and live with him as a wife should live with her husband, and you shall be the cause of all this."

This seemed to the noble lady no small request, for she feared that some dishonor could, perhaps, fall upon her daughter; but she considered what an honorable thing it would be to assist the good woman in regaining her husband, for in doing this she would be working toward an honorable goal. And so, trusting the good and genuine affection of the Countess, she not only promised the Countess to help her, but within a few days' time acting with secrecy and caution and following the plan devised by the Countess, she had the ring (in spite of the fact that the Count was most reluctant to give it away), and in the place of her daughter she had skillfully managed to put the Countess to lie with the Count. In the course of their first couplings, lovingly sought after by the Count, it pleased God that the lady became pregnant with two male children, as was clear when the time for her delivery arrived. It was not only on one occasion that the noble lady managed to please the Countess with the embraces of her husband, but many times, working so secretly that never a word was learned about it, the Count all the while believing himself to have been in bed not with his wife but rather with the lady he loved; and when it was time to leave her in the morning, the Count would always present her with beautiful and precious jewels, all of which the Countess guarded most carefully.

When she knew that she was pregnant, the Countess no longer wished to trouble the noble lady with such services any further, and she said to her:

"Madam, thanks to God and to you, I have what I wanted, and now it is time for me to do whatever you wish me to do, so that afterward I may take my leave."

The noble lady told her she was happy that the Countess had obtained what she desired, but that she had not acted in the hopes of receiving any recompense but only because she felt it was her duty to support a good cause.

To this the Countess said:

"Madam, your intentions please me very much, but for my part, I have no intention of giving you something as a reward; but rather, I give you whatever you ask for supporting a good cause, for I believe that things should be done in this fashion."

Constrained by necessity, and with the greatest embarrassment, the noble lady then asked the Countess for a hundred pounds in order to marry her daughter. The Countess, understanding her embarrassment and hearing her modest request, gave her five hundred pounds as well as a quantity of beautiful and precious jewels amounting, perhaps, to as much again; the noble lady, more than satisfied, thanked the Countess profusely. Then the Countess left and returned to the inn. So that Beltramo would no longer have any excuse to send messages or visit her home, the noble lady went with her daughter to the country home of her relatives, and shortly thereafter, Beltramo was recalled home by his vassals and, having heard that the Countess had left the place, he returned there.

When the Countess learned that he had left Florence and had returned to his domain, she was very happy; she remained in Florence until the time for her delivery arrived, and she gave birth to two sons, both of whom very much resembled their father. She had them carefully nursed, and when she thought the time was right, she set out without being recognized by anyone and reached Montpellier; she rested there for a few days, making inquiries about the Count and his whereabouts, and when she learned that on All Saints' Day he was to give a great banquet for his ladies and knights in Rossiglione, she made her way there, still dressed in the pilgrim's clothing she had worn the day she left home.

And hearing that the ladies and knights gathered together in the Count's palace were about to sit down at the table, without changing her clothes and with the two little boys in her arms, she entered the dining hall, and she moved from one guest to another until, finding the Count, she threw herself at his feet, saying in tears:

"My lord, I am your unfortunate bride, who in misery has wandered about a long time in order to allow you to return and live in your own home. I beg you in God's name to observe the conditions imposed upon me by the two knights whom I sent to you: here in my arms is not one of your sons but two, and here is your ring. So the time has come for you to accept me as your wife according to your promise."

When he heard this, the Count was much confused, but he recognized his ring and even his sons, for they resembled him so, but he still asked: "How could this have happened?"

To the utter astonishment of the Count and of all the others who were present, the Countess recounted in detail how everything happened; because of this, he knew she was telling the truth, and seeing her perseverance and her intelligence and, moreover, two such handsome sons, the Count, in order to keep his promise as well as please his men and their ladies, all of whom begged him to receive and honor her as his legitimate wife, set aside his obstinate severity, raised the Countess to her feet, and embracing and kissing her, recognized her as his legitimate bride and her children as his own sons. Then he had her dressed in more suitable garments, to the greatest pleasure of all who were present and of all his other vassals who heard the news, and he gave a magnificent banquet which lasted not only that entire day but several days afterward; and from that day on, always honoring her as his bride and wife, he loved her and held her most dear.

· ❧ ·

Fourth Day, Introduction

Dearest ladies, both from what I have heard wise men say and from things I have often seen and read about, I used to think that the impetuous and fiery wind of envy would only batter high towers and the topmost part of trees, but I find that I was very much mistaken in my judgment. I flee and have always striven to flee the fiery blast of this angry gale, by trying to go about things quietly and unobtrusively not only through the plains but also through the deepest valleys. This will be clear to anyone who reads these short stories which I have written, but not signed, in Florentine vernacular prose, and composed in the most humble and low style possible; yet for all of this, I have not been able to avoid the terrible buffeting of such a wind which has almost uprooted me, and I have been nearly torn to pieces by the fangs of envy. Therefore, I can very easily attest to what wise men say is true: only misery is without envy in this world.

There have been those, discerning ladies, who have read these stories and have said that you please me too much and that it is not fitting for me to take so much pleasure from pleasing and consoling you, and, what seems to be worse, in praising you as I do. Others, speaking more profoundly, have stated that at my age it is not proper to pursue such matters, that is, to discuss women or to try to please them. And many, concerned about my reputation, say that I would be wiser to remain with the Muses on Parnassus than to get myself involved with you and these trifles. And there are those still who, speaking more spitefully than wisely, have said that it would be more practical if I were to consider where my daily bread was coming from rather than to go about "feeding on wind" with this foolishness of mine. And certain others, in order to belittle my labors, try to demonstrate that the things I have related to you did not happen in the way I told you they did.

Thus, worthy ladies, while I battle in your service, I am buffeted, troubled, and wounded to the quick by such winds and by such fierce, sharp teeth as these. God knows, I hear and endure these things with a tranquil mind, and however much my defense depends upon you in all of this, I do not, nevertheless, intend to spare my own forces; on the contrary, without replying as much as might be fitting, I shall put forward some simple answer, hoping in this way to shut my ears to their complaints, and I shall do this without further delay, for if I have as yet completed only a third of my task, my enemies are numerous and presumptuous, and before I reach the end of my labors, they will have multiplied—unless they receive some sort of reply before that time; and if this is not done, then their least effort will be enough to overcome me; and even your power, great as it may be, would be unable to resist them.

But before I reply to my critics, I should like to tell not an entire tale (for in doing so it might appear that I wished to mix my own stories with those of so worthy a group as I have been telling you about) but merely a portion of a tale, so that its very incompleteness will separate it from any of the others in my book.

For the benefit of those who criticize me, then, let me tell you about a man named Filippo Balducci, who lived in our city a long time ago. He was of rather modest birth, but he was rich, well versed, and expert in those matters which were required by his station in life; and he had a wife whom he dearly loved, and she loved him, and together they lived a tranquil life, always trying to please one another. Now it happened, as it must happen to all of us, that the good woman passed from this life and left nothing of herself to Filippo but an only child, whom she had conceived with him and who was now almost two years old.

No man was ever more disheartened by the loss of the thing he loved than Filippo was by the loss of his wife; and seeing himself deprived of that companionship which he most cherished, he decided to renounce this world completely, to devote himself to serving God, and to do the same for his little boy. After he had given everything he owned to charity, he immediately went to the top of Mount Asinaio, and there he lived in a small hut with his son, surviving on alms, fasts, and prayers. And with his son, he was careful not to talk about worldly affairs or to expose him to them; with him he would always praise the glory of God and the eternal life, teaching him nothing but holy prayers. They spent many years leading this kind of life, his son restricted to the hut and denied contact with everyone except his father.

The good man was in the habit of coming into Florence from time to time, and he would return to his hut after receiving assistance from the friends of God according to his needs. Now, one day, when his son was eighteen years of age, Filippo happened to tell him that he was going into the city, and his son replied:

"Father, you are now an old man and can endure hardship very poorly. Why don't you take me with you one time to Florence so that you can introduce me to your friends and to those devoted to God? Since I am young and can endure hardship better than you, I can, from then on, go to Florence whenever you like to tend to our needs, and you can remain here."

The worthy man, realizing that this son of his was now grown up and was already so used to serving God that only with great difficulty could the things of this world have any effect on him, said to himself: "He is right." And since he had to go away, he took his son along with him.

When the young man saw the palaces, the houses, the churches, and all the other things that filled the city, he was amazed, for he had never seen such things in his life, and he kept asking his father what this one and that one was called. His father told him, and no sooner was one question answered than he would ask about something else. As they went along this way, the son asking and the father explaining, by chance they ran into a group of beautiful and elegantly dressed young women who were returning from a wedding feast; when the young man saw them, he immediately asked his father what they were. To this his father replied:

"My son, lower your eyes and do not look, for they are evil."

Then the son asked: "What are they called?"

In order not to awaken some potential or anything-but-useful desire in the young man's carnal appetite, his father did not want to tell his son their proper name, that is to say "women," so he answered:

"Those are called goslings."

What an amazing thing to behold! The young man, who had never before seen a single gosling, no longer paid any attention to the palaces, oxen, horses, mules, money, or anything else he had seen, and he quickly said:

"Father, I beg you to help me get one of those goslings."

"Alas, my son," said the father, "be quiet; they are evil."

To this the young man replied:

"Are evil things made like that?"

"Yes," his father replied.

And his son answered:

"I do not understand what you are saying or why they are evil. As far as I know, I have never seen anything more beautiful or pleasing than they. They are more beautiful than the painted angels which you have pointed out to me so many times. Oh, if you care for me at all, do what you can to take one of these goslings home with us, and I will take care of feeding it."

His father replied:

"I will not, for you do not know how to feed them!"

Right then and there the father sensed that Nature had more power than his intelligence, and he was sorry for having brought his son to Florence. But let what I have recounted of this tale up to this point suffice, so that I may return to those for whom it was meant.

Well, young ladies, some of my critics say that I am wrong to try to please you too much, and that I am too fond of you. To these accusations I openly confess, that is, that you do please me and I do try to please you. But why is this so surprising to them? Putting aside the delights of having known your amorous kisses, your pleasurable embraces, and the delicious couplings that one so often enjoys with you, sweet ladies, let us consider merely the pleasure of seeing you constantly: your elegant garments, your enchanting beauty, and the charm with which you adorn yourselves (not to mention your feminine decorum). And so we see that someone who was nurtured and reared in the confines of a small cave upon a lonely and uncivilized mountaintop without any companions except for his father desired only you, asked for only you, gave only you his affection.

Will my critics blame me, bite and tear me apart if I—whose body heaven made most ready to love you with, and whose soul has been so disposed since my childhood when I first experienced the power of the light from your eyes, the softness of your honeylike words, and the flames kindled by your compassionate sighs—will they blame me for trying to please you and for the fact that you delight me, when we see how you, more than anything else, pleased a hermit, and what's more, a young man without feeling, much like a beast? Of course, those who do not love you and do not desire to be loved by you (people who neither feel nor know the pleasures or the power of natural affection) are the ones who blame me for doing this, but I care very little about them. And those who go around talking about my age show that they know nothing about the matter, for though the leek may have a white top, its roots can still be green. But joking aside, I reply by saying to them that I see no reason why I should be ashamed of delighting in these pleasures and in the ladies that give them, before the end of my days, since Guido Cavalcanti and Dante Alighieri (already old men) and Messer Cino da Pistoia[14] (a very old man indeed) considered themselves honored in striving to please the ladies in whose beauty lay their delight. And if it were not a departure from the customary way of arguing, I certainly would cite from history books and show you that they are full of ancient and worthy men who in their most mature years strove with great zeal to please the ladies—if my critics are not familiar with such cases, they should go and look them up! I agree that remaining with the Muses on Parnassus is sound advice, but we cannot always dwell with the Muses any more than they can always dwell with us. If it sometimes happens that a man leaves them, he should not be blamed if he delights in seeing something resembling them: the Muses are ladies, and although ladies are not as worthy as Muses, they do, nevertheless, look like them at first glance; and so for this reason, if for no other, they should please me. Furthermore, the fact is that ladies have already been the reason for my composing thousands of verses, while the Muses were in no way the cause of my writing them. They have, of course, assisted me and shown me how to compose these thousands of verses, and it is quite possible that they have been with me on several occasions while I was writing these stories of mine, no matter how insignificant they may be—they came to me, it could be said, out of respect for the affinity between these ladies and themselves. Therefore, in composing such stories as these, I am not as far away from Mount Parnassus or the Muses as some people may think.

But what shall we say about those who feel so much compassion for my hunger that they advise me to find myself a bit of bread to eat? All I know is that if I were to ask myself what their reply would be if I were forced to beg them for a meal, I imagine that they would tell me, "Go look for it among your fables!" And yet, poets have found more of it in their fables than many rich men have in their treasures, and many more still, by pursuing their fables, have lengthened their lives, while, on the contrary, others have lost them early in the search for more bread than they needed. What more, then? Let these people drive me away if ever I ask bread of them—thanks be to God, as yet I have no such need. And if ever the need arises, I know, in the words of the Apostle, how to endure both in abundance as well as in poverty.[15] And let no one mind my business but myself!

And as for those who say that these things did not happen the way I say they did in my stories, I should be very happy if they would bring forward the original versions, and if these should be different from what I have written, I would call their reproach justified and would try to correct myself; but until they produce something more than words, I shall leave them to their own opinions and follow my own, saying about them what they say about me.

Most gracious ladies, let this suffice as my reply for the time being, and let me say that armed with the aid of God and that of yourselves, in which I place my trust, with patience I shall proceed with my task, turning my back on that wind and letting it blow, for I do not see what more can happen to me than what happens to fine dust in a windstorm—either it does not move from the ground, or it does move from the ground; and if the wind sweeps it up high enough, it will often drop on the heads of men, the crowns of kings and emperors, and sometimes on high palaces and lofty towers; if it falls from there, it cannot go any lower than the spot from which it was lifted up. And if I have in the past striven with all my might to please you in some way, now I shall do so even more, for I realize that no reasonable person could say that I and the others who love you act in any way but according to Nature, whose laws (that is, Nature's) cannot be resisted without exceptional strength, and they are often resisted not only in vain but with very great damage to the strength of the one who attempts to do so. I confess that I do not possess nor wish to possess such strength, and if I did possess it, I would rather lend it to others than employ it myself. So let those critics of mine be silent, and if they cannot warm up to my work, let them live numbed with the chill of their own pleasures, or rather with their corrupt desires, and let me go on enjoying my own for this short lifetime granted to us. But we have strayed a great deal from where we departed, beautiful ladies, so let us return now and follow our established course.

The sun had already driven every star from the sky and the damp shadow of night from the earth when Filostrato arose and made his whole company stand, and they went into the beautiful garden, where they began to amuse themselves; and when it was time to eat, they breakfasted there where they had eaten supper the previous evening. When the sun was at its highest, they took their naps and then arose, and in their usual manner, they sat around the beautiful fountain. Then Filostrato ordered Fiammetta to tell the first story of the day; and without waiting to be told again, she began in a graceful fashion as follows:

————————— · ❧ · —————————

Fourth Day, First Story

Tancredi, Prince of Salerno, kills the lover of his daughter and sends her his heart in a gold goblet; she pours poisoned water on it, drinks it, and dies.

Today our King has given us a sad topic for discussion, especially when you consider that having come here to enjoy ourselves, we are now obliged to tell stories about the sorrows of others, ones which cannot be told without arousing the pity of those who tell them as well as of those who listen to them. Perhaps he did this in order to temper somewhat the happiness we have enjoyed during the past few days; but, since it is not for me to question his motives or try to change his wishes, I shall tell you about an incident that is not only pitiful but also disastrous and one worthy of your tears.

Tancredi, Prince of Salerno, was a most humane lord with a kindly spirit, except that in his old age he stained his hands with lovers' blood. In all his life he had but one daughter, and he would have been more fortunate if he had not had her. This girl was as tenderly loved by her father as any daughter ever was; and this tender love of his prevented her from leaving his side; and she had not yet married, in spite of the fact that she had passed by many years the suitable age for taking a husband. Then, finally, he gave her in marriage to a son of the Duke of Capua, who a short time later left her a widow, and she returned to her father. She was as beautiful in body and face as any woman could be, and she was both young and vivacious, and wiser, perhaps, than any woman should be. She lived like a great lady with her loving father in the midst of great luxury, and since she was aware that her father, because of the love he bore her, was not concerned about giving her away in marriage again, and since she felt it would be immodest of her to request this of him, she decided to see if she could secretly find herself a worthy lover.

In her father's court she was able to observe many of those men, both noble and otherwise, who frequent such courts, and after studying the manners and habits of many of them, one more than any of the others attracted her—a young valet of her father's whose name was

Guiscardo, a man of very humble birth but one whose virtues and noble bearing pleased her so much that she silently and passionately fell in love with him, and the more she saw him, the more she admired him. The young man, who among other things was not slow of wit, soon noticed her attention toward him, and he took her so deep into his heart that he could hardly think of anything else but his love for her.

And so they were secretly in love with each other, and the young girl desired nothing more than to find herself alone with him, and since she was unwilling to confide in anyone about her love, she thought of an unusual scheme for letting him know how they could meet. She wrote him a letter, and in it she told him what he had to do the following day in order to be with her; then she put it in the hollow of a reed and as if in jest, she gave it to Guiscardo, saying:

"Make a bellows of this tonight for your serving girl to keep the fire burning."

Guiscardo took it, and realizing that she would not have given it to him and spoken as she did without some reason, he brought it home with him and after examining the stick, he found that it was hollow, and opening it, he found her letter inside; when he read it and learned what he had to do, he was the happiest man that ever lived, and he carefully prepared to meet her in the way she had described to him in her letter. Near the Prince's palace was a cave hollowed out of a hill a long time before, and it was lit by a small opening in the side of the hill; the cave had been abandoned for so long that the opening was almost covered over by brambles and weeds. One could reach this cave by a secret stairway blocked by a strong door which led from one of the rooms on the ground floor of the palace which the young lady occupied. Hardly anyone alive remembered that the stairway existed, for it had not been used for so long a time. But Love, from whose eyes no secret can remain concealed, brought back the stairway to this young lady's enamored mind.

For many days, the young lady tried with tools to open that door in such a way that no one might suspect, finally she succeeded, and once the door was open, she was able to walk down into the cave and see the outer entrance; then she sent word to Guiscardo that he should try to come there, indicating to him the probable height from the opening to the floor of the cave below. In order to accomplish this, Guiscardo immediately prepared a rope with knots and loops in it so that he would be able to climb up and down with it; then, wrapped in a leather skin to protect himself from the brambles, without anyone knowing about it, the following night he made his way to the cave opening. He tied one of the loops of the rope firmly to a tree stump at the mouth of the opening, and with it he lowered himself into the cave and waited there for the lady.

The next day, pretending that she wished to rest, the young lady sent her ladies-in-waiting away and, alone, she closed herself in her bedroom. Then, opening the stairway door, she descended into the cave, where she found Guiscardo, and they welcomed each other with great joy; later, they went to her bedroom, where they remained most of that day, to their greatest pleasure. Having made arrangements to keep their love affair a secret, Guiscardo returned to the cave, and the lady locked the door and came out to rejoin her attendants. Then, when night came, Guiscardo climbed up his rope and left the cave through the same opening that he had entered and returned home. Having learned the way, he was to return frequently in the course of time.

But Fortune, jealous of so long and great a pleasure, turned the happiness of the two lovers into a sorrowful event: Tancredi was sometimes in the habit of visiting his daughter's bedroom to spend a little time talking to her, and then he would leave. One day after eating, while the lady (whose name was Ghismunda) was in her garden with all her attendants, he went there without being observed or heard by anyone and entered her bedroom. Finding the windows closed and the bed curtains drawn back, and not wishing to take her away from her amusement, Tancredi sat down on a small stool at the foot of the bed; he leaned his head back on the bed and drew the bed curtain around him—almost as if he were trying to hide himself on purpose—and there he fell asleep. Ghismunda, who unfortunately that day had sent for Guiscardo, left her ladies-in-waiting in the garden and quietly entered her bedroom, where Tancredi was sleeping; she locked her door without noticing that someone was there and opened the door to Guiscardo, who was waiting for her, and they went to bed together, as they had always done, and while they were playing together and enjoying each other, Tancredi happened to awaken, and he heard and saw what Guiscardo and his daughter were doing. It grieved him beyond all measure, and at first he wanted to cry out, but then he decided to be silent and remain hidden, if he could, so that he could do with less shame what he had already decided must be done. The two lovers remained together for a long time, as they were accustomed to do, without noticing Tancredi; when they felt it was time, they got out of bed and Guiscardo returned to the cave and the lady left her room. Although he was an old man, Tancredi left the room by climbing through a window down to the garden, and, unnoticed, he returned, grief-stricken, to his room.

That night while all were asleep, on Tancredi's orders Guiscardo was seized by two guards just as he was emerging, hindered by his leather skin, from the cave opening, and in secret he was taken to Tancredi, who, almost in tears when he saw him, said:

"Guiscardo, my kindness toward you did not deserve the outrage and the shame which you have given me this day and which I witnessed with my very own eyes!"

To this, Guiscardo offered no other reply but:

"Love is more powerful than either you or I."

Then Tancredi ordered him to be guarded secretly in a nearby room, and this was done. The following day, while Ghismunda was still ignorant of all this, and after Tancredi had considered all sorts of diverse solutions, shortly after eating, as was his custom, he went to his daughter's room; he had her summoned, and locking himself inside with her, he said to her in tears:

"Ghismunda, I thought I knew your virtue and honesty so well that it never would have occurred to me, no matter what people might have said, that you could submit to any man who was not your husband, or even think of doing so, if I had not witnessed it with my own eyes; and thinking of it, I shall grieve for the duration of that little bit of life my old age still allows me. Since you had to bring yourself to such dishonor, would to God you had chosen a man who was worthy of your nobility. From among all the men that frequent my court you chose Guiscardo, a young man of very low class, who was raised at our court from the time he was a small child until today almost as an act of charity. You have caused me the greatest of worry, for I do not know what to do: as he left the cave opening last night, I had him arrested and now he is in prison; I have already made my decision about what to do with Guiscardo, but with you—God knows what I should do with you! On the one hand, the love I have always felt for you—more love than any father ever had for a daughter—urges me in one direction; on the other hand, my righteous indignation over your great folly urges me in the other; my love tells me to forgive you and my wrath tells me, against my own nature, to punish you. But before I make a decision, I should like to hear what you have to say about the matter."

Having said this, he lowered his head, and wept like a child who had been severely beaten. Ghismunda, hearing her father's words and realizing not only that her secret affair had been discovered but that Guiscardo had been seized, felt measureless grief, which she was very near to showing with cries and tears, as most women do; but her proud spirit conquered this cowardice, and her face remained the same through her miraculous strength of will, and knowing that her Guiscardo was already as good as dead, she decided that rather than offering excuses for her behavior, she preferred not to go on living; therefore, without a trace of feminine sorrow or contrition for her misdeed, she faced her father as a brave and unafraid young lady, and with a tearless, open,. and unperturbed face, she said to him:

"Tancredi, I am disposed neither to deny nor to beg, since the former would not avail me, and I do not wish to avail myself of the latter; moreover, in no way do I intend to appeal to your kindness and your love but, rather, I shall confess the truth to you, first defending my reputation with sound arguments, and then, with deeds, I shall follow the boldness of my heart. It is true that I loved and still do love Guiscardo, and as long as I shall live, which will not be long, I shall love him; and if there is love after death, then I shall continue loving him. I was moved to act this way not so much by my womanly weakness but by your own lack of interest in marrying me, as well as by Guiscardo's own worth. It is clear, Tancredi, that you are made of flesh and blood and that you have fathered a daughter made of flesh and blood, not one of stone or of iron; and though you are old now, you should have remembered the nature and power of the laws of youth; although, as a man, you spent the best part of your years soldiering in the army, you should, nevertheless, know how idleness and luxurious living can affect the old as well as the young.

"And I was fathered by you and am of flesh and blood, and have not lived so long that I am yet old—for both these reasons I am full of amorous desire, which has also been greatly increased by my marriage, which taught me how pleasurable it is to satisfy such desires. Unable to resist their power, and being both young and a woman, I decided to follow where they led me, and I fell in love. And though I had made up my mind to commit this natural sin, I tried as best I could to avoid bringing shame on you and on myself. Compassionate Love and kindly Fortune revealed to me a secret way to fulfill my desires without anyone knowing. And no matter who told you or how you found out, I make no denial of any of this. I did not choose Guiscardo at random, as many women do, but I chose him over all others with deliberate consideration and careful forethought, and the two of us have enjoyed the satisfaction of our desires for some time now. Besides reproving me for having sinned in loving, you reprove me even more bitterly—preferring, in so doing, to follow a common fallacy rather than the truth—in stating that I consorted with a man of lowly birth, as if to say you would not have been angry had I chosen a man of noble birth as a lover. You fail to see that it is Fortune you should blame and not my sin, for it is Fortune that most frequently raises the unworthy to great heights and casts down the most worthy.

"But let us leave all that aside and look rather to the principles of things: you will observe that we are all made of the same flesh and that we are all created by one and the same Creator with equal powers and equal force and virtue. Virtue it was that first distinguished differences among us, even though we were all born and are still being born equal; those who possessed a greater portion of virtue and were devoted to it were called nobles, and the rest remained commoners. And although a custom contrary to this practice has made us forget this natural law, yet it is not discarded or broken by Nature and good habits; and a person who lives virtuously shows himself openly to be noble, and he who calls him other than noble is the one at fault, not the noble man.

"Look at all your noblemen, and compare their lives, customs, and manners on the one hand to those of Guiscardo on the other; if you judge without prejudice, you will declare him most noble and those nobles of yours mere commoners. I do not trust the judgment of any other person concerning the virtue and valor of Guiscardo—I trust only what you yourself have said about him and what I have seen with my own eyes. Who has praised him more than you in all those praiseworthy matters worthy of a valiant man? You were certainly not mistaken; and unless my eyes deceive me, you never praised him for anything he did not clearly achieve in a manner more admirable than your words could express. If in this matter I was deceived in any way, then I was deceived by you. Will you say, then, that I consorted with a man of lowly condition? Then you do not speak the truth; you may, by chance, say that he is a poor man, and this I grant you—but only to your shame, for that is the condition in which you kept a valiant servant of yours. Poverty does not diminish anyone's nobility, it only diminishes his wealth! Many kings and great rulers were once poor, and many of those who plow the land and watch the sheep were once very rich, and they still are.

"As for your last problem—what to do with me—in no way should you hesitate: if in your old age you are inclined to do what you did not do as a young man—that is, to turn to cruelty—then turn your cruelty upon me. I shall not beg for leniency, for I am the true cause of this sin, if it be a sin; and I assure you that if you do not do to me what you have done or plan to do to Guiscardo, my own hands will do it for you. Now go, shed your tears with women, and if you must be cruel, if you feel we deserve death, then kill both of us with one blow!"

The Prince recognized his daughter's greatness of soul, but he did not believe she was as resolute as her words implied; therefore, having left her and given up all thought of punishing her cruelly, he thought he could cool her burning love with different punishment: he ordered the two men who were guarding Guiscardo to go in secret and strangle him that night and to cut out his heart and bring it to him. They did just as they were ordered to do, and the following day, the Prince sent for a large, handsome goblet of gold, and in it he put Guiscardo's heart; he sent it to his daughter by one of his most trusted servants, who was instructed to say the following words when he gave it to her:

"Your father sends you this to console you for the loss of that which you loved the most, just as you have consoled him for the loss of what he loved the most."

Ghismunda, firm in her desperate resolution, had had poisonous herbs and roots brought to her as soon as her father departed, and she distilled and reduced them to a liquid, in order to have them available if what she feared actually did occur. When the servant arrived and delivered the Prince's gift and his words, she took the goblet with a determined look, uncovered it, and seeing the heart and hearing the words, she knew for certain that this was Guiscardo's heart. Turning to the servant, she said:

"There is no burial place more worthy for such a heart than one of gold; in this regard, my father has acted wisely."

And saying this, she raised the cup to her lips and kissed it, and then continued speaking to the servant:

"I have always found my father's love for me to be most tender in every respect as I do now, even in this extreme moment of my life, but here it shows itself to be even more so than ever; and thanking him for the last time on my behalf, I bid you tell him how grateful I am to him for so precious a gift as this."

Then, looking into the goblet, which she held firmly in her hand, gazing at the heart, she sighed and said:

"Ah! Sweetest abode of all my pleasures, cursed be the cruelty of he who has forced me to look at you with the eyes of my body! It was already too much to gaze upon you constantly even with the eyes of my mind. Your life has run the course that Fortune has bestowed upon you; you have reached the goal toward which all men race; you have abandoned the miseries and trials of the world and have received from your very enemy the burial that your valor deserved. Nothing is lacking in your last rites except the tears of the one who loved you while you were alive. So that you might have them, God moved my pitiless father to send you to me, and I shall give you those tears, even though I was determined to die without them, and I will give them with a serene face; as soon as I have wept for you, I shall act in such a way that my soul will join yours without further delay, and may you, heart, accept my soul which once was so dear to you. In what company could I go more happily or more securely to unknown places than in yours? I am sure that your soul is still here and continues to look upon the places where we took our pleasure, and as I am certain that your soul loves me still, may it wait for my soul, which loves it so deeply."

And when this was said, she bent over the goblet and without a womanly show of grief, she began to weep in a way marvelous to behold, pouring forth her tears as if from a fountain as she kissed the dead heart countless times. Her attendants, who stood all around her, did not understand whose heart it was or what her words meant, but overcome with compassion they all began to weep; they asked her most pityingly why she was weeping, and they sought to comfort her as best they knew how, but it was all in vain. Then, when she felt she had wept enough, she raised her head, dried her eyes, and said:

"Oh, most beloved heart, now that I have fulfilled all my duties to you, nothing more remains for me but to come to you and join my soul to yours."

When she had said this, she took the phial she had prepared the day before containing the liquid, and pouring it into the goblet where the heart was bathed with her many tears, with no trepidation whatsoever, she lifted it to her lips and drank all of it. Having done this, she climbed upon her bed, with the goblet in her hand, and as modestly as possible she arranged her body upon the bed and placed the heart of her dead lover against her own, and without saying another word she waited for death.

Although her ladies-in-waiting had seen and heard all these things, they did not understand, nor did they know that the liquid she had drunk was poison; they sent word to Tancredi about it, and he, fearing what might happen, immediately went down to his daughter's bedroom. He arrived there just as she was arranging herself on her bed; observing her condition, he tried to comfort her (only too late) with sweet words and began to weep most sorrowfully. And the lady said:

"Tancredi, save those tears for a less fortunate fate than this, and do not shed them on my account, for I do not want them. Who ever heard of someone weeping over what he himself wished for? But if you still retain anything of that love you once had for me, grant me one last gift: since it displeased you that I once lived quietly in secret with Guiscardo, let my body be publicly laid to rest beside his, wherever you choose to cast his remains."

The anguish of his weeping did not allow the Prince to answer. Then, when the young woman felt her death was near, she drew the dead heart to her breast and said:

"God be with you, for now I leave you."

And closing her eyes, her senses left her, and she departed from this sorrowful existence. Thus, just as you have heard it, the sad love of Guiscardo and Ghismunda came to an end; and then Tancredi, who wept much and repented of his cruelty too late, amid the grief of all the people of Salerno, had them buried together honorably in one tomb.

· ❦ ·

Fifth Day, Eighth Story

Nastagio degli Onesti, in love with a girl from the Traversari family, squanders all his wealth without being loved in return; his relatives beg him to leave for Chiassi; there he sees a knight hunting down a young lady, who is killed and devoured by two dogs; he invites his relatives and the lady he loves to dine with him, and when she sees this same young lady torn to pieces, fearing a similar fate, she takes Nastagio as her husband.

When Lauretta fell silent, at the Queen's command Filomena began as follows:

Charming ladies, just as our compassion is praised, so, too, is our cruelty punished severely by divine justice. In order to prove this to you and to give you reason to drive all such cruelty completely from your hearts, I would like to tell you a story which is no less moving than it is entertaining.

In Ravenna, that most ancient city of Romagna, there once lived many a noble gentleman, among whom was a young man named Nastagio degli Onesti, who was left rich beyond all measure by the deaths of his father and one of his uncles. And as often happens to young men who have no wife, he fell in love with one of the daughters of a certain Paolo Traversaro, a girl of a far nobler family than his own, but whose love he hoped to win by means of his accomplishments. But no matter how magnificent, splendid, and praiseworthy these were, they not only did him little good but, on the contrary, they seemed to do him harm—so cruel, harsh, and unfriendly did the young girl he loved act toward him;

perhaps because of her singular beauty or perhaps because of her exalted rank, she became so haughty and disdainful that she disliked everything about him and anything he liked. Such behavior was so difficult for Nastagio to bear that he often considered, after grieving much over it, taking his own life in despair; but yet he held back, at times deciding to give her up altogether or to learn to hate her just as she hated him. But such resolutions were taken in vain, for it appeared that the less hope of success he enjoyed, the more his love increased.

And so then, as the young man persisted in loving and in spending lavishly, there were certain friends and relatives of his who thought that he was on the brink of wasting away both himself and his fortune; and so they would often beg and advise him to leave Ravenna and to stay for a while in some other place, for in doing this, both his passion and his expenses might be diminished. Nastagio consistently made fun of their advice, but they begged him so insistently that he was no longer able to refuse, and so he agreed to do as they said; and having made great preparations, as if he were going to France or Spain or some other faraway land, he climbed upon his horse, and accompanied by his many friends, left the city and went about three miles outside Ravenna to a place called Chiassi, where he had his pavilions and tents set up, informing those who had ridden with him that he wished to stop there and that they were free to return to Ravenna. So then Nastagio, having established himself there, began to lead the finest and most elegant life that anyone could possibly lead, inviting different groups of friends to dine or lunch with him, as was his custom.

Now it happened to be around the beginning of May and the weather was beautiful when Nastagio began to brood over his cruel lady, and having ordered all his servants to leave him alone so that he could think about her at his pleasure, step by step, lost in his thoughts, he wandered into the pine woods. And it was already past the fifth hour of the day[16] when, having walked at least half a mile into the pine forest, not mindful of eating or anything else, he suddenly seemed to hear a terrible cry and the most horrible shrieks of a woman; his sweet train of thoughts being thus interrupted, he raised his head to see what it was and discovered to his astonishment that he was in a pine forest. Moreover, as he looked straight in front of him, he saw a very beautiful girl, naked, her hair all disheveled, her flesh torn by the briars and thorns, running toward him through a wood thick with bushes and briars, weeping and crying out for mercy; then he saw running behind her two huge and ferocious mastiffs that every so often would catch up with her and bite her savagely; and even farther behind her, he could see a dark-looking knight, his face flushed with anger, riding a black steed and holding a sword in his hand, threatening her with death in horrible and abusive language.

This sight filled his soul with both wonder and fear as well as with compassion for the unfortunate woman, and from his compassion was born a desire to save her, if he could, from such anguish and threat of death. On finding himself without weapons, he used the branch of a tree as a club and prepared to confront the dogs and the knight.

But when the knight saw this, he shouted to him from a distance:

"Nastagio, don't interfere; leave it to me and these dogs to give this wicked female what she deserves!"

No sooner had he said this than the dogs seized the girl firmly by her thighs and stopped her, and the knight, reaching that spot, dismounted from his horse, as Nastagio went up to him and said:

"I do not know who you are or how you happen to know me, but let me tell you how base an act it is for an armed knight to try to kill a naked woman and to set dogs upon her as if she were a savage beast. I certainly shall defend her to the best of my ability."

The knight then said:

"Nastagio, I was from the same town as you, and you were still a small child when I, Messer Guido degli Anastagi, fell too passionately in love with this woman, far more so than you are with this Traversari girl of yours; her arrogance and cruelty led me to such a wretched state that one day with this very sword you see in my hand, I killed myself out of desperation, and I am now condemned to eternal punishment. Nor was it long afterward that this woman, who rejoiced at my death beyond all measure, also died, and for the sin of her cruelty and for the delight she took in my sufferings, unrepentant as she was and convinced that she deserved to be rewarded rather than punished for them, she, too, was and continues to be condemned to the pains of Hell. When she descended into Hell, both of us received a punishment: she was to flee from me and I, who had loved her so much, was to pursue her as if she were my mortal enemy and not the woman I loved; and every time I catch up to her, with this sword, the one I used to kill myself, I kill and split her back open, and that hard and cold heart, into which neither love nor compassion ever entered, I tear from her body along with her other entrails, as you will see presently, and give them to these dogs to devour. Then, after a short space of time as decreed by the justice and power of God, she is resurrected, as if she had never been dead, and she begins her painful flight all over again, with the dogs and me pursuing her. And every Friday around this time I catch up with her at this spot, and here I slaughter her as you are about to witness; but do not think that we rest on other days, for I catch up with her then in other places where she thought or acted cruelly toward me; and having changed from her lover to her enemy, as you see, in this role I must pursue her for as many years as the number of months she was cruel to me. Now, allow me to carry out the sentence of divine justice and do not try to oppose what you are helpless to prevent."

When Nastagio heard these words, he became quite frightened, and there was not a hair on his head which was not standing on end, and stepping back, he watched the wretched girl and waited in fear to see what the knight would do to her; when the knight finished speaking, with sword in hand, like a mad dog, he pounced on the girl, who was kneeling and screaming for mercy as the two mastiffs held her tightly, and with all his might, he stabbed her in the middle of her breast, the blade passing through to the other side. When the girl received this blow, she fell to the ground, still weeping and screaming, and the knight, having laid hold of a dagger, slit open her back, ripped out her heart and everything else around it, and threw it all to the two mastiffs, who, ravenous with hunger, devoured it instantly. Nor was it long before the girl, almost as if nothing had happened, suddenly rose to her feet and began to run off in the direction of the sea with the dogs still tearing at her flesh; and the knight, having remounted his horse and taken up his sword again, also began to chase her, and in a short time, they were so far away that Nastagio could no longer see them.

After witnessing these events, Nastagio remained in that spot for a long while, caught up in his feelings of compassion and fear, but after a while it occurred to him that this spectacle, since it took place every Friday, might well be useful to him; and so, after marking the spot, he returned to his servants, and then, when the time seemed right, he sent for a number of his relatives and friends and said to them:

"For a long time now, you have been trying to persuade me to stop loving this hostile lady of mine and to put an end to my spending, and this I am prepared to do on condition that you do one favor for me, which is this: that on this coming Friday, you arrange for Messer Paolo Traversaro, his wife and daughter, and all their womenfolk, as well as anyone else you wish, to dine in this spot with me. Why I wish to do this, you will see when the time comes."

They all felt that this was not much to ask of them, and returning to Ravenna, at the appropriate time, they invited the people Nastagio requested, and although it was not at all easy to convince the girl Nastagio loved to go with them, she nevertheless went along with the other ladies. Nastagio arranged for a magnificent banquet to be prepared, and he had all the tables placed under the pine trees near the spot where he had seen the slaughter of the cruel lady; and in seating the men and the ladies at the table, he organized things in such a way that the girl he loved was placed directly in front of the place where the event was to occur.

And so it was that just after the last course was served, everyone began to hear the desperate cries of the girl who was being pursued. Everyone was very astonished and asked what it was, but since nobody seemed to know, they all got up to see what was happening for themselves, and they caught sight of the suffering girl, the knight, and the dogs; and in a matter of no time at all, they found them in their very midst.

They began screaming loudly at the dogs and the knight, and many of them stepped forward to help the girl, but the knight, speaking to them just as he had spoken to Nastagio, not only forced them to draw back but filled them with terror and amazement; and after he had done to the girl what he had done the other time, all of the ladies present (many of whom were relatives either of the suffering girl or of the knight and who remembered his love affair and his death) began to weep piteously, as if what they had witnessed had actually been inflicted upon themselves. When the scene came to an end and the lady and the knight had vanished, they all began to discuss what they had observed, with many different interpretations. But among those who were the most terrified was the cruel girl Nastagio loved, for she had clearly seen and heard every detail and realized that these things concerned her far more than anyone else who was present, inasmuch as she recalled the cruelty she had always inflicted upon Nastagio; as a result, she already felt herself fleeing from his rage and the mastiffs lunging at her sides.

So great was the terror aroused in the lady by this spectacle that in order to avoid a similar fate herself, she changed her hatred into love, and as soon as the proper occasion presented itself (which was that very evening), in secret she sent one of her trusted maidservants to Nastagio, begging him on her behalf to be so kind as to come to her, for she was now prepared to do everything he wished. To this request, Nastagio sent a reply saying that this was most gratifying but that he preferred to take his pleasure, preserving her honor; that is, to take her as his wife in marriage, if she would agree. The girl, who knew she alone was to blame for the fact that she and Nastagio were not already married, sent him a message that she would be delighted. And so, acting as her own intermediary, she told her father and mother that she would be happy to become Nastagio's bride, which pleased them immensely.

And so on the following Sunday, Nastagio married her, and having celebrated their nuptials, they lived happily together for a long time to come. Nor was this the only good that came from this terrible apparition, for all the ladies of Ravenna became so frightened that from then on they became a good deal more amenable to men's pleasure than they ever had been in the past.

· ❧ ·

Sixth Day, Seventh Story

Madonna Filippa is discovered by her husband with a lover of hers, and when she is called before a judge, with a ready and amusing reply she secures her freedom and causes the statute to be changed.

Fiammetta had finished speaking, and everyone was still laughing over the strange argument Scalza had used to ennoble the Baronci above every other family when the Queen called upon Filostrato to tell a story; and he began, saying:

Worthy ladies, it is good to know how to say the right thing at the right time, but I think it is even better when you know how to do so at a moment of real necessity. There was a noble lady, about whom I intend to tell you, who accomplished this so well that she not only provided her listeners with amusement and laughter, but she also managed to slip out of the clutches of a shameful death, as you shall hear.

In the city of Prato, there was once a statute—in truth, no less harsh than it was worthy of criticism—which, without any extenuating circumstances whatsoever, required that any woman caught by her husband committing adultery with a lover should be burned alive, just the way a woman who goes with a man for money would be. And while this statute was in effect, it happened that a noble lady named Madonna Filippa, who was beautiful and more in love than any woman could be, was discovered in her own bedroom by her husband, Rinaldo de' Pugliesi, in the arms of Lazzarino de' Guazzagliotri, a noble and handsome young man from that city, whom she loved more than herself. When Rinaldo discovered this, he was extremely angry and could hardly restrain himself from rushing at them and murdering them, and had he not been so concerned over what might happen to him if he were to follow the impulse of his anger, he would have done so. While able to restrain himself from doing this, he was, however, unable to refrain from claiming the sentence of Prato's statute, which he was not permitted to carry out by his own hand, that is, the death of his wife.

And so, in possession of very convincing evidence of his wife's transgression, when day broke, without thinking further about the matter, he denounced the lady and had her summoned to the court. The lady, who was very courageous, as women truly in love usually are, was determined to appear in court, and in spite of the fact that she was advised against this by many of her friends and relatives, she decided that she would rather confess the truth and die with a courageous heart than, fleeing like a coward, live in exile condemned *in absentia* and show herself unworthy of such a lover as the man in whose arms she had rested the night before. Escorted by a large group of women and men, all of whom were urging her to deny the charges, she came before the *podestà* and, with a steady gaze and a firm voice, demanded to know what he wanted of her. Gazing at the lady and finding her to be most beautiful and very well-bred as well as most courageous, indeed, as her own words bore witness, the *podestà* took pity on her and was afraid she might confess to something which would force him, in order to fulfill his duty, to condemn her to death.

But since he could not avoid questioning her about what she had been accused of doing, he said to her:

"Madam, as you can see, your husband Rinaldo is here and has lodged a complaint against you, in which he states that he has found you in adultery with another man; and because of this he demands that I punish you by putting you to death in accordance with the statute which requires such sentence here in Prato. But since I cannot do this if you do not confess, I suggest you be very careful how you answer this charge; now, tell me if what your husband accuses you of is true."

Without the slightest trace of fear, the lady, in a lovely tone of voice, replied:

"Sir, it is true that Rinaldo is my husband and that this past night he found me in Lazzarino's arms, where, because of the deep and perfect love I bear for him, I have many times lain; nor would I ever deny this; but, as I am sure you know, the laws should be equal for all and should be passed with the consent of the people they affect. In this case these conditions are not fulfilled, for this law applies only to us poor women, who are much better able than men to satisfy a larger number; furthermore, when this law was put into effect, not a single woman gave her consent, nor was any one of them ever consulted about it; therefore, it may quite rightly be called a bad law. And if, however, you wish, to the detriment of my body and your own soul, to put this law into effect, that is your concern; but, before you proceed to any judgment, I beg you to grant me a small favor: that is, to ask my husband whether or not I have ever refused, whenever and however many times he wished, to yield my entire body to him."

To this question, without waiting for the *podestà* to pose it, Rinaldo immediately replied that without any doubt, the lady had yielded to his every pleasure whenever he required it.

"So then," the lady promptly continued, "I ask you, Messer *Podestà*, if he has always taken of me whatever he needed and however much pleased him, what was I supposed to do then, and what am I to do now, with what is left over? Should I throw it to the dogs? Is it not much better to give it to a gentleman who loves me more than himself, rather than let it go to waste or spoil?"

The nature of the case and the fact that the lady was so well known brought almost all of Prato's citizens flocking to court, and when they heard such an amusing question posed by the lady, after much laughter, all of a sudden and almost in a single voice, they cried out that the lady was right and had spoken well; and before they left the court, with the *podestà*'s consent, they changed the cruel statute, modifying it so that it applied only to those women who were unfaithful to their husbands for money. And Rinaldo, confused by the whole mad affair, left the courtroom, and the lady, now free and happy, and resurrected from the flames, so to speak, returned to her home in triumph.

———————————— · 🦃 · ————————————

Sixth Day, Tenth Story

Brother Cipolla promises some peasants that he will show them a feather from the Angel Gabriel; but finding only bits of charcoal in its place, he tells them that these were the ones used to roast Saint Lorenzo.

Each member of the company having told a story, Dioneo realized that it was now his turn, and so, without waiting for any formal command, he imposed silence upon those who were praising Guido's clever reply and began:

Pretty ladies, although I enjoy the privilege of speaking on whatever subject I please, I have no intention of straying from the topic on which all of you have spoken so admirably today; on the contrary, I intend to follow in your footsteps and show you how one of the friars of Saint Anthony managed with a quick solution to avoid a trap set for him by two young men. Nor should it bother you if, in order to tell the story as it should be told, I have to speak at some length, for if you will look up at the sun, you will discover it is still mid-heaven.

Certaldo, as you may have heard, is a fortified city in the Valdelsa, within our own territory, which, no matter how small it may be now, was inhabited at one time by noble and well-to-do people. Because it was such good grazing ground, one of the brothers of Saint Anthony used to go there once a year to collect the alms that people were stupid enough to give him. He was called Brother Cipolla,[17] and was warmly welcomed there no less, perhaps, because of what his name stood for than for religious reasons, since that area of the country produced onions which were famous throughout Tuscany.

Brother Cipolla was short, redheaded, with a cheerful face, and he was the nicest scoundrel in the world; and despite the fact that he had no education, he was such a skillful and quick talker that whoever did not know him would not only have taken him for a great master of eloquence but would have considered him to be Cicero himself or perhaps even Quintilian; and if he was not the godfather of almost everyone in the district, he was at least their friend or acquaintance.

Now, as was his custom, he went there for one of his regular visits in the month of August; and one Sunday morning, when all the good men and women of the surrounding villages were gathered together in the parish church to hear Mass, Brother Cipolla stepped forward at the proper time and said:

"Ladies and gentlemen, as you know, it is your practice every year to send some of your grain and crops—some of you more and others less, according to your capacity and your piety—to the poor brothers of our blessed lord Saint Anthony, so that the blessed Saint Anthony may keep your oxen, your donkeys, your pigs, and your sheep safe from all danger; furthermore, you are used to paying, especially those of you who are enrolled in our order, those small dues which are paid once a year. To collect these contributions, I have been sent by my superior, that is, by Messer Abbot; and so, with God's blessing, after nones, when you hear the bells ring, you will come here to the front of the church, where in my usual manner I shall preach my sermon and you will kiss the cross. Moreover, since I know you all to be most devoted to my lord Messer Saint Anthony, as a special favor, I shall show you a most holy and beautiful relic which I myself brought back from the Holy Land, overseas: it is one of the feathers of the Angel Gabriel, precisely the one which was left in the Virgin Mary's bedroom when he came to perform the Annunciation before her in Nazareth."

He said this, and then he stopped talking and returned to the Mass. When Brother Cipolla was making this announcement, there happened to be, among the many others in the church, two young men who were most clever: one called Giovanni del Bragoniera and the other Biagio Pizzini, both of whom, after quite a bit of laughing over Brother Cipolla's relic, decided to play a trick on him and his feather, even though they were old and close friends of his. They found out that Brother Cipolla would be eating that day in the center of town with a friend; when they figured it was around the time for him to be at the table, they took to the street and went to the inn where the friar was staying. The plan was this: Biagio would keep Brother Cipolla's servant occupied by talking to him while Giovanni was to look for this feather, or whatever it was, among the friar's possessions and steal it from him, in order to see just how he would be able to explain its disappearance to the people later on.

Brother Cipolla had a servant, whom some called Guccio the Whale, others Guccio the Mess, and still others Guccio the Pig; he was such a crude individual that even Lippo Topo[18] himself would not have been able to do him justice. Brother Cipolla would often joke about him with his friends, and say:

"My servant has nine qualities, and if any one of them had existed in Solomon, Aristotle, or Seneca, it would have sufficed to spoil all of their virtue, intelligence, and holiness. Just think, then, what kind of man he must be, having nine such qualities, but no virtue, intelligence, or holiness!"

And when he was asked what these nine qualities were, he would recite them in a kind of doggerel verse:

"I'll tell you. He's lying, lazy, and lousy; negligent, disobedient, and foul-tongued; heedless, careless, and bad-mannered; besides this, he has other various little defects that are best left unmentioned. And what is most amusing about him is that wherever he goes, he wants to take a wife and set up housekeeping; and because he has a big, black, greasy beard, he thinks he is very handsome and attractive—in fact, he imagines that every woman who sees him falls in love with him, and if it were up to him, he'd lose his pants chasing after them all. And it is true that he is of great assistance to me, for he never lets anyone burden me with secrets without getting his share of an earful, and if someone happens to ask me a question about something, he is so afraid that I will not know how to reply that he quickly answers yes or no for me as he sees fit."

Brother Cipolla had left his servant back at the inn and had ordered him to make sure that no one touched his belongings, and especially his saddlebags, for the sacred objects were inside them. But Guccio the Mess was happier to be in a kitchen than a nightingale was to be on the green branches of a tree, especially if he knew that some servant girl was also there. When he noticed the innkeeper's maid, who was a fat, round, short, and ill-shapen creature with a pair of tits that looked like two clumps of cowshit and a face like one of the Baronci family,[19] all sweaty, greasy, and covered with soot, Guccio left Brother Cipolla's rooms unlocked and all his possessions unguarded as he swooped down into the kitchen just like a vulture pouncing on some carcass. Although it was still August, he took a seat near the fire and began to talk with the girl, whose name was Nuta, telling her that he was a gentleman by procuration, that he had more than a thousand hundreds of florins[20] (not counting those he had to give away to others), and that he knew how to do and say so many things more than even his very master ever dreamed of doing and saying. And with absolutely no concern for his cowl, which was covered with so much grease it would have seasoned all the soup kettles in Altopascio, or his torn and patched-up doublet, covered with sweat stains all around his collar and under his arms and in more spots and colors than a piece of cloth from India or China ever had, or his shoes, which were all worn out, or his hose, which were full of holes, he spoke to her as if he were Milord of Châtillons, talking about how he wanted to buy her new clothes and take her away from all this drudgery and into the service of someone else, and how he would give her the hope for a better life, even if he did not have much to offer, and he told her many other things in this very amorous way, but, like most of his undertakings, this one, too, amounted to nothing but hot air.

And so, when the two young men found Guccio the Pig busy with Nuta (something which made them very happy, since this meant that half of their task was done), without anyone to stop them, they entered Brother Cipolla's bedroom, which they found unlocked, and the first thing they picked up to search through was the saddlebag in which the feather was kept; they opened it, and discovered a little casket wrapped in an extravagant length of silk, and when they lifted the lid, they found a feather inside, just like the kind you find on a parrot's tail; and they realized that it had to be the one that Brother Cipolla had promised the people of Certaldo. And it certainly would have been easy for him to make them believe his story, for in those times the luxurious customs of Egypt had not yet made their way to any great degree into Tuscany, as they were later to do throughout all of Italy, much to its ruin; and if these feathers were known to just a few, those few certainly were not among the inhabitants of that area. On the contrary, as long as the crude customs of their forefathers endured there, not only had they never seen a parrot, but most of the people there had never heard of one.

The young men were happy to have discovered the feather. They took it out, and in order not to leave the container empty, they filled it with some charcoal that they found in a corner of the room.

They shut the lid and arranged everything just as they had found it, and unnoticed, they merrily departed with the feather and then waited to hear what Brother Cipolla would say when he found charcoal in place of the feather. The simpleminded men and women who were in church, having heard that they were going to see one of the Angel Gabriel's feathers after nones, returned home when the Mass was finished; friends and neighbors spread the news from one to another, and when everyone had finished eating, so many men and women rushed to town to see this feather that there was hardly enough space for them all.

After a hearty meal and a short nap, Brother Cipolla got up a little after nones, and when he heard that a great crowd of peasants was gathering to see the feather, he ordered Guccio the Mess to come along with him to ring the church bells and to bring the saddlebags with him. With great reluctance, he left Nuta and the kitchen and made his way there very slowly; he arrived there panting, for having drunk so much water he had bloated his stomach. But on Brother Cipolla's order, he went to the door of the church and began to ring the bells loudly.

When all the people were gathered together, Brother Cipolla began his sermon, unaware that any of his belongings had been tampered with, preaching in a way that served his own personal ends, and when it came time to reveal the Angel Gabriel's feather, first he had the congregation solemnly recite the *Confiteor* and had two candles lighted, then after drawing back his cowl, he very gently unwound the silk and took out the box; after pronouncing several words of praise about the Angel Gabriel and his relic, he opened the box. When he saw it was full of charcoal, he did not suspect that Guccio the Whale had done this to him, for he knew him too well to believe he was capable of such tricks, nor did he even blame him for not keeping others from doing this; he merely cursed himself silently for having made him guardian of his belongings when he knew him to be so negligent, disobedient, careless, and absent-minded—nevertheless, without the slightest change of color on his face, he raised his face and hands to heaven, and spoke so that all could hear him:

"O Lord, may Thy power be praised forever!" Then he closed the box and turned to the people, saying:

"Ladies and gentlemen, I want you to know that when I was very young, I was sent by my superior to those parts of the earth of the rising sun, and I was charged by express order to discover the special privileges of the Porcellana, which, although they cost nothing to seal, are much more useful to others than to ourselves. I set out on my way, leaving from Venice and passing through Greekburg, then riding through the kingdom of Garbo and on through Baldacca, and I came to Parione, whereupon, not without some thirst, I reached, after some time, Sardinia.

"But why do I go on listing all the countries that I visited? After passing the straits of St. George, I came to Truffia and Buffia, lands heavily populated with a great many people, and from there I came to Liarland, where I discovered many of our friars and those of others who scorned a life of hardship for the love of God, who cared little about the troubles of others, following their own interests, and who spent no money other than that which had not yet been coined in those countries; and afterward I came to the land of Abruzzi where men and women walk around on mountaintops in wooden shoes and dress their pigs in their own guts. And farther on I discovered people who carry bread twisted around sticks and wine in goatskins; then I arrived at the Baskworms' mountains, where all the streams run downhill.

"To make a long story short, I traveled so far that I came to Parsnip, India, where I swear by the habit I wear on my back that I saw feathers fly, an incredible thing to one who has not witnessed it; and Maso del Saggio, whom I found there cracking nuts and selling the husks retail, was witness to the fact that I do not lie about this matter. But, not able to find there what I was seeking, and since to travel further would have meant going by sea, I turned back and came to the Holy Land, where cold bread in the summer costs four cents and you get the heat for nothing; and there I found the venerable father Messer Blamemenot Ifyouplease, the most worthy patriarch of Jerusalem, who, out of respect for the habit of our lord Messer Saint Anthony, which I have always worn, wanted me to see all the holy relics he had there with him; and they were so numerous that if I had counted them all, I would have finished up with a list several miles long; but in order not to disappoint you, let me tell you about some of them.

"First he showed me the finger of the Holy Spirit, as whole and as solid as it ever was, and the forelock of the seraphim which appeared to Saint Francis, and one of the nails of the cherubim, and one of the ribs of the True-Word-Made-Fresh-at-the-Windows, and vestments of the holy Catholic faith, and some of the beams from the star which appeared to the three wise men in the East, and a phial of the sweat of Saint Michael when he fought the Devil, and the jawbones from the death of Saint Lazarus, and many others.

"And since I was happy to give him copies of the *Slopes of Monte Morello* in the vulgar tongue as well as several chapters of the *Caprezio*,[21] for which he had been hunting a long time, he gave me in return part of his holy relics, presenting me with one of the teeth of the Holy Cross, and a bit of the sound of the bells from the temple of Solomon, in a little phial, and the feather from the Angel Gabriel which I already told you I have, and one of the wooden shoes of Saint Gherardo da Villamagna, which I gave, not long ago in Florence, to Gherardo de' Bonsi, who holds it in the greatest reverence. And he also gave me some of the charcoal upon which the most holy martyr Saint Lorenzo was roasted alive. All these articles I most devoutly brought back with me, and I have them all.

"The truth is that my superior has never permitted me to show them until they were proven to be authentic, but now, because of certain miracles that were performed through them and letters received from the Patriarch, he is now sure that they are authentic, and he has allowed me to display them to you. And since I am afraid to trust them to anyone else, I always carry them with me. As a matter of fact, I carry the feather from the Angel Gabriel in one box, in order not to damage it, and the coals over which Saint Lorenzo was roasted in another, and both boxes are so much alike that I often mistake the one for the other, and this is what happened to me today; for while I thought that I had brought the box containing the feather here, instead I brought the one with the charcoal. But I do not consider this to be an error; on the contrary, it is the will of God, and He Himself placed the box in my hands, reminding me in this way that the Feast of Saint Lorenzo is only two days away; and since God wished me to show you the charcoal in order to rekindle in your hearts the devotion that you owe to Saint Lorenzo, rather than the feather that I had wanted to show you, He made me take out these blessed charcoals that were once bathed in the sweat of that most holy body. And so, my blessed children, remove your cowls and come forward, devoutly, to behold them. But first, I want each of you to know that whoever makes the sign of the cross on himself with this charcoal will live for one year safe in the knowledge that he will not be cooked by fire without his feeling it."

And after he said those words, he sang a hymn in praise of Saint Lorenzo, opened the box, and displayed the charcoal. The foolish throng gazed upon it in reverent admiration, and they crowded around him and gave him larger offerings than they ever had before, begging him to touch each one of them with the coals. And so Brother Cipolla took these charcoals in his hand and on their white shirts and doublets and on the women's veils he made the largest crosses possible, announcing that, as he had proved many times, no matter how much the charcoals were consumed in making those crosses, afterward they would always return to their former size no sooner than they were placed back in the box.

And in this manner, and with great profit for himself, Brother Cipolla turned the entire population of Certaldo into crusaders and, by means of his quick wit, tricked those who thought they had tricked him by stealing his feather. The two young men, having been present at his sermon and having heard the fantastic story he had invented, laughed so hard that they thought their jaws would break, for they knew how farfetched his story was; and after the crowd dispersed, they went up to him and got the greatest joy in the world out of telling him what they had done; then they gave him back his feather, with which, by the way, he happened to rake in for himself all during the following year no less than the charcoal had that day.

· ❧ ·

Eighth Day, Sixth Story

Bruno and Buffalmacco steal a pig from Calandrino; pretending to help him find it again by means of a test using ginger cookies and Vernaccia wine, they give him two such cookies one after the other, made from cheap ginger seasoned with bitter aloes, thus making it appear that he stole the pig himself; then, they forced him to pay them a bribe by threatening to tell his wife about the affair.

Filostrato's story, which gave the group a good laugh, had no sooner reached its conclusion than the Queen ordered Filomena to continue the storytelling; and she began:

Gracious ladies, just as Filostrato was moved by the mention of Maso's name to tell the story you have just heard, in like manner, I am inspired by the mention of the names of Calandrino and his companions to tell you another tale about them which, I believe, will amuse you.

There is no need for me to explain to you who Calandrino, Bruno, and Buffalmacco were, for you have already heard a great deal about them in an earlier tale; and so getting on with my story, let me say that Calandrino owned a little farm not far from Florence, which he had acquired by way of his wife's dowry, and from it, along with the other produce which he collected there, every year he received a pig; and it was his regular custom to go to the country around December with his wife to slaughter the pig, and to have it salted there.

Now it happened once, at a time when his wife was not feeling very well, that Calandrino went by himself to slaughter the pig; when Bruno and Buffalmacco heard about this and learned that his wife was not going to be there with him, they went to stay for a few days with a priest who was a great friend of theirs and who lived near Calandrino. On the very morning of their arrival, Calandrino had slaughtered the pig; seeing them with the priest, he called them over and said: "I bid you welcome. I would like you to see what a good farmer I am," and he took them into the house and showed them this pig.

When they saw what a fine pig it was and learned from Calandrino that he intended to salt it for his family, Bruno said to him:

"Hey! You must be crazy! Sell it and let's enjoy the money and tell your wife it was stolen from you."

Calandrino replied:

"No, she won't believe me, and she'll run me out of the house. Stay out of this. I'd never do anything like that."

They tried to convince him with all sorts of arguments, but it was no use. Then Calandrino invited them to supper, but so begrudgingly that they refused to eat with him, and off they went, leaving him there.

Bruno said to Buffalmacco: "What would you say to stealing that pig of his tonight?"

Buffalmacco replied: "And how could we do that?"

Bruno replied: "I've already figured out how to do it, provided he doesn't move it from where it was just now."

"Well," concluded Buffalmacco, "let's do it; why shouldn't we do it? And then we can all enjoy it here together, you, me, and the priest."

The priest declared that this plan was very much to his liking; then Bruno said:

"Now this calls for a bit of skill. Buffalmacco, you know how greedy Calandrino is and how happy he is to have a drink when somebody else pays the bill; let's go and take him to the tavern; let the priest pretend to be our host and pay for all the drinks; we won't let him pay for anything, and Calandrino will drink himself silly, and then the rest will be easy, since there is no one else in the house."

And so they did just as Bruno suggested. Calandrino, seeing that the priest would not allow him to pay, began to drink in earnest, and while usually it never took much to get him drunk, this time he drank a great deal. It was already late in the evening when he left the tavern, and, not wishing to eat supper, he went home, and thinking that he had locked the door, he left it open and went to bed. Buffalmacco and Bruno went to eat supper with the priest; after they had eaten, they collected the tools they needed to get into Calandrino's house the way Bruno had planned, and they quietly made their way there; but when they found the door open, they went straight in and carried the pig off to the priest's home, where they stowed it away and then went off to bed.

In the morning, after the wine had cleared from his brain, Calandrino got up, and when he went downstairs, he looked around and saw that his pig was gone and the door wide open; and so he asked a number of people if they knew who had taken his pig, but unable to find it, he began making a racket, crying, "Ah, poor me, my pig has been stolen." When Bruno and Buffalmacco got out of bed they went straight over to Calandrino's to hear what he would have to say about his pig. When Calandrino saw them, he called them over and on the verge of tears he said: "Oh, my friends, my pig has been stolen from me!"

Bruno drew close to him and whispered: "I'm amazed; so you finally got smart for once in your life."

"Oh, no," said Calandrino, "I'm really telling the truth."

"That-a-boy, that's the way," Bruno said, "tell it loud and clear so it looks the way it should."

Then Calandrino started shouting louder and saying:

"God's body, I'm speaking the truth, it has been stolen from me!"

And Bruno replied:

"Well put, that's perfect, just right, scream louder, make yourself heard, it'll seem truer that way!"

Calandrino insisted:

"You'll drive my soul to the devil: I'm telling the truth and you don't believe me, but I swear, may I be hanged by the neck, if my pig hasn't been stolen!"

Then Bruno said:

"Ah, how can this be? I saw it here just yesterday; do you think you can make me believe it just flew out of here?"

Calandrino answered: "It's just like I'm telling you."

"Ah," remarked Bruno, "how can that be?"

"That's it, yes sirree," declared Calandrino, "and now that's the end of me, and I don't know how I can go home now. My wife will never believe me, and even if she does, I'll have no peace from her for a year."

Then Bruno said:

"God help me, if it's true, this is a serious matter; but you know,

Calandrino, this is exactly what I told you to say yesterday. You wouldn't be trying to fool your wife and us at the same time, would you?"

Calandrino began to scream and say:

"Ah, why are you driving me crazy and making me curse God, His saints, and everything else? I'm telling you that the pig was stolen from me last night."

Then Buffalmacco said:

"If that's the case, we must try to find some way to get it back again if possible."

"And what way," asked Calandrino, "is there?"

Then Buffalmacco replied:

"Well, for sure, nobody came all the way from India to steal this pig from you; one of these neighbors of yours must have done it, and so, if you can bring them all together, I can perform the bread-and-cheese test,[22] and then we'll see at once who has the pig."

"Just great," said Bruno, "you'll do splendidly with your bread-and-cheese test, especially with the fine people that live around here! It's clear that one of them stole it, and they would catch on to what we're doing and refuse to come."

"What can we do, then?" asked Buffalmacco.

Bruno replied:

"We could do it with some nice ginger cookies, and some good Vernaccia wine, and invite them all for a drink. They won't think anything of it and will come, and then we can bless the ginger cookies just as if they were bread and cheese."

Buffalmacco said:

"Yep, that's it for sure! And you, Calandrino, what do you say? Are we going to do it?"

Calandrino replied:

"By all means, I beg you, for the love of God, go ahead and do it; I wouldn't feel half so bad, if only I knew who took my pig."

"Well, that's it," Bruno said, "I'm prepared to go all the way into Florence for the things you need, if you give me the money."

Calandrino had around forty copper pennies, which he gave to Bruno. And Bruno went to Florence to a friend of his who was an apothecary and bought a pound of excellent ginger cookies, having him prepare two of them from cheaper ginger, which he had mixed into a confection of fresh hepatic aloes. Then he had them sprinkled with sugar just like the other cookies and in order not to lose them or mix them up with the others, he had them marked with a certain sign, by which he could easily recognize them; and after purchasing a flask of good Vernaccia wine, he returned to the country and said to Calandrino:

"You must invite all those you suspect to come and have a drink with you tomorrow morning: it's a holiday, and everyone will be happy to come, and this evening, along with Buffalmacco, I'll cast the spell on the ginger cookies and bring them to your house tomorrow morning, and for your sake, I, myself, will give them out and do and say what must be done and said."

Calandrino did just that. And the next morning, after he gathered together around the elm in front of the church a considerable group of farm laborers and whatever young Florentines happened to be staying in the country at the time, Bruno and Buffalmacco came around with the box of cookies and the flask of wine; and getting them all to stand in a circle, Bruno announced:

"Gentlemen, I must tell you the reason why you are here, so that if anything happens to cause you displeasure, you will not blame it on me. Last night, Calandrino, who is right here, was robbed of one of his fine pigs, and he has not been able to discover who took it; and since it could have been stolen only by someone here, in order to find out who has taken it, he is going to give each of you in turn one of these cookies to eat and something to drink. I warn you in advance that the one who stole the pig will be unable to swallow the cookie. On the contrary, it will taste more bitter than poison to him, and he will spit it out; and so, in order not to disgrace himself in the presence of so many people, perhaps it would be better for the person who stole the pig to confess now to the priest, and I can forget the entire affair."

Everyone there said they would gladly eat one of the cookies, and so Bruno lined them up, placing Calandrino among them, and beginning at one end of the line, he started giving a ginger cookie to each of them; and when he reached Calandrino, he took one of the special cookies and put it in his hand. Calandrino, without hesitating, popped it into his mouth and began to chew, but his tongue had no sooner tasted the bitter aloes than Calandrino, unable to stand the bitter taste, spit it out. Everyone was looking at everyone else to see who was going to spit his out; Bruno, who had not yet finished handing them out, pretended not to notice anything, when he heard a voice behind him say: "Hey, Calandrino, what's the meaning of this?" He quickly turned around and, seeing that Calandrino had spit his out, he declared: "Wait a minute, perhaps something else caused him to spit; try another one." Picking out the second one, he stuck it into Calandrino's mouth and then went on to finish handing out the rest of them. If the first one had seemed bitter to Calandrino, this second one seemed even more bitter; but since he was ashamed to spit it out, he chewed it a bit and kept it in his mouth, until his eyes began to produce tears the size of hazelnuts; and finally, when he could bear it no longer, he spit it out as he had done with the first one. Buffalmacco was pouring out drinks for the group, as was Bruno, and when they and all the others saw what happened, everyone said that it had to be Calandrino himself who had stolen the pig; and there were even some in the group who reproached him harshly.

But when the crowd had broken up, leaving Bruno and Buffalmacco behind with Calandrino, Buffalmacco began to say:

"I was certain right from the start that it was you who stole it yourself, and that you were trying to make us believe that it had been stolen from you just so you wouldn't have to stand us to a round of drinks with the money you received from the profits."

Calandrino, who had still not spat out the bitterness of the aloes, began swearing he had not taken it.

But Buffalmacco said, "Come on now, buddy, tell us how much you got out of it. Did it fetch six florins?"

When Calandrino heard this, he was at the point of despair, but then Bruno said to him:

"Listen to this, Calandrino. There was a fellow in the group we were eating and drinking with today who told me you had a young girl up here you were keeping for your amusement and that you gave her whatever you could scrape together, and he was convinced you had sent her this pig. You've really become quite a trickster! There was that time you led us along the Mugnone River to pick up those black stones, and after leading us on a wild-goose chase, you took off for home and then tried to make us believe you had really made the discovery! And now, once again, you think with your oaths you can make us believe that this pig, which you either gave away or sold, was actually stolen from you. We've caught on to your tricks by now; you can't fool us anymore! And to tell you the truth, that's why we took so much trouble to cast the spell, and now, unless you give us two brace of capons we mean to tell Monna Tessa everything."

Seeing that they would not believe him, and feeling that he had enough trouble as it was without letting himself in for a battle with his wife's temper, Calandrino gave them the two brace of capons; and after they had salted the pig they took back everything with them to Florence, leaving Calandrino behind with a loss and the expense of their laughter.

· ❦ ·

Tenth Day, Tenth Story

The Marquis of Sanluzzo is urged by the requests of his vassals to take a wife, and in order to have his own way in the matter, he chooses the daughter of a peasant and by her he has two children, whom he pretends to have put to death. Then, under the pretense that she has displeased him, he pretends to have taken another wife, and has their own daughter brought into the house as if she were his new wife, having driven out his real wife in nothing more than her shift. Having found that she has patiently endured all this, he brings her back home, more beloved than ever, shows their grown children to her, honors her, and has others honor her, as the Marchioness.

The lengthy tale of the King, which, judging by the expression on everyone's face seemed to have pleased them all, came to an end, and laughing, Dioneo said:

"The good fellow who was looking forward to lowering the ghost's stiff tail the following night wouldn't have given you two cents for all the praises you are lavishing upon Messer Torello."[23] And then, realizing that he alone remained to speak, Dioneo began:

Gentle ladies of mine, it seems to me this day has been devoted to kings, sultans, and people like that; therefore, in order not to stray too far from your path, I should like to tell you about a marquis and not about a generous act of his but, rather, about his insane cruelty, which, while good did result from it in the end, I would never advise anyone to follow as an example, for I consider it a great shame that he derived any benefit from it at all.

A long time ago, there succeeded to the Marquisate of Sanluzzo the firstborn son of the family, a young man named Gualtieri, who, having no wife or children, spent his time doing nothing but hawking and hunting, never thinking of taking a wife or of having children—a very wise thing to do on his part. This did not please his vassals, and they begged him on many an occasion to take a wife so that he would not be without an heir and they without a master; they offered to find him a wife born of the kind of mother and father that might give him good expectations of her and make him happy. To this Gualtieri answered:

"My friends, you are urging me to do something that I was determined never to do, for you know how difficult it is to find a woman with a suitable character, and how plentiful is the opposite kind of woman, and what a wretched life a man would lead married to a wife that was not suitable to him. And to say that you can judge daughters by examining the characters of their fathers and mothers (which is the basis of your argument that you can find a wife to please me) is ridiculous, for I do not believe that you can come to know all the secrets of the father or mother; and even if you did, a daughter is often unlike her father and mother. But since it is your wish to tie me up with these chains, I shall do as you request; and so that I shall have only myself to blame if things turn out badly, I want to be the one who chooses her, and I tell you now that if she is not honored by you as your lady—no matter whom I choose—you will learn to your great displeasure how serious a matter it was to compel me with your requests to take a wife against my will." His worthy men replied that they would be happy if only he would choose a wife.

For some time Gualtieri had been impressed by the manners of a poor young girl who lived in a village near his home, and since she seemed very beautiful to him, he thought that life with her could be quite pleasant; so, without looking any further, he decided to marry her, and he sent for her father, who was extremely poor, and made arrangements with him to take her as his wife. After this was done, Gualtieri called all his friends in the area together and said to them:

"My friends, you wished and continue to wish for me to take a wife, and I am ready to do this, but I do so more to please you than to satisfy any desire of mine to have a wife. You know what you promised me: to honor happily anyone I chose for your lady; therefore, the time has come for me to keep my promise to you, and for you to do the same for me. I have found a young girl after my own heart, very near here, whom I intend to take as my wife and bring home in a few days. So, make sure that the wedding celebrations are splendid and that you receive her honorably, so that I may consider myself as happy with your promise as you are with mine."

The good men all happily replied that this pleased them very much and that, whoever she was, they would treat her as their lady and honor her in every way they could; and soon after this, they all set about preparing for a big, beautiful, and happy celebration, and Gualtieri did the same. He had an enormous and sumptuous wedding feast prepared, and he invited his friends and relatives and the great lords and many others from the surrounding countryside. And besides this, he had beautiful and expensive dresses cut out and tailored to fit a young girl whom he felt was about the same size as the young girl he had decided to marry; he also saw to it that girdles and rings were purchased and a rich and beautiful crown and everything else a new bride might require. When the day set for the wedding arrived, Gualtieri mounted his horse at about the middle of tierce, and all those who had come to honor him did the same; when all was arranged, he said:

"My lords, it is time to fetch the new bride."

Then he with his entire company set out, and eventually they arrived at the little village; they came to the house of the girl's father and found her returning from the well in great haste in order to be in time to go and see the arrival of Gualtieri's bride with the other women; when Gualtieri saw her, he called her by name—that is, Griselda—and asked her where her father was; to this she replied bashfully:

"My lord, he is in the house."

Then Gualtieri dismounted and ordered all his men to wait for him; alone, he entered that poor, little house, and there he found Griselda's father, who was called Giannucole, and he said to him:

"I have come to marry Griselda, but before I do, I should like to ask her some things in your presence."

And he asked her, if he were to marry her, would she always try to please him, and would she never become angry over anything he said or did, and if she would always be obedient, and many other similar questions—to all of these she replied that she would. Then Gualtieri took her by the hand, led her outside, and in the presence of his entire company and all others present, he had her stripped naked and the garments he had prepared for her brought forward; then he immediately had her dress and put on her shoes, and upon her hair, disheveled as it was, he had a crown placed; then, while everyone was marveling at the sight, he announced:

"My lords, this is the lady I intend to be my wife, if she will have me as her husband."

And then, turning to Griselda, who was standing there blushing and perplexed, he asked her:

"Griselda, do you take me for your husband?"

To this she answered: "Yes, my lord."

And he replied: "And I take you for my wife."

In the presence of them all he married her; then he had her set upon a palfrey and he led her with an honorable company to his home. The wedding feast was great and sumptuous, and the celebration was no different from what it might have been if he had married the daughter of the King of France. The young bride seemed to have changed her soul and manners along with her clothes: she was, as we have already said, beautiful in body and face, and as she was beautiful before, she became even more pleasing, attractive, and well mannered, so that she seemed to be not the shepherdess daughter of Giannucole but, rather, the daughter of some noble lord, a fact that amazed everyone who had known her before. Moreover, she was so obedient and indulgent to her husband that he considered himself the happiest and the most satisfied man on earth. And she was also so gracious and kind toward her husband's subjects that there was no one who was more beloved or gladly honored than she was; in fact, everyone prayed for her welfare, her prosperity, and her further success. Whereas everyone used to say that Gualtieri had acted unwisely in taking her as his wife, they now declared that he was the wisest and cleverest man in the world, for none other than he could have ever recognized the noble character hidden under her poor clothes and peasant dress.

In short, she knew how to comport herself in such a manner that before long, not only in her husband's marquisate but everywhere else, her virtue and her good deeds became the topic of discussion, and for anything that had been said against her husband when he married her, she now caused the opposite to be said. Not long after she had come to live with Gualtieri, she became pregnant, and in the course of time she gave birth to a daughter, which gave Gualtieri much cause for rejoicing. But shortly afterward, a new thought entered his mind: he wished to test her patience with a long trial and intolerable proofs. First, he offended her with harsh words, pretending to be angry and saying that his vassals were very unhappy with her because of her low birth and especially now that they saw her bear children; they were most unhappy about the daughter that had been born, and they did nothing but mutter about it. When the lady heard these words, without changing her expression or intentions in any way, she answered:

"My lord, do with me what you think best for your honor and your happiness, and no matter what, I shall be happy, for I realize that I am of lower birth than they and am not worthy of this honor which your courtesy has bestowed upon me."

This reply was very gratifying to Gualtieri, for he realized that she had not become in any way haughty because of the respect which he or others had paid her. A short time later, having told his wife in vague terms that his subjects could not tolerate the daughter to whom she had given birth, he spoke to one of her servants and then sent him to her, and he, with a very sad look on his face, said to her:

"My lady, since I do not wish to die, I must do what my lord commands. He had commanded me to take this daughter of yours and to . . ." And he could say no more.

When the lady heard these words and saw her servant's face, she remembered what her husband had said to her and understood that her servant had been ordered to murder the child; so she quickly took the girl from the cradle, kissed her and blessed her, and although she felt great pain in her heart, showing no emotion, she placed her in her servant's arms and said to him:

"There, do exactly what your lord and mine has ordered you to do, but do not leave her body to be devoured by the beasts and birds unless he has ordered you to do so."

The servant took the child and told Gualtieri what the lady had said, and he was amazed at her perseverance; then he sent the servant with his daughter to one of his relatives in Bologna, requesting that she raise and educate the girl carefully but without ever telling whose daughter she was. Shortly after this, the lady became pregnant again, and in time she gave birth to a male child, which pleased Gualtieri very much; but what he had already done to his lady was not enough to satisfy him, and he wounded the lady with even a greater blow by telling her one day in a fit of feigned anger:

"Lady, since you bore me this male child, I have not been able to live with my vassals, for they bitterly complain about a grandson of Giannucolo's having to be their lord after I am gone. Because of this, I am very much afraid that unless I want to be driven out, I must do what I did the other time, and then, finally, I shall have to leave you and take another wife."

The lady listened to him patiently and made no other reply than this:

"My lord, think only of making yourself happy and of satisfying your desires and do not worry about me at all, for nothing pleases me more than to see you happy."

After a few days, Gualtieri sent for his son in the same way he had sent for his daughter, and, again pretending to have the child killed, he sent him to be raised in Bologna as he had his daughter; and the lady's face and words were no different from what they were when her daughter had been taken, and Gualtieri was greatly amazed at this and remarked to himself that no other woman could do what she had done. If he had not seen for himself how extremely fond she was of her children as long as they found favor in his sight, he might have thought that she acted as she did in order to get rid of them, but he realized that she was doing it out of obedience.

His subjects, believing he had killed his children, criticized him bitterly and regarded him as a cruel man, and they had the greatest compassion for the lady; but she never said anything to the women with whom she mourned the deaths of her children. Then, not many years after the birth of their daughter, Gualtieri felt it was time to put his wife's patience to the ultimate test: he told many of his vassals that he could no longer bear having married Griselda and that he realized he had acted badly and impetuously when he took her for his wife, and that he was going to do everything possible to procure a dispensation from the Pope so that he could marry another woman and abandon Griselda; he was reprimanded for this by many of his good men, but the only answer he gave them was that this was the way it had to be.

When the lady heard about these matters and it appeared to her that she would be returning to her father's house (perhaps even to guard the sheep as she had previously done) and that she would have to bear witness to another woman possessing the man she loved, she grieved most bitterly; but yet, as with the other injuries of Fortune which she had suffered, she was determined to bear this one, too, with firm countenance. Not long afterward, Gualtieri had forged letters sent from Rome, and he showed them to his subjects, pretending that in these letters the Pope had granted him the dispensation to take another wife and to abandon Griselda; and so, having his wife brought before him, in the presence of many people he said to her:

"Lady, because of a dispensation which I have received from the Pope, I am able to take another wife and to abandon you; and because my ancestors were great noblemen and lords of these regions while yours have always been peasants, I wish you to be my wife no longer and to return to Giannucolo's home with the dowry that you brought me, and I shall then bring home another more suitable wife, whom I have already found."

When the lady heard these words, she managed to hold back her tears only with the greatest of effort (something quite unnatural for a woman), and she replied:

"My lord, I have always known that my lowly origins were in no way suitable to your nobility, and the position I have held with you I always recognized as having come from God and yourself; I never made it mine or considered it given to me—I always kept it as if it were a loan. If you wish to have it back again, it must please me, which it does, to return it to you: here is your ring with which you married me; take it. You order me to take back with me the dowry I brought you, and to do this no accounting on your part, nor any purse or beast of burden, will be necessary, for I have not forgotten that you received me naked; and if you judge it proper that this body which bore your children should be seen by everyone, I shall leave naked; but I beg you, in the name of my virginity which I brought here and which I cannot take with me, that you at least allow me to take away with me just one shift in addition to my dowry."

Gualtieri, who felt closer to tears than anyone else there, stood, nevertheless, with a stern face and said:

"You may take a shift."

Many of those present begged him to give her a dress, so that this woman who had been his wife for more than thirteen years would not be seen leaving his home so impoverished and in such disgrace as to leave clad only in a shift; but their entreaties were in vain, and in her shift, without shoes or anything on her head, the lady commended him to God, left his house, and returned to her father, accompanied by the tears and the weeping of all those who witnessed her departure.

Giannucolo, who had never believed that Gualtieri would keep his daughter as his wife, and who had been expecting this to happen any day, had kept the clothes that she had taken off that morning when Gualtieri married her; he gave them back to her, and she put them on and began doing the menial tasks in her father's house as she had once been accustomed to doing, suffering with brave spirit the savage assaults of a hostile Fortune.

Once Gualtieri had done this, he then led his vassals to believe that he had chosen a daughter of one of the Counts of Panago for his new wife; and while great preparations were being made for the wedding, he sent for Griselda to come to him, and when she arrived he said to her:

"I am bringing home the lady I have recently chosen as my wife, and I want to give her an honorable welcome when she first arrives; you know that I have no women in my home who know how to prepare the bedrooms or do the many chores that are required by such a grand celebration, and since you understand these matters better than anyone else in the house, I want you to make all the arrangements: invite those ladies whom you think should be invited, and receive them as if you were the lady of the house; then when the wedding is over, you can return to your home."

These words were like a dagger in Griselda's heart, for she had not yet been able to put aside the love she felt for him as she had learned to live without her good fortune, and she answered:

"My lord, I am ready and prepared."

And so in a coarse peasant dress she entered that house which she had left a short time before dressed only in a shift, and she began to clean and arrange the bedrooms, to put out hangings and ornamental tapestries on the walls, to make ready the kitchen, and to put her hands to everything, just as if she were a little servant girl in the house; and she never rested until she had organized and arranged everything as it should be. After this, she had invitations sent in Gualtieri's name to all the ladies of the region and then waited for the celebration; when the day of the wedding came, though the clothes she wore were poor, with the courtesy and graciousness of a lady, she cheerfully welcomed all the women who arrived for the celebration.

Gualtieri had seen to it that his children were raised with care in Bologna by one of his relatives who had married into the family of the Counts of Panago. His daughter was already twelve years old and the most beautiful thing ever seen; the boy was six. He sent a message to his relative in Bologna, requesting him to be so kind as to come to Sanluzzo with his daughter and his son, and to see to it that a fine and honorable retinue accompany them, and not to reveal her identity to anyone but to tell them only that he was bringing the girl as Gualtieri's bride.

The nobleman did what the Marquis had asked him: he set out, and after several days he arrived at Sanluzzo at about suppertime with the young girl, her brother, and a noble following, and there he found all the peasants and many other people from the surrounding area waiting to see Gualtieri's new bride. She was received by the ladies and then taken to the hall where the tables were set, and there Griselda, dressed as she was, cheerfully met her and said to her:

"Welcome, my lady!"

The ladies, many of whom had begged Gualtieri (but in vain) either to allow Griselda to stay in another room or that some of the clothing that had once been hers be lent to her so that she would not have to meet his guests in such condition, sat down at the table and were served. Everyone looked at the young girl and agreed that Gualtieri had made a good exchange; but it was Griselda above all who praised her as well as her little brother.

Gualtieri, who felt that he now had enough evidence of his wife's patience, having seen that these unusual circumstances had not changed Griselda one bit, and certain that her attitude was not due to stupidity, for he knew her to be very wise, felt that it was time to remove her from the bitterness he knew to be hidden behind her impassive face, and so he had her brought to him, and in the presence of everyone, he said to her with a smile:

"What do you think of my new bride?"

"My lord," replied Griselda, "she seems very beautiful to me; and if she is as wise as she is beautiful, which I believe she is, I have no doubt that living with her will make you the happiest man in the world. But I beg you with all my heart not to inflict those wounds upon her which you inflicted upon that other woman who was once your wife, for I believe that she could scarcely endure them, not only because she is younger but also because she was reared in a more refined way, whereas that other woman lived in continuous hardship from the time she was a little girl."

When Gualtieri saw that she firmly believed the girl was to be his wife, and in spite of this said nothing but good about her, he made her sit beside him, and he said:

"Griselda, it is time now for you to reap the fruit of your long patience, and it is time for those who have considered me cruel, unjust, and bestial to realize that what I have done was directed toward a preestablished goal, for I wanted to teach you how to be a wife, to show these people how to know such a wife and how to choose and keep one, and to acquire for myself lasting tranquillity for as long as I lived with you. When I decided to marry, I greatly feared that the tranquillity I cherished would be lost, and so, to test you, I submitted you to the pains and trials you have known. But since I have never known you to depart from my wishes in either word or deed, and since I now believe I shall receive from you that happiness which I always desired, I intend to return to you now what I took from you for a long time and with the greatest of delight to soothe the wounds that I inflicted upon you. And so, with a happy heart receive this girl, whom you suppose to be my bride, and her brother as your very own children and mine; they are the ones you and many others have long thought I had brutally murdered; and I am your husband, who loves you more than all else, for I believe I can boast that no other man exists who could be as happy with his wife as I am."

After he said this, he embraced and kissed her, and she was weeping for joy; they arose and together went over to their daughter, who was listening in amazement to these new developments; both of them tenderly embraced first the girl and then her brother, thus dispelling their confusion as well as that of many others who were present. The ladies, who were most delighted, arose from the tables, and they went with Griselda to her room, and with a more auspicious view of her future, they took off her old clothes and dressed her in one of her noble garments, and then they led her back into the hall as the lady of the house, which she, nonetheless, appeared to be even when she wore rags.

Everyone was very happy with the way everything had turned out, and Griselda with her husband and children celebrated in great style, with the joy and feasting increasing over a period of several days; and

Gualtieri was judged to be the wisest of men (although the tests to which he had subjected his wife were regarded as harsh and intolerable), and Griselda the wisest of them all.

The Count of Panago returned to Bologna several days later, and Gualtieri took Giannucolo from his labor, setting him up in a way befitting his father-in-law so that he lived the rest of his days with honor and great comfort. After giving their daughter in marriage to a nobleman, Gualtieri lived a long and happy life with Griselda, always honoring her to the best of his ability.

What more can be said here, except that godlike spirits do sometimes rain down from heaven into poor homes, just as those more suited to governing pigs than to ruling over men make their appearances in royal palaces. Who besides Griselda could have endured the severe and unheard-of trials that Gualtieri imposed upon her and remain with a not only tearless but a happy face? It might have served Gualtieri right if he had run into the kind of woman who, once driven out of her home in nothing but a shift, would have allowed another man to warm her wool in order to get herself a nice-looking dress out of the affair!

NOTES

· ❦ ·

1. This title of Greek derivation means "ten days" and refers to the total number of days spent telling stories; it is modeled on that of a work by St. Ambrose, *Hexameron*, as well as on medieval treatises on the six days of the world's creation.

2. According to Arthurian legend and medieval literary tradition, Galeotto acted as go-between in the love affair of Lancelot and Queen Guinevere; here Boccaccio refers specifically to a line in Dante's *Inferno* (V, 137), where a book described as the instigator of the fatal love affair between Paolo and Francesca is compared to Galeotto's role in bringing Lancelot and Guinevere together.

3. In Boccaccio's day, Florentines began the first of each year not with the first of January, as is done today, but rather with the traditional date of the Annunciation (March 25).

4. *Gavoccioli*—or *bubboni*, in modern Italian—are called "buboes" in modern English, the source of the phrase "bubonic plague." The plague of 1348 is often known as the Black Plague or Black Death because of the black spots Boccaccio describes.

5. There is no general agreement on the meaning of the names Boccaccio gives his storytellers. Some critics suggest they are allegories, representations of the seven virtues, or symbols of other moral qualities; it has also been suggested that the names reflect, in a general manner, Boccaccio's literary background.

6. Unlike the women's names, the names of the three men are usually explained etymologically: "completely in love" (Panfilo); "overcome by love" (Filostrato); and "lustful" (Dioneo).

7. A popular round dance, usually accompanied by music and song.

8. Charles (1270–1325), Count of Valois, Maine, and Anjou, and third son of Philip III, King of France. Upon the request of Pope Boniface VIII (Benedetto Caetani, 1235?–1303), Charles crossed the Alps in 1301 to assist Guelph forces in Italy.

9. Ser, the shortened form of Messer(e), is the equivalent of Sir, Mister, or Master. A similar expression commonly used to address women of a certain position is Madonna, meaning "my lady," also found in the shortened forms Mona or Monna.

10. This ruler (1137–93) enjoyed a legendary reputation for courtesy and magnanimity throughout medieval Europe, in spite of the fact that he reconquered Jerusalem (1187) and opposed the Crusaders.

11. This ill-famed district of Naples actually existed in Boccaccio's day, and its name might best be rendered into English as "Evilhole."

12. The Guelphs, supporters of the papacy, were opposed by the Ghibellines, the imperial party in medieval Italy. The names are derived from Welf and Waiblingen, the names of two twelfth-century families heading rival parties in the Holy Roman Empire.

13. Spitfire (*Buttafuoco*) is called a *scarbone* by the two men in the original Italian, meaning an important figure in the local criminal underworld—what is known today as the Camorra, a Neapolitan equivalent of the Sicilian Mafia.

14. Cavalcanti (1250?–1300) was a friend of Dante and a poet known for his philosophical view of love; Dante Alighieri (1265–1321) was the author of the *Divine Comedy*; Cino (1270–1336) was a poet and distinguished jurist.

15. Philippians 4:12.

16. That is, between eleven in the morning and noon.

17. It is interesting to note that this virtuoso storyteller (whose name, Cipolla, means "onion" in Italian) came from Certaldo, possibly Boccaccio's birthplace.

18. Probably a reference to a mediocre painter of the period.

19. A reference to the Sixth Day, Sixth Story, where the Baronci family's ugliness is mentioned. This story has been omitted from this anthology.

20. Guccio invents this amount, as well as the previous phrase "by procuration," in order to impress his lady.

21. These imaginary book titles have been seen by some scholars as a veiled reference to sodomitic practices.

22. According to some traditional beliefs, special prayers or spells could be performed over bread and cheese, making it impossible for thieves to swallow the morsels which had been so treated.

23. A reference to the story of Gianni Lotteringhi (Seventh Day, First Story) as told by Emilia. This story and that of Messer Torello (Tenth Day, Ninth Story) are not included in this anthology.

LEON BATTISTA ALBERTI
1404–72

A FLORENTINE HUMANIST, ARCHITECT, ART THEORIST, POET, PAINTER, AND mathematician, Alberti was a member of one of the most prominent and prosperous merchant and banking families of the bourgeois aristocracy of Florence. However, by the time Leon Battista went to Bologna in 1421 to study canon law, both his father and his paternal uncle had died, and his relatives appropriated his inheritance, refusing to support him. Nevertheless, he persevered in his studies, particularly those of the Greek and Latin classics.

In 1432, while in Rome, Alberti gained an appointment as apostolic abbreviator, or secretary, in the papal chancery at the court of Pope Eugenius IV, a position he was to hold until 1464. There, amid the ancient ruins of Rome's architectural splendor, he developed many of the principles for his treatise *De re aedificatoria* (begun 1449, printed in 1485, *Ten Books of Architecture*). Another major treatise, *De pictura* (1436, *On Painting*), urges the painter to imitate nature and to work with perspective in order to exploit a sense of space in painting.

While Alberti is perhaps best known for his influential treatises on art and architecture, his *Book of the Family* (1433–39), one of the few works by him written in the vernacular rather than in the more learned humanist Latin, represents a very important expression of the ideals of the middle-class merchants and businessmen who created the Renaissance in fifteenth-century Italy. Here Alberti argues, among other things, that wealth is not to be despised but is, rather, a most necessary part of good citizenship. Moreover, this work's prologue presents one of the most optimistic views of the relationship of man and Fortune that was expressed during the Italian Renaissance—obviously indebted to the kind of thinking which produced Pico della Mirandola's *Oration on the Dignity of Man* and quite different from the darker and more pessimistic views of Fortune in either Machiavelli or Guicciardini.

The *Book of the Family* is, like so many other Renaissance works, a dialogue in four books. The first book treats the problem of paternal responsibility and conjugal love, the bond holding the family together. In Book II, attention turns to a treatment of marriage. Book III examines the economic basis of the family and presents an important analysis of *masserizia*—economy, thrift, and good management, the essence of the mercantile ethos. The final book (actually written considerably later than the others) discusses friendship.

BIBLIOGRAPHY

Leon Battista Alberti, *The Family in Renaissance Florence*, trans. Renée Watkins (Columbia, S.C.: University of South Carolina Press, 1969), and *On Painting and On Sculpture*, trans. Cecil Grayson (London: Phaidon, 1972); Joan Gadol, *Leon Battista Alberti: Universal Man of the Renaissance* (Chicago: University of Chicago Press, 1969).

—————————————— · ❦ · ——————————————

Prologue

Remembering how much ancient history and the recollection of our ancestors together can teach us, how much we are able to see in our own times both in Italy and elsewhere, and how not a few families used to be most happy and glorious but have now disappeared and died out, I often marveled to myself and was saddened over how much power Fortune's unfairness and malignity wielded over men; and how Fortune was permitted with her will and temerity to seize families well provided with the most virtuous of men, abounding in everything precious, expensive, and most desired by men, and endowed with many honors, fame, great praise, authority, and public favor; and how she would deprive them of every happiness, place them in a state of poverty, loneliness, and misery, reduce them from a great number of wealthy ancestors to only a few descendants and from countless riches to the direst straits, and, from the most glorious splendor, subject them to so many calamities, casting them down into abject, dark, and tempestuous adversity. Ah! How many families we see today which are fallen and ruined! It would not be possible to count or to describe all of the noblest families among the ancients, such as the Fabii, the Decii, the Drusii, the Grachii, and the Marcelli, or others, who existed for a long time in our land, supporting the public good and the maintenance of liberty, and who conserved the authority and the dignity of their homeland both in peacetime and in wartime—very modest, prudent, and strong families, such that they were feared by their enemies and loved and revered by their friends. Of all these families, not only their magnificence and their grandeur but the very men themselves, and not only the men but their very names and their memories, have shrunk and faded away, and every trace of them has been completely blotted out and obliterated.

Thus it is not without good reason that I have always thought it well worth knowing whether or not Fortune possesses such power over human affairs and whether this supreme license is really hers that with her instability and inconstancy she may destroy the grandest and most respectable of families. I think about this question without much emotion, detached and free of every passion, and I think to myself, O, young Albertis, how our own Alberti family has been subject to so many adversities for such a long time now and how with the strongest of spirits it has persevered and with what complete reason and good counsel our Albertis have been able to cast off and with firm determination endure our own bitter misfortunes and the furious blows of our unjust fates, and I note that many blame Fortune without just cause as being most often the reason, and I observe that many who through their own stupidity have fallen upon bad times have blamed Fortune and have complained of being buffeted by her stormy waves when they themselves in their foolishness brought about their problems. And in this way, many inept people claim that some other force was the cause of their own errors.

But if anyone who would investigate with care what it is that exalts and increases the family and what it is which also maintains the family in the highest ranks of honor and happiness, that person would soon discover how men usually are the cause of their every good or their every evil, nor will they ever attribute the reasons for their acquisition of praise, greatness, or fame more to Fortune than to their own ability. This is true, and if we examine republics or recall all the past principalities, we will discover that in acquiring and increasing as well as in maintaining and conserving the majesty and the glory already achieved, Fortune was never more influential than the good and holy disciplines of living. Who can doubt this? Just laws and virtuous principles, prudent counsel, and strong and constant actions, love of country, faith, diligence, the impeccable and most laudable customs of the citizens—these have always been able, even without Fortune's favor, to earn and to acquire fame, or with Fortune's assistance, to expand and to increase one's country gloriously and to commend themselves to posterity, achieving immortality. . . .

So then, it can be said that Fortune is incapable and most weak in taking from us even the least part of our character, and we must judge ability as itself sufficient to attain and maintain every sublime and most excellent thing—the grandest of principalities, the most supreme praise, eternal fame, and immortal glory. And you can be sure that whatever you seek or hold dear, no matter what it may be, there is nothing easier for you to acquire or obtain than this nobility. Only the man who does not desire it is without it. And there, if we admit that character, discipline, and manly behavior are man's possessions insofar as they desire them, good counsel, prudence, strong, constant, and persevering spirits, reason, order and method, good arts and discipline, equity, justice, diligence are within reach and embrace so much dominion that they ultimately climb to the highest degree and heights of glory. Oh, young Albertis, who among you would think it an easy task to persuade me that, given the often observed changeability and inconstancy of weak and mortal things, ability—which cannot be denied to men insofar as their free will and willpower seize it and make it part of them—can easily be taken away from its most diligent and vigilant possessors or its many strong defenders? We shall always be of the opinion, just as I believe you also are, since you are all prudent and wise, that in political affairs and in the lives of men, reason is more important than Fortune, and prudence more powerful than blind chance. Nor would any man ever seem wise or prudent to me who placed his hope less in his own ability than in fortuitous events. Anyone will recognize that hard work, good skills, constant enterprises, mature counsel, honest endeavor, just will, and reasonable expectations have increased and enlarged, adorned, maintained, and defended both republics and principalities, and with these qualities any dominion may arise to glory, while without them, it may remain deprived of all its majesty and honor; if we recognize that desire, inertia, lasciviousness, perfidy, cupidity, inequity, libido, and the raw and unbridled passions of human spirits contaminate, divert, and undermine every grandiose, solid, and stable human accomplishment, we shall also recognize that the same rules apply to families as they do to principalities, and we must confess that families rarely fall into unhappy times for any other cause except their lack of prudence and diligence.

And thus, since I know this to be the case, Fortune with its most cruel of floods may overcome and submerge the families which, throwing themselves upon the mercies of such waves, have either not known how to control or contain themselves in times of prosperity or have not been prudent and strong in sustaining and regulating themselves when they were buffeted by adversities; and because I do not doubt in the least that solicitous and diligent fathers of families may render their families most grand and extremely happy by their careful management, good practices, honest customs, humanity, openness, and civility, it has therefore seemed worthwhile to me to investigate with every care and concern what useful precepts are appropriate for instructing fathers and the entire family on how they may finally reach the heights of supreme happiness and not be forced in time to succumb to inequitable and unforeseen Fortune. And as much free time as I have permitted to take from my other affairs, I have been delighted to have spent in searching among the ancient writers as many precepts as they have left us which are apt and useful for the good, honor, and growth of families; and since I discovered many perfect lessons there, I felt it my duty to collect them together and set them in some order so that, gathered together in one place, you might come to know them with less effort, and in coming to know them, you might follow them. I also think, after you have reviewed with me the sayings and authority of these good ancient writers on the one hand, and have considered, on the other, the excellent customs of our Alberti ancestors, you will come to this same conclusion and will conclude for yourselves that ability determines all your fortune. Nor will it delight you any the less in reading me to discover the good ancient manners of our Alberti house, for when you recognize that the counsel and the remembered customs of our older Albertis are completely applicable and most perfect, you will believe their precepts and embrace them. You will learn from them in what manner the family is increased, with what skills it becomes both fortunate and blessed, and with which type of procedures it acquires grace, good will, and friendship, and by means of what discipline it grows and spreads honor, fame, and glory, and in what ways it commends the family's name to eternal praise and immortality. . . .

[After Alberti's prologue, Book I opens during a single afternoon and evening in May 1421 as a number of the Alberti family gathers at a home in Padua, where they are visiting the dying Lorenzo Alberti (Leon Battista's father). The first book contains a discourse by Lorenzo on the role of the father in the family, the relative responsibilities of the old and the young, and the importance of education for the children.]

· ❦ ·

Book II

[Book II discusses the important question of taking a wife, an act which was usually more concerned with economic questions than with romantic love. For the middle-class family man, the choice of a wife involved complicated issues—gaining alliances with the family and relatives of the bride, receiving the all-important dowry along with the bride, and—most important—fathering the legitimate children who would guarantee the continuity of the all important family line. In this book, the dying Lionardo offers advice to the young Leon Battista, who would have been seventeen years of age when the fictitious dialogue was supposed to have taken place—thus, a young man of marriageable age.]

... Let a man take a wife for two reasons: the first is to perpetuate himself with children, and the second is to have a steady and constant companion for his entire life. Therefore, you must seek to have a woman capable of bearing children and pleasing enough to serve as your perpetual companion.

It is said that in taking a wife, you must look for beauty, relatives, and wealth. ... I think beauty in a woman may be judged not only in her charms and in the gentleness of her face but even more in her person, which should be shaped and adapted for carrying and giving birth to a great number of beautiful children. And among the beauties of a woman, above all, are her good manners; for while an unkempt, wasteful, greasy, and drunken woman may have a beautiful body, who would call her a beautiful wife? And the most important manners worthy of praise in a woman are modesty and purity. Thus Marius, that most illustrious Roman citizen, in his first speech to the Roman people declared: "Purity in women and work from men." And it certainly seems so to me as well. There is nothing more repulsive than an untidy, filthy woman. Who is so stupid as not to realize that a woman who does not take pleasure in appearing clean and neat not only in her clothes and her body but in her every act and word is not to be considered well mannered? And who cannot see that a badly mannered woman is only very rarely a virtuous one? How damaging women without virtue are to families will be considered and discussed elsewhere, but I would not know which would be the greatest misfortune for families—complete sterility or a woman without virtue. Thus, in a bride one must first look for beauty of spirit—that is, good behavior and virtue—and then one should seek in her physical appearance loveliness, grace, and charm, but also try to find someone well suited for bearing children with the kind of body that guarantees healthy and tall ones. There is an ancient proverb which says: "When you want children, pick your wife accordingly," and every virtue of hers will show forth greater in her beautiful children. This saying is very common among the poets: "A beautiful character comes from a beautiful body." Doctors urge that a wife not be too thin nor too overloaded with fat, for the latter are full of chills, menstrual occlusions, and are slow to conceive. They also prefer that a woman be by nature happy, fresh, and lively in her blood and in her whole being. Nor are they displeased if the girl is dark-complexioned. However, they do not accept girls who are too black, nor do they like small ones or praise those who are too large or too slender. They consider it most useful for the woman to have well-balanced and well-developed limbs if she is to give birth to many children. And they always prefer a young woman, for reasons which need not be explained here, but especially because they have a more adaptable character. Young girls are pure because of their age, they are not malicious by habit, and they are by nature bashful and free of all maliciousness; they are well disposed to learning quickly and they follow the habits and wishes of their husbands without stubbornness. These things, therefore, are what follows from our discussion and are the concerns that should be most usefully kept in mind when selecting the proper, prolific wife. To these considerations should be added that it would be an excellent sign if the young girl has a great number of brothers, since you can hope that when she is yours, she will be like her mother in bearing male children.

Now we have spoken about beauty. The wife's lineage is the next problem, and here we shall consider what things are proper and to be preferred. I believe that in choosing relatives, the first thing to do is to examine the lives and the customs of all one's prospective relatives. Many marriages have brought about the utter ruin of numerous families, according to what we hear or read about every day, because they involved relatives who were quarrelsome, picky, arrogant, and full of ill will. . . . Therefore, to sum up this issue in a few words, since I wish to be brief on this question, it is important to acquire new relatives who are not of vulgar birth, who can boast a patrimony which is not insignificant, who exercise a profession which is not vile, and who are modest and respectable in all their affairs, people who are not too superior to you, so that their greatness will not eclipse your own honor and dignity, or disturb your peace and tranquillity and that of your family, and also because if one of your new relatives fails, you will be able to give him your support and sustain him without too much difficulty and without sweating too much under the weight of the burden you are carrying. Nor would I wish for these same new relatives to be inferior to you, for while the first condition of superiority places you in a state of servitude to them, this second condition of inferiority will cause you expense. Let them be, therefore, your equals, and as we have already said, modest and respectable. Next is the problem of the dowry, which, it seems to me, should be not excessive but certain and prompt rather than enormous, doubtful, and remote. . . .

[With some reluctance and obvious embarrassment, the writer then turns to the actual engendering of children, the primary function of a proper bourgeois union.]

But let us consider our first topic of discussion. I have noted what kind of woman is most suitable for bearing children; now I believe we should next treat the question of how best children may be conceived, a subject which might well be avoided on account of certain considerations of modesty. But in this nevertheless vital matter, I shall be so circumspect and so very brief that anyone expecting to find this matter dealt with at this point will not be disappointed. Husbands should not couple with their wives in an agitated state of mind or when they are perturbed by fears or other like preoccupations, for such emotions as these that afflict the spirit deaden and weaken our vital spirits, and the other passions which inflame the spirit disturb and effect those vital seeds which then must produce the human image. Thus, one may observe how a father who is impetuous and strong and knowledgeable has engendered a son who is timid, weak, and foolish, on the one hand, while another father who is moderate and reasonable has given birth to a son who is crazy and brutish. In addition, it is necessary not to couple if the body and all its members are not well disposed and healthy. Doctors declare, with good reason, and offer examples to prove that if fathers and mothers are either sluggish, deadened by debauchery, or weakened by bad blood, as well as made feeble or devoid of vigor and pulse, it is reasonable to expect that their children, as is often the case, will turn out leprous, epileptic, disgusting, and misshapen or lacking in their bodily parts—all qualities which are not desirable in one's children. As a result, doctors recommend that such couplings be undertaken in a sober, tranquil, and as happy a state of mind as possible, and they believe that the best hour of the night occurs right after the first digestion is completed, at which time you are neither empty nor filled with bad foods but, rather, well along in your digestion and refreshed with sleep. They also recommend during this coupling to make yourself intensely desired by the woman. They have yet many other recommendations, such as when it is excessively hot or when seeds and roots are hidden in the soil and frozen there; then one must wait for more temperate weather. But it would take too long a time to recite all their prescriptions, and perhaps I should keep better in mind to whom I am speaking. You are only young men, after all; perhaps this argument, which can be excused by the fact that I was drawn into it accidentally by the course of my discussion, is something I should examine explicitly. But even if I am to be blamed and should excuse myself for it, I am delighted that my error may nevertheless have served some useful purpose, and because of this, I consider what I have done less offensive than if I had delved more deeply into the question. . . .

Book III

[Book III celebrates the crucial middle-class values of Alberti's era, thrift and good management. Alberti uses a distant relative of Lorenzo, a man named Giannozzo, as the spokesman for his economic vision of the family.]

GIANNOZZO: . . . In those days I was young and spent and threw around my money.

LIONARDO: And now?

GIANNOZZO: Now, my dear Lionardo, I am prudent, and I realize that anyone who throws away his possessions is crazy. The man who has never experienced how miserable and fruitless it is to go about seeking the charity of others in times of need will never know just how useful money is. And the man who has not experienced the great difficulty with which money is acquired will spend it too easily. And the man who is not measured in his spending is usually quickly impoverished. And anyone in this world who lives in poverty, my children, will suffer many hardships and many deprivations, and he would perhaps be better off dying than living in misery and in want. Therefore, my dear Lionardo, believe me as a person who knows by experience and could not be any surer of the truth of this proverb of our peasants: "He who finds no money in his own purse will find even less in another's." My children, if you wish to be thrifty, you should protect yourself against superfluous expenses as if from a mortal enemy.

LIONARDO: Nevertheless, Giannozzo, I do not think that in your desire to avoid expenses, you would like to be or appear to be avaricious.

GIANNOZZO: God preserve me from that! Let our enemies be avaricious. There is nothing so contrary to fame or grace in men than avarice. What virtue could be so clear and noble as not to be obscured and rendered unrecognizable under the cloak of avarice? And as for the continuous anxiety which characterizes men who are too tight and stingy, it is a most odious thing; for they first expend a great deal of trouble in accumulating their wealth and are then made unhappy by spending it, the worst thing which inevitably occurs to the stingy. I never see them happy, they never enjoy any part of their fortune.

LIONARDO: But to avoid seeming cheap, people think it is necessary to spend extravagantly?

GIANNOZZO: And to avoid appearing mad, one must be thrifty. But why, God help us, should anyone not prefer to appear thrifty rather than extravagant? Believe me, as I have had experience and knowledge of these matters, such expenditures as these which are not very necessary are not praised by wise men, and I have never witnessed (nor do I believe you will ever witness) a great, lavish, and magnificent expenditure that has not been criticized for countless shortcomings by countless people: there is always too much of this, or not enough of that. See for yourself. If a person plans a banquet, although a banquet is a most civilized expense and a kind of tax or a tribute we pay to preserve the goodwill and the bonds among friends, yet aside from the confusion, the worry, and the other anxieties—this is required, that is needed, and this too is necessary—the bother and the worry wear you out before you have even begun your preparations; and besides all this, there is the throwing away of things, the damaging effects of sweeping and washing the entire house: nothing can stay locked up, one thing is lost, another is needed, you seek here, borrow from others, buy, spend, spend some more, and waste. And then, you add the regrets and the many second thoughts that trouble you during the banquet itself and afterward, which are worrisome and inestimable inconveniences, as well as too expensive, and yet, by the time the smoke in the kitchen has disappeared, all the favor you have gained from the banquet is gone, Lionardo—every bit of it—and you'll hardly be noticed for what you've done! If things were done moderately, few people will praise you for its avoidance of ostentation, but many will criticize you for your lack of extravagance. And these many are certainly right. For any expenditure which is not absolutely necessary, in my opinion, can come from nothing but madness. And if a man goes mad in any respect, he should go completely mad in that regard, since to seek to be reasonably mad has always been a double and completely incredible insanity. But let us ignore all these things, since they are minor compared to these other matters, which I shall now discuss. These expenditures for the entertainment and honoring of your friends can come only one or two times a year, and they bear with them an excellent cure for anyone who has tried them once, and if that person is not entirely out of his mind, I believe he will avoid a second try. Lionardo, consider the matter yourself and think about it a moment. Consider whether there is anything more likely to destroy not only a family but a community or a country than those—what do they call them in those books of yours, those people who spend without reason?

LIONARDO: Prodigals.

GIANNOZZO: Call them what you wish. If I were to invent a name for them, what could I call them but completely misguided souls? They are completely misguided themselves, and they lead others astray as well. Since it is the unhappy inclination of the young to frequent dens of iniquity rather than the workshops and to spend their time more willingly among lavish young spenders than among thrifty older people, other young people see these "prodigals" of yours abounding in every sort of delight, and they immediately run to join them, giving themselves over to lasciviousness, to overly refined pleasures, and to idleness while they avoid praiseworthy enterprises, placing their glory and happiness in the wasting away of their resources, no longer seeking praise for being virtuous and holding every principle of good management in low esteem. To tell the truth, who among them could ever become virtuous, living as they do, in the midst of so many flattering gluttons and liars, and besieged by the most vile and dishonest men, musicians, players, dancers, buffoons, pimps, and beribboned dressers in livery and frills? Perhaps this entire crowd does not run to sit on the doorstep of anyone who is "prodigal," as if at school or in a factory for vices, so that as a result young men used to such a life cannot leave? Oh, good God! To continue, what evil do such people not do? They steal from their fathers, parents, and friends, they pawn and they sell. Who could even tell the half of the perversities they commit? Every day you hear new complaints, every hour some fresh infamy springs up, and they continuously spread about greater hatred, envy, enmity, and disgrace. Finally, my Lionardo, these "prodigals" find themselves impoverished in their old age, without honor, and with very few friends—actually none at all; for those flattering hangers-on, whom they considered their friends when they gave themselves over to lavish expenditures and who called spending (that is, becoming poor) "virtue," those who with their glass in hand swore and promised to lay down their lives for them—all of these people act like fishes: as long as the bait swims on the water and stays afloat, a great school of fish will swarm around, but when the bait disappears, everything is empty and deserted. I don't want to go on and on with these arguments, nor to give you examples of such people, nor to recount to you how many people I have seen with my very eyes who have at first been very wealthy and who have then become impoverished because of their poor management; Lionardo, that story would be too long to tell, and even the entire day would not suffice. In order to be brief, let me say this: just as prodigality is evil, thrift is good, useful, and praiseworthy. Thrift causes harm to no one, and it is useful, to the family. And let me tell you, I know that thrift alone is sufficient to maintain you in such a way that you will never need anyone else. Thrift is a holy thing, and how many lascivious desires, how many dishonest appetites does thrift put behind us! Prodigal and lascivious youth, my dear Lionardo, has always been the cause of the ruin of every family. Older thrifty and modest men are the salvation of the family. One must be thrifty if only because in this fashion, you gain the peace of mind of knowing that you live very well with what Fortune has given you. For whoever lives contented with whatever he possesses, in my opinion, does not deserve to be called avaricious. These spendthrifts, instead, are the avaricious, for they do not know how to satisfy themselves with their spending, and thus, they are never content with their acquisitions and seek to prey upon others. However, do not think that I admire any excessive stinginess. Let me say only this: I cannot criticize too harshly a father of a family who lives more like a thrifty person than a lavish spender.

LIONARDO: If you dislike spendthrifts, Giannozzo, people who do not spend money should please you. But avarice, which according to what wise writers say, consists in desiring too much wealth, also consists in not spending.

GIANNOZZO: You speak the truth.

LIONARDO: Yet you do not like avarice?

GIANNOZZO: I certainly do not.

LIONARDO: Well, then, what would this thrift of yours consist of?

GIANNOZZO: You know, Lionardo, I am not a man of letters. I have tried all my life to understand things more by experience than by what others have said, and what I know I have learned more from the truth of experience than from the arguments of others. And when one of those people who spend all day reading books tells me "that's the way things are," I do not believe him unless I see an obvious reason for doing so, a reason which moves me to accept the argument rather than one which forces me to do so. And if another person, one who is uneducated, cites the same reason for the same things to me, I will believe him without his citing written authorities, just as much as I would a man who uses the testimony from a book, since I consider anybody who writes a book a man like myself. But perhaps I would not be able to reply to you in the organized fashion you would, since you always spend the day with a book in your hands. But look here, Lionardo, these spendthrifts about whom I was speaking a moment ago displease me because they spend without reason, and the avaricious also annoy me because they do not use things when they have need of them and also because they desire wealth too much. Do you know the kind of man I like? The kind of man who employs his possessions as much as he needs to and not a bit more; such a man saves the surplus; and such men I call thrifty.

LIONARDO: I understand you perfectly—you mean those men who know how to hold the mean between two little and too much.

GIANNOZZO: Yes, that's it.

LIONARDO: But how can we know what is too much and what is too little?

GIANNOZZO: Easily—by the ruler in our hand.

LIONARDO: I am waiting and anxious to see this ruler.

GIANNOZZO: Lionardo, this is very easily and usefully explained. With every expenditure, you must only make sure that the cost is no greater nor more burdensome nor larger than necessity demands, nor should it be less than honesty requires.

LIONARDO: Oh, Giannozzo, how much more useful in the affairs of this world is an experienced and practical man such as yourself than an unexperienced man of letters!

GIANNOZZO: What are you saying? Haven't you read these things in your books? And yet, people say that they find everything in books.

LIONARDO: That may be true, but I don't ever remember finding them. And if you knew, Giannozzo, how useful and to the point you have been, you would be amazed.

GIANNOZZO: Is that so? I am delighted if I have been of some help to you.

GIOVANNI PICO DELLA MIRANDOLA
1463–94

THE YOUNGER SON OF AN OLD AND WEALTHY NOBLE FAMILY, PICO BEGAN HIS studies at home and continued them at a number of universities (Bologna, Ferrara, Padua, Paris), being especially interested in Aristotelianism, Platonism, and a number of languages, including Hebrew, Greek, Latin, and his native Italian. While the Christian Latin tradition provided a frame of reference for all his work, Pico came to believe that Greek philosophy and the Judeo-Christian tradition participated in a single universal truth, arrived at through Greek reason and Christian revelation. He also believed that there existed an occult or hermetic tradition of religious truth stemming from Hermes Trismegistus, Orpheus, and Pythagoras which could be subjected to allegorical interpretation by those who were capable of extracting the secret meanings from the texts. Furthermore, Pico's study of Hebrew brought him into contact with the cabala, a Jewish tradition of Biblical interpretation. Such an ecclectic philosophical view was a novelty at the time.

His vast learning culminated in the writing of nine hundred theses or *conclusiones* which were printed in December 1486 and which he presented at Rome in order to involve many scholars in a public disputation on January 1487. It was for this debate that he prepared his *Oratio*, now known as the *Oration on the Dignity of Man*, which was to serve as an introduction to the disputation. The work was printed only in 1495–96, after Pico's death. The actual debate never took place, for when Pope Innocent VIII had a commission investigate the theses, they condemned thirteen propositions as heretical. Pico subsequently became involved in a conflict with church authorities, fled Italy, and was arrested in France. He was returned to Italy on parole in the custody of Lorenzo de' Medici, and he remained in that ruler's care until his death.

The title is somewhat misleading, since the *Oration* as a whole justifies the study and practice of philosophy as the idea of a universal harmony among philosophies. However, this brief section of the work remains the most influential expression of the Renaissance optimism which viewed man as creation's finest adornment. It is also the most radical statement in favor of human free will produced by the Italian Renaissance and may be compared with similar discussions in Leon Battista Alberti's *Book of the Family* or the far more pessimistic views in either Machiavelli or Guicciardini. Among Pico's other works are the *Heptaplus* (1489) and the treatise *On Being and the One* (1491): the first work is a commentary on Genesis, illustrating his method of interpreting the Scriptures; the second attempts a synthesis of the works of Plato and Aristotle.

BIBLIOGRAPHY

Giovanni Pico della Mirandola, *On the Dignity of Man, On Being and the One, Heptaplus*, trans. Paul J. W. Miller et al. (Indianapolis: Bobbs-Merrill, 1965); Eugenio Garin, *Portraits from the Quattrocento* (New York: Harper, 1972); Paul Kristeller, *Eight Philosophers of the Italian Renaissance* (Stanford: Stanford University Press, 1964); Charles Trinkaus, *In Our Image and Likeness: Humanity and Divinity in Italian Renaissance Thought* (Chicago: University of Chicago Press, 1970).

SELECTIONS FROM THE
ORATION ON THE DIGNITY OF MAN

· ❧ ·

I have read in the ancient annals of the Arabians, most reverend Fathers, that when asked what on the world's stage could be considered most admirable, Abdala the Saracen[1] answered that there is nothing more admirable to be seen than man. In agreement with this opinion is the saying of Hermes Trismegistus: "What a great miracle, O Asclepius, is man!"[2]

When I had thought over the meaning of these maxims, the many reasons for the excellence of man advanced by many men failed to satisfy me—that man is the intermediary between the creatures, the intimate of the higher beings and the lord of those below him; the interpreter of nature by the sharpness of his senses, by the discernment of his reason, and by the light of his intellect; the intermediate point between fixed eternity and fleeting time; and, as the Persians say, the bond or rather the marriage song of the world, but little lower than the angels according to David's testimony.[3] These are weighty reasons, indeed, but they are not the principal reasons, that is, those which should be accorded boundless admiration. For why should we not admire more the angels themselves and the most blessed choirs of heaven?

At last, it seems to me that I have understood why man is the most fortunate living thing worthy of all admiration and precisely what rank is his lot in the universal chain of being, a rank to be envied not only by the brutes but even by the stars and by minds beyond this world. It is a matter past faith and extraordinary! Why should it not be so? For it is upon this account that man is justly considered and called a great miracle and a truly admirable being. But hear, Fathers, exactly what man's rank is, and as friendly listeners by virtue of your humanity, forgive any deficiencies in this, my work.

God the Father, the supreme Architect, had already built this cosmic home which we behold, this most majestic temple of divinity, in accordance with the laws of a mysterious wisdom. He had adorned the region above the heavens with intelligences, had quickened the celestial spheres with eternal souls and had filled the vile and filthy parts of the lower world with a multitude of animals of every kind. But when the work was completed, the Maker kept wishing that there were someone who could examine the plan of so great an enterprise, who could love its beauty, who could admire its vastness. On that account, when everything was completed, as Moses and Timaeus both testify, He finally took thought of creating man.[4] However, not a single archetype remained from which he might fashion this new creature, not a single treasure remained which he might bestow upon this new son, and not a single seat remained in the whole world in which the contemplator of the universe might sit. All was now complete; all things had been assigned to the highest, the middle, and the lowest orders. But it was not in the nature of the Father's power to fail in this final creative effort, as though exhausted; nor was it in the nature of His wisdom to waver in such a crucial matter through lack of counsel; and it was not in the nature of His Beneficent Love that he who was destined to praise God's divine generosity in regard to others should be forced to condemn it in regard to himself. At last, the Supreme Artisan ordained that the creature to whom He could give nothing properly his own should share in whatever He had assigned individually to the other creatures. He therefore accepted man as a work of indeterminate nature, and placing him in the center of the world, addressed him thus:

"O Adam, we have given you neither a place nor a form nor any ability exclusively your own, so that according to your wishes and your judgment, you may have and possess whatever place, form, or abilities you desire. The nature of all other beings is limited and constrained in accordance with the laws prescribed by us. Constrained by no limits, in accordance with your own free will, in whose hands we have placed you, you shall independently determine the bounds of your own nature. We have placed you at the world's center, from where you may more easily observe whatever is in the world. We have made you neither celestial nor terrestrial, neither mortal nor immortal, so that with honor and freedom of choice, as though the maker and molder of yourself, you may fashion yourself in whatever form you prefer. You shall have the power to degenerate into the inferior forms of life which are brutish; you shall have the power, through your soul's judgment, to rise to the superior orders which are divine."

O supreme generosity of God the Father! O highest and most admirable felicity of man to whom it is granted to have whatever he chooses, to be whatever he wills! From the moment of their birth, or as Lucilius says,[5] from their mother's womb, the beasts bring with them all that they will ever possess. The highest spirits, either from the beginning of time or soon thereafter, become what they are to be throughout eternity. In man alone, at the moment of his creation, the Father placed the seeds of all kinds and the germs of every way of life. Whatever seeds each man cultivates will mature and bear their own fruit in him; if vegetative, he will be like a plant; if sensitive, he will become a brute; if rational, he will become a celestial being; if intellectual, he will be an angel and the son of God. And if content with the lot of no creature he withdraws into the center of his own unity, his spirit, made one with God, in the solitary darkness of the Father who is placed above all things, will surpass them all.

Who would not admire this our chameleon? Or who could admire any other being more greatly than man? Asclepius the Athenian justly says that man was symbolized in the mysteries by the figure of Proteus, because of his ability to change his character and transform his nature.[6] This is the origin of those metamorphoses or transformations celebrated among the Hebrews and the Pythagoreans.[7] For the occult theology of the Hebrews sometimes transforms the holy Enoch into an angel of divinity and sometimes transforms other people into other divinities.[8] The Pythagoreans transform impious men into beasts and, if Empedocles is to be believed, even into plants. Echoing this, Mohammed often had this saying on his lips: "He who deviates from divine law becomes a beast," and he was right in saying so. For it is not the bark that makes the plant but its dumb and insentient nature; neither is it the hide that makes the beast of burden but its irrational and sensitive soul; neither is it the spherical form which makes the heavens, but their undeviating order; nor is it the freedom from a body which makes the angel but its spiritual intelligence.

If you see one abandoned to his appetites crawling along the earth on his belly, it is a plant, not a man, which you see; if you see one enchanted by the vain illusions of fancy, as if by the spells of Calypso, and seduced by these tempting wiles, a slave to his own senses, it is a beast and not a man you see. However, if you see a philosopher who discerns all things by means of right reason, you will venerate him: he is a celestial, not an earthly being. If you see a pure contemplator, unmindful of the body and wholly withdrawn into the inner reaches of the mind, he is neither a terrestrial nor a celestial being; he is a higher spirit clothed in mortal flesh and most worthy of respect.

Are there any who will not admire man? In the sacred Mosaic and Christian writings, man, not without reason, is sometimes described by the name of "all flesh" and sometimes by that of "every creature," since man molds, fashions, and transforms himself according to the form of all flesh and the character of every creature.[9] For this reason, the Persian Evantes, in describing Chaldean theology, writes that man does not have an inborn and fixed image of himself but many which are external and foreign to him; whence comes the Chaldean saying: "Man is a being of varied, manifold, and inconstant nature."[10]

But why do we reiterate all these things? To the end that from the moment we are born into the condition of being able to become whatever we choose, we should be particularly certain that it may never be said of us that, although born to a privileged position, we failed to realize it and became like brutes and mindless beasts of burden,[11] but that the saying of Asaph the prophet might be repeated: "You are all gods and the sons of the Most High."[12] Otherwise, abusing the most indulgent generosity of the Father, we shall make that freedom of choice which He has given to us into something harmful rather than something beneficial.

Let some holy ambition invade our souls, so that, dissatisfied with mediocrity, we shall eagerly desire the highest things and shall toil with all our strength to obtain them, since we may if we wish. Let us disdain earthly things, despise heavenly things, and finally, esteeming less all the things of this world, hasten to that court beyond the world which is nearest to the Godhead. There, as the sacred mysteries relate, Seraphim, Cherubim, and Thrones occupy the first places.[13] Let us emulate their dignity and glory, intolerate of a secondary position for ourselves and incapable of yielding to them the first. If we have willed it, we shall be inferior to them in nothing.

But how shall we proceed and what in the end shall we do? Let us observe what they do, what sort of lives they live. For if we also come to live like them, and we are able to do so, we shall then equal their destiny.

NOTES

· ❦ ·

1. Possibly 'Abd-Allah Ian al Muqaffa (718–75), a cousin of Mohammed, noted for his translations of Medo-Persian writings into Arabic.

2. Hermes Trismegistus was the Greek name for the Egyptian god Troth and the reputed author of writings on the occult dating from the first three centuries of the Christian era; supposedly he invented a magic seal to make vessels airtight by sealing them completely.

3. See Psalms 8:5.

4. See Genesis 2:1 and Plato's *Timaeus*, 41b ff.

5. A Roman satirist (180–102 B.C.), whose poetry influenced Horace, Juvenal, and Persius but which survives only in fragments.

6. Sometimes said to be the son of Poseidon, sometimes his attendant, Proteus had the power of foretelling the future and of changing his shape at will.

7. Followers of Pythagoras, a Greek philosopher of the sixth century B.C., who expounded a syncretistic philosophy distinguished primarily by its description of reality in terms of arithmetical relationships.

8. Book of Enoch 40:8.

9. See Genesis 6:12; Numbers 27:16; and Mark 16:15.

10. Scholars have not been able to identify this Evantes with certainty, and the source of the quotation has not been discovered.

11. See Psalms 49:20.

12. See Psalms 49:20.

13. In medieval angelology, there were nine orders of spiritual beings, the highest of which were seraphim, cherubim, and thrones, and then in descending order, dominions or dominations, virtues, powers, principalities, archangels, and angels.

LEONARDO DA VINCI
1452–1519

AN ARTIST, SCIENTIST, AND WRITER, LEONARDO IS NATURALLY BEST KNOWN for his numerous drawings and paintings. He was, however, a prodigious writer who set his ideas about numerous topics down in a rather disorganized fashion. Furthermore, the Vincian manuscripts are so scattered and often so provisional that it is impossible to identify even one authentic chapter, not to mention a separate book on a single subject. After his death, Leonardo's manuscripts were scattered, and an unknown number were lost or destroyed. Some twelve hundred folios were assembled by the sixteenth-century collector Pompeo Leoni to form what is known as the Codex Atlanticus now located in the Ambrosiana Library in Milan. Other important codices include the Codex Trivulzianus in Milan; a small codex on the flight of birds in Turin; a group of drawings in Venice; a rich collection of drawings in the Royal Collection at Windsor Castle; and two recently discovered notebooks (Codex Madrid I and II) that reappeared in 1965 after having been lost for 135 years.

Leonardo's contributions to painting and science are far more decisive than his contribution to Renaissance literature. Yet, the enigma of Leonardo's strange and mysterious personality, which has attracted generations of readers and scholars, is perhaps best revealed by his curious notebooks (which, incidentally, Leonardo wrote backward as if to hide his innermost secrets). In the brief selection contained in this anthology, the reader will catch a glimpse of Leonardo and his most important ideas—his rejection of book learning and his preference for observation and experience, his famous self-description as a man without erudition, his preference for painting over sculpture, his general views on the proper way to approach this craft, his contempt for useless contemporaries who failed to embrace his love of work and study, and his profound unhappiness. Leonardo was a man of almost unlimited talents, and the draft of a letter he sent to Ludovico Sforza, Duke of Milan, is perhaps the best example we have of the self-conscious Renaissance paragon—the "universal man."

LEONARDO DA VINCI

With all his genius, Leonardo was a profoundly tragic figure who never completed a host of major projects and often concealed from the world the full scope of his genius. Even though what he did accomplish amazed an age accustomed to works of brilliance, Leonardo could nevertheless include in one of his last notebooks a note of despair which questioned it all: "Tell me if anything was ever done." Perhaps his own evaluation of his life, which lay hidden in the Codex Madrid I for a number of years, is his best epitaph: "Peruse me, reader, if you find pleasure in my work, since this profession very seldom returns to this world, and the perseverance to pursue it and to invent such things afresh is discovered in very few people. And come, men, to see the marvels which may be discovered in nature by such study."

BIBLIOGRAPHY

Leonardo da Vinci, *The Madrid Codices*, ed. Ladislao Reti, 5 vols. (New York: McGraw-Hill, 1974), and *The Notebooks of Leonardo da Vinci*, ed. Jean Paul Richter, 2 vols. (New York: Dover, 1970); Kenneth Clark, *Leonardo da Vinci* (Baltimore: Penguin, 1973); Martin Kemp, *Leonardo da Vinci: The Marvelous Works of Nature and Man* (Cambridge: Harvard University Press, 1981); Carlo Pedretti, *The Literary Works of Leonardo da Vinci: A Commentary to Jean Paul Richter's Edition*, 2 vols. (Berkeley: University of California Press, 1977).

———————— · 🐝 · ————————

3

Let no man who is not a mathematician read the elements of my work.

———————— · 🐝 · ————————

4

Begun at Florence, in the house of Piero di Braccio Martelli, on the 22nd day of March 1508. And this is to be a collection without order, taken from the many papers which I have copied here, with the hope of arranging them later on each in its own place, according to the subjects of which they treat.[1] But I think that before I come to the end of this work I shall have to do the same things a number of times; for which, O reader! do not blame me, since the subjects are many and memory cannot retain all of them, and say: "I will not write this because I wrote it before." And if I should wish to avoid committing this error, it would be necessary in every case when I wanted to copy [something] that, in order not to repeat myself, I should read over all that had gone before; and all the more since the intervals between writing one time and the next are long.

———————— · 🐝 · ————————

Introduction

I am fully conscious that, since I am not a literary man, certain presumptuous persons will think it quite proper to blame me, alleging that I am not a man of letters.[2] Foolish people! Do they not realize that I might well answer as Marius did the Roman Patricians by saying that they who deck themselves out in the labors of others will not allow me my own. They will say that since I have no literary ability, I cannot properly express what I wish to deal with, but what they do not know is that my subjects are to be dealt with by experience rather than by words; and experience has always been the mistress of those who wrote well. And so, as mistress in this, I will cite her in all cases.

— • ❧ • —

11

Even though I may not, like them, be able to quote other authors, I shall rely on what is far greater and more worthy: on experience, the mistress of their Masters.[3] They go about puffed up and pompous, dressed and decorated not in their own labors, but in those of others. And they will not allow me my own. They will scorn me as an inventor, but how much more might they—who are not inventors but braggarts and declaimers of the works of others—be blamed.

— • ❧ • —

19
Of the Mistakes Made by Those Who Practice Without Knowledge

Those who love practice without knowledge are like the sailor who gets into a ship that has no rudder or compass and who can never be sure of where he is going. Practice must always be founded on sound theory, and to this perspective is the guide and the gateway; and without this nothing good can be done when it comes to drawing.

483

The young artist should learn about perspective first, then the proportions of objects. Then he may copy from some good master, to accustom himself to find forms, and then from nature, to confirm by practice the rules he has learned; then observe for a while the works of a number of different masters; then get into the habit of putting his art into practice and work.

488
Of Painting

It is indispensable to a painter, in order to be thoroughly familiar with the limbs in all the positions and actions of which they are capable in the nude, to know the anatomy of the sinews, bones, muscles, and tendons so that, in their various movements and exertions, he may know which nerve or muscle is the cause of each movement and show only those as prominent and swelled, and not all the others in limb, as many do who, in order to appear as great artists, draw their nude figures looking like wood, and lacking in grace—you would think you were looking at a sack of walnuts rather than the human form, or a bundle of radishes rather than bare muscles.[4]

651

A beautiful object that is mortal passes away, but not so with art.

· ❦ ·

652
He Who Despises Painting Loves Neither Philosophy Nor Nature

If you condemn painting, which is the only imitator of all of nature's visible works, you will certainly despise a subtle invention which brings philosophy and subtle speculation to the consideration of the nature of all forms—seas and land, trees, animals, plants and flowers—which are surrounded by shade and light. And this is true knowledge and the legitimate offspring of nature; for painting is born of nature—or, to be more correct, we will say it is the grandchild of nature; for all visible things are produced by nature, and these, her children, have given birth to painting. Hence we may justly call it the grandchild of nature and related to God.

· ❦ ·

653
That Painting Surpasses All Human Works by the Subtle Considerations Belonging to It

The eye, which is called the window of the soul, is the principal means by which the central sense can most completely and fully appreciate the infinite works of nature; and the ear is the second, which acquires dignity by hearing of the things the eye has seen. If you, historians, or poets, or mathematicians, had not seen things with your eyes, you would have been able to write about them poorly. And if you, O poet, tell a story with your pen, the painter with his brush can tell it more easily, with simpler completeness, and it would be less tedious to understand. And if you call painting dumb poetry, the painter may call poetry blind painting. Now which is the worse defect, to be blind or dumb? Though the poet is as free as the painter in the invention of his stories, they are not so satisfactory to men as paintings, for, though poetry is able to describe forms, actions, and places in words, the painter deals with the actual similitude of the forms in order to represent them. Now tell me which is closer to man himself: the name of man or the image of man. The name of a man may differ from country to country, but a man's form is never changed except by death.

655

That Sculpture Is Less Intellectual Than Painting, and Lacks Many Characteristics of Nature

Since I myself have practiced the art of sculpture no less than that of painting, doing both of them to the same degree, it seems to me that I, without invidiousness, can give my opinion as to which of the two is most worthy, difficult, and perfect. To begin with, sculpture requires a certain light (that is, from above), while a picture carries with it throughout its own light and shade. Thus sculpture owes its importance to light and shade, and the sculptor is assisted in this by nature, by the relief which is inherent in it, while the painter whose art expresses the accidental aspects of nature places his effects in the spots where nature would reasonably have put them. The sculptor cannot change his work by means of the various natural colors that objects contain, but painting is not defective in any particular. The perspective used by sculptors never appears to be true; that of the painter can appear to be a hundred miles beyond the picture itself. Their sculpted works have no aerial perspective whatever; they cannot represent luminous bodies, nor reflected lights, nor lustrous bodies—as mirrors and similar polished surfaces—nor mists, nor dark skies, nor an infinite number of things which I need not mention for fear of becoming tedious. As regards the capability to resist time, though they do have this resistance, a picture painted on thick copper covered with white enamel on which it is painted with enamel colors and then put back into the fire and baked will last forever compared to sculpture. It may be said that if a mistake is made it is not easy to correct it, but it is a poor argument to try to prove that a piece of work is nobler because oversights are irremediable; I would say rather that it is more difficult to improve the mind of the master who makes such mistakes than to fix the work he has ruined.

· ❦ ·

660

That Painting Declines and Deteriorates from Age to Age, When Painters Have No Other Standard Than Painting Already Done

The painter will produce pictures of little worth if he takes for his standard the pictures of others. But if he will learn from the objects of nature he will bear good fruit; this we have seen in the painters following the Romans who always imitated both, and their art continued to decline from age to age. After these came Giotto the Florentine, who was not content with imitating the works of Cimabue, his master. Born in solitude and in the mountains inhabited only by goats and the like, and guided by nature to his art, he began by drawing on the rocks the movements of the goats of which he was keeper. And then he began to draw all types of animals found in the country, and he did so in such a way that after much study he excelled not only all the masters of his time but all those of many centuries past. Later this art declined once more, because everyone imitated the pictures already existing; and so it went from century to century until Tommaso of Florence, nicknamed Masaccio, showed by his perfect works how those who take for their standard anyone but nature, the mistress of all masters, labor in vain.[5] And I would say concerning these mathematical studies that those who study only the authorities and not the works of nature are nephews but not sons of nature, the mistress of all good authors. Oh! how great is the folly of those who accuse artists who learn from nature, setting aside those authorities who themselves were the disciples of nature.

· ❦ ·

661

The first drawing was nothing but a line going around the shadow of a man cast by the sun on a wall.

· ❦ ·

1162

Now you see how the hope and desire of returning home and to one's former state is like the moth to the light, and that the man who with constant longing awaits with joy the coming of each new springtime, each new summer, each new month and new year—and it seems that the things he longs for are always too late in coming—does not perceive that he is longing for his own destruction. But this desire is the very quintessence, the spirit of the elements, which finding itself imprisoned within the soul always longs to return to its giver. And I want you to know that this same longing is that quintessence, the companion of nature, and that man is the image of the world.

· ❦ ·

1179

There are some who are nothing more than a passage for food and augmentors of excrement and fillers of privies, because through them no other things in the world, nor any good effects, are produced, since nothing but full privies results from them.

· ❦ ·

1340
(To Ludovico Sforza, Duke of Milan)[6]

Having now, most illustrious Lord, sufficiently seen the specimens of all those who consider themselves master craftsmen of instruments of war, and that the invention and operation of such instruments are no different from those in common use, I shall now endeavor, without offending anyone, to explain myself to your Excellency by revealing to your Lordship my secrets, and then offering them for your pleasure and approbation to work with effect at the opportune time as well as all those things which, in part, shall be briefly noted below.

1. I have the kind of bridges that are extremely light and strong, made to be carried with great ease, and with them you may pursue, and, at any time, flee from the enemy; and there are others, that are safe, indestructible by fire and battle, easy and convenient to lift and set up; and also methods of burning and destroying those of the enemy.

2. I know how, when a place is under attack, to eliminate the water from the trenches, and make endless variety of bridges, and covered ways and ladders, and other machines pertaining to such expeditions.

3. If, because of the height of the banks, or the strength of the place and its position, it is impossible, when besieging a place, to follow a plan of bombardment, I have methods for destroying every rock or other fortress, even if it were built on rock, etc.

4. I also have other kinds of mortars that are most convenient and easy to carry; and with these small stones can be thrown creating the effect of a storm; and the smoke produced by this will strike terror into the hearts of the enemy to his great detriment and confusion.

9. And if it should be a sea battle, I have many kinds of machines that are most efficient for offense and defense; I also have vessels which will resist the attack of the largest guns and powder and fumes.

5. I also have means that are noiseless to reach a designated area by secret and tortuous mines and ways, even if they had to pass under a trench or river.

6. I will make covered chariots, safe and unattackable, which can penetrate the enemy with their artillery, and there is no body of men strong enough to prevent them from breaking through. And behind these, infantry could advance unharmed and without any hindrance.

7. In case of need I will make big guns, mortars, and light ordnance of fine and useful forms that are out of the ordinary.

8. If the operation of bombardment should fail, I would contrive catapults, mangonels, trabocchi, and other machines of marvelous efficacy and unusualness.[7] In short, I can, according to each case in question, contrive various and endless means of offense and defense.

10. In time of peace I believe I can give perfect satisfaction that is equal to any other in the field of architecture and the construction of buildings, public and private, and in directing water from one place to another.

I can execute sculpture in marble, bronze, or clay, and also in painting I do the best that can be done, and as well as any other, whoever he may be.

Again, the bronze horse may be taken up, which is to be to the immortal glory and eternal honor of the happy memory of the prince, your father, and of the illustrious house of Sforza.

And if any of the above-named things appear to anyone to be impossible or not feasible, I am more than ready to test the experiment in your park or in whatever place may please your Excellency, to whom I commend myself with the utmost humility, etc.

NOTES

·❧·

1. Leonardo seems to have planned a general treatise on painting and had a number of possible introductions in mind. Given the state of the extant manuscripts, the disorderly nature of Leonardo's original plan has been intensified by the loss or dispersal of many of his original manuscripts.

2. This passage, one of the possible introductions mentioned above in note 1, contains Leonardo's famous self-description as an unlettered (but not unlearned) man. Leonardo rejected the bookish science of the universities for the practical experience of personal observation.

3. Leonardo anticipates Francesco Guicciardini's attack upon the book learning of Renaissance thought. Whereas Leonardo rejects studying ancient classical scientific texts, since they obscure our perception of the natural world around us (and are often simply incorrect), Guicciardini (see selections in this anthology) will reject abstract, bookish political schemes (like those of his friend Machiavelli) in favor of practical experience in government.

4. Leonardo's own skill as a painter was due, in large measure, to his incomparable gift of noticing the details of every object or body contained in his paintings or sketches.

5. In this fragment, Leonardo anticipates the theory of the development of Italian art in the Renaissance usually associated with Giorgio Vasari's *Lives of the Artists*. However, he stresses the fact that Giotto and Masaccio imitated nature, not their predecessors.

6. Leonardo left Florence in 1481 and went to Milan, then ruled by the dashing Ludovico Sforza (known as "Il Moro," 1451–1508), who was the virtual ruler of Milan, since his nephew and the heir to the city's rule, Gian Galeazzo Sforza, was only thirteen years old. Ludovico needed an architect and military engineer as much as he required an artist, and Leonardo's letter of presentation to him stresses his many practical talents. The bronze horse mentioned was to be an equestrian monument to commemorate Ludovico's father, Francesco Sforza (1401–66), sixth Duke of Milan. The extant manuscript of this letter is not in Leonardo's hand and may have been only a draft.

7. Mangonels and trabocchi are technical terms for different kinds of military catapults or mortars frequently employed in Leonardo's time in besieging a city or fortress.

BALDESAR CASTIGLIONE
1478–1529

A MANTUAN COURTIER, DIPLOMAT, WRITER ON COURTESY AND MANNERS, and occasional poet, Castiglione spent his early years in his native city before being sent to the court of Ludovico "il Moro" in Milan in 1492 to finish his training. There, in the company of humanists and artists such as Bramante and Leonardo da Vinci, Castiglione polished his education. With the fall of Milan to the French in 1499, Castiglione first tried unsuccessfully to obtain a place at the Gonzaga court in Mantua; then in 1504 he was permitted to enter the service of Guidobaldo di Montefeltro, Duke of Urbino, and he served this court from 1504 to 1513, under both Guidobaldo and his successor, Francesco Maria della Rovere. Because Francesco Maria was the nephew of Pope Julius II, Castiglione was often sent to Rome on diplomatic missions for the Duchy of Urbino. In Rome, he developed close friendships with Raphael and a number of humanists at the Roman court. In 1524, Castiglione was made papal nuncio to the Spanish court of Charles V, but his last years were unhappy ones, particularly since the sack of Rome in 1527 by troops of Charles V caused some of Castiglione's enemies to accuse him of having failed to warn Pope Clement VII of this impending disaster. Castiglione died in Spain only a year after he had been made Bishop of Avila.

The *Book of the Courtier* first appeared in a final version in 1528, although shorter versions were published earlier. The book presents the ideal portrait of the perfect courtier, a figure inspired by humanism as well as chivalric ideals from the past. It is written in the form of a dialogue, a literary genre that became popular in the Renaissance in imitation of works by Cicero or Plato. In this relatively informal literary form, moreover, Castiglione's readers could also catch a glimpse of the type of ideal court (supposedly that of Urbino in March 1507) to which they were supposed to aspire.

The European reputation of the *Book of the Courtier* would be difficult to minimize. Along with Machiavelli's portrait of the ideal political leader in *The Prince*, with which it has a number of affinities, it became one of the most popular books in the Renaissance period, read by almost every educated individual and translated into a number of languages. While naive readers saw in it only a handbook of manners, most astute readers of Castiglione would find in his pages an engaging analysis of the dialectic between reality and appearance that would fascinate readers of Machiavelli as well.

BIBLIOGRAPHY

Baldesar Castiglione, *The Book of the Courtier*, trans. George Bull (New York: Penguin, 1967); Julia Cartwright Ady, *Baldassare Castiglione, The Perfect Courtier: His Life and Letters, 1478–1529*, 2 vols. (London: Murray, 1908); Peter Bondanella, "Baldesar Castiglione," in William T. H. Jackson, ed., *European Writers: The Middle Ages and the Renaissance* (New York: Scribner's, 1983); Wayne A. Rebhorn, *Courtly Performances: Masking and Festivity in Castiglione's Book of the Courtier* (Detroit: Wayne State University Press, 1978); J. R. Woodhouse, *Baldesar Castiglione: A Reassessment of "The Courtier"* (Edinburgh: Edinburgh University Press, 1978).

SELECTIONS FROM THE
BOOK OF THE COURTIER

·❦·

To the Reverend and Illustrious Don Miguel da Silva, Bishop of Viseo[1]

1. When Signor Guidobaldo of Montefeltro, Duke of Urbino, departed from this life, I together with some other noblemen who had served him remained in the service of Duke Francesco Maria della Rovere, his heir and successor in the state;[2] and as the reminiscence of his virtue was fresh in my mind as well as the satisfaction that I had felt during those years spent in the loving company of such excellent people as then happened to be present at the court of Urbino, I was moved by the memory of it to write this book of The Courtier, which I did in a few days, with the intention of correcting in the course of time those errors which arose from my desire to repay this debt quickly. But for many years now, fortune has continuously kept me overburdened with such constant toil that I could never find the time to bring these books to the point that my feeble judgment was satisfied with them.

Then finding myself in Spain and being informed by someone in Italy that Signora Vittoria della Colonnna, Marchioness of Pescara,[3] to whom I had already presented a copy of the book, had, contrary to her promises, allowed a large part of it to be transcribed, I could not help feeling somewhat annoyed, fearing the many problems that might well arise in such cases. Nonetheless, I trusted that the wisdom and prudence of that lady, whose virtue I have always admired as something divine, would suffice to prevent any harm from happening to me for having obeyed her commands. In the end I found out that many people in Naples already had that part of the book, and as men are always eager for new things, it seemed that some of these people were trying to have it printed. Wherefore, frightened by this danger, I decided to revise very quickly the small part of the book that time would allow with the intention of publishing it, judging it less harmful to let it be seen slightly corrected by my hand than greatly mutilated by the hands of others.

Thus, to carry out this decision, I began to reread it, and immediately, because of its title, I was seized by an uncommon sadness, which increased considerably as I read along and remembered that most of those introduced in the discussions were already dead, for, besides those who are mentioned in the preface to the last book, even Alfonso Ariosto,[4] to whom the book is dedicated, is dead—an affable young man, discreet, well mannered, and able in all that befits a man who lives at court. Likewise, Duke Giuliano de' Medici,[5] whose goodness and noble courtesy deserved to be enjoyed a little longer by the rest of the world. Messer Bernardo, Cardinal of Santa Maria in Portico,[6] who charmed anyone who met him with a sharp, pleasing, and ready wit, too, is dead. Also dead is Signor Ottaviano Fregoso,[7] a man most rare in our times, magnanimous, religious, full of goodness, wit, prudence, and courtesy, and truly a friend of honor and virtue and so worthy of esteem that even his enemies were forced to praise him; and those misfortunes that he endured with the greatest constancy were indeed enough to prove that Fortune is, as she always was, even today, the enemy of virtue. Also dead are many others named in the book, to whom nature seemed to promise a very long life. But what should not be recounted without tears is that our lady, the Duchess, is dead as well, and if my mind is troubled over the loss of so many friends and lords who have left me behind in this life of solitude so full of sorrows, it is understandable that I feel far more sorrowful over the death of the Duchess[8] than over those of any of the others, because she was more worthy than all the others, and I was much more obligated to her than to any of them. In order, therefore, not to delay in repaying what I owe to the memory of such an excellent lady as well as the others who no longer live, and prompted also by the threat to my book, I have had it printed and published in such a fashion as the brevity of time has allowed.

And because you had no knowledge of either the Duchess or the others while they were alive (except for Duke Giuliano and the Cardinal of Santa Maria in Portico), in order to acquaint you with them, insofar as I can, after their death, I am sending you this book as a portrait of the court of Urbino, not by the hand of Raphael or Michelangelo, but by that of a lowly man who is capable only of sketching the main lines, without adorning the truth with beautiful colors or making, by means of the art of perspective, what truly is appear to be what it is not. And although I have tried to show with these discussions the qualities and conditions of those who are named herein, I confess that I have not even hinted at, let alone expressed, the virtues of the Duchess, because not only is my style insufficient to express them, but my mind cannot even conceive of them; and if I am censured for this or any other thing worthy of blame (and well do I know that many such things are not lacking in this book), I shall not be contradicting the truth. . . .

3. Others say that since it is so difficult and almost impossible to find a man as perfect as I wish the courtier to be, it is a waste of time to write of him, because it is futile to teach what cannot be learned. To such persons I answer (putting aside any debate about the Intelligible World or Ideas) that I will be content to have erred with Plato, Xenophon, and Cicero, and just as, according to the opinion of these writers, there is the idea of the perfect republic, the perfect king, and the perfect orator, so likewise there is also that of the perfect courtier.[9] And if I have not been able to approximate the image of the latter with my style, then courtiers will find it far less difficult to approximate with their deeds the end and goal I have proposed for them in this book I have written, and if, for all that, they cannot attain the perfection, such as it is, that they have tried to express, the one who comes nearest to it will be the most perfect, just as when many archers shoot at a target and none of them hits the bull's-eye, the one who comes closest to it is, without a doubt, better than the others. There are still others who say that I, using myself as a model, have convinced myself that the qualities I attribute to the courtier are all in me. To such people, I will not deny having attempted to describe all that I would want the courtier to know—and I think that anyone who did not have some knowledge of the things discussed in the book, however erudite he may be, could hardly have written about them—but I am not so lacking in judgment and self-knowledge as to presume to know all that I would wish to know.

Thus, for the present I leave the defense against these accusations, and perhaps against many others, to the consensus of public opinion, because most of the time, the majority, even though lacking perfect knowledge, have instinctively a natural sense for what is good and bad, and without being able to explain why, they enjoy and love one thing while they reject and hate another. Hence, if the book is generally pleasing, I shall take it to be good, and I shall think that it is to survive; if, once again, it does not please, I will take it to be bad and at once believe that it is to be forgotten. And if my accusers are not yet satisfied with this public judgment, then let them be content at least with that of time, which, in the end, reveals the hidden defects of all things, and, by being the father of truth and an impartial judge, is inclined to pronounce a just sentence of life or death on all writing.

BALDESAR CASTIGLIONE

· ❧ ·

Book I

[At the beginning of Book I, Castiglione announces that the book follows classical tradition in the way it recounts what the author was told of the discussion that took place at the court of Urbino.]

2. On the slopes of the Apennines, almost in the center of Italy and toward the Adriatic Sea, sits, as everyone knows, the little city of Urbino, and although it lies among hills which are not, perhaps, as pleasant as some we see in many other places, still Heaven has so greatly favored it that the countryside all around is most fertile and productive, so that, besides the healthiness of the air, everything necessary for human life is found there in abundance. But among the greatest sources of happiness that can be attributed to it, I believe this to be the chief one: that for so long a time, it has always been ruled by the best lords, although it was for a time deprived of them during the universal calamity of the wars in Italy. But without looking any further, we can bear witness to the glorious memory of Duke Federico,[10] who, in his day, was the light of Italy; nor are there lacking numerous and reliable witnesses still living who can testify to his prudence, humanity, justice, liberality, his unconquerable soul, and his military discipline, the principal proof of which lies in his many victories, the capture by siege of impregnable places, the instant readiness of his expeditions, the many times he routed large and very powerful armies with few men, and the fact that he was never the loser in any battle; so that not without reason may we compare him to many famous men of ancient times. This man, among his other praiseworthy deeds, built on the rugged site of Urbino a palace which is, according to many, the most beautiful to be found in all of Italy, and he furnished it not only with what was ordinarily in fashion, such as silver vases, hangings in the richest cloth of gold, silk and other such fabrics, but for decoration he added an infinite number of ancient statues of marble and bronze, unique paintings, and musical instruments of every sort; nor did he want anything there that was not the rarest and most excellent of quality. Then, at very great expense, he collected a large number of the most excellent and rare books in Greek, Latin, and Hebrew, all of which he adorned with gold and silver, considering them to be the supreme excellence of his magnificent palace.

3. Following the natural course of things, this man, who was already sixty-five years old, died as gloriously as he had lived, leaving as his heir his only male child, who was a boy of ten without a mother—that is, Guidobaldo. This boy appeared to be heir to all his father's virtues as well as to his state, and immediately his wondrous nature began to promise so much more than seemed possible to expect from any mortal; so men judged none of Duke Federico's other noteworthy deeds to be greater than having fathered such a son. But Fortune, jealous of such worth, set herself against this glorious beginning with all her might, so that before Duke Guido reached the age of twenty, he fell ill with the gout, which, growing worse with atrocious pains, so crippled all his members that in a short time he could not stand on his feet or move by himself. Thus, one of the fairest and most well-proportioned bodies in the world was deformed and ruined in the flower of its youth. And still not content with this, Fortune opposed him so in his every undertaking that only on rare occasions did he succeed in realizing what he wished to do; and although he was very wise in council and his soul indomitable, it seemed that anything he undertook to do, great or small, dealing with arms or otherwise, always ended in failure. This is attested to by his many and diverse calamities, all of which he always bore with such great strength of mind that his spirit was never overcome by Fortune. On the contrary, scorning her tempests with valiant courage, he lived in sickness as if in health and in adversity as if in great good fortune, with dignity and the esteem of all; so that though infirm in body as he was, he served on the most honorable terms with the Serene Highnesses Kings Alfonso[11] and Ferdinand the Younger[12] of Naples, and later with Pope Alexander VI,[13] as well as the Venetian and Florentine lords. Once Julius[14] ascended to the papacy, he was made Captain of the Church and, at that time, following his usual style, he managed, above all, to fill his house with very noble and talented gentlemen, with whom he lived on the most familiar terms, finding pleasure in their company, in which the pleasure he gave others was not less than he received from them, being so learned in Latin and Greek and combining affability and charm with the knowledge of so vast a number of things. Besides this, so much did his greatness of soul spur him on that even though he could not personally perform deeds of chivalry as he had formerly done, he still took the greatest pleasure in seeing them performed by others; and by his words, now criticizing, now praising each man according to his merits, he clearly demonstrated how much judgment he had in these matters. As a result, in jousts, tournaments, riding, handling of all kinds of arms, as well as in festivals, games, musical performances, in short, in all the

exercises befitting noble cavaliers, everyone tried to prove himself deserving of being judged worthy of such noble company as his.

4. All the hours of the day, therefore, were divided among honorable and pleasant exercises both of the body and the mind, but because, owing to his infirmity, the Duke usually went to sleep quite early after supper, everyone usually repaired to wherever the Duchess Elisabetta Gonzaga was at that hour and where Signora Emilia Pia[15] was also to be found, who, being endowed with such lively wit and judgment, as you know, seemed the mistress of all, and all seemed to take on wisdom and worth from her. Here, then, courteous discussions and honest witticisms were heard, and on everyone's face a joyous good humor was seen displayed, so much so that this house could be called the very abode of gaiety; nor do I believe that the sweetness derived from dear and beloved company could be enjoyed more in any other place than it once was there, for, leaving aside how great an honor it was for each of us to serve such a lord as the one I have described, we all felt enormous pleasure arise within our hearts whenever we came into the presence of the Duchess. And it seemed that this was a chain that held all of us united in love in such a way that never was there more harmony of will or cordial friendship among brothers than that which prevailed among all of us there.

The same was true among the ladies with whom one had the most free and honest relationships, for each of us was permitted to talk, sit, joke, and laugh with anyone he pleased, but so great was the reverence felt for the wishes of the Duchess, that this same liberty was also a great restraint, nor was there anyone who did not judge it to be the greatest pleasure in the world to be able to please her and the greatest pain to displease her. For this reason, the most decorous of customs were joined there with the greatest of liberty, and games and laughter in her presence were seasoned not only with witty jests but with a gracious and stern dignity; for that modesty and grandeur which regulated all the acts, words, and gestures of the Duchess, in jest and laughter, caused even someone who had never seen her before to recognize her as a very great lady. And thus in making an impression on those around her, it seemed that she tempered all to her own image and quality, so that everyone tried to imitate her style, deriving, as it were, a standard of fine behavior from the presence of so virtuous a lady, whose best qualities I do not intend to narrate at this point, this not being my aim, since they are quite well known to all the world and much more than I could express either with my tongue or my pen; and those which may have remained somewhat concealed, Fortune, as if the admirer of such rare virtues, decided to reveal through many adversities and the sting of misfortunes, in order to demonstrate that in the tender breast of a woman accompanied by singular beauty, there may exist prudence and strength of spirit and all those virtues that even in the sternest of men are most rare.

5. But leaving this aside, let me say that the custom of all the gentlemen of the house was to go immediately after dinner to the Duchess, where, amid the pleasing festivities and the music and dancing which were customary, excellent topics for discussion were often proposed and sometimes ingenious games (now at the request of one, now of another) in which, under various pretexts, those present revealed their thoughts allegorically to whomever they wished. Sometimes other debates would arise on various topics or there would be a sharp exchange of witty retorts; and often they made up "emblems," as we call them today. And great pleasure was taken in such marvelous discussions, the house being full, as I have said, of the most noble talents, among which, as you know, the most celebrated were Signor Ottaviano Fregoso; Messer Federico, his brother;[16] the Magnifico Giuliano de' Medici; Messer Pietro Bembo;[17] Messer Cesare Gonzaga;[18] Count Ludovico da Canossa;[19] Signor Gaspar Pallavicino;[20] Signor Ludovico Pio;[21] Signor Morello da Ortona;[22] Pietro da Napoli;[23] Messer Roberto da Bari;[24] and countless other very noble gentlemen. Besides these, there were many others who, although they did not, as a rule, remain there permanently, spent most of their time there, such as Messer Bernardo Bibbiena; the Unico Aretino;[25] Giancristoforo Romano;[26] Pietro Monte;[27] Terpandro;[28] and Messer Niccolò Frisio.[29] So that there was always to be found gathered there at court agreeable men and the finest kind of every talent to be found in Italy.[30]

* * *

[The arrival of Pope Julius II and his entourage provides the pretext for the discussions recorded in Book I of *The Courtier*.]

6. . . . Thus, the day after the departure of the Pope, the company had retired at the usual hour to the customary place, and the Duchess, after much pleasant discussion, wished for Signora Emilia to begin the games; and she, after having declined the task several times, spoke as follows: "Madam, since it is your wish for me to be the one to begin the games for this evening, and since I cannot rightly fail to obey you, I have decided to propose a game for which I think I shall have little blame and even less work; and this will be for everyone to propose a game according to his own liking that has not yet been played; and then we will choose the one which seems most worthy of being played in this company."

And speaking thus, she turned to Signor Gaspar Pallavicino, enjoining him to tell his choice, and he immediately replied: "It is for you, Madam, to tell yours first."

Signora Emilia said: "I have already told it to you, but now you, Duchess, bid him to obey."

Then the Duchess said, laughing: "So that everyone will be bound to obey you, I make you my deputy, and give you all my authority."

* * *

[The group considers and rejects a number of suggested pastimes.]

12. Everyone was waiting for Signora Emilia's answer; without saying a word to Bembo, she turned to Federico Fregoso and asked him to suggest his game, and he immediately began in this fashion: "Signora, I would like to be allowed, as sometimes happens, to submit to someone else's judgment, since I, for one, will approve with pleasure any of the games proposed by these gentlemen, because truly it seems to me that all of them would be amusing; still, so as not to break the rules of the game, I will say that whoever wishes to praise our court—apart from the merits of our Duchess, which alone with her divine virtue would be enough to lift the basest souls in the world from earth to heaven—might well say, without any suspicion of flattery, that in all of Italy, it would be difficult to find an equal number of cavaliers as distinguished and as excellent in a variety of things beyond their principal profession of chivalry as are found here; on that account, if in any place there are men who deserve to be called good courtiers and who know how to judge what belongs to the perfection of courtiership, it is only right to think that they are here present. So then, in order to silence those many fools, who through their presumptuousness and ineptitude believe they can acquire the name of good courtiers, I would like our game for this evening to be this—that one of this company be elected and to this person be given the task of forming with words a perfect courtier, describing all the conditions and special qualities that are required of anyone who deserves this name; and that everyone be allowed to contradict those things which do not seem appropriate to him, just as in the schools of the philosophers it is permitted to raise objections to anyone maintaining a thesis."

Messer Federico was continuing with his discourse, when Signora Emilia, interrupting him, said: "This, if it pleases the Duchess, will be our game for now."

The Duchess answered: "I am pleased."

Then nearly all of those present began to say, both to the Duchess and among themselves, that this was the finest game that could be played; and without waiting for each other's answers, they all pressed

Signora Emilia to decide who should be the one to begin. Turning to the Duchess, she said: "Madam, will you command the one who pleases you most to assume this task, for I do not wish, through choosing one rather than another, to appear to decide which person I judge more capable than the others in this matter, and in so doing offend anyone."

The Duchess replied: "Please make the choice yourself, and take care not to set an example for the others by disobeying, so that they are even less obedient."

13. Then Signora Emilia, laughing, said to Count Ludovico da Canossa: "In order, therefore, not to lose more time, you, Count, will be the one to take on this task in the way Messer Federico has said; and certainly not because we think that you are so good a courtier that you know what befits one, but because, if you say anything to the contrary, as we hope you will do, the game will be all the more amusing, because everyone will have something to which he may respond; whereas, if another who has more knowledge than you had this task, nothing that he said could be contradicted, because he would speak the truth, and thus the game would be tedious."

The Count answered at once: "Signora, there could be no danger that opposition would be lacking against whoever tells the truth, so long as you are present here," and once everyone had laughed awhile at his repartee, he went on: "But truly, milady, I would most willingly escape this task, since it seems too difficult for me, and I well know to be true what you have in jest said of me; namely, that I do not know what befits a good courtier. And I do not seek to prove this by any other testimony than by the fact that since I do not act like a good courtier, it can be judged that I have no knowledge of the subject; hence, I believe that I am less blameworthy, since, without a doubt, it is worse not to wish to act well than not to know how to do so. Still, since it so pleases you that I undertake this charge, I cannot, nor do I wish to, refuse it, so as not to contravene our regulations or your judgment, which I value far more than my own."

Then Messer Cesare Gonzaga said: "Since it is already rather late, and we have many other kinds of amusements at hand, perhaps we would do well to postpone this discussion until tomorrow and give the Count time to think about what he is going to say, for, truly, it is a difficult thing to improvise on such a subject."

The Count replied: "I do not wish to be like the man who having stripped down to his doublet, jumped less far than he had with his cloak on. And so, as far as I am concerned, it is fortunate that the hour is so late, because due to the brevity of time, I shall be forced to say very little, and not having given this matter any thought, I will be excused and allowed to say, without censure, anything that comes to my mind. Therefore, in order not to bear this burden of obligation on my shoulders any longer, let me say that in all things it is so difficult to know what true perfection is that it is nearly impossible, and this is due to the diversity of our opinions. Thus, there are many who welcome a man who talks a great deal, and they will call him pleasing; some will prefer a more modest man; others an active and restless man; still others someone who shows calm and deliberation; and so everyone praises or blames according to his own opinion, always hiding a vice with the name of the corresponding virtue, or a virtue with the name of the corresponding vice; for example, calling an arrogant man frank, a modest man uninteresting, a simple-minded man good, a rascal discreet, and so on and so forth. Yet, I do think that there is perfection for everything, even though it be hidden, and that this perfection can be revealed with reasonable arguments by someone who has knowledge of the subject. And because, as I have said, the truth often remains hidden and I cannot boast of having this knowledge, I can only praise the sort of courtier I most value and approve to what seems to my weak judgment to be closest to the truth; and you may follow my judgment if it seems good to you, or you may well hold to your own, if it differs from mine. Nor will I contend that mine is better than yours, for not only can you think one thing and I another, but I myself may sometimes think one thing and sometimes another.

14. "And so, I would want our courtier to be of noble birth and good family, because it matters much less for the common man if he fails to perform virtuously than for a nobleman, who, should he stray from the path of his ancestors, stains the family name and not only fails to achieve anything but loses what has already been achieved. For nobility is like a bright lamp which makes manifest and visible both good deeds and bad ones, kindling and spurring on to virtue as much for fear of infamy as for hope of praise; and since the deeds of the common men do not show forth such noble brilliance, they lack both that stimulus and that fear of dishonor, nor do they feel obligated to go beyond what their ancestors have done, while to the nobles it seems blameworthy not to attain at least the standard set them by their forebears. Thus, in general, both in arms and in other virtuous actions, those who are most distinguished are of noble birth, because Nature has implanted in all things that hidden seed which gives a certain strength and quality of its own essence to all that arises from it, making it similar to itself—as we see not only in breeds of horses and other animals, but also in trees, the shoots of which

almost always resemble the trunk; and if they sometimes degenerate, the fault lies with the bad farmer. And so it happens with men, who, if they are cultivated and well raised, are nearly always similar to those from whom they come, and often they are better; but if they lack someone to look after them properly, they become wild and never attain their full growth. It is true that be it through the goodwill of the stars or Nature, some are born endowed with so many graces that it seems that they were not born at all but rather that some god, with his own hands, fashioned and adorned them with all the graces of mind and body; similarly, there are as many to be found who are so inept and crude that it is hard not to conclude that Nature brought them into the world simply out of spite and mockery. Just as the latter, usually, will bear little fruit even with unending diligence and good training, so the former with minimal effort arrive at the summit of excellence.

"And to give you an example, see Signor Don Ippolito d'Este, Cardinal of Ferrara,[31] who was accompanied at birth with so many good qualities that this person, his appearance, his words, and all his movements are so much in conformity with this grace of his that although he is young, he carries among the most venerable prelates such a grave authority that he seems more ready to teach than needful of learning. Likewise, in conversing with men and women of every sort, in play, in laughter, and in jest, he possesses a certain sweetness and such gracious manners that it is inevitable that anyone who speaks with him or even lays eyes on him becomes eternally fond of him.

"But returning to our subject, I say that between this excellent grace and that senseless stupidity, a means can be found; and those who are not so perfectly endowed by nature can with study and hard work polish and, in great part, correct their natural defects. So then, besides being of noble birth, I should like the courtier to be fortunate in this respect, too, and to receive from Nature not only the talent and beauty of person and face but also that certain grace which we call an 'air' that will make him immediately agreeable and charming to whoever sees him; and let this be an adornment which harmonizes with and accompanies all his actions, giving the promise from his outward appearance of being someone worthy of the company and favor of every great lord."

15. Then, without waiting any longer, Signor Gaspar Pallavicino said: "So that our game may have the prescribed form and that it will not appear that we have so little esteem for the authority given us to oppose what is set forth, let me say that to me this nobility of birth does not seem all that necessary in the courtier; and if I thought I were saying something new to any of us, I would cite numerous examples of people

born with noble blood, who are full of vices, and, on the contrary, many lowborn individuals who have made their posterity illustrious through their virtue. And if what you said just now is true, that is, that there is in all things that hidden force of the first seed, then we should all be of the same condition by reason of having had the same origin, nor would one person be more noble than another. But I believe that there are many other causes for our diversity and the degrees of elevation and lowliness, among which I judge Fortune to be the chief one, because over all the things of this world, we see her hold sway and, as it seems, amuse herself in often raising to the heavens someone who seems to be without merit and in burying in the depths those most worthy of being exalted. I can attest to what you say about the happiness of those who are endowed at birth with blessings of the mind and body, but this we find in the humble as well as the noble, because Nature does not make such subtle distinctions; rather, as I have said, often the loftiest gifts of Nature can be seen in the most humble persons. Therefore, since this nobility is acquired neither by talent nor by strength or skill, and more often results from the merits of our ancestors than from our own, it seems to me most strange to insist that if the parents of our courtier are of humble birth, then all his good qualities are ruined, and that those other qualities you have named would not quite suffice to bring him to the height of perfection; these qualities being talent, beauty of countenance, personal appearance, and the grace which will make him at first sight most pleasing to everyone."

16. Then Count Ludovico replied: "I do not deny that these same virtues can rule in the man of low birth as in the man of noble family, but in order not to repeat what we have already said along with many other arguments which might be advanced in praise of nobility, which is always honored by everyone, because it stands to reason that good should be born from good, and since it is our purpose to create a courtier who has no defects whatsoever and possesses all that is praiseworthy, I feel it is necessary to have him be of noble birth, not only for many other reasons but also for public approval, which immediately sides with nobility. For, given that there are two courtiers, who have not previously given any impression of themselves through either good deeds or bad, no sooner than the one is understood to have been born a gentlemen and the other not, the one who is lowborn will be much less valued by everyone than the noble, and will need much more time and greater effort to impress upon the minds of men the good opinion of himself that the other will have given in an instant and solely by being a gentleman. And everyone can easily comprehend how important these impressions

are, for, to speak of ourselves, we have seen men arrive at this house who, though rather stupid and very awkward, have had the reputation throughout Italy of being great courtiers; and although they were in the end found out, they still deceived us for many days and maintained in our minds that opinion of themselves which they already found imprinted there, even though they behaved in accordance with their little worth. We have also seen others who at first enjoyed little esteem, and who, in the end, succeeded brilliantly.

"And the causes of these errors are diverse, including the obstinacy of lords, who, in the hope of achieving miracles, sometimes resolve to show favor to someone who seems to them to deserve disfavor. And then again they too are often deceived, but since princes always have countless imitators, their favor produces a great fame which, for the most part, our judgments will normally follow. And if we discover something which seems contrary to common opinion, we fear we must be deceiving ourselves and we always expect a revelation of sorts, because we think that such universal opinions must somehow be founded on the truth and arise from reasonable causes; moreover, our minds are very quick to love and hate, as can be seen in the public combats or games or in any other sort of competition, where the spectators for no obvious reason will often become fond of one of the parties, showing the greatest desire that his choice should win and the other lose. Then, as for the general opinion concerning a man's qualities, it is good or ill repute that moves our minds to one of these two passions. Hence, it happens that, for the most part, we judge on the basis of love or hate. So you see, then, how important this first impression is, and how anyone who wishes to win the rank and name of a good courtier must strive from the start to make a favorable impression on princes.

17. "But to come to some particulars, I believe that the principal and true profession of the courtier must be that of arms, which, above all, I would have him exercise with passion; and also let him stand out from all the rest as being bold and valiant and faithful to whomever he serves. And the fame of these good qualities will be acquired by exercising them whenever and wherever possible, inasmuch as failure to do so will incur the greatest blame. And just as among women chastity, once sullied, is never restored, so the fame of a gentleman who bears arms, if ever in the slightest way he sullies himself through cowardice or some other disgrace, always remains contemptible to the world and full of ignominy. Therefore, the more our courtier excels in this art, the more worthy of praise he will be, although I do not think it necessary for him to have the perfect professional knowledge of things and the other

qualities that are appropriate to a military leader. However, since the subject of what makes a great captain might put us on too rough a sea, we shall be content for the courtier to show complete loyalty and undaunted spirit and for him always to be seen to have these qualities. For often a man's courage is known from small things rather than from great ones. And often in the face of grave dangers, and where there are many witnesses, there are some men who, although their heart may stop dead out of fear, still spurred on by the fear of shame or the company present, press forward with eyes shut, as it were, and do their duty, God knows how; and in things that matter little and where it seems they can avoid putting themselves in danger without being observed, they happily allow themselves to settle for what is safe. But those men who, even when they think they will not be observed, or seen, or recognized by anyone, show courage and avoid nothing, however slight, for which they could be blamed, have that quality of spirit that we are seeking in our courtier.

"We do not, however, want him to make a show of being so fierce that he is forever boasting of what he has done, declaring that he has taken his cuirass for his wife, and threatening with such fierce looks as we have often seen Berto[32] do, for to such as these one may say what a clever lady in noble company jokingly once said to a certain man (whom I do not now want to name), whom she invited to dance in order to honor him, and who not only refused her offer but who would not even listen to music or take part in the many other entertainments offered him, declaring all along that such frivolous things were not his business. And when, at length, the lady asked him, 'What then is your business?' he answered with a scowl, 'Combat.' The lady replied at once: 'Well, I should think it a good thing now that since you are not away at war or engaged in fighting at the moment, you have yourself well greased and, together with all your armor, put back into storage in some closet, so that you will not grow any rustier than you already are!' And thus, with great laughter among those present, she ridiculed him in his stupid presumption. Therefore, the man we are seeking should be extremely fierce, harsh, and always among the first wherever the enemy is seen, and everywhere else he should be humane, modest, and reserved, fleeing, above all, ostentation, and the impudent praise of himself, by which a man always arouses hatred and disgust in whoever hears him."

18. "And I," replied Signor Gasparo, "I have known few men who are excellent in anything whatsoever who do not praise themselves, and it seems to me that it is only right that they be permitted to do so, because anyone who feels himself to be of some worth and sees that his

deeds are ignored is offended that his own worth is buried, and he cannot help disclosing it in some way lest he feel cheated of the honor that is the true reward of virtuous labors. Thus, among the ancient writers, rarely does someone of great worth abstain from praising himself. Those who praise themselves even though they lack merit really are intolerable, but we do not presume that our courtier will be of that type."

Then the Count said: "If you noticed, I blamed extravagant and indiscriminate praise of oneself, but certainly, as you say, one must not have a bad opinion of a worthy man who praises himself modestly; on the contrary, one must accept it as better evidence than if it came from another's mouth. What I am saying, then, is that whoever praises himself in a correct manner and in doing so does not generate annoyance or envy in those who hear him is, indeed, a discreet man, and he deserves the praise of others besides the praise he gives himself, because this is a very difficult matter."

Then Signor Gasparo said: "This you have to teach us."

The Count answered: "Among the ancient writers, there is no lack of those who taught this, but in my opinion it all depends on saying things in such a way that it does not seem they are spoken with that end in mind, but are rather so appropriate that one cannot help saying them, and on always giving the impression of avoiding self-praise while practicing it—but not in the manner of those braggarts who open their mouths and let the words pour out at random. As one of our friends did the other day who when, after he had his thigh run through by a lance in Pisa, he said that he thought a fly had bitten him; and another who said that he did not keep a mirror in his room because when he got angry his appearance became so frightful that seeing himself in the mirror he would frighten himself to death."

Everyone laughed at this point, but Messer Cesare Gonzaga added: "What are you laughing at? Do you not know that Alexander the Great, upon hearing a certain philosopher's opinion that there were countless other worlds, began to weep, and when asked why, responded: 'Because I have not yet conquered even one'—as if he had had the intention of taking them all? Does it not seem to you that this is even a greater boast than the one about the fly's bite?"

Then the Count said: "And Alexander was a greater man than the one who mentioned the fly. But truly one has to pardon excellent men when they presume too much about themselves, because a man who must achieve great things must himself have the courage to do them and must have confidence in himself. And he should not be abject or cowardly but modest, rather, in his words, demonstrating that he presumes less of himself than he accomplishes, provided that such presumption does not turn into foolhardiness."

19. Then the Count paused briefly, and Messer Bernardo Bibbiena said, laughing: "I remember you said a short time ago that this courtier of ours should be naturally endowed with a beautiful face and person and with a kind of grace which makes him attractive. As for grace and beauty of face, I am quite certain I have it, and it is for that reason so many ladies, as you know, love me madly; but when it comes to the beauty of my person, I am rather doubtful, especially these legs of mine, which in truth do not seem to me as suitable as I would wish; I remain, however, quite content with my chest and the rest. So please explain a little more in detail what shape of body one should have, so that I can extricate myself from this doubt and put my mind at ease."

After some laughter at this, the Count added: "Certainly that grace of countenance you can honestly be said to possess, nor will I adduce any other example than this one to make clear what that grace is, because without a doubt we do see that your aspect is very agreeable and pleasing to everyone, even if your features are not very delicate—but then again, there is something both virile and graceful about it; and this is a quality found in many different types of faces. And I want the appearance of our courtier to be of this sort, not so soft and feminine as many try to have, who not only curl their hair and pluck their eyebrows, but dress themselves in those ways that the most lascivious and shameful women of the world adopt. They appear so tender and languid in the way they walk, stand, and in all their gestures that their limbs seem about to fall off, and they pronounce their words so limply that it seems they are about to expire on the spot, and the more they find themselves with men of standing, the more they use such devices. Since Nature did not make them into the ladies they want to seem to be, these men should be treated not as good women but as common whores and driven not only from the courts of great lords but also from the society of all noble men.

20. "Coming then to the qualities of one's body, let me say that it is enough for it to be neither too small nor too large, because both of these conditions bring with them a certain scornful wonder, and men of this sort are stared at as if they were monstrous things; however, having to choose between the two extremes, then it is better to be a bit small than to be of unreasonable size, for men so huge of body, apart from the fact that they are often found to have dull minds, are also unsuited for every exercise requiring agility, which I think is most important for the courtier. So, then, I would like him to have a good build and his limbs to be well proportioned, and to show strength and agility and ease of move-

ment, and to know all the physical exercises befitting a man of war; and in this, I think his first duty must be to know how to handle well every kind of weapon on foot and on horse, and to know the advantages of each kind, and especially to be well acquainted with those arms ordinarily used among gentlemen, because apart from making use of them in war (where perhaps so many subtleties are not necessary), there often arise differences between one gentleman and another, resulting in duels, and very often the weapons used are those which are at hand at the moment. Hence, knowledge of them is a very safe thing. Nor am I indeed one of those who say that the skill is forgotten at the moment of need, since certainly whosoever loses his skill at such times shows that he has already lost his heart and head out of fear.

21. "I also believe that knowing how to wrestle is of considerable importance, because it often accompanies the use of weapons on foot. And then both for himself and for his friends, he must understand the quarrels and differences that can arise and should be capable of seizing the advantage, and in all this, he should always show both courage and prudence; nor should he be anxious to get into such fights, except insofar as he is compelled by his honor, for apart from the great danger that uncertain fate carries with it, whoever rushes into such things precipitously and without urgent cause deserves the greatest reproach, even if he is successful at it. However, when one finds oneself to be so involved that he cannot withdraw without reproach, he must be very deliberate in both the preliminaries to the duel and in the duel itself, and always show readiness and courage; nor must he do as those who spend their time in quibbling and arguing over points of honor and, when they have the choice of weapons, choose those which can neither cut nor pierce, and arm themselves as if they were expecting to face a cannonade, and thinking it enough not to be defeated, remain constantly on the defensive and on the retreat, exhibiting extreme cowardice, and in this way making themselves the laughingstock of children, like those two men from Ancona who, a short time ago, fought a duel at Perugia and made everyone who saw them laugh."

"And who were they?" said Signor Gasparo Pallavicino.

Messer Cesare answered: "Two cousins."

Then the Count said: "In their fighting, they appeared to be true brothers." Then, he added: "Weapons are also often used in times of peace in various sports, and gentlemen are seen in such public spectacles in the presence of the people, ladies, and great lords. Therefore, I would like our courtier to be a perfect horseman in every kind of saddle, and besides having a knowledge of horses and what pertains to riding, he should put every effort and great diligence into going slightly beyond others in all things, so that he may always be recognized as excellent in comparison to others. And just as we read of Alcibiades, who surpassed all the peoples among whom he lived, and each one in whatever they considered themselves best at, so this courtier of ours should surpass all others, and each one in whatever is his special profession. And since it is the particular excellence of the Italians to ride well with the rein and to manage spirited horses with special skill, to tilt and joust, then he must be among the best of the Italians in this. In tournaments, in holding a position, in trying to overcome obstacles, he should compare with the best of the French; in casting lances, in bullfighting, and in casting spears and darts, he should be excellent in comparison to the Spaniards. But, above all, let his every movement be accompanied by a certain good judgment and grace, if he wishes to deserve that universal recognition which is so highly valued.

22. "There are also many other sports, which although not directly dependent upon weapons still have many connections with them and require rather significant manly exertion; and chief among these, it appears to me, is the hunt, because it has a certain similarity to war; and in addition to this, it is the true pleasure of great lords and suitable for a man at court, and we know that it was also quite in fashion among the ancients. It is also appropriate for the courtier to know how to swim, jump, run, throw stones, for, besides the usefulness one might derive from this in war, it is very often necessary to show one's ability in such things in order to enhance one's reputation, especially with the crowd, with whom one must always come to terms. One more noble sport and most suitable for a man at court is the game of tennis, which displays the disposition of the body and the quickness and nimbleness of every member, and all the other qualities needed to play nearly every other sport. Nor do I consider vaulting on horseback to be less praiseworthy, which, although it is tiring and difficult, makes more than anything else a man agile and skillful; and besides its usefulness, if such ability is accompanied by grace, it makes, in my opinion, a finer spectacle than any of the others.

"If, then, our courtier is more than ordinarily skilled in these sports, I think that he should give up the others, such as doing cartwheels, tightrope walking, and the like, which have something of the buffoon in them and are rather unsuitable for a gentleman. But since one cannot always be engaged in such strenuous activities (apart from the fact that insistence satiates and eliminates the admiration that is attached to rare things), we must always give variety to our lives with diverse activities.

Therefore, I would like the courtier sometimes to descend to more calm and restful games, and to avoid envy and enter into pleasant conversations with everyone by doing all that others do, without, nevertheless, ever departing from commendable conduct and always following that good judgment which will not allow him to become involved in anything foolish. Let him laugh, joke, banter, play, dance, but in a manner that always reflects his geniality and discretion, and let him be graceful in everything he says or does."

23. "Certainly," Messer Cesare Gonzaga then said, "no one should interrupt the course of this discussion, but if I were to remain silent, I would not be taking advantage of my privilege to speak and satisfy my desire to learn something. May I be pardoned if I ask a question instead of speaking in opposition, for I believe I may be allowed to do so after the example set by our Messer Bernardo, who, in his excessive desire to be considered a handsome man, has broken the rules of our game by asking a question instead of saying something in opposition to what has been said."

"You see," the Duchess then said, "how from a single error many may follow. Therefore, whoever breaks the rules and sets a bad example, as Messer Bernardo has done, deserves to be punished not only for his own failure but also for that of the others."

Then Messer Cesare answered: "So then, Madam, I shall be exempt from punishment, since Messer Bernardo is to be punished both for his own error and for mine."

"On the contrary," said the Duchess, "both of you must receive a double punishment: he for his own failure and for having led you to fail; you for your own failure and for having imitated one who failed."

"Madam," answered Messer Cesare, "as yet, I have not failed; therefore, in order to leave all this punishment to Messer Bernardo alone, I shall remain silent."

And he was already silent, when Signora Emilia, laughing, said: "Say whatever you please, for, with the permission of the Duchess, I pardon both the one who has failed and the one who is going to fail in such a small way."

"So be it, then," the Duchess went on, "but take care not to deceive yourself by thinking it is perhaps more meritorious to be clement than to be just, for forgiving too easily the one who fails injures the one who does not fail. Nevertheless, I would not have my present austerity in finding fault with your indulgence to cause us to lose the opportunity of hearing Messer Cesare's question."

And so, having been given a sign by the Duchess and Signora Emilia, Messer Cesare said at once:

24. "If I remember well, it seems to me, Count, that this evening you have repeated several times that the courtier has to accompany with grace his actions, gestures, habits, in short his every movement; and it seems to me that you consider this to be the seasoning for everything, without which all the other properties and good qualities are of little worth.[33] And I truly believe that everyone would easily allow himself to be persuaded of this, because, by the very meaning of the word, it can be said that he who has grace finds grace with others. But since you have said that this is often a gift of nature and the heavens, and even that when it is not so perfect it can be much enhanced by care and hard work, those men who are born as fortunate and as rich in such treasure as some we know, it seems to me, have little need in this of another teacher, because that benign favor from heaven raises them almost in spite of themselves higher than they might have desired and makes them both pleasing and admirable to everyone. I am not, therefore, discussing this, since it is not in our power to acquire it by ourselves. But regarding those who by nature have only so much that their actions can be graceful only through hard work, industry, and care, I would like to know by means of what art, with what discipline, and with what means they can acquire this grace, both in physical exercise, in which you consider it to be necessary, and also in all the other things they say or do. Therefore, since you have, by praising this quality so highly, generated in all of us, I believe, an ardent desire to pursue it, according to the task set before you by Lady Emilia, you are still obliged to satisfy that desire by instructing us about it."

25. "I am not obliged," said the Count, "to teach you how to become graceful or anything else, but only to show you what a perfect courtier should be. Nor would I take on the task of teaching you how to acquire this perfection, especially since a little while ago I said that the courtier should know how to wrestle, vault, and so many other things, which, never having learned them myself, I realize that you all know quite well just how I would be able to teach them to you. Let it suffice to say that just as a good soldier knows how to tell the blacksmith what shape, style, and quality his armor must have and yet would not know how to teach him to make it or to hammer or temper it, just so I, perhaps, shall be able to tell you what a perfect courtier should be but not be able to teach you what you have to do to become one. Yet, in order to give you an answer to your question insofar as it is in my power, and given the fact that it is almost proverbial that grace is not

learned, let me say that anyone who wishes to be graceful in physical exercises (presupposing first of all that he is not by nature incapable) must begin early and learn the principles from the best teachers. How important this seemed to King Philip of Macedonia can be seen from the fact that it was Aristotle, so famous a philosopher and perhaps the greatest the world has ever known, that he wanted to teach the first elements of letters to his son Alexander. And among the men we know today, consider how well and gracefully Signor Galeazzo Sanseverino, Grand Equerry of France,[34] performs all physical exercises, and this because, besides the natural inclination he has for this, he has made every effort to learn from good teachers and always to have near him excellent men, taking from each of them the best they have to offer. Thus, just as in wrestling, vaulting, and in the handling of many kinds of weapons he took our Messer Pietro Monte as a guide, who is, as you know, the only true master of every kind of strength and agility that can be learned, so too in riding, jousting, and whatever other activity, he has always kept before his eyes the men known to be most perfect in those professions.

26. "Anyone, therefore, who would like to be a good pupil, must, besides doing things well, always take great care to resemble his master, and, if it is possible, to transform himself into his master. And when he feels that he has made good progress, he will find it very useful to observe different men of the same profession, and governing himself with the good judgment that must always be his guide, he should choose various qualities now from one man and now from another. And just as the bee in the green meadows goes about among the tall grass robbing the nectar from the flowers, so our courtier must steal this grace from those who seem to have it and from each that part which is most commendable— not doing as a friend of ours, whom all of you know, who thought himself to be much like King Ferdinand the Younger of Aragon and took care to imitate him in nothing other than in the way he frequently would raise his head, twisting a corner of his mouth, a habit which the King had contracted through illness. And there are many men like this who think it is enough, if they could only resemble a great man in some one thing; and often they choose the man's only bad habit.

"But having already thought often about the source of this grace, and leaving aside those who have received it from their stars, I have discovered a universal rule, which in this matter seems to apply more than any other in all human actions, whether they be said or done: that is, to avoid affectation as much as possible as if it were a rough and dangerous reef, and (to coin a new term for it, perhaps) to practice in all things a certain *sprezzatura* or nonchalance,[35] which conceals all signs of artistry and makes whatever one does or says seem effortless and unstudied. I believe that grace is truly derived from this, because everyone knows the difficulty of accomplishing well something which is difficult, and for this reason facility in such things generates the greatest wonder;[36] and, on the other hand, to labor over something or, as we say, "to pull your hair out" over something, reveals the greatest lack of grace and causes everything, no matter what its worth may be, to be considered of little value.

"Therefore, what does not seem to be art may be called true art; nor must one take more care in anything than in concealing it, because if it is exposed, this discredits a man completely and causes him to be held in slight esteem. I remember having once read about certain excellent orators of antiquity who, among their other clever accomplishments, tried to make everyone believe that they had no knowledge of letters, and, hiding their knowledge, they made their orations appear to be composed in a most simple manner and according to what nature and truth offered them rather than art and effort; for had their skill been recognized, it would have created fear in the minds of the people that they were being deceived by it. So you see how art and intense effort, once it is revealed, deprive everything of grace. Who among you does not laugh when our Messer Pierpaolo[37] dances the way he does with those hops and skips of his, legs rigid and on tiptoes, never moving his head, as if he were a stick of wood, and all with such care that he actually appears to be counting his steps? What eye is so blind as not to see in this the lack of grace in affectation and not see the grace of that easy manner (for in reference to bodily movements many call it that) found in many of the men and women present here, who in their manner of speaking or laughing or posture show that they do not care and appear to be thinking more about everything else but that, so as to make anyone watching them believe that they neither know how nor are capable of making a mistake?"

* * *

[After a brief discussion of affectation, the Count observes that affectation is detrimental in all pursuits, both military and cultural, and that "this excellence—which is the opposite of affectation, and which, at the moment, we are calling *sprezzatura* or nonchalance—besides being the real source from which grace springs, brings with it another adornment which, when it accomplishes any human action, however small, not only discloses at once how much the person knows who does it, but often causes it to be judged much greater than it actually is, since it impresses upon the minds of the onlookers the opinion that he who performs well with so much facility must possess even greater skill than this, and that if he were to devote care and effort to what he does, he could do it far better." This discussion is followed by the conclusion that the courtier must be able to express himself gracefully and must be knowledgeable. They debate whether or not Tuscan is the preferred linguistic model. Then the Count returns to the subject of grace and the cultivation of the soul.]

42. "But, besides goodness, I think that the true and principal adornment of the mind is, for everyone, letters, although the French recognize only the nobility of arms and consider all the rest worthless, so that not only do they not value learning but they abhor it and hold all men of letters in contempt, believing that it is a great insult to call anyone a scholar."

Then the Magnifico Giuliano responded: "What you are saying is true—that this error has prevailed now for a long time among the French; but if kind fate wills that Monseigneur d'Angoulême[38] succeeds to the crown as is hoped, then I believe that just as the glory of arms now flourishes and shines forth in France, so also must that of letters flourish there with supreme elegance, because not long ago, when I was at that court, I saw this lord, and it seemed to me that, besides the disposition of his body and the beauty of his face, he had in his bearing such greatness—yet accompanied with a certain gracious humanity—that it made the realm of France seem rather insignificant compared to him. I have heard since then from many gentlemen, both French and Italian, much about his most noble manners, his greatness of spirit, his valor and liberality, and I was told, among other things, that he loved and esteemed letters in the highest degree and held all men of letters in the highest regard; and that he condemned the French themselves for being so opposed to this profession, especially since they have in their midst a university as noble as that of Paris, which is frequented by students from all over."

Then the Count said: "It is a great wonder that at such a tender age, guided solely by natural instinct, against the usual custom of his country, he on his own should have chosen such a good path; and since subjects always follow the customs of their superiors, it may be that, as you say, the French will yet come to esteem letters for their true worth, which they can be easily persuaded to do if they will listen to reason, since nothing is more naturally desired by men, or more characteristic of them, than knowledge, and it is great folly to say or believe that knowledge is not always a good thing.

43. "And if I could speak with them or with others who were of an opinion contrary to mine, I would try to show them how useful and necessary to our life and dignity letters are, for they were bestowed upon men by God as a supreme gift; nor would I lack examples of a great many military commanders of ancient times, who joined the glory of letters to their courage in arms. For, as you know, Alexander[39] held Homer in such veneration that he always kept the *Iliad* by his bed, and he gave the greatest attention not only to these studies but to philosophical speculations as well under the instruction of Aristotle.[40] Alcibiades[41] increased and enhanced his good qualities through letters and the teachings of Socrates.[42] The attention that Caesar gave to studies is also witnessed by those divinely written works of his which have survived. Scipio Africanus,[43] it is said, always had the book of Xenophon in his hands, wherein a perfect king under the name of Cyrus is described.[44] I could tell you of Lucullus, Sulla, Pompey, Brutus,[45] and many other Romans and Greeks, but I shall only mention so excellent a commander as Hannibal,[46] who was by nature fierce and a stranger to humanity, treacherous and contemptuous of both men and gods, but who had, nonetheless, the rudiments of letters and knowledge of Greek. And, if I am not mistaken, it seems to me I read once that he even left a book which he himself wrote in Greek.

"But to tell you this is superfluous, for I am well aware that you all know how the French deceive themselves into thinking that letters are harmful to arms. You know that the true stimulus of great and bold deeds in war is the desire for glory, and whoever is moved to that for gain or any other motive, not only fails to accomplish anything worthwhile, but deserves to be called a wretched merchant and not a gentleman. And it is true glory that is entrusted to the sacred treasury of letters, as everyone knows, except those unhappy ones who have never tasted them.

"What soul is so modest, timid, and abject that when reading about the deeds and the greatness of Caesar, Alexander, Scipio, Hannibal, and many others, he does not truly burn with ardent desire to be like these men and would not relinquish this fleeting life of a few days' duration to acquire an almost perpetual life of fame, which, despite death, makes him live on more renowned than before? But anyone who does not taste the sweetness of letters cannot know how great is the glory so long preserved by them, and measures it only by the life of one or two men, because his own memory is so limited; hence, he cannot value this brief life of glory as he could one which is almost eternal if, by misfortune, he was denied the knowledge of it; and since he does not esteem it as much as one who has knowledge of it, it is reasonable to believe that he will not risk such danger to win it as one would who knows of it.

"I would not want some adversary to cite instances to the contrary in order to refute my opinion, alleging that with all their knowledge of letters, the Italians have shown little worth in arms for some time now, which is, unfortunately, only too true. But certainly it may be said that here the fault of a few men has inflicted grave harm along with eternal infamy on the many, and that they have been the true cause of our ruin and of the prostrate—if not dead—virtue of our spirits. Yet, it would be even more shameful for us to make this public than it is for the French to be ignorant of letters; hence, it is better to pass over in silence what cannot be remembered without pain and, leaving this subject which I took up unwillingly, to return to our courtier.

44. "I would like him to be more than ordinarily learned in letters, at least in those studies which we call the humanities; and that he have a knowledge not only of the Latin language but also of Greek, because of the many different things that are so beautifully written in that language. Let him be versed in the poets and no less in the orators and historians and also experienced in writing verse and prose, particularly in our own language, for, besides the pleasure that he himself will take in this, he will never, in this way, be at a loss in conversing pleasantly with ladies, who usually like such things. And if because of his other affairs or through too little study, he is unable to attain such perfection that his writings are worthy of great praise, let him be careful to suppress them, so that others will not laugh at him, and show them only to a friend who can be trusted; because at least they will be of some use to him in that, through such practice, he will know how to judge the writings of others. For, in fact, it rarely happens that someone who is not accustomed to writing, however learned he may be, can ever completely understand the toil and diligence of writers or taste the sweetness and excellence of styles, and those intrinsic subtleties that are often found in the writers of ancient times.

"Moreover, these studies will make him well informed and (as Aristippus[47] said to the tyrant) bold and self-confident with everyone. I would, however, insist that our courtier keep one precept firmly in mind—that is, that in this and in every other thing, to be diffident and reserved rather than forward, and take care not to convince himself falsely that he knows what he does not know, because we are all by nature more avid for praise than we should be, and more than any other sweet song or sound, our ears love the melody of words that praise us;

and thus, like sirens' voices, they are often the cause of shipwreck to one who does not stop up his ears to such beguiling harmony. There were among ancient sages those who, recognizing this danger, wrote books to show how the true friend can be distinguished from the flatterer. But of what value is it if many, indeed countless, persons, are well aware that they are being flattered, and yet love the one who flatters them and hate the one who tells them the truth? And often finding the one who praises them to be too sparing in his words, they themselves help him along by saying such things about themselves that even the most outrageous flatterer himself must feel ashamed.

"Let us leave these blind ones in their error and decide that our courtier has such good judgment that he will not let himself be told that black is white or presume of himself more than he clearly knows to be true, and particularly in those things which, if you remember well, Messer Cesare in his game reminded us we had often used as the means of revealing the folly of one person and another. In fact, if he knows the praises bestowed on him are true, he should, in order to avoid error, not assent to them too openly, nor confirm them without some protest, but rather, let him disclaim them modestly, always giving the impression and truly esteeming arms as his principal profession, and that all his other good qualities serve merely to decorate them; this he should do especially among soldiers, in order not to act as those who in the world of scholarship wish to appear as soldiers or those who among soldiers wish to appear as men of letters. In this way, for the reasons we have given, he will avoid affectation and even the ordinary things he does will appear to be very great."

45. Then Messer Pietro Bembo replied: "I do not know, Count, why you expect this courtier, who is lettered and who has so many other virtuous qualities, to regard everything as an embellishment for arms and not regard arms and the rest as an embellishment for letters, which, without any other accompaniment, are as superior to arms in dignity as the soul is to the body, since the practice of letters is properly related to the soul, even as the practice of arms is related to the body."

Then the Count replied: "On the contrary, the practice of arms belongs to the soul as well as the body. But I would not have you be the judge in such a case, Messer Pietro, because you would be far too suspect of partiality by one of the parties. And since this debate has long been carried on by very wise men, there is no need to renew it; but I consider it settled in favor of arms, and since I may form our courtier the way I would like him to be, I would have him be of the same opinion. And if you are of the contrary opinion, then wait until you hear about a contest in which the one who defends the argument for arms is permitted to use arms, just as those who defend letters make use of letters in their defense; for if each one avails himself of his own tools, you will see that the men of letters will lose."

"Ah," said Messer Pietro, "you earlier condemned the French for placing so little value on letters, and you spoke of how greatly they have enlightened men and how they make men immortal, and now it appears that you have changed your mind. Do you not remember that

> Once Alexander had come to the famous tomb
> of the proud Achilles, sighing, he said:
> "O fortunate one, who found so clear a trumpet,
> And one who could write of you in so lofty a fashion!"
> [Petrarch, *Canzoniere*, sonnet 187]

And if Alexander envied Achilles, not for his deeds but for the fortune which had granted him the blessing of having his actions celebrated by Homer, we can see that he esteemed Homer's letters more than Achilles' arms.[48] What other judge, therefore, would you have, or what other verdict on the worth of arms and letters than the one pronounced by one of the greatest commanders who has ever lived?"

46. Then the Count replied: "I blame the French for thinking that letters are detrimental to the profession of arms, and I hold that to no one is it more fitting to be learned than to a soldier, and I would like these two qualities to be tightly united in our courtier, and each an aid to the other, as is most fitting. Nor does this mean that I have changed my opinion. But, as I have said, I do not wish to debate which of the two is more worthy of praise. Let it suffice to say that men of letters almost never choose to praise anyone but great men and glorious deeds, which in themselves deserve praise because of the inherent essential virtue from which they derive; besides this, they provide a truly noble theme for writers, and are in themselves a great embellishment and, in part, the reason why these writings endure, which perhaps would not be so much read or valued if they lacked the noble subject, but would be empty and of little moment.

"And if Alexander envied Achilles for being praised by Homer, you should not, however, conclude that he esteemed letters more than arms; if he thought himself to be as far below Achilles in these things as he judged all those who were to write of him must be below Homer, I am certain that he would have much preferred carrying out his own fine deeds than hearing praise from others. Hence, I believe that what he said was tacit praise of himself and a desire for what it seemed to him he lacked, that is, the supreme excellence of a writer, and not for what he presumed himself to have already achieved, that is, prowess in arms, in which he did not at all judge Achilles to be his superior; therefore, he called him fortunate, as if to indicate that if in the future his own fame was not as celebrated in the world as Achilles', which was made bright and illustrious by such an inspired poem, this did not come about because his valor and merits were fewer and less worthy of praise, but because of the way fortune had offered Achilles such a miracle of nature to be the glorious trumpet for his deeds. And perhaps he also wished to rouse some noble talent to write about him, showing that his pleasure in this would be equal to his love and veneration for the sacred monuments of letters about which we have now spoken quite enough."

"On the contrary," replied Signor Ludovico Pio, "far too much, because I believe it impossible to find a vessel that is capable of containing all the things you want to put into our courtier."

Then the Count said: "Wait a bit, for there are still many more to come."

Pietro da Napoli remarked: "In this case, Grasso de' Medici[49] will have a great advantage over Messer Pietro Bembo."

* * *

[Everyone laughs at Pietro's witty remark, and at the end of the first book, the Count goes on to advocate that the courtier should also have a good, practical knowledge of music and painting.]

Book II

[In Book II, Castiglione once again raises the problem of the passing of time, observing that courts of the present are as praiseworthy as those in the past. Federico Fregoso is charged with the duty of explaining how the courtier ought to exercise his good qualities and do the things that have been said will benefit him. Among other things, the courtier must have the good judgment to avoid arousing envy. He must avoid showy affectation in public or private activities, such as the exercise of arms or dancing, tennis, games, and conversation, and in his relations with his prince he should avoid flattery, although justified praise is acceptable. Federico's discussion of the courtier's relation to his prince leads him to conclude that a courtier should always be worthy of the prince's favors.]

21. Here Vincenzio Calmeta[50] said: "Before you go any further, if I have understood correctly, it seems to me you said earlier that the best way to gain favors is to deserve them, and that the courtier ought to wait until they are offered to him rather than seeking them presumptuously. I rather think that this rule is hardly appropriate, and it seems to me that experience very clearly shows the contrary, because nowadays few are favored by lords, except the presumptuous, and I know you can testify that some, who, failing to find themselves quite in the good graces of their princes, have pleased them only through presumption. If there are some who have risen through modesty, I for my part know of none, and I will even give you time to think about this, for I am confident that you will find few. And if you consider the court of France, which today is one of the noblest in Christendom, you will discover that all those who enjoy universal favor there tend to be presumptuous, and not only with one another, but also with the King himself."

"Do not say that," replied Messer Federico. "There are, on the contrary, very modest and courteous gentlemen in France; it is true that they are accustomed to a certain liberty and an unceremonious familiarity which is right and natural for them and should not, therefore, be called presumption, because in this particular manner of theirs, although they laugh and mock the presumptuous, they still value highly those they believe to be worthy and modest."

Calmeta replied: "Look at the Spaniards, who seem to be masters of courtiership, and consider how many you find, who are not extremely presumptuous both with ladies and with gentlemen, and even more than the French insofar as they first display extreme modesty; and in doing so, they are truly discerning, because, as I have said, the princes of our time all favor only those who have such manners."

22. Then Messer Federico answered: "I certainly do not wish to tolerate your efforts to place this blame on the princes of our times, Messer Vicenzio, because there are still many who love modesty, although, I do not say that this alone will suffice to make a man pleasing; I do say, however, that when it is joined to great worth, it honors the one who possesses it greatly; and although worth is silent about itself, praiseworthy deeds speak loudly, and are much more admirable than if they were accompanied by presumption and rashness. I certainly do not wish to deny that there are many presumptuous Spaniards, but I will say that those who are highly esteemed are very modest for the most part. Then there are certain others who remain so aloof that they shun the company of men to a degree that exceeds a certain mean, so much so that they cause themselves to be considered either too timid or too proud; and I do

not praise such as these in any way, nor do I wish modesty to be so dry and arid that it becomes boorishness.

"But let the courtier be eloquent when it meets his purpose, and prudent and wise in political discussions, and let him have the good judgment to know how to come to terms with customs of the countries in which he happens to be staying; then, let him be entertaining in less important matters, and let him be well spoken on any subject. But above all, let him always be inclined toward what is good, never envious or slanderous; and never let him bring himself to seek grace or favor by corrupt or dishonest means."

Then Calmeta said: "I assure you that all the other means are far more uncertain and more time-consuming than these you are finding fault with, because, to repeat myself, our princes today love only those who take such a path."

"Do not say such a thing," Messer Federico then replied, "because that would be too clear an argument that the princes of our times are all corrupt and evil, which is not so, because there are actually some good ones among them. But if our courtier finds himself by chance in the service of one who is corrupt and malicious, let him leave that person's service as soon as he discovers this, so that he does not experience the bitter anguish all good men feel who serve the wicked."

"We must pray God," responded Calmeta, "to give us good men to serve, since once we have them, we must endure them as they are, because countless considerations compel a gentleman to remain with his patron once he has entered his services. The misfortune lies in ever having begun, and in that case, courtiers are in the same circumstances as those unfortunate birds that are born in some gloomy vale."

"It seems to me," said Messer Federico, "that duty must be more important than all other considerations. And a gentleman must not leave his patron when he is at war or in adversity, for then it could be thought that he did so to better his own fortunes or that he apparently lost the means for some gainful profit; but at any other time, I believe he has the right to quit, and should quit, the service which is sure to disgrace him in the eyes of good men, because everyone assumes that anyone who serves the good is good, and anyone who serves the wicked is wicked."

23. Signor Ludovico Pio then said: "I would like you to clear up one of my doubts; that is, whether a gentleman, while he serves a prince, is obligated to obey him in everything he commands, even if it is something dishonest and dishonorable."

"In dishonest things we are not obliged to obey anyone," responded Messer Federico.

"And," continued Signor Ludovico, "if I happen to be in the service of a prince who treats me well, and who trusts that I will do for him whatever possible, and he were to command me to go and kill a man or something of the sort, am I to refuse to do it?"

"You ought to obey your lord," answered Messer Federico, "in all the things that are useful and honorable to him, not in those that are harmful and shameful; thus, if he should command you to do something treacherous, not only are you not obligated to do it, but you are obligated not to do it, both for your own sake and in order not to be the minister of your lord's shame. It is true that many things which are evil appear, at first sight, to be good, and many things which seem evil are good; hence, it is sometimes permissible to kill not just one man in the service of one's lord but ten thousand, and to do many other things, which might seem evil to someone who did not think them through, but which are not evil at all."

Then Signor Gaspar Pallavicino said: "Oh! I beg you, discuss this a little further, and teach us how what is truly good can be distinguished from what appears to be good."

"Pardon me," said Messer Federico, "I do not wish to go into that, for there would be too much to say; I prefer the whole matter be left to your discretion."

* * *

[Following the discussion of the courtier's relationship with his lord, Federico leads the group to consider the courtier's dealings with his equals as well as his attire, his choice of friends, witty conversation, the definition of man as an animal who laughs, the role of laughter, and the decorous mean in the courtier's behavior.]

41. [Federico continues.] "Therefore, in one's manner of living and in one's conversation, the safest thing is always to act according to a certain respectable mean, which truly provides a very great and strong shield against envy, which is always to be avoided as much as is possible. I would have our courtier take care not to acquire the name of a liar or a boaster, which can sometimes happen to even those who do not deserve it; therefore, in all his discussions, let him always be careful not to go beyond the bounds of verisimilitude, and not to tell too often those truths that have the appearance of being lies, like many who never speak of anything but miracles and who want to be held in such authority that every incredible thing they say must be believed. There are others who at

the beginning of a friendship, in order to gain favor with their new friend, swear, on the first day they speak with him, that there is no one in the world whom they love more than him, and that they would willingly die to do him some service and other such unreasonable things; and when they leave him, they make a show of crying and being unable to speak a word because of their grief. So, in wanting to be thought of as very loving, they allow themselves to be thought of as liars and foolish flatterers.

"But it would be too long and troublesome to try to discuss all the faults that can occur in one's conversation; therefore, as for what I desire in the courtier, let it suffice to say, beyond the things that have already been said, that he should be one who is never lacking in things to say that are good and suited to those with whom he is conversing, and that he know how to restore with a certain sweetness the minds of his listeners and induce them discreetly to merriment and laughter with pleasant witticisms and humor, so that, without ever being tedious or boring, he may continually give pleasure."

* * *

[Federico explains that some people are more witty by nature than others, and that there are two kinds of pleasantry, one characteristic of lengthy discussions and the other of brief, pointed remarks. Bibbiena carries on the discussion of pleasantries, and Signora Emilia finally asks Bernardo how pleasantries are to be used.]

45. [Bernardo continues.] "I shall say as briefly as I can whatever occurs to me on the subject of what moves us to laughter, which is so characteristic of mankind,[51] that in order to describe man, we are in the habit of saying that he is an animal who is inclined towards laughter. For laughter is found only in men and nearly always shows evidence of a certain good humor which is felt inwardly in the mind, and which by nature is attracted to pleasure and desires rest and recreation; wherefore we take note of many things devised by men for this purpose, such as festivals and many and varied kinds of spectacles. And because we tend to like those who are the source of such recreation, it was the custom of ancient kings, the Romans, Athenians, and many others, in order to win the goodwill of the people and feed the eyes and minds of the multitude, to build great theaters and other public buildings, and there they would show new games, horse and chariot races, combats, strange animals, comedies, tragedies, and mimes; nor were austere philosophers opposed to such sights, and they would often, by means of spectacles of this kind and at banquets, relax their minds, which were exhausted by their lofty

discussions and inspired thoughts—which is also something all kinds of men willingly do—for not only farmers, sailors, and all those who carry on hard and rough work with their hands, but holy men of religion, and prisoners awaiting death from hour to hour, all go in search of some remedy and medicine to restore themselves. Therefore, everything that elicits laughter exhilarates man's soul and gives pleasure, and for a moment in time allows us to forget the bothersome worries of which our life is so full. Thus, as you see, laughter is most pleasing to everyone, and anyone who elicits it at the right time and in the right way is much to be praised. But what laughter is, where it dwells, and in what way it sometimes takes possession of our veins, our eyes, our mouths, and sides, and seems to want to make us burst, so that no matter what power we exert upon it, it is impossible to hold it back—I will leave that argument to Democritus, who, even if he were to promise to do so, would not know how to explain it.

46. "Now then, the place and approximate source from which the ridiculous arises consists in a certain deformity, because one not only laughs at those things which contain elements of incongruity and that seem to be wrong without really being so. I do not know how to state it differently, but if you think about it, you will see that what we laugh at is nearly always something that is not quite proper but yet is not wrong.

"Now, as far as the means the courtier ought to use to make others laugh and within what limits, I shall try to tell you, insofar as my judgment allows, for it is not always proper for the courtier to make people laugh, nor should he do so in the manner of madmen, drunks, fools, bumblers, or buffoons. And although these kinds of men seem to be in demand at the courts, still, they do not deserve to be called courtiers, but each should be called by his proper name and judged for what he is.

"The limits and extent of provoking laughter by making fun of someone must also be carefully considered, as well as who it is that we make fun of, because there is nothing to laugh at in deriding some miserable wretch, or notorious scoundrel, since the latter seems to deserve a greater punishment than being ridiculed, and people are not inclined to make fun of the wretched unless, in their misfortune, they are boastful, proud, and presumptuous. One must also take care not to mock those who are universally favored and loved by all and who are powerful, because sometimes a man can engender dangerous enmities by doing so. But it is proper to ridicule and laugh at the vices found in people who are neither so wretched that they excite compassion nor so wicked that they would seem to deserve being condemned to capital punishment, nor of so high a station that their slightest anger could do us great harm.

47. "You must also know that the same situations from which amusing witticisms are extracted can likewise provide serious maxims for praising and blaming, and sometimes in the same words: just as in praising a generous man who shares all his belongings with his friends, it is customary to say that what he has is not his own; and the same can be said to condemn someone who has stolen or acquired through some other evil means what he possesses. It is also said, 'She is very much a lady,' by one who wishes to praise her for prudence and goodness; the same could be said by someone who wanted to condemn her, indicating that she is the lady of many. But more often it is a matter of exploiting the same situations rather than the same words; just as recently while a lady was at Mass in a church with three noblemen, one of whom served her in love, a poor beggar appeared, and, having placed himself before her, begged her for alms; and, though he repeatedly begged her with much tiresome persistence and a pitiful voice and moans, with all this, she never gave him alms or even dismissed him by making a sign that he should go with God, but stood there completely lost in thought as if she were thinking about something else. Then the cavalier who was in love with her said to his two companions: 'You see what I can hope for from my lady, who is so cruel that she gives no alms to that poor, starving, destitute man who begs with so much passion and with such insistence, but she does not even dismiss him—so much does she enjoy seeing before her a man who languishes in misery and asks for mercy in vain.'

"One of his two friends replied: 'That is not cruelty but this lady's tacit way of teaching you to understand that she is never pleased with anyone who begs with too much persistence.'

"The other answered: 'On the contrary, it is a warning to him that, although she does not give what is asked of her, she still likes to be begged for it.'

"So there you have it! From the fact that this lady did not give the poor man leave arises a saying of severe censure, one of modest praise, and another of biting sarcasm.

48. "Turning back now, to explain the kind of pleasantries that pertain to our subject, I say that in my opinion, there are to be found three kinds, even though Messer Federico has mentioned only two; that is, that long narrative, urbane and pleasing, that recounts the outcome of an action; and the other, the spontaneous, sharp readiness of a single remark. On that account, we shall add a third kind, which are

called 'practical jokes,' which include in them both long narratives and short sayings, as well as a certain amount of action sometimes.

"Now the first kind which consists of a continuous narrative is almost like a short story. And to give you an example. At the time when Pope Alexander the Sixth died and Pius the Third was made Pope, Messer Antonio Agnello, your fellow Mantuan, my Duchess, being at Rome and in the Vatican Palace, while talking about the death of one and the creation as Pope of the other, and making various judgments on all that with certain of his friends, said: 'Gentlemen, even in Catullus' time, doors began to speak without tongues and to hear without ears, and, in this way, to expose adulteries; now, although men are not as worthy as they were in those times, it may be that doors, many of which, at least here in Rome, are made of ancient marble, have the same properties that they had then; and, for my part, I believe that these two here could clear up all our doubts, if we wished to learn from them.'

"Then, the gentlemen there became rather curious, waiting to find out what the outcome of all this would be. Messer Antonio, continuing to walk back and forth, suddenly lifted his eyes to look at one of the doors in the hall in which they were walking, and after stopping a moment, with his finger, he pointed out to his companions the inscription above it, which bore the name of Pope Alexander, at the end of which was a V and an I, signifying, as you know, the Sixth, and he said: 'You see what this door says: *Alexander Pope VI*, which means that he became Pope by means of the violence he employed, and that he made more use of violence than reason.[52] Now let us see if we can learn something about the new Pope from this other door,' and turning as if by chance to that other door, he pointed out the inscription NPPV, which signified Nicolas Papa Quintus; and he said at once: 'Alas, bad news; you see how this door tells us *Nihil Papa Valet*.' "[53]

* * *

[The remainder of Book II is devoted to an exploration of the different forms of wit and their proper use in courtly conversation. Messer Bernardo warns that impiety must be avoided in jests. The book ends in a discussion of women, including an attack upon them by Messer Ottaviano Fregoso and Messer Gasparo Pallavicino, and a discussion of the courtier's relationships with them. The Duchess suggests that the Magnifico Giuliano speak on the qualities desirable in a woman. He replies as follows.]

100. "Madam," replied the Magnifico, "I do not know how well advised you are to assign me an undertaking of such importance, which

in truth, I do not feel equal to; nor am I like the Count and Messer Federico, who with their eloquence have created a courtier who never existed and perhaps never can exist. Nevertheless, if it pleases you for me to bear this burden, at least let it be on the same terms that these other gentlemen enjoyed: that is, that anyone may contradict me whenever he pleases, and I shall regard this not as a contradiction but as assistance, and perhaps through the correction of my errors, we shall discover the perfection of the courtly lady we are seeking."

Book III

[At the beginning of Book III, Castiglione restates his purpose of immortalizing through his writings the court of Urbino, which, he tells us, is superior to all others in Italy. When the discussions are renewed the next day, the noble company decides that the courtly lady is indispensable both to the atmosphere of a court and to the actions and behavior of the courtier.]

4. . . . Then the Magnifico, turning to the Duchess, said: "Since it pleases you, Madam, I will say what I must say, but with the great fear that I shall give no satisfaction, and certainly it would be a much lesser task to create a lady who deserved to be queen of the world than a perfect court lady, for I do not know where to find the model for the latter, whereas for the queen, I would not have to look very far, since it would be enough for me only to imagine the divine attributes of a lady whom I know, and, in contemplating those, to direct all my thoughts to expressing clearly in words what many see with their eyes, and if I could do no more, I would have discharged my duty by merely mentioning her name."[54]

Then the Duchess said: "Do not exceed our limits, Signor Magnifico, but keep to the order given and create the court lady, so that such a noble lady may have someone who can serve her in a fitting manner."

The Magnifico continued: "Then, Madam, in order to assure you that your commands can induce me to attempt even to do what I still do not know how to do, I shall describe this excellent lady as I would like her to be, and once I have created her in my own way, and since I may not then have another, I will take her, like Pygmalion, for my own. And although Signor Gasparo has said that the same rules given for the courtier serve also for the lady, I am of a different opinion; for although some qualities are common to both and are as necessary to the man as to the woman, there are yet others that are more suited to the woman than to the man, and some more fitting to a man, to which a woman should be a complete stranger. I say the same for physical exercises, but, above all, it seems to me that in her style, manners, words, gestures, and bearing, the woman should be very different from the man, for just as it is fitting for him to show a certain strong, solid manliness, so it is well for the woman to have a soft and delicate tenderness, with a sweet feminine manner in her every movement, which in her going and staying and in whatever she says always makes her seem a woman, without any similarity to a man.

"Adding this note of caution to the rules which these gentlemen have taught the courtier, then, I think that she should be able to make use of many of them and adorn herself with the best accomplishments, as Signor Gasparo says. For I hold that many virtues of the mind are as necessary to a woman as to a man: to be of noble birth; to avoid affectation; to be naturally graceful in all her actions; to be well mannered, witty, prudent, but not arrogant, envious, slanderous, vain, contentious, or inept; to know how to gain and hold the favor of her mistress and all others; to perform well and gracefully the exercises suitable for women. I do think that beauty is more important to her than to the courtier, for truly much is lacking to that woman who lacks beauty. Also, she must be more circumspect and more careful not to give anyone the opportunity to speak ill of her, and conduct herself so that not only may she avoid being sullied by guilt, but also by even the suspicion of it, for a woman does not have as many ways of defending herself against false accusations as a man does. But since Count Ludovico has explained in minute detail the principal profession of the courtier, and has insisted that it be that of arms, I think it is only right to say what I consider to be that of the court lady; and when I have done this in a satisfactory manner, I believe I shall have discharged the greater part of my duty.

5. "Leaving aside, then, those virtues of the mind which she is to have in common with the courtier, such as prudence, magnanimity, continence, and many others, and likewise those qualities that are fitting to all women, such as goodness, discretion, the ability to manage her husband's property, his house and children (if she is married), and all the qualities that are required in a good mother, I say that, in my opinion, a lady who is at court should have, above all else, a certain pleasing

affability, whereby she will know how to entertain graciously every kind of man with charming and respectable conversation appropriate to the time and place and to the social standing of the person with whom she speaks, joining to gentle and modest manners and to the candor that should always govern all her actions a quick liveliness of wit, by which she will show herself a stranger to all boorishness, but with such a kind manner that she causes herself to be thought no less chaste, prudent, and gracious than pleasing, witty, and discreet. Thus, she must observe a certain mean (difficult to achieve and, in a way, composed of contraries), and be careful not to go beyond certain fixed limits.

"Now this lady, in her desire to be thought chaste and virtuous, must not be so shy or appear to abhor company and conversation that is a little frivolous to the point that she withdraws when she finds herself involved, because it could easily be thought that she was feigning such austerity in order to hide something about herself which she feared others might find out; for such unsociable manners are always odious. Yet, on the other hand, in order to seem free and agreeable, she must not utter indecent words or engage in any unrestrained or excessive familiarity or in actions which might cause others to believe about her what is perhaps not true; but when she finds herself in the midst of such discussions, she should listen with a slight blush of shame.

"Likewise, she should flee from an error into which I have seen many fall, which is to gossip and willingly listen to anyone who speaks evil of others, because those women who, when they hear stories about the immodest behavior of other women, become upset and pretend not to believe it, and show that to them such an immodest woman is quite a monster, provide a pretext for thinking that, since this defect seems so enormous to them, they themselves might be guilty of it. And those who always go about prying into the love affairs of other women and telling about them in such detail and with such delight appear to be envious and anxious for everyone to know about it, so that the same thing by mistake may not be attributed to them; and so they give in to a certain kind of laughter and assume certain mannerisms that make it evident that they are taking the greatest delight over it all. And as a result men, although it appears that they listen to them willingly, generally have a bad opinion of such women and have little respect for them, and men take these ways of theirs as an invitation to go further, and then they often do pass beyond the limits which deservedly brings them to shame, and, in the end, men esteem them so little that they care nothing for their company and find them rather distasteful. On the other hand, there is no man so shameless and brash that he has no reverence for those women who are judged to be chaste and virtuous, for that gravity tempered with wisdom and goodness is like a shield against the insolence and bestiality of presumptuous men; and thus we see that a word, a laugh, an act of kindness, however small it may be, coming from an honest woman, is more prized by everyone than all the affectations and caresses of those who without reserve show their lack of shame—and, if they are not unchaste, with their unrestrained laughter, loquacity, insolence, and such scurrilous manners of this sort, they give the impression of being so."

* * *

[Following the Magnificos' discourse upon the suitable traits of a court lady, Signor Gasparo asks him what physical exercises are proper for her, how she ought to converse, and what she should know. The Magnifico replies that a lady should participate in no strenuous exercises and must be graceful and slow to move. She must be gay and know how to dress, have a knowledge of letters, music, painting, and dance. He refutes Gasparo's contention that women represent an imperfection in nature, concluding that the lady must be knowledgeable in the discourse of love and in judging who truly loves her. Outside marriage, she should seek only spiritual and honorable love.]

Book IV

[At the beginning of Book IV, the narrator laments the loss of three of the participants in these discussions—Gaspar Pallavicino, Cesare Gonzaga, and Roberto da Bari—observing that Fortune often prevents us from completing our designs. The members of the court continue their discussion of the courtier, and Signor Ottaviano suggests that the activities of the courtier must have a praiseworthy purpose.]

5. "The aim, therefore, of the perfect courtier (which up to now we have not mentioned) is, I believe, to win for himself, by means of the qualities ascribed to him by these gentlemen, the goodwill and mind of that prince whom he serves, so that he may be able to tell him (and always will tell him) the truth about everything he needs to know without fear or danger of displeasing him; and when he knows that the mind of the prince is inclined to do something unsuitable, that he may

dare to contradict him, and in a gentle way, avail himself of the favor acquired with his excellent accomplishments, so as to deter him from every evil purpose and lead him to the path of virtue. And thus, while having within himself the goodness these gentlemen ascribed to him along with readiness of wit and charm, prudence and knowledge of letters and of many other things, the courtier will in every situation possess the skill to make his prince see how much honor and profit will come to him and his family from the justice, liberality, magnanimity, gentleness, and other virtues that are proper to a good prince; and, on the contrary, how much infamy and injury proceed from the vices opposed to these virtues. Therefore, I think that just as music, festivals, games, and other pleasant circumstances are, as it were, the flower, so to lead or help one's prince toward the good and frighten him away from the evil is the true fruit of courtiership. And because the merit of good deeds consists mainly in two things, one of which is to choose a truly good end to which we can direct our intentions, and the other of which is to know how to find timely and suitable means in order to attain that good end, it is certain that the man who sees to it that his prince is deceived by no one, listens to no flatterers or slanderers or liars, and is well acquainted with good and evil, loving the one and hating the other, is aiming at the best end of all."[55]

* * *

[After their discussion of the courtier's true purpose and how the prince can be taught to love the good and to do it, they examine what kind of government is best. Ottaviano also argues that although the courtier instructs the prince, he is not necessarily of greater dignity, since, after all, Plato and Aristotle performed their works of courtiership with Alexander the Great and the tyrants of Sicily. Finally Gasparo remembers that in their discussion of the preceding evening, they wished the courtier to be in love, and he wonders how this can be fitting, especially if he is an older man. Messer Pietro Bembo is asked by the Duchess to explain courtly love.]

51. Then, Messer Pietro, having at first kept silent, composing himself as if he were about to speak of something important, said: "Gentlemen, in order to show that old men can love not only without blame but sometimes more happily than the young, I shall have to present a short discourse explaining what love is and what is the nature of the happiness that lovers experience; so, I beg you to listen to me attentively, because I hope to make you see that there is no man here to

whom it is unseemly to be in love, even though he may be fifteen or twenty years older than Signor Morello."[56]

And then, after some laughter from the company, Messer Pietro added: "Let me say, therefore, that, according to the way it is defined by ancient sages, love is nothing other than a certain desire to enjoy beauty, and because our desire longs only for things that are known, knowledge must always precede desire, which by its nature wants the good but is in itself blind and does not know the good. Therefore, nature has so ordained that to every cognitive power there will be joined an appetitive power; and since there are three modes of knowledge in our soul, that is, by means of the senses, by reason, and by intellect, so from the senses arise the appetites, which we have in common with the animals; from reason arises choice, which is proper to man; from the intellect, through which man can share in the nature of the angels, arises will.[57] Thus, accordingly, just as the senses know only sensible things, appetite desires these things only; and just as the intellect is turned to nothing but the contemplation of intelligible things, the will feeds only upon spiritual goods. Man, rational by nature, and placed in the middle between these two extremes, can, by choice, descending to the senses or rising toward the intellect, turn his desire now in one direction, now in the other. In either of these ways, therefore, man can long for beauty, the concept of which is appropriate to all things, whether natural or artificial, that are made up with that good proportion and due measure required by their nature.

52. "But speaking of the beauty we have in mind, that only which appears in the human body and chiefly in the face, and which prompts this ardent desire we call love, we shall argue that it is an influx of the divine goodness, which, although it is diffused over all created things like the light of the sun,[58] still, when it finds a face well proportioned and composed of a certain joyous harmony of various colors and enhanced by light and shadow and a prescribed symmetry and definition, infuses itself therein and appears most beautiful, and adorns and illuminates with a grace and a wonderful splendor the object wherein it shines, in the manner of a sunbeam which strikes a beautiful vase of polished gold set with precious gems. In this way, it pleasantly attracts the eyes of men to itself, and penetrating through them, impresses itself upon the soul, which it moves and delights throughout with a new sweetness; and by kindling it, it inspires it to desire itself.

"Then being seized with the desire to enjoy this beauty as something good, the soul, if it allows itself to be guided by the judgment of the senses, makes a very serious error and judges that the body in which the beauty is seen is its principal cause, and because of this, it deems it necessary, in order to enjoy this beauty, to join itself as intimately as possible to that body, which is wrong; and therefore, whoever thinks he will enjoy beauty by possessing the body deceives himself and is moved not by true knowledge through rational choice but by false opinion through sensual appetite; whence, the pleasure that ensues from it is also necessarily false and defective. Consequently, all those lovers who satisfy their unchaste desires with the women they love encounter one of two evils: for either, as soon as they have reached the desired goal, they not only feel satiety and disgust, but they can also develop hatred for the beloved object, as if appetite repented of its error and recognized how it was deceived by the false judgment of the senses, through which it believed that evil is good; or else, they remain in the same state of desire and eagerness, like those who have not really reached the end they were seeking; and although, through their own blind approach with which they have become intoxicated, they think they are feeling pleasure at that moment, just as a sick man dreams that he is drinking at some clear spring, still, they are not satisfied, nor are they calm. And because peace and satisfaction always arise from possessing the desired good in the soul of the possessor, if that were the true and good end of their desire, they would remain tranquil and satisfied upon possessing it, but they do not; on the contrary, deceived by that similarity, they quickly return to their unbridled desire, and with the same turmoil they felt before, they find themselves once again with that furious and burning thirst for what in vain they hope to possess perfectly. Such lovers as these, therefore, love most unhappily, for either they never attain their desires, which is a source of great unhappiness, or if they do attain them, they find that they have attained their sorrow, and their miseries end up by becoming even greater; because both in the beginning and in the middle of this love, they never feel anything other than suffering, torment, pain, toil, and hardship; so that to be pale, dejected, constantly weeping and sighing, to be always silent or lamenting, to long for death, in short, to be most unhappy, are the conditions that are said to be proper to lovers.

53. "The cause, therefore, of this calamity in man's soul is principally the senses, which are most potent in youth, because the vigor of the flesh and blood during that stage of life give them as much strength as it takes away from reason, and thus easily induces the soul to follow appetite; for finding itself buried in an earthly prison and deprived of spiritual contemplation, the soul cannot of itself clearly perceive the truth when carrying out the function of governing the body; wherefore, in order to have knowledge of things, it has to go begging for it to the

senses for its first notions, and so it believes the senses and bows down before them and allows itself to be guided by them, particularly when they are so vigorous that they almost force it; and because the senses are so deceptive, they fill it with errors and false opinions.

"For this reason, it nearly always happens that young men are wrapped up in this sensual love which is in every way a rebel against reason, and so they make themselves unworthy of enjoying the graces and benefits which love gives to its true subjects; nor do they feel any pleasures in love except for the same ones that unreasoning animals feel, though their sufferings are much more painful.

"Given this premise, therefore, which is a most valid one, let me say that the contrary happens to those who are at a more mature stage of life. For if the latter, when the soul is already less oppressed by the weight of the body and when the natural ardor begins to cool off, are inflamed by beauty and direct their desire to it, guided by rational choice, they are not deceived then and they manage to acquire perfect possession of beauty; thus, nothing but good arises from the possession of it, because beauty is good, and, consequently, true love of beauty is most good and holy and always produces good effects in the souls of those who, with the bridle of reason, restrain the wickedness of the senses—something which the old can do much more easily than the young.

54. "It is not, therefore, unreasonable to say also that the old can love without blame and more happily than the young; without taking this word 'old,' however, in the sense of 'decrepit' or as when the organs of the body are already so weak that the soul cannot exercise its powers through them, but as meaning when knowledge in us is in its true prime. I will not be silent about this as well: while I think that sensual love is bad at every age, I feel that in the young it deserves to be excused, and perhaps in some sense, it is permissible; for, even if it brings them suffering, danger, hardship, and that unhappiness we have mentioned, there are still many who, to win the favor of the ladies they love, do worthy things which, although they are not directed to a good end, are still in themselves good; and thus, from much bitterness they extract a little sweetness, and through the adversities which they endure they eventually recognize their error. So, just as I think that those youths who control their appetites and love with reason are heroic, I likewise excuse those who allow themselves to be overcome by sensual love, to which they are so inclined by human weakness, provided that in this love they show tenderness, courtesy, and worthiness, and all the other noble qualities that these gentlemen have mentioned and that when they are no longer young, they abandon it altogether, renouncing this sensual

desire as the lowest rung on that ladder by which one can ascend to true love.[59] But if even when they are old, they keep the fire of the appetites in their cold hearts and subject strong reason to the weak senses, it is not possible to say how much they should be blamed, for, like senseless fools, they deserve to be numbered among the animals that lack reason, for the thoughts and ways of sensual love are most unseemly to a mature stage of life."

* * *

[Bembo pauses and there is a brief discussion among the group about old men loving in a purely intellectual fashion. Signor Morello wonders how it is possible to possess beauty without a body, especially among young men. In paragraph 57, Bembo explains that "beauty springs from God and is like a circle, the center of which is goodness. And hence as there cannot be a circle without a center, there cannot be beauty without goodness. Thus, a wicked soul rarely inhabits a beautiful body, and for that reason, external beauty is a true sign of inner goodness; and that grace is imprinted upon the bodies more or less according to the character of the soul, by which it is recognized outwardly, just as with trees in which the beauty of the blossoms bears witness to the goodness of the fruit; and the same principle operates in bodies, for we see that the physiognomists often recognize in the face the habits and sometimes the thoughts of men." Bembo continues in 58: "Hence, the ugly are for the most part also wicked and the beautiful good; and it can be said that beauty is the graceful, merry, pleasing, and desirable face of the good, and ugliness the dark, troublesome, displeasing, and wretched face of evil; and if you consider all things, you will find that those which are good and useful always have the grace of beauty as well." After discussing the beauty and harmony of the created world, Bembo describes man as a microcosm: "Think now of the figure of man, who may be called a little world, in whom it is obvious that every part of the body is precisely designed with skill and not by chance, and then the form taken as a whole is so beautiful that it would be difficult to decide whether it is utility or grace which is given more to the human face and the rest of the body by its various parts, such as the eyes, nose, mouth, ears, arms, chest, and all the other parts. The same can be said of all the animals. Look at the feathers of birds, the leaves and branches of trees, which nature gives them to preserve their being, and yet they also have the greatest loveliness." Bembo next compares men to the building of ships, palaces, or temples in which both beauty and utility are essential. He concludes that "beauty is the true trophy of the soul's victory, when, with divine strength she holds sway over material nature and with her light conquers the darkness of the body." After a discussion concerning the extent of chastity in beautiful women, Bembo continues his discussion of how the courtier ought to love "beyond the manner of the vulgar crowd."]

61. ". . . I say, therefore, that since human nature in its period of youth is so greatly inclined toward the senses, the courtier may be allowed to love sensually while he is young, but if in later years he happens to be inflamed by such an amorous desire, he must be very cautious and take care not to deceive himself by letting himself be led into those calamities which in the young deserve more compassion than blame, and, on the contrary, in the old more blame than compassion.

62. "Therefore, when the graceful appearance of some beautiful woman presents itself to his eye, joined to such elegant behavior and gentle manners that he, as an expert in love, recognizes that his feeling accords with hers, and as soon as he perceives that his eyes seize upon her image and carry it to his heart, and when his soul begins to contemplate her with pleasure and to feel that influence within itself that moves and warms it little by little, and as soon as those lively spirits which shine forth through her eyes continue to add new fuel to the fire, then he must, at the beginning, provide a prompt remedy, and arouse his reason and therewith arm the fortress of his heart, thus closing the pathways to the senses and appetites so that they cannot enter there either by force or by deception. Thus, if the flame is extinguished, the danger, too, is extinguished, but if it persists and grows, then the courtier, feeling himself caught, must be utterly resolved to avoid all the ugliness of vulgar love and must enter into the divine path of love with reason as his guide. And he must first consider that the body, wherein that beauty shines, is not the source from which it springs, but rather, that beauty, being an incorporeal thing and, as we have said, a heavenly ray, loses much of its dignity when it is joined with base and corruptible matter, because the more perfect it is, the less it partakes of matter and is most perfect when it is completely separated from it; and he must also consider that just as one cannot hear with his palate or smell with his ears, so also one cannot enjoy beauty in any way or satisfy the desire that it excites in our souls through the sense of touch, but only by means of that sense of which beauty is the true object, namely, the faculty of sight.

"Let him, therefore, remove himself from the blind judgment of the senses and enjoy with his eyes that splendor, that grace, those amorous sparks, the smiles, the manners, and all the other pleasant ornaments of his lady's beauty; likewise, with his hearing let him enjoy the sweetness of her voice, the modulations of her words, the harmony of her music (if the beloved lady is a musician); and thus, his soul will nourish itself on the sweetest food by means of these two senses—which contain little of the corporeal and are the ministers of reason—without allowing desire for the body to arouse in him any unchaste appetite. Then, let him obey, please, and honor his lady with all reverence and hold her dearer than himself, and put her every convenience and pleasure before his own, and love in her the beauty of the mind no less than that of her body; let him, therefore, take care not to allow her to fall into any error, but with admonishments and good precepts let him seek always to lead her to modesty, temperance, and true chastity, and make certain that in her no thoughts arise except those that are pure and free of all the ugliness of vice; and thus, by sowing virtue in the garden of that beautiful mind, he will also gather fruits of the most beautiful behavior and will taste them with wondrous delight; and this will be the true engendering and expression of beauty in beauty, which is said by some to be the end of love.

"In such a way, our courtier will be most pleasing to his lady, and she will always show herself obedient, sweet, and affable to him, and as desirous of pleasing him as of being loved by him; and the wishes of both will be most virtuous and harmonious and, consequently, they will both be very happy."

63. Here, Signor Morello said: "The begetting of beauty in beauty effectively would be the begetting of a beautiful child in a beautiful woman; and pleasing him in this would appear to me a much clearer sign that she loved her lover than through that affability of which you were speaking."

Bembo laughed and said: "You must not go beyond proper bounds, Signor Morello, nor does the woman give little indication of her love, when she gives the lover her beauty, which is so precious a thing, and by the paths that are the gateway to the soul (that is, sight and hearing) sends the glances of her eyes, the image of her face, her voice, her words, which penetrate into the lover's heart and give him proof of her love."

Signor Morello replied: "Glances and words can be and often are false evidence; therefore, anyone who has no better token of love is, in my judgment, most uncertain; and truly I was expecting you to make this lady of yours a little more courteous and liberal toward the courtier than the Magnifico has made his own, but it seems to me that both of you are acting in the same way as those judges who pronounce sentences against their friends in order to appear wise."

64. Bembo answered: "I am quite willing for this lady to be more courteous to my courtier who is no longer young than the Magnifico's is to the younger one, and with reason, because my courtier will only desire seemly things, and therefore, the lady can, without blame, grant them all to him, but Signor Magnifico's lady, who is not so sure of the young courtier's modesty, must grant him only seemly things and deny him the unseemly ones; therefore, my courtier, who is granted what he requests, is happier than the other to whom part is granted and part denied.

"And so that you may understand better that rational love is happier than sensual love, let me say that sometimes the same things should be denied in sensual love and granted in rational love, because they are unseemly in the one and seemly in the other; therefore, to please her good lover, besides granting him pleasant smiles, intimate and secret discussions, and permission to joke, jest, and touch her hand, the lady may reasonably without blame go even as far as the kiss, which in sensual love, according to the Magnifico's rules, is not permitted; for, since the kiss is the union of the body and soul, there is the danger that the sensual lover may be more inclined toward the body than toward the soul, whereas the rational lover knows that although the mouth is part of the body, it nonetheless gives rise to words which are the interpreters of the soul as well as to that inward breath which itself is even called 'soul.' And for that reason, the lover delights in joining his mouth to that of his beloved in a kiss, not in order to excite in himself any unseemly desire, but because he feels that bond is the mutual gateway to their souls, into which, drawn by the desire for each other, they pour themselves by turn, each into the other's body, and mingle together in such a way that each of them has two souls, and a single soul thus composed of these two rules, as it were, two bodies; whence the kiss may more readily be said to be a union of souls rather than of bodies, because it exerts such power over the soul that it draws it to itself and almost separates it from the body. For this reason, all chaste lovers desire the kiss as a union of souls, and thus the divinely enamored Plato says that in kissing, the soul came to his lips in order to escape from the body. And because the separation of the soul from perceptible things to the senses and its complete union with spiritual things can be signified by the kiss, Solomon, in his divine book of the *Song of Songs*, says, 'Let him kiss me with the kiss of his mouth,' to explain his desire that his soul be transported by divine love to the contemplation of heavenly beauty in such a way that by uniting itself intimately with that love, it might abandon the body."

65. All remained most attentive to Bembo's discourse, and he, pausing briefly and seeing that the others were not speaking, said: "Since

you have made me begin to show the nature of truly happy love to our courtier who is not young, I want to lead him a little further still, for it is very dangerous to remain at this point, considering that, as we have said several times, the soul is most inclined toward the senses; and although reason may choose well through proper argument and know that such beauty does not originate in the body and, on that account, put a bridle on unseemly desires, still the continual contemplation of physical beauty often perverts sound judgment. And even if no other evil results from this, remaining absent from the loved one brings with it much distress, because the influence of that beauty, when it is present, gives the lover wondrous delight, and by warming his heart, awakens and melts certain dormant and frozen powers in his soul, which, being nourished by the amorous warmth, spread and well up around the heart and send forth through the eyes those spirits that are most subtle vapors, made of the purest and brightest part of the blood which receive the image of her beauty and shape it with a thousand various ornaments. As a result, the soul takes delight, and, with a certain wonder it is frightened and yet rejoices, and, as if dazed, it feels, together with enjoyment, that fear and reverence which we are accustomed to have for sacred things, and it believes it has entered into its own paradise.

66. "Therefore, the lover who considers beauty only in the body loses this good and this happiness as soon as the beloved lady, by being absent, leaves his eyes deprived of their splendor and, consequently, the soul widowed of its good. For since her beauty is far away, that amorous influence does not warm his heart as it did in her presence, wherefore his pores remain arid and dry, yet the memory of her beauty still stirs those powers of his soul a little, so that they seek to scatter the spirits, and these, finding the ways blocked, have no outlet, and yet seek to escape; and shut in this way, they prick the soul with these goads and cause it the most bitter pains, as children experience when their teeth begin to come through the tender gums. And from this come the tears, the sighs, the suffering, and the torments of lovers, because the soul is in constant torment and distress and almost in a furor until that dear beauty appears to it once again; and then suddenly it becomes calm and breathes easily and, entirely intent on that beauty, it nourishes itself on sweet food, nor would it ever wish to depart from so enticing a vision.

"In order, therefore, to escape the torment of this absence and to enjoy beauty without suffering, the courtier, with the aid of reason, must turn his desire completely away from the body and to beauty alone, and insofar as he is able, contemplate it in its own simplicity and purity, and give it a shape distinct from all matter in his imagination; and thus he will make it pleasing and dear to his soul, and there enjoy it and have it with him day and night in every time and place without fear of ever losing it, remembering always that the body is something very different from beauty which not only does not increase beauty but diminishes its perfection.

"In this way, our courtier who is no longer young will be out of reach of all the bitterness and calamities that the young almost always feel in the form of jealousy, suspicion, disdain, anger, desperation, and certain furors full of such rage that they are often led into such error that some not only beat the women they love, but take their own lives; he will do no injury to the husband, father, brothers, or relatives of the lady he loves; he will never cause her shame; he will never be forced to curb, sometimes with the greatest difficulty, his eyes and tongue in order not to disclose his desires to others, or to endure the pain of partings or absences; for he will always carry his precious treasure with him enclosed in his heart and will also by the power of imagination make that beauty far more beautiful than it is in reality.

67. "But among these blessings the lover will find another much greater still, if he will use this love as a step by which to ascend to a love far more sublime; this he will succeed in doing if he continually considers within himself how tight a bond it is always having to contemplate the beauty of one body alone; and so in order to go beyond such narrow limits, he will add to his idea of beauty little by little so many adornments that by uniting all forms of beauty, he will create a universal concept and reduce the multitude of these individual beauties to the unity of that single beauty which sheds its light over human nature as a whole. Thus, he will no longer contemplate the particular beauty of one woman but rather that universal beauty which adorns all bodies; and so, dazzled by this greater light, he will not be concerned with the lesser one, and burning in a more perfect flame, he will put little value on what he had at first so greatly prized.

"This degree of love, although it is very noble and such that few can attain it, can still not be called perfect, for the imagination is a corporeal faculty and has no knowledge if not through those principles that are provided to it by the senses, and so it is not wholly purged of material darkness, and, hence, although it may consider this universal beauty in the abstract and in itself alone, yet it does not discern that beauty clearly or without some ambiguity, because of the similarity that the mental images have with the body; thus, those who attain this love are like little birds beginning to grow feathers, which, although with their weak wings can lift themselves a little in flight, still dare not go too far from their nest or expose themselves to the winds and open sky.

68. "Therefore, when our courtier shall have reached this goal, although he may be called a very happy lover in comparison with those who are submerged in the misery of sensual love, still I do not wish him to be content, but rather to go boldly forward along that sublime path, following behind the guide that leads him to the goal of true happiness; and, thus, instead of going outside himself in thought, as anyone must who wishes to consider corporeal beauty, let him turn within himself to contemplate that beauty, seen with the eyes of the mind, which begins to become sharp and clear when those of the body lose the flower of their delight; and in this way, estranged from all evil, purified by the study of true philosophy, immersed in the spiritual life, and trained in the things of the intellect, the soul, turning itself to the contemplation of its own substance, as if awakened from the profoundest sleep, opens those eyes which all have but few utilize and perceives in itself a ray of that light which is the true image of the angelic beauty imparted to it, and of which it, in turn, imparts a faint image to the body.

"Thus, once grown blind to earthly things, the soul has eyes only for celestial things; and sometimes when the motive powers of the body are abstracted by assiduous contemplation, or are bound by sleep, then, no longer fettered by them, the soul senses a certain hidden savor of true angelic beauty, and, ravished by the splendor of that light, begins to be inflamed and follows it so eagerly that it becomes, as it were, drunk and beside itself in its desire to unite with that beauty, believing to have found the footprint of God in the contemplation of which, as in its blessed end, it seeks to find its final rest. And so, burning with this most happy flame, it rises to its noblest part, which is the intellect; and there, no longer darkened by the obscure night of earthly things, it beholds divine beauty; but it still does not yet quite enjoy that beauty wholly and perfectly, because it only contemplates it in its own particular intellect, which is not capable of comprehending universal beauty in its immensity.

"Wherefore, not fully content with bestowing this benefit, love bestows a greater happiness upon the soul; for, just as from the particular beauty of one body it guides the soul to the universal beauty of all bodies, so in the highest grade of perfection, it guides the soul from the particular intellect to the universal intellect. Hence, the soul, burning in the holy fire of true divine love, flies to unite itself with the angelic nature and not only wholly abandons the senses, but no longer has any need of the discourse of reason, for, transformed into an angelic being, it understands all intelligible things, and without any veil or cloud beholds the wide sea of pure divine beauty and receives it into itself and enjoys that supreme happiness that by way of the senses is incomprehensible.

69. "If, then, the beauties which we see every day with these clouded eyes of ours in corruptible bodies (and which are nothing but dreams and the faintest shadows of beauty) seem to us so lovely and graceful that they often kindle a most ardent fire in us and one of such delight that we deem no happiness capable of equaling what we sometimes feel at a single glance that comes to us from the eyes of a lady we love—what happy wonder then, what blessed awe must we think is that which fills the soul when it attains the vision of divine beauty! What sweet fire, what delightful burning must we believe that to be which springs from the fountain of supreme and true beauty, the source of every other beauty which never increases or diminishes: always beautiful and in itself most simple and equal in every part, like only to itself, and partaking of none other, but so beautiful that all other beautiful things are beautiful because they derive their beauty from it.

"This is that beauty, indistinguishable from the highest good, which by its light calls and draws all things to itself and not only gives intellect to intellectual things, reason to rational things, sense and the desire to live to sensual things, but also transmits to plants and to stones motion and that natural instinct peculiar to them, as a vestige of itself. Therefore, this love is as much greater and happier than the others as the cause that moves it is more excellent; and so, just as material fire refines gold, so this most sacred fire in our souls destroys and consumes what is mortal therein and quickens and beautifies that celestial part which in the soul was at first deadened and buried by the senses. This is the pyre on which, the poets write, Hercules was burned at the summit of Mount Oeta and through whose burning he became divine and immortal after death; this is the chariot of Elias which doubles the grace and happiness in the souls of those who are worthy to see it when they depart from this earthly baseness and fly toward Heaven.

"Therefore, let us direct all thoughts and powers of our soul to this most sacred light which shows us the path that leads to Heaven; and following after it and divesting ourselves of the human passions in which we were clothed when we fell, let us ascend by the ladder which bears the imprint of sensual beauty at its lowest rung, to the sublime place where heavenly, gracious, and true beauty dwells, which lies hidden in the innermost secret recesses of God, so that profane eyes cannot behold it. And here we shall find a most happy end to our desires, true rest from our labors, a sure remedy to our miseries, a wholesome medicine for our infirmities, and the safest port away from the dark storms of this life's tempestuous sea.

70. "O most holy Love, what mortal tongue, then, can praise you worthily? Most beautiful, most good, most wise, you flow from the union of beauty and goodness, and there in that union you dwell, and by that union you return to it there, as in a circle. Sweetest bond of the universe midway between celestial and terrestrial things, with gracious disposition and just proportion, you direct the celestial powers to govern the lower ones and, turning the minds of mortals back to their source, you join them to it. You unite the elements in harmony, move nature to produce, and move whatever is born to the continuation of life. You join things that are separate, give perfection to the imperfect, likeness to the unlike, friendship to the hostile, fruit to the earth, calm to the sea, vital light to the heavens. You are father of true pleasures, of all grace, of peace, of gentleness and benevolence, enemy of rude cruelty and vileness—in short, you are the beginning and end of all good. And because you delight in residing in the flower of beautiful bodies and souls and from there sometimes consent to reveal yourself a little to the eyes and minds of those who are worthy of seeing you, I believe that you now dwell among us.

"Deign, then, O Lord, to hear our prayers, infuse yourself in our hearts and with the splendor of your most sacred fire illuminate our darkness and like a faithful guide, in this blind maze, show us the true path. Correct the falsity of our senses and after our long delirium give us the true and substantial good; make us savor those spiritual odors that quicken the powers of the intellect and hear the celestial harmony with such accord that discord of passion may no longer exist in us; intoxicate us at that inexhaustible fountain of contentment that always delights, never satiates, and always gives a taste of true blessedness to anyone who drinks from its living and limpid waters; with the rays of your light purge our eyes of dark ignorance so that they no longer value mortal beauty but know that the things they first seemed to see are not and that those they did not see truly are. Accept our souls which are offered to you in sacrifice; burn them in that living flame which consumes all material ugliness so that, wholly separated from the body, they may be united with divine beauty in an everlasting and most sweet bond, and that we, being separated from ourselves, may, like true lovers, be able to become one with the beloved, and rising up beyond the earth, be admitted to the banquet of angels, where, nourished on ambrosia and immortal nectar, we may at last die a most happy death in life, as did those ancient fathers whose souls you seized by the most ardent power of contemplation from the body, and unite with God."

71. Having spoken thus far with so much vehemence that he seemed almost in a trance and beside himself, Bembo remained quiet and immobile, keeping his eyes turned toward Heaven, as if enraptured. And then Signora Emilia, who along with the others had been very attentively listening to his discourse, took the hem of his robe and, shaking him a little, said: "Take care, Messer Pietro, that with these thoughts your soul, too, does not part from your body."

"Madam," replied Messer Pietro, "that would not be the first miracle that love has worked in me."[60]

* * *

[Afterward, the others urge Bembo to continue, but he says he no longer feels inspired. Signor Gasparo asserts that this path to happiness will be difficult for men and impossible for women. Then they propose that Bembo address the question of whether or not women are as capable of divine love for the next evening, when they all discover to their great surprise that it is already dawn, and the book ends with them going to their chambers, still reflecting upon Signor Gasparo's attitude toward women.]

NOTES

•❧•

1. Dom Miguel da Silva (c. 1480–1556), to whom the book was dedicated, was a Portuguese nobleman and cleric who served as an ambassador to Popes Leo X, Adrian VI, and Clement VII in Rome, where he became friends with Castiglione. He earned a certain reputation for his writings and was made a cardinal in 1541.

2. Guidobaldo of Montefeltro (1472–1508), the son of Federico of Montefeltro (1422–82) and Battista Sforza, succeeded his father as Duke of Urbino in 1482. He married Elisabetta Gonzaga in 1486 but had no children. He adopted his nephew Francesco Maria della Rovere (1490–1538) as his heir in 1504. Francesco inherited the duchy in 1508 upon Guidobaldo's death.

3. Vittoria della Colonna (1492–1547) was the wife of the Marquis of Pescara and a renowned poetess and woman of letters who exchanged lyrics with Michelangelo.

4. This elegiac enumeration of his dead friends includes Alfonso Ariosto (1475–1525), distantly related to the poet Ludovico Ariosto. Alfonso was apparently the one who encouraged Castiglione to write his *Book of the Courtier* at the suggestion of Francis I of France. The book was originally dedicated to Alfonso, who was himself a model courtier. At his death, the book was rededicated to da Silva.

5. Giuliano de' Medici (1479–1516) resided for lengthy periods of time at the court of Urbino while the Medici were exiled from Florence (1494–1512). The youngest son of Lorenzo de' Medici, Il Magnifico, he was made Duke of Nemours by Francis I of France. Niccolò Machiavelli originally dedicated *The Prince* to Giuliano but was forced to change the dedication after his death in 1516 (see note 1 to *The Prince*).

6. Bernardo Dovizi da Bibbiena (1470–1520) served Giovanni de' Medici, Giuliano's brother, who made him a cardinal after his election to the papacy as Leo X. Bibbiena's influence on Leo was so profound that he became known as "the other Pope." A patron of Raphael and a friend of Castiglione, he was also the writer of one of the new comedies imitative of Plautus, *La Calandria*.

7. A nobleman and politician from Genoa, Ottaviano Fregoso (1470–1524), like Giuliano de' Medici, sought refuge in Urbino, where he was exiled from his native city in 1497. After serving Francesco Maria della Rovere as ambassador to

France, he was elected Doge of Genoa in 1513 and had French protection until 1522, when he was taken prisoner by the Marquis of Pescara. He died in exile.

8. Elisabetta Gonzaga (1471–1526), the second daughter of the Marquis Federico Gonzaga of Mantua, married Duke Guidobaldo in 1489. She was greatly admired for her elegance, wit, strength, and virtue. Because of her husband's poor health, she was a dominant figure at the court of Urbino.

9. Castiglione refers here to Plato's *Republic*, Xenophon's *Cyropaedia*, and Cicero's *De oratore*.

10. Federico of Montefeltro (1422–82), famous for military skill, his wise rule, and his love of arts and letters, was in 1474 made Duke of Urbino and Captain General of the church by Pope Sixtus IV. His wife, Battista Sforza, niece of Duke Francesco Sforza of Milan, gave him several daughters and one son, Guidobaldo. He built the enchantingly beautiful palace of Urbino, where the *Book of the Courtier* takes place.

11. Alfonso II of Aragon (1448–95), the Duke of Calabria, became King of Naples in 1494.

12. Ferdinand II of Aragon (1469–96) was King of Naples.

13. Pope Alexander VI (1431–1503) was elected in 1492. The former Rodrigo Borgia, a Spanish cardinal, Alexander VI was the father of the famous Borgia discussed in Machiavelli's *The Prince*.

14. Pope Julius II (1443–1513), Giuliano della Rovere, was elected Pope in 1503 and was known as the "warrior pope" as well as a famous patron of the arts. Michelangelo painted the Sistine Chapel for Julius.

15. Emilia Pia (d. 1528), born the daughter of Marco Pio of Carpi, lived in Urbino after the death of her husband, Antonio da Montefeltro (a natural brother of Guidobaldo), as the duchess's constant companion. Like her mistress, she was known for her wit, gaiety, and virtue.

16. Federico Fregoso (1480–1541), younger brother of Ottaviano and nephew of Duke Guidobaldo, was a soldier, respected diplomat, courtier, and active politician who first supported and then opposed his brother Ottaviano during his rule in Genoa. Julius II made him Archbishop of Salerno in 1507 and Pope Paul III made him a cardinal in 1539. Federico was a close friend of many writers of the time, including Castiglione, as well as a student of languages.

17. Pietro Bembo (1470–1547) came from a noble Venetian family and lived in Florence as a child. An authority on language, style, and platonic love, and a poet in the Petrarchan tradition, Bembo was one of the most respected men of letters in the Renaissance. He spent the years between 1506 and 1512 at the court of Urbino. He moved to Rome and became a papal secretary for Pope Leo X in 1512 and was made a cardinal in 1539. He corrected the proofs for the *Book of the Courtier*.

18. Cesare Gonzaga (1475–1512) was related to the Gonzaga family of Mantua and a cousin of Castiglione. Reputed a man of great valor, he served the rulers of Urbino as a soldier and diplomat. His friendship with Castiglione and Bembo was very strong and close.

19. Count Ludovico da Canossa (1476–1532) came from a noble family of

Verona and was a close friend and relation of Castiglione. From 1496 on, he spent time at the court of Urbino and served first the papacy, then King Francis I of France as a diplomat. A man of notable ability and culture, he was also a friend of Erasmus and Raphael. He became Bishop of Bayeux in 1516.

20. Gasparo Pallavicino (1486–1511) was a Lombard, a descendant of the Marquis of Cortemaggiore, near Piacenza. One of the youngest members of the court, he was always ill and died at an early age.

21. Ludovico Pio (d. 1512) was a distant cousin of Emilia Pia, who probably met Castiglione in Milan. He was a brave soldier and eventually died after being wounded in a battle.

22. Sigismondo Morello da Ortona came from the Abruzzi region and may have belonged to the Ricciardi family. The misogynist of the group, he served Guidobaldo well as a soldier and courtier. He is the only old courtier depicted by Castiglione, and he exhibits an irritability unusual in the other courtiers.

23. Pietro da Napoli briefly appears in the Book of the Courtier to tell a joke. Little is known of him, although he apparently accompanied Julius II to Viterbo after the Bologna expedition.

24. Roberto da Bari (d. 1512) belonged to the Massimi family of Bari. A young and elegant courtier, he was another of Castiglione's good friends.

25. Bernardo Accolti (1458–1535) was known as the "Unico Aretino" because he was born in Arezzo, the son of a famous lawyer and historian, Benedetto Accolti, and gained acclaim as a great improviser of poetry in courts from Milan to Naples. He grew to have a rather inflated opinion of his own talents. Both Julius II and Leo X were his patrons.

26. Giancristoforo Romano (c. 1465–1512), a noted sculptor, medal-maker, goldsmith, architect, and musician, visited the court of Urbino in 1506 and 1507.

27. Pietro Monte served Duke Guidobaldo for a time as Master of the Horse in charge of the tournaments. Little is known about him except that his work in Urbino was praiseworthy.

28. Antonio Maria Terpandro, a friend of Bembo and Bibbiena, probably came from Rome and spent time in Urbino at the time Julius II was Pope. He was a singer and a musician, and thus his nickname appropriately recalls Terpander of Lesbos, the father of Greek classical music and lyric poetry.

29. Niccolò Frisio (or Frigio) was a German friend of Castiglione and Bembo who was a man of culture and a skilled diplomat. In 1510, he retired to a monastery in Naples.

30. The court of Urbino described by Castiglione represents a microcosm of Italian society.

31. Ippolito d'Este (1479–1520), the son of Duke Ercole of Ferrara, was a friend of Leonardo da Vinci and a patron of Ludovico Ariosto. He was made a cardinal by Pope Alexander VI in 1493.

32. A popular buffoon and jester at the papal court.

33. Central to Castiglione's conception of the courtier are the attributes of grace and sprezzatura, or nonchalance. Grace (grazia) is the key quality of the

courtier and refers to the harmonious elegance and refinement that Giorgio Vasari viewed as a product of genius. In his *Lives of the Artists*, Vasari describes the style of Raphael as "gracious." Grace is true art which does not seem to be art; it is a special gift which can be enhanced by application and effort, beginning when one is young. The selection of appropriate models to imitate is important, but the complete assimilation of what one learns is crucial (note the simile of the bee gathering nectar that the Count employs in the second paragraph of his response to Messer Cesare). Without grace, all the courtier's actions will be rendered worthless.

34. Galeazzo Sanseverino (d. 1525) served as a military officer for Ludovico Sforza in Milan before being appointed grand equerry by King Louis XII of France in 1506.

35. *Sprezzatura*, or nonchalance, is a term coined by Castiglione to describe the ability to conceal all effort or art in one's words or actions, an ability without which the courtier cannot achieve true grace. Castiglione uses the word *disinvoltura*, "ease," as a synonym. The courtier must always appear natural.

36. The feeling of wonder, *meraviglia*, on the part of the onlooker is the result of seeing the courtier's true grace.

37. A gentleman at the court of Urbino who has never been completely identified.

38. Monseigneur d' Angoulême (1494–1547) became King Francis I of France in 1515 and was a great patron of the arts and letters.

39. Alexander the Great (356–323 B.C.); his regard for Homer was noted by Plutarch in his *Parallel Lives*.

40. Aristotle (384–322 B.C.) was a pupil of Plato and tutor of Alexander the Great.

41. Alcibiades (c. 450–404 B.C.), the Athenian general and politician, was the pupil and friend of Socrates. See Plutarch's *Parallel Lives*.

42. Socrates (469–399 B.C.) was the most famous Greek philosopher; his ideas are known mainly through the works of Plato and Xenophon. He was put to death by the state for sedition but came to be idealized for his virtue and honesty.

43. Scipio Africanus the Younger (d. 129 B.C.), or Scipio Aemilianus, conquered Carthage in 146 B.C., completing the efforts of Scipio Africanus the Elder (237–183 B.C.), who had defeated Hannibal at Zama. Polybius tells us that the younger Scipio was worthy of the great Africanus (he was his adopted grandson) in his virtue, courage, vigor, and intellect. He was a patron of the arts and of such writers as the playwright Plautus and the philosopher Panaetius.

44. The Greek historian Xenophon (c. 430–c. 355 B.C.) wrote the *Cyropaedia* (*The Education of Cyrus*), a moralistic account of the life of Cyrus the Great, King of Persia, which influenced generations of readers and writers. Machiavelli uses Cyrus as an example of a worthy prince (see *The Prince*, chapter 6) who acquired power by his own skill and not as a result of fortune's fickle favor.

45. To bolster his claim that a courtier should study the humanities, the Count refers to various great military leaders in these paragraphs. This list of other great Roman generals and political figures includes Lucullus (106–57

B.C.), Lucius Cornelius Sulla (138–78 B.C.), Gnaeus Pompeius Magnus (Pompey the Great, 106–48 B.C.), and Marcus Junius Brutus (c.85–42 B.C.). All were known variously for military skills, humanistic learning, devotion to old Roman virtues, and courage.

46. Hannibal (247–183 B.C.) was the Carthaginian general defeated by Scipio Africanus at the battle of Zama in 203 B.C. near Carthage. Trained as a leader from an early age by his father, Hamilcar Barca, he was thoughtful and shrewd in his dealings with the Romans, who thought him exceedingly cruel.

47. Aristippus (c.435–356 B.C.), a friend and student of Socrates, is known as the founder of the Cyrenaic School of hedonism; he lived and taught at the court of Dionysius, the ruler of Syracuse in Sicily.

48. Achilles, the son of Peleus, King of Phthia, and a sea goddess, Thetus, was educated by Phoenix, who taught him to speak well and fight bravely, and by Chiron, who taught him the art of healing. As the hero of Homer's epic poem the *Iliad*, he reveals intelligence, courage, and intense feelings. His anger is the subject of the poem, but he is also loyal and even wise in dealing with others.

49. Grasso ("Fatso") was the nickname given to a man in the service of the Medici family. He was well known in Urbino.

50. Vincenzio Colli, Il Calmeta (d. 1508), was a poet and writer from Castelnuova.

51. Bernardo goes beyond the traditional definitions of man as a supremely rational animal or a sinful one to characterize the human being as a risible animal. Laughter plays an important part in his society.

52. The numeral VI could be read as the ablative form of Latin *vis*, which means "force," "might," or "violence." The play on words suggests that Alexander VI became Pope by violence or *vi*.

53. These comments on two worthy popes, Nicholas V, a saintly man and theologian, and the gentle and good Pius III, seem rather harsh. Perhaps *Nihil Papa Valet*, "The Pope is capable of nothing," refers to Pius' kindliness and the brevity of his reign.

54. In the third book, Magnifico Giuliano defends women against the misogyny of Gasparo Pallavicino.

55. In Book IV, Ottaviano questions the goals of the courtier in the previous book and offers a new goal with a social purpose. Through the proper education, a courtier can come to know the good and the true.

56. Bembo published the *Asolani* in 1505; it contained, in Book III, the first literary expression of Neoplatonist views which became the common property of artists, courtiers, and writers. The classical source of these views was Plato's *Symposium*, but, in Marsilio Ficino's translation and commentary (written in 1469 and published in 1484 in Latin), "platonic" love was introduced into the European vocabulary. Ficino views this emotion not as homosexuality but as an intellectual love between friends based on man's love for God. Love is always aroused by sight, whether it is bestial, human, or divine.

57. Bembo's description of the human soul conforms to the traditional Christian model. In *De Officiis*, Cicero distinguishes between the two essential

activities or forces of the soul: appetite, which "impels a man this way or that"; and reason, "which teaches and explains what should be done."

58. The simile of the sun comes from Plato's *Republic*, Book VI, where he compares the good to the sun. It is also comparable to the illumination experienced by St. Augustine at his conversion in his *Confessions*. Bembo's eloquent concluding speech combines Christian and Platonic images and concepts derived from Plato and works by Ficino and Bembo himself.

59. Bembo's discourse on platonic love is often discussed in terms of the famous metaphor of the "ladder," of which sensual love is only the first step or rung in the ascent to true or divine love.

60. This ironic conclusion raises questions about this ideal love.

NICCOLÒ MACHIAVELLI
1469–1527

NICCOLÒ MACHIAVELLI WAS BORN IN FLORENCE, BUT VERY LITTLE IS KNOWN about his early life before he entered the Florentine Chancery in 1498, where he was to serve the city's republican government until 1512. We do know, however, that Machiavelli's early reading included a copy of Livy's history of republican Rome and that his later characteristic tendency to compare great events or men from the classical past with contemporary affairs must have been born during his childhood readings of the Roman historians. Even though his contribution to modern political theory has always been primarily connected to the influence of his little treatise on the principality, *The Prince* (written in 1513; published posthumously in 1532), Machiavelli was himself an avowed republican and was even imprisoned and tortured in 1513 by the Medici rulers of Florence who overturned the republican government which he served.

In fact, Machiavelli considered *The Prince* an occasional work, one which owed its relevance to fortuitous historical circumstances which characterized the year 1513. At that time, the son of Lorenzo de' Medici, Giovanni de' Medici, was elected to the papacy, taking the title Leo X. The Pope's brother, Giuliano de' Medici, Duke of Nemours, seemed destined to rule Florence and Tuscany. For a brief time, it seemed to Machiavelli that Medici power in Tuscany might unite with Medici control of the papacy to form the nucleus of an Italian alliance (perhaps even a nation-state) to liberate Italy from her "barbarian" invaders. In *The Prince*, much the same kind of situation is described as Machiavelli discusses his prototype for the Renaissance ruler, Cesare Borgia, whose military adventures in central Italy benefited from the control exercised over the papacy by his father, Alexander VI. To employ Machiavelli's own terms, the Medici were presented with a historical opportunity (*occasione*) that constituted a challenge to their ability and ingenuity (*virtù*), a challenge which was the gift of a fleeting fortune (*fortuna*).

In the process of discussing the ideal princely ruler, rather than the form of government closer to his own preferences—that of a republic, which he treated in his more lengthy book *The Discourses on the Decades of Livy* (written 1513–19; published posthumously in 1531)—Machiavelli covered a wide range of important philosophical and ethical questions relating to politics. He is most original and most provocative when he deals with the sometimes amoral or immoral means by which power is seized, administered, and lost. A good deal of the appeal of this book lay in its unabashed pragmatism, in Machiavelli's willingness to discuss the dark underside of the nature of power.

As a result of Machiavelli's ventures into such dangerous waters, his reputation has for centuries been colored by attacks upon his morality. Elizabethan England saw in *The Prince* a compendium of maxims fit only for tyrants, and in the nearly four hundred references to Machiavelli in the drama of the period, the terms "Machiavellian" and "Machiavellianism" were introduced into the English language. Not only Protestants condemned the book; Catholics placed it on the Index in 1559. And Machiavelli's first name was even associated with a preexisting nickname for the devil: Old Nick. This *succès de scandale* guaranteed a clamorous reception for the treatise, and, after the Bible, it was probably the most widely read book on the entire European continent during the Renaissance. The style of *The Prince* is still as fresh as when it first appeared in print, and modern commentators still hotly debate the significance of Machiavelli's sometimes shocking definition of the relationship between politics and morality.

BIBLIOGRAPHY

Niccolò Machiavelli, *The Portable Machiavelli*, eds. and trans. Peter Bondanella and Mark Musa (New York: Viking Penguin, 1979); Peter Bondanella, *Machiavelli and the Art of Renaissance History* (Detroit: Wayne State University Press, 1974); Felix Gilbert, *Machiavelli and Guicciardini: Politics and History in Sixteenth-Century Florence* (Princeton: Princeton University Press, 1965); J.G.A. Pocock, *The Machiavellian Moment: Florentine Political Thought and the Atlantic Republican Tradition* (Princeton: Princeton University Press, 1975); Roberto Ridolfi, *The Life of Niccolò Machiavelli* (London: Routledge & Kegan Paul, 1963); Quentin Skinner, *The Foundations of Modern Political Thought*, Vol. 1 (Cambridge: Cambridge University Press, 1978).

SELECTIONS FROM
THE PRINCE •

· ❦ ·

Dedicatory Preface
Niccolò Machiavelli to Lorenzo de' Medici, the Magnificent[1]

In most instances, it is customary for those who desire to win the favor
of a Prince to present themselves to him with those things they value
most or which they feel will most please him; thus, we often see princes
given horses, arms, vestments of gold cloth, precious stones, and similar
ornaments suited to their greatness. Wishing, therefore, to offer myself to
Your Magnificence with some evidence of my devotion to you, I have
not found among my belongings anything that I might value more or
prize so much as the knowledge of the deeds of great men, which I have
learned from a long experience in modern affairs and a continuous study
of antiquity; having with great care and for a long time thought about
and examined these deeds, and now having set them down in a little
book, I am sending them to Your Magnificence.

And although I consider this work unworthy of your station, I am
sure, nevertheless, that your humanity will move you to accept it, for
there could not be a greater gift from me than to give you the means to
be able, in a very brief time, to understand all that I, in many years and
with many hardships and dangers, have come to understand and to
appreciate. I have neither decorated nor filled this work with fancy
sentences, with rich and magnificent words, or with any other form of
rhetorical or unnecessary ornamentation which many writers normally
use in describing and enriching their subject matter; for I wished that
nothing should set my work apart or make it pleasing except the variety
of its material and the seriousness of its contents. Neither do I wish that
it be thought presumptuous if a man of low and inferior station dares to
debate and to regulate the rule of princes; for, just as those who paint
landscapes place themselves in a low position on the plain in order to
consider the nature of the mountains and the high places and place

---

•These selections are from Niccolò Machiavelli, *The Prince*, ed. Peter
Bondanella and trans. Peter Bondanella and Mark Musa (Oxford: Oxford Uni-
versity Press, 1985).

themselves high atop mountains in order to study the plains, in like manner, to know well the nature of the people one must be a prince, and to know well the nature of princes one must be of the people.

Accept, therefore, Your Magnificence, this little gift in the spirit that I send it; if you read and consider it carefully, you will discover in it my most heartfelt desire that you may attain that greatness which fortune and all your own capacities promise you. And if Your Magnificence will turn your eyes at some time from the summit of your high position toward these lowlands, you will realize to what degree I unjustly suffer a great and continuous malevolence of fortune.

* * *

[In Chapter I, Machiavelli distinguishes between different kinds of principalities—hereditary or new ones without long traditions. Chapter II discusses the first type, which do not really interest Machiavelli. He is most concerned with the "new" principality, the subject of Chapter III, since most Renaissance rulers of the day in Italy fell into this category. Chapters IV and V discuss some historical examples taken from the period of Alexander the Great and Greek, Roman, or modern Florentine history.]

———— · ❦ · ————

CHAPTER VI

*On New Principalities Acquired by
One's Own Arms and Skill*

No one should marvel if, in speaking of principalities that are totally new as to their prince and organization, I use the most illustrious examples; since men almost always tread the paths made by others and proceed in their affairs by imitation, although they are not completely able to stay on the path of others nor attain the skill of those they imitate, a prudent man should always enter those paths taken by great men and imitate those who have been most excellent, so that if one's own skill does not match theirs, at least it will have the smell of it; and he should proceed like those prudent archers[2] who, aware of the strength of their bow when the target they are aiming at seems too distant, set their sights much higher than the designated target, not in order to reach to such a height with their arrow but rather to be able, with the aid of such a high aim, to strike the target.

I say, therefore, that in completely new principalities, where there is a new prince, one finds in maintaining them more or less difficulty according to the greater or lesser skill of the one who acquires them. And because this act of transition from private citizen to prince presupposes either ingenuity or fortune,[3] it appears that either the one or the other of these two things should, in part, mitigate many of the problems; nevertheless, he who relies upon fortune less maintains his position best. Things are also facilitated when the prince, having no other dominions to govern, is constrained to come to live there in person. But to come to those who, by means of their own skill and not because of fortune, have become princes, I say that the most admirable are Moses, Cyrus, Romulus, Theseus, and the like.[4] And although we should not discuss Moses, since he was a mere executor of things ordered by God, nevertheless he must be admired, if for nothing but that grace which made him worthy of talking with God. But let us consider Cyrus and the others who have acquired or founded kingdoms; you will find them all admirable; and if their deeds and their particular institutions are considered, they will not appear different from those of Moses, who had so great a guide. And examining their deeds and their lives, one can see that they received nothing from fortune except the opportunity, which gave them the material they could mold into whatever form they desired; and without that opportunity the strength of their spirit would have been extinguished, and without that strength the opportunity would have come in vain.

It was therefore necessary for Moses to find the people of Israel in Egypt slaves and oppressed by the Egyptians in order that they might be disposed to follow him to escape this servitude. It was necessary for Romulus not to stay in Alba and to be exposed at birth so that he might become King of Rome and founder of that nation. It was necessary for Cyrus to find the Persians discontented with the empire of the Medes, and the Medes soft and effeminate after a lengthy peace. Theseus could not have shown his skill if he had not found the Athenians scattered. These opportunities, therefore, made these men successful, and their outstanding ingenuity made that opportunity known to them, whereby their nations were ennobled and became prosperous.

Like these men, those who become princes through their skill acquire the principality with difficulty, but they hold on to it easily; and the difficulties they encounter in acquiring the principality grow, in part, out of the new institutions and methods they are obliged to introduce in order to found their state and their security. And one should bear in mind that there is nothing more difficult to execute, nor more dubious of success, nor more dangerous to administer than to introduce a new order of things; for he who introduces it has all those who profit from the old order as his enemies, and he has only lukewarm allies in all those who might profit from the new. This lukewarmness partly stems from fear of their adversaries, who have the law on their side, and partly from the skepticism of men, who do not truly believe in new things unless they have actually had personal experience of them. Therefore, it happens that whenever those who are enemies have the chance to attack, they do so enthusiastically, whereas those others defend hesitantly, so that they, together with the prince, are in danger.

It is necessary, however, if we desire to examine this subject thoroughly, to observe whether these innovators act on their own or are dependent on others: that is, if they are forced to beg or are able to use power in conducting their affairs. In the first case, they always come to a bad end and never accomplish anything; but when they depend on their own resources and can use power, then only seldom do they find themselves in peril. From this comes the fact that all armed prophets were victorious and the unarmed came to ruin. Besides what has been said, people are fickle by nature; and it is simple to convince them of something but difficult to hold them in that conviction; and, therefore, affairs should be managed in such a way that when they no longer believe, they can be made to believe by force. Moses, Cyrus, Theseus, and Romulus could not have made their institutions long respected if they had been unarmed; as in our times happened to Brother Girolamo Savonarola,[5] who was ruined by his new institutions when the populace began no longer to believe in them, since he had no way of holding steady those who had believed nor of making the disbelievers believe. Therefore, such men have great problems in getting ahead, and they meet all their dangers as they proceed, and they must overcome them with their skill; but once they have overcome them and have begun to be respected, having removed those who were envious of their merits, they remain powerful, secure, honored, and happy.

To such noble examples I should like to add a minor one; but it will have some relation to the others, and I should like it to suffice for all similar cases: and this is Hiero of Syracuse.[6] From a private citizen, this man became the prince of Syracuse; he did not receive anything from fortune except the opportunity, for since the citizens of Syracuse were oppressed, they elected him as their leader; and from that rank he proved himself worthy of becoming their prince. And he was so skillful while still a private citizen that someone who wrote about him said that "he lacked nothing to reign save a kingdom." He did away with the old militia and established a new one; he put aside old friendships and made new ones; and since he had allies and soldiers that depended on him, he was able to construct whatever building he wished on such a foundation; so that it cost him great effort to acquire and little to maintain.

· ❦ ·

CHAPTER VII

On New Principalities Acquired with the Arms of Others and by Fortune

Those private citizens who become princes through fortune alone do so with little effort, but they maintain their position only with a great deal; they meet no obstacles along their way since they fly to success, but all their problems arise when they have arrived. And these are the men who are granted a state either because they have money or because they enjoy the favor of him who grants it: this occurred to many in Greece in the cities of Ionia and the Hellespont, where Darius created princes in order that he might hold these cities for his security and glory; in like manner were set up those emperors who from private citizens came to power by bribing the soldiers. Such men depend solely upon two very uncertain and unstable things: the will and the fortune of him who granted them the state; they do not know how and are not able to maintain their position. They do not know how, since if men are not of great intelligence and ingenuity, it is not reasonable that they know how to rule, having always lived as private citizens; they are not able to, since they do not have forces that are friendly and faithful. Besides, states that rise quickly, just as all the other things of nature that are born and grow rapidly, cannot have roots and ramifications; the first bad weather kills them, unless these men who have suddenly become princes, as I have noted, are of such ability that they know how to prepare themselves quickly and to preserve what fortune has put in their laps, and to construct afterward those foundations that others have built before becoming princes.

Regarding the two methods just listed for becoming a prince, by skill or by fortune, I should like to offer two recent examples: these are Francesco Sforza and Cesare Borgia. Francesco, through the required means and with a great deal of ingenuity, became Duke of Milan from his station as a private citizen, and that which he had acquired with countless hardships he maintained with little trouble. On the other hand, Cesare Borgia (commonly called Duke Valentino) acquired the state through the favor and help of his father, and when this no longer existed, he lost it,[7] and this despite the fact that he did everything and used every means that a prudent and skillful man ought to use in order to root himself securely in those states that the arms and fortune of others had granted him. Because as stated above, anyone who does not lay his foundations beforehand could do so later only with great skill, although this would be done with inconvenience to the architect and danger to the building. If, therefore, we consider all the steps taken by the Duke, we shall see that he laid sturdy foundations for his future power; and I do not judge it useless to discuss them, for I would not know of any better precepts to give to a new prince than the example of his deeds; and if he did not succeed in his plans, it was not his fault but was instead the result of an extraordinary and extreme instance of ill fortune.

Alexander VI, in his attempts to advance his son, the Duke, had many problems, both present and future. First, he saw no means of making him master of any state that did not already belong to the church; and if he attempted to seize anything belonging to the church, he knew that the Venetians and the Duke of Milan would not agree to it because Faenza and Rimini were already under the protection of the Venetians. Moreover, he saw that the troops of Italy, and especially those he would have to use, were in the hands of those who had reason to fear the Pope's power; and he could not count on them, since they were all Orsini, Colonnesi, and their allies.[8] Therefore, he had to disturb the order of things and cause turmoil among these states in order securely to make himself master of a part of them. This was easy for him to do, for he found that the Venetians, moved by other motives, had decided to bring the French back into Italy; not only did he not oppose this, but he rendered it easier by annulling King Louis' first marriage. The King, therefore, entered Italy with the aid of the Venetians and the consent of Alexander; and no sooner was he in Milan than the Pope procured troops from him for the Romagna campaign; these were granted to him because of the reputation of the King.

Having seized, then, Romagna and having beaten the Colonna, the Duke, wishing to maintain his gain and to advance further, was held back by two things: first, his troops' lack of loyalty; second, the will of France; that is, the troops of the Orsini, which he had been using, might let him down and not only keep him from acquiring more territory but even take away what he had already conquered; and the King, as well, might do the same. He had one experience like this with the Orsini soldiers, when, after the seizure of Faenza, he attacked Bologna and saw them go reluctantly into battle; as for the King, he learned his purpose when he invaded Tuscany after the capture of the Duchy of Urbino; the King forced him to abandon that campaign. As a consequence, the Duke decided to depend no longer upon the arms and favor of others. And his first step was to weaken the Orsini and Colonna factions in Rome; he won over all their followers who were noblemen, making them his own noblemen and giving them huge subsidies; and he honored them, according to their rank, with military commands and civil appointments; as a result, in a few months their affection for the factions died out in their hearts and all of it was turned toward the Duke. After this, he waited for the opportunity to do away with the Orsini leaders, having already scattered those of the Colonna family; and good opportunity arose and the use he put it to was even better: for when the Orsini later realized that the greatness of the Duke and of the Church meant their ruin, they called together a meeting at Magione, in Perugian territory. From this resulted the rebellion of Urbino and the uprisings in Romagna, and endless dangers for the Duke, all of which he overcame with the aid of the French. And when his reputation had been regained, placing no trust either in France or other outside forces, in order not to have to test them, he turned to deceptive methods. And he knew how to falsify his intentions so well that the Orsini themselves, through Lord Paulo, made peace with him; the Duke did not fail to use all kinds of gracious acts to reassure Paulo, giving him money, clothing, and horses, so that the stupidity of the Orsini brought them to Sinigaglia and into his hands.[9] Having killed these leaders and having changed their allies into his friends, the Duke had laid very good foundations for his power, having all of Romagna along with the Duchy of Urbino, and, more important, it appeared that he had befriended Romagna and had won the support of all of its populace once the people began to taste the beneficial results of his rule.

And because this matter is notable and worthy of imitation by others, I shall not pass it over. After the Duke had taken Romagna and had found it governed by powerless lords who had been more anxious to plunder their subjects than to govern them and had given them reason for disunity rather than unity, so that the entire province was full of thefts, fights, and of every other kind of insolence, he decided that if he wanted to make it peaceful and obedient to the ruler's law it would be necessary to give it good government. Therefore, he put Messer Remirro de Orco,[10] a cruel and able man, in command there and gave him complete authority. This man, in little time, made the province peaceful and united, and in doing this he made for himself a great reputation.

Afterward, the Duke decided that such great authority was no longer required, for he was afraid that it might become odious; and he set up in the middle of the province a civil court with a very distinguished president, wherein each city had its own counselor. And because he realized that the rigorous measures of the past had generated a certain amount of hatred, he wanted to show, in order to purge men's minds and to win them to his side completely, that if any form of cruelty had arisen, it did not originate from him but from the harsh nature of his minister. And having found the occasion to do this, one morning at Cesena he had Messer Remirro placed on the piazza in two pieces with a block of wood and a bloody sword beside him. The ferocity of such a spectacle left those people satisfied and amazed at the same time.

But let us return to where we digressed. I say that the Duke, finding himself very powerful and partially secured from present dangers, having armed himself the way he wanted to, and having in large measure destroyed those nearby forces that might have harmed him, still had to take into account the King of France if he wished to continue his conquests, for he realized that the King, who had become aware of his error too late, would not support further conquest. And because of this, he began to seek out new allies and to temporize with France during the campaign the French undertook in the Kingdom of Naples against the Spaniards who were besieging Gaeta. His intent was to make himself secure against them; and he would have quickly succeeded in this if Alexander had lived.

And these were his methods concerning present things. But as for future events, he had first to fear that a new successor in control of the Church might not be his friend and might try to take away from him what Alexander had given him. Against this possibility he thought to secure himself in four ways: first, by putting to death all the relatives of those lords that he had dispossessed in order to prevent the Pope from employing that opportunity; second, by gaining the friendship of all the noblemen of Rome, as already mentioned, in order to hold the Pope in check by means of them; third, by making the college of Cardinals as much his own as he could; fourth, by acquiring such a large territory before the Pope died that he would be able to resist an initial attack without need of allies. Of these four things, he had achieved three by the time of Alexander's death; the fourth he had almost achieved, for he killed as many of the dispossessed noblemen as he could seize, and very few saved themselves; and he had won over the Roman noblemen; and he had a great following in the College of Cardinals; and as for the acquisition of new territory, he had planned to become lord of Tuscany and was already in possession of Perugia and Piombino and had taken Pisa under his protection. And as soon as he no longer needed to respect the wishes of France (for he no longer had to, since the French had already been deprived of the kingdom by the Spaniards, so that it was necessary for both of them to purchase his friendship), he would attack Pisa. After this, Lucca and Siena would have immediately surrendered, partly to spite the Florentines and partly out of fear, and the Florentines would have had no means of preventing it. If he had carried out these designs (and he would have brought them to fruition during the same year that Alexander died), he would have gathered together so many forces and such a reputation that he would have been able to stand alone and would no longer have had to rely upon the favor and forces of others, but rather on his own power and ingenuity. But Alexander died five years after he had drawn his sword. He left his son, gravely ill, with only the state of Romagna secured and with all the others up in the air, between two very powerful enemy armies. And there was in the Duke so much ferocity and so much ability, and so well did he understand how men can be won or lost, and so firm were the foundations that he had laid in such a short time, that if he had not had those armies upon him or if he had been healthy, he would have overcome every difficulty. And that his foundations were good is witnessed by the fact that Romagna waited more than a month for him; in Rome, although only half alive, he was safe; and although the Baglioni, the Vitelli, and the Orsini came to Rome, they found none of their allies opposed to him; if he could not set up a Pope he wanted, at least he could act to ensure that it would not be a man he did not want. But if he had been healthy at the time of Alexander's demise, everything would have been simple. And he himself said to me, on the day when Julius II was made Pope, that he had thought of what might happen on his father's death, and he had found a remedy for everything, except he never dreamed that at the time of his father's death he too would be at death's door.

Now, having summarized all of the Duke's actions, I would not know how to censure him; on the contrary, I believe I am correct in proposing that he be imitated by all those who have risen to power through fortune and with the arms of others. Because he, possessing great courage and high aims, could not have conducted himself in any other manner; and his plans were frustrated solely by the brevity of Alexander's life[11] and by his own illness. Anyone, therefore, who determines it necessary in his newly acquired principality to protect himself from his enemies, to win friends, to conquer either by force or by fraud, to make himself loved and feared by the people, to be followed and respected by his soldiers, to put to death those who can or may do him harm, to replace ancient institutions with new ones, to be severe and gracious, magnanimous and generous, to do away with unfaithful soldiers and to select new ones, to maintain the friendship of kings and of princes in such a way that they must assist you gladly or offend you with caution—that person cannot find more recent examples than this man's deeds. One can only censure him for making Julius Pope; in this he made a bad choice, since, as I said before, not being able to elect a Pope of his own, he could have kept anyone he wished from the papacy; and he should have never agreed to raising to the papacy any cardinal he might have offended or who, upon becoming Pope, might have cause to fear him. For men do harm either out of fear or hatred. Those he had injured were, among others, San Pietro ad Vincula, Colonna, San Giorgio, Ascanio;[12] any of the others, upon becoming Pope, would have to fear him, except for Rouen and the Spaniards; the latter because they were related to him and were in his debt, the former because of his power, since he was joined to the kingdom of France. Therefore, the Duke, above all else, should have made a Spaniard Pope; failing in that, he should have agreed to the election of Rouen[13] and not to that of San Pietro ad Vincula. And anyone who believes that new benefits make men of high station forget old injuries is deceiving himself. The Duke, then, erred in this election, and it was the cause of his ultimate downfall.

———————————————— • ❦ • ————————————————

CHAPTER VIII

On Those Who Have Become Princes Through Wickedness

But because there are yet two more ways one can from an ordinary citizen become prince, which cannot completely be attributed to either fortune or skill, I believe they should not be left unmentioned, although one of them will be discussed at greater length in a treatise on republics. These two are: when one becomes prince through some wicked and nefarious means or when a private citizen becomes prince of his native city through the favor of his fellow citizens. And in discussing the first way, I shall cite two examples, one from classical times and the other from recent days, without otherwise entering into the merits of this method, since I consider them sufficient for anyone forced to imitate them.

Agathocles the Sicilian,[14] not only from being an ordinary citizen but from being of low and abject status, became King of Syracuse. This man, a potter's son, lived a wicked life at every stage of his career; yet he joined to his wickedness such strength of mind and of body that, when he entered upon a military career, he rose through the ranks to become commander of Syracuse. Once placed in such a position, having decided to become prince and to hold with violence and without any obligations to others what had been granted to him by universal consent, and having made an agreement with Hamilcar the Carthaginian, who was waging war with his armies in Sicily, he called together one morning the people and the senate of Syracuse as if he were going to discuss things concerning the state; and with a prearranged signal, he had his troops kill all the senators and the richest citizens; and when they were dead, he seized and held the rule of the city without any opposition from the citizenry. And although he was twice defeated by the Carthaginians and eventually besieged, not only was he able to defend his city but, leaving part of his troops for the defense of the siege, with his other men he attacked Africa, and in a short time he freed Syracuse from the siege and forced the Carthaginians into dire straits: they were obliged to make peace with him and to be content with possession of Africa and to leave Sicily to Agathocles.

Anyone, therefore, who examines the deeds and the life of this man will observe nothing or very little that can be attributed to fortune; since, as was said earlier, not with the aid of others but by rising through the ranks, which involved a thousand hardships and dangers, did he come to rule the principality which he then maintained by many brave and dangerous actions. Still, it cannot be called ingenuity[15] to kill one's fellow citizens, to betray friends, to be without faith, without mercy, without religion; by these means one can acquire power but not glory. For if one were to consider Agathocles's ability in getting into and out of dangers, and his greatness of spirit in supporting and in overcoming adversaries, one can see no reason why he should be judged inferior to any most excellent commander; nevertheless, his vicious cruelty and inhumanity, along with numerous wicked deeds, do not permit us to honor him among the most excellent of men. One cannot, therefore, attribute to either fortune or skill what he accomplished without either the one or the other.

In our own days, during the reign of Alexander VI, Oliverotto of Fermo, who many years before had been left as a child without a father, was brought up by his maternal uncle, Giovanni Fogliani. While still very young he was sent to serve as a soldier under Paulo Vitelli so that, once he was versed in that skill, he might attain some outstanding military position. Then, after Paulo died, he served under his brother, Vitellozzo; and in a very brief time, because of his intelligence and his vigorous body and mind, he became the commander of his troops. But since he felt it was servile to work for others, he decided to seize Fermo with the aid of some citizens of Fermo who preferred servitude to the liberty of their native city, and with the assistance of the followers of Vitellozzo; and he wrote to Giovanni Fogliani that, having been away many years from home, he wished to come to see him and his city and to inspect his own inheritance; and since he had exerted himself for no other reason than to acquire glory, he wanted to arrive in honorable fashion, accompanied by an escort of a hundred horsemen from among his friends and servants so that his fellow citizens might see that he had not spent his time in vain; and he begged his uncle to arrange for an honorable reception from the people of Fermo, one which might bring honor not only to Giovanni but also to himself, being his pupil. Giovanni, therefore, in no way failed in his duty toward his nephew: he had him received in honorable fashion by the people of Fermo, and he gave him rooms in his own house. Oliverotto, after a few days had passed and he had secretly made the preparations necessary for his forthcoming wickedness, gave a magnificent banquet to which he invited Giovanni Fogliani and all of the first citizens of Fermo. And when the meal and all the other entertainment customary at such banquets were completed, Oliverotto, according to plan, began to discuss serious matters, speaking of the greatness of Pope Alexander and his son, Cesare, and of their undertakings. After Giovanni and the others had replied to his comments, he suddenly rose up, announcing that these were matters to be discussed in a more secluded place; and he retired into another room, followed by Giovanni and all the other citizens. No sooner were they seated than from secret places in the room out came soldiers who killed Giovanni and all the others. After this murder, Oliverotto mounted his horse, paraded through the town, and besieged the chief officials in the government palace; so that out of fear they were forced to obey him and to constitute a government of which he made himself prince. And when all those were killed who, because they were discontented, might have harmed him, he strengthened himself by instituting new civil and military institutions; so that, in the space of the year that he held the principality, not only was he secure in the city of Fermo, but he had become feared by all its neighbors. His expulsion would have been as difficult as that of Agathocles if he had not permitted himself to be tricked by Cesare Borgia, when at Sinigaglia, as was noted above, the Duke captured the Orsini and the

Vitelli; there he, too, was captured, a year after he committed the parricide, and together with Vitellozzo, who had been his teacher in ingenuity and wickedness, he was strangled.

One might wonder how Agathocles and others like him, after so many betrayals and cruelties, could live for such a long time secure in their cities and defend themselves from outside enemies without being plotted against by their own citizens; many others, using cruel means, were unable even in peaceful times to hold on to their state, not to speak of the uncertain times of war. I believe that this depends on whether cruelty be well or badly used. Well used are those cruelties (if it is permitted to speak well of evil) that are carried out in a single stroke, done out of necessity to protect oneself, and are not continued but are instead converted into the greatest possible benefits for the subjects. Badly used are those cruelties which, although being few at the outset, grow with the passing of time instead of disappearing. Those who follow the first method can remedy their condition with God and with men as Agathocles did; the others cannot possibly survive.

Wherefore it is to be noted that in taking a state its conqueror should weigh all the harmful things he must do and do them all at once so as not to have to repeat them every day, and in not repeating them to be able to make men feel secure and win them over with the benefits he bestows upon them. Anyone who does otherwise, either out of timidity or because of poor advice, is always obliged to keep his knife in his hand; nor can he ever count upon his subjects, who, because of their fresh and continual injuries, cannot feel secure with him. Injuries, therefore, should be inflicted all at the same time, for the less they are tasted, the less they offend; and benefits should be distributed a bit at a time in order that they may be savored fully. And a prince should, above all, live with his subjects in such a way that no unforeseen event, either good or bad, may make him alter his course; for when emergencies arise in adverse conditions, you are not in time to resort to cruelty, and that good you do will help you little, since it will be judged a forced measure and you will earn from it no thanks whatsoever.

* * *

[Chapter IX treats the "civil" principality, a prince who rules with the support of his fellow citizens. Chapter X discusses how the strength of a principality may be measured: military power is the answer Machiavelli provides. Chapter XI analyzes the special problem of principalities connected with the Church, and concludes that they are in an entirely different category from the others he has discussed. In Chapter XII, Machiavelli attacks the use of mercenary troops, preferring the use of citizen soldiers in Chapter XIII. In Chapter XIV, he defines the prince's most important activity as planning for and studying warfare, although the prince should read history books to train his mind as well.]

———————————— · ❦ · ————————————

CHAPTER XV

On Those Things for Which Men, and Particularly Princes, Are Praised or Blamed

Now there remains to be examined what should be the methods and procedures of a prince in dealing with his subjects and friends. And because I know that many have written about this, I am afraid that by writing about it again I shall be thought of as presumptuous, since in discussing this material I depart radically from the procedures of others. But since my intention is to write something useful for anyone who understands it, it seemed more suitable to me to search after the effectual truth of the matter rather than its imagined one.[16] And many writers have imagined for themselves republics and principalities that have never been seen nor known to exist in reality; for there is such a gap between how one lives and how one ought to live that anyone who abandons what is done for what ought to be done learns his ruin rather than his preservation: for a man who wishes to profess goodness at all times will come to ruin among so many who are not good. Hence it is necessary for a prince who wishes to maintain his position to learn how not to be good, and to use this knowledge or not to use it according to necessity.

Leaving aside, therefore, the imagined things concerning a prince, and taking into account those that are true, I say that all men, when they are spoken of, and particularly princes, since they are placed on a higher level, are judged by some of these qualities which bring them either blame or praise. And this is why one is considered generous, another miserly (to use a Tuscan word, since "avaricious" in our language is still used to mean one who wishes to acquire by means of theft; we call "miserly" one who excessively avoids using what he has); one is considered a giver, the other rapacious; one cruel, another merciful; one treacherous, another faithful; one effeminate and cowardly, another bold and courageous; one humane, another haughty; one lascivious, another chaste; one trustworthy, another frivolous; one religious, another unbelieving; and the like. And I know that everyone will admit that it would be a very praiseworthy thing to find in a prince, of the qualities mentioned above, those that are held to be good; but since it is neither possible to have them nor to observe them all completely, because the human condition does not permit it, a prince must be prudent enough to know how to escape the bad reputation of those vices that would lose the state for him, and must protect himself from those that will not lose it for him, if this is possible; but if he cannot, he need not concern himself unduly if he ignores the less serious vices. And, moreover, he need not worry about incurring the bad reputation of those vices without which it would be difficult to hold his state; since, carefully taking everything into account, he will discover that something which appears to be a virtue, if pursued, will end in his destruction; while some other thing which seems to be a vice, if pursued, will result in his safety and his well-being.

CHAPTER XVI

On Generosity and Miserliness

Beginning, therefore, with the first of the above-mentioned qualities, I say that it would be good to be considered generous; nevertheless, generosity used in such a manner as to give you a reputation for it will harm you; because if it is employed virtuously and as one should employ it, it will not be recognized and you will not avoid the reproach of its opposite. And so, if a prince wants to maintain his reputation for generosity among men, it is necessary for him not to neglect any possible means of lavish display; in so doing such a prince will always use up all his resources and he will be obliged, eventually, if he wishes to maintain his reputation for generosity, to burden the people with excessive taxes and to do everything possible to raise funds. This will begin to make him hateful to his subjects, and, becoming impoverished, he will not be much esteemed by anyone; so that, as a consequence of his generosity, having offended many and rewarded few, he will feel the effects of any slight unrest and will be ruined at the first sign of danger; recognizing this and wishing to alter his policies, he immediately runs the risk of being reproached as a miser.

A prince, therefore, being unable to use this virtue of generosity in a manner which will not harm himself, if he is known for it, should, if he is wise, not worry about being called a miser; for with time he will come to be considered more generous once it is evident that, as a result of his parsimony, his income is sufficient, he can defend himself from anyone who makes war against him, and he can undertake enterprises without overburdening his people, so that he comes to be generous with all those from whom he takes nothing, who are countless, and miserly with all those to whom he gives nothing, who are few. In our times we have not seen great deeds accomplished except by those who were considered miserly; the others were failures. Pope Julius II, although he made use of his reputation for generosity in order to gain the papacy, then decided not to maintain it in order to be able to wage war; the present King of France has waged many wars without imposing extra taxes on his subjects, only because his habitual parsimony has provided for the additional expenditures; the present King of Spain, if he had been considered generous, would not have engaged in or won so many campaigns.

Therefore, in order not to have to rob his subjects, to be able to defend himself, not to become poor and contemptible, and not to be forced to become rapacious, a prince must consider it of little importance if he incurs the reputation of being a miser, for this is one of those vices that permits him to rule. And if someone were to say: Caesar with his generosity achieved imperial power, and many others, because they were generous and known to be so, achieved very high positions; I would reply: you are either already a prince or you are on the way to becoming one; in the first instance such generosity is damaging; in the second it is very necessary to be thought generous. And Caesar was one of those who wanted to gain the principality of Rome; but if, after obtaining this, he had lived and had not moderated his expenditures, he would have destroyed his rule. And if someone were to reply: there have existed many princes who have accomplished great deeds with their armies who have been reputed to be generous; I would answer you: a prince either spends his own money and that of his subjects or that of others; in the first case he must be economical; in the second he must not restrain any part of his generosity. And for that prince who goes out with his soldiers and lives by looting, sacking, and ransoms, who controls the property of others, such generosity is necessary; otherwise he would not be followed by his troops. And with what does not belong to you or to your subjects you can be a more liberal giver, as were Cyrus, Caesar, and Alexander; for spending the wealth of others does not lessen your reputation but adds to it; only the spending of your own is what harms you. And there is nothing that uses itself up faster than generosity, for as you employ it you lose the means of employing it, and you become either poor and despised or else, in order to escape poverty, you become rapacious and hated. And above all other things a prince must guard himself against being despised and hated; and generosity leads you to both one and the other. So it is wiser to live with the reputation of a miser, which produces reproach without hatred, than to be forced to incur the reputation of rapacity, which produces reproach along with hatred, because you want to be considered generous.

. ❦ .

CHAPTER XVII

On Cruelty and Mercy, and Whether It Is Better to Be Loved Than to Be Feared or the Contrary

Proceeding to the other qualities mentioned above, I say that every prince must desire to be considered merciful and not cruel; nevertheless, he must take care not to misuse this mercy. Cesare Borgia was considered cruel; nonetheless, his cruelty had brought order to Romagna, united it, restored it to peace and obedience. If we examine this carefully, we shall see that he was more merciful than the Florentine people, who, in order to avoid being considered cruel, allowed the destruction of Pistoia.[17] Therefore, a prince must not worry about the reproach of cruelty when it is a matter of keeping his subjects united and loyal; for with a very few examples of cruelty he will be more compassionate than those who, out of excessive mercy, permit disorders to continue, from which arise murders and plundering; for these usually harm the community at large, while the executions that come from the prince harm particular individuals. And the new prince, above all other princes, cannot escape the reputation of being called cruel, since new states are full of dangers. And Virgil, through Dido, states: "My difficult condition and the newness of my rule make me act in such a manner, and to set guards over my land on all sides."[18]

Nevertheless, a prince must be cautious in believing and in acting, nor should he be afraid of his own shadow; and he should proceed in such a manner, tempered by prudence and humanity, so that too much trust may not render him imprudent nor too much distrust render him intolerable.

From this arises an argument: whether it is better to be loved than to be feared, or the contrary. I reply that one should like to be both one and the other; but since it is difficult to join them together, it is much safer to be feared than to be loved when one of the two must be lacking. For one can generally say this about men: that they are ungrateful, fickle, simulators and deceivers, avoiders of danger, greedy for gain; and while you work for their good they are completely yours, offering you their blood, their property, their lives, and their sons, as I said earlier,[19] when danger is far away; but when it comes nearer to you they turn away. And that prince who bases his power entirely on their words, finding himself completely without other preparations, comes to ruin; for friendships that are acquired by a price and not by greatness and nobility of character are purchased but are not owned, and at the proper moment they cannot be spent. And men are less hesitant about harming someone who makes himself loved than one who makes himself feared because love is held together by a chain of obligation which, since men are wretched creatures, is broken on every occasion in which their own interests are concerned; but fear is sustained by a dread of punishment which will never abandon you.

A prince must nevertheless make himself feared in such a manner that he will avoid hatred, even if he does not acquire love; since to be feared and not to be hated can very well be combined; and this will always be so when he keeps his hands off the property and the women of his citizens and his subjects. And if he must take someone's life, he should do so when there is proper justification and manifest cause; but, above all, he should avoid seizing the property of others; for men forget more quickly the death of their father than the loss of their patrimony. Moreover, reasons for seizing their property are never lacking; and he who begins to live by stealing always finds a reason for taking what belongs to others; on the contrary, reasons for taking a life are rarer and disappear sooner.

But when the prince is with his armies and has under his command a multitude of troops, then it is absolutely necessary that he not worry about being considered cruel; for without that reputation he will never keep an army united or prepared for any combat. Among the praiseworthy deeds of Hannibal[20] is counted this: that, having a very large army, made up of all kinds of men, which he commanded in foreign lands, there never arose the slightest dissension, neither among themselves nor against their leader, both during his good and his bad fortune. This could not have arisen from anything other than his inhuman cruelty, which along with his many other qualities, made him always respected and terrifying in the eyes of his soldiers; and without that, to attain the same effect, his other qualities would not have sufficed. And the writers of history, having considered this matter very little, on the one hand admire these deeds of his and on the other condemn the main cause of them.

And that it is true that his other qualities would not have been sufficient can be seen from the example of Scipio, a most extraordinary man not only in his time but in all recorded history, whose armies in Spain rebelled against him; this came about from nothing other than his excessive compassion, which gave to his soldiers more liberty than military discipline allowed. For this he was censured in the senate by Fabius Maximus,[21] who called him the corruptor of the Roman militia. The Locrians, having been ruined by one of Scipio's officers, were not avenged by him, nor was the arrogance of that officer corrected, all because of his tolerant nature; so that someone in the senate who tried to apologize for him said that there were many men who knew how not to err better than they knew how to correct errors. Such a nature would have, in time, damaged Scipio's fame and glory if he had continued to command armies; but, living under the control of the senate, this harmful characteristic of his not only was concealed but brought him glory.

I conclude, therefore, returning to the problem of being feared and loved, that since men love at their own pleasure and fear at the pleasure of the prince, a wise prince should build his foundation upon that which belongs to him, not upon that which belongs to others: he must strive only to avoid hatred, as has been said.

CHAPTER XVIII

How a Prince Should Keep His Word

How praiseworthy it is for a prince to keep his word and to live by integrity and not by deceit everyone knows; nevertheless, one sees from the experience of our times that the princes who have accomplished great deeds are those who have cared little for keeping their promises and who have known how to manipulate the minds of men by shrewdness; and in the end they have surpassed those who laid their foundations upon loyalty.

You must, therefore, know that there are two means of fighting:[22] one according to the laws, the other with force; the first way is proper to man, the second to beasts; but because the first, in many cases, is not sufficient, it becomes necessary to have recourse to the second. Therefore, a prince must know how to use wisely the natures of the beast and the man. This policy was taught to princes allegorically by the ancient writers, who described how Achilles and many other ancient princes were given to Chiron the Centaur[23] to be raised and taught under his discipline. This can only mean that, having a half-beast and half-man as a teacher, a prince must know how to employ the nature of the one and the other; and the one without the other cannot endure.

Since, then, a prince must know how to make good use of the nature of the beast, he should choose from among the beasts the fox and the lion;[24] for the lion cannot defend itself from traps and the fox cannot protect itself from wolves. It is therefore necessary to be a fox in order to recognize the traps and a lion in order to frighten the wolves. Those who play only the part of the lion do not understand matters. A wise ruler, therefore, cannot and should not keep his word when such an observance of faith would be to his disadvantage and when the reasons which made him promise are removed. And if men were all good, this rule would not be good; but since men are a contemptible lot and will not keep their promises to you, you likewise need not keep yours to them. A prince never lacks legitimate reasons to break his promise. Of this one could cite an endless number of modern examples to show how many pacts, how many promises have been made null and void because of the infidelity of princes; and he who has known best how to use the fox has come to a better end. But it is necessary to know how to disguise this nature well and to be a great hypocrite and a liar: and men are so simple-minded and so controlled by their present needs that one who deceives will always find another who will allow himself to be deceived.

I do not wish to remain silent about one of these recent instances. Alexander VI did nothing else, he thought about nothing else, except to deceive men, and he always found the occasion to do this. And there never was a man who had more forcefulness in his oaths, who affirmed a thing with more promises, and who honored his word less; nevertheless, his tricks always succeeded perfectly since he was well acquainted with this aspect of the world.

Therefore, it is not necessary for a prince to have all of the above-mentioned qualities, but it is very necessary for him to appear to have them. Furthermore, I shall be so bold as to assert this: that having them and practicing them at all times is harmful; and appearing to have them is useful; for instance, to seem merciful, faithful, humane, trustworthy, religious, and to be so; but his mind should be disposed in such a way that should it become necessary not to be so, he will be able and know how to change to the contrary. And it is essential to understand this: that a prince, and especially a new prince, cannot observe all those things for which men are considered good, for in order to maintain the state he is often obliged to act against his promise, against charity, against humanity, and against religion. And therefore, it is necessary that he have a mind ready to turn itself according to the way the winds of fortune and the changeability of affairs require him; and, as I said above, as long as it is possible, he should not stray from the good, but he should know how to enter into evil when necessity commands.

A prince, therefore, must be very careful never to let anything slip from his lips which is not full of the five qualities mentioned above: he should appear, upon seeing and hearing him, to be all mercy, all faithfulness, all integrity, all kindness, all religion. And there is nothing more necessary than to seem to possess this last quality. And men in general judge more by their eyes than their hands; for everyone can see but few can feel. Everyone sees what you seem to be, few touch upon what you are, and those few do not dare to contradict the opinion of the many who have the majesty of the state to defend them; and in the actions of all men, and especially of princes, where there is no impartial arbiter, one must consider the final result.[25] Let a prince therefore act to conquer and to maintain the state; his methods will always be judged honorable and will be praised by all; for ordinary people are always deceived by appearances and by the outcome of a thing; and in the world there is nothing but ordinary people; and there is no room for the few, while the many have a place to lean on. A certain prince of the present day,[26] whom I shall refrain from naming, preaches nothing but peace and faith, and to both one and the other he is entirely opposed; and both, if he had put them into practice, would have cost him many times over either his reputation or his state.

· ❦ ·

CHAPTER XIX

On Avoiding Being Despised and Hated

But now that I have talked about the most important of the qualities mentioned above, I would like to discuss the others briefly in this general manner: that the prince, as was noted above, should concentrate upon avoiding those things which make him hated and despised; and when he has avoided this, he will have carried out his duties and will find no danger whatsoever in other vices. As I have said, what makes him hated above all else is being rapacious and a usurper of the property and the women of his subjects; he must refrain from this; and in most cases, so long as you do not deprive them of either their property or their honor, the majority of men live happily; and you have only to deal with the ambition of a few, who can be restrained without difficulty and by many means. What makes him despised is being considered changeable, frivolous, effeminate, cowardly, irresolute; from these qualities a prince must guard himself as if from a reef, and he must strive to make everyone recognize in his actions greatness, spirit, dignity, and strength; and concerning the private affairs of his subjects, he must insist that his decision be irrevocable; and he should maintain himself in such a way that no man could imagine that he can deceive or cheat him.

That prince who projects such an opinion of himself is greatly esteemed; and it is difficult to conspire against a man with such a reputation and difficult to attack him, provided that he is understood to be of great merit and revered by his subjects. For a prince should have two fears: one, internal, concerning his subjects; the other, external, concerning foreign powers. From the latter he can defend himself by his good troops and friends; and he will always have good friends if he has good troops; and internal affairs will always be stable when external affairs are stable, provided that they are not already disturbed by a conspiracy; and even if external conditions change, if he is properly organized and lives as I have said and does not lose control of himself, he will always be able to withstand every attack, just as I said that Nabis the Spartan did. But concerning his subjects, when external affairs do not change, he has to fear that they may conspire secretly: the prince secures himself from this by avoiding being hated or despised and by keeping the people satisfied with him; this is a necessary accomplishment, as was treated above at length. And one of the most powerful remedies a prince has against conspiracies is not to be hated by the masses; for a man who plans a conspiracy always believes that he will satisfy the people by killing the prince; but when he thinks he might anger them, he cannot work up the courage to undertake such a deed; for the problems on the side of the conspirators are countless. And experience demonstrates that there have been many conspiracies but few have been concluded successfully; for anyone who conspires cannot be alone, nor can he find companions except from amongst those whom he believes to be dissatisfied; and as soon as you have revealed your intention to one malcontent, you give him the means to make himself content, since he can have everything he desires by uncovering the plot; so much is this so, that, seeing a sure gain on the one hand and one doubtful and full of danger on the other, if he is to maintain faith with you he has to be either an unusually good friend or a completely determined enemy of the prince. And to treat the matter briefly, I say that on the part of the conspirator there is nothing but fear, jealousy, and the thought of punishment that terrifies him; but on the part of the prince there is the majesty of the principality, the laws, the defenses of friends and the state to protect him; so that, with the good will of the people added to all these things, it is impossible for anyone to be so rash as to plot against him. For, where usually a conspirator has to be afraid before he executes his evil deed, in this case he must be afraid even after the crime is performed, having the people as an enemy, nor can he hope to find any refuge because of this.

One could cite countless examples on this subject; but I shall be satisfied with only the one which occurred during the time of our fathers. Messer Annibale Bentivogli,[27] prince of Bologna and grandfather of the present Messer Annibale, was murdered by the Canneschi family, who conspired against him; he left behind no heir except Messer Giovanni, then only a baby. As soon as this murder occurred, the people rose up and killed all the Canneschi. This came about because of the goodwill that the house of the Bentivogli enjoyed in those days; this goodwill was so great that with Annibale dead, and there being no one of that family left in the city who could rule Bologna, the Bolognese people, having heard that in Florence there was one of the Bentivogli blood who was believed until that time to be the son of a blacksmith, went to Florence to find him, and they gave him the control of that city; it was ruled by him until Messer Giovanni became of age to rule.

I conclude, therefore, that a prince should not be too concerned with conspiracies when the people are well disposed toward him; but when the populace is hostile and regards him with hatred, he must fear everything and everyone. And well-organized states and wise princes have, with great diligence, taken care not to anger the nobles and to satisfy the common people and keep them contented; for this is one of the most important concerns that a prince has.

Among the kingdoms in our times that are well organized and well governed is that of France: in it one finds countless good institutions upon which depend the liberty and the security of the king; of these the foremost is the parliament and its authority. For he who organized that kingdom, recognizing the ambition of the nobles and their insolence, and being aware of the necessity of keeping a bit in their mouths to hold them back, on the one hand, while, on the other, knowing the hatred, based upon fear, of the populace for the nobles, and wanting to reassure them, did not wish this to be the particular obligation of the king. In order to relieve himself of the difficulties he might incur from the nobles if he supported the common people, and from the common people if he supported the nobles, he established a third judicial body that might restrain the nobles and favor the masses without burdening the king. There could be no better nor more prudent an institution than this, nor could there be a better reason for the safety of the king and the kingdom. From this one can extract another notable observation: that princes must delegate distasteful tasks to others; pleasant ones they should keep for themselves. Again I conclude that a prince must respect the nobles but not make himself hated by the common people.

Perhaps it may seem to many who have studied the lives and deaths of some Roman emperors that they afford examples contrary to my point of view; for we find that some of them always lived nobly and demonstrated great strength of character yet nevertheless lost their empire or were killed by their own subjects who plotted against them. Wishing, therefore, to reply to these objections, I shall discuss the traits of several emperors, showing the reasons for their ruin, which are not different from those which I myself have already deduced; and I shall bring forward for consideration those things which are worthy of note for anyone who reads about the history of those times. And I shall let it suffice to choose all those emperors who succeeded to the throne from Marcus the philosopher to Maximinus: these were Marcus, his son Commodus, Pertinax, Julian, Severus, Antoninus Caracalla his son, Macrinus, Heliogabalus, Alexander, and Maximinus.[28] And it is first to be noted that while in other principalities one has only to contend with the ambition of the nobles and the arrogance of the people, the Roman emperors had a third problem: they had to endure the cruelty and the avarice of the soldiers. This created such difficulties that it was the cause of the downfall of many of them, since it was hard to satisfy both the soldiers and the populace; for the people loved peace and quiet and because of this loved modest princes, while the soldiers loved the prince who had a military character and who was arrogant, cruel, and rapacious; they wanted him to practice such qualities on the people so that they might double their pay and give vent to their avarice and cruelty. As a result of this situation, those emperors always came to ruin who by nature or by guile did not have so great a reputation that they could keep both the people and the soldiers in check; and most of them, especially those who came to power as new princes, recognizing the difficulty resulting from these two opposing factions, turned to appeasing the soldiers, caring little about injuring the people. Such a decision was necessary; since princes cannot avoid being hated by somebody, they must first seek not to be hated by the bulk of the populace; and when they cannot achieve this, they must try with every effort to avoid the hatred of the most powerful group. And therefore, those emperors who had need of extraordinary support because of their newness in power allied themselves with the soldiers instead of the people; nevertheless, this proved to their advantage or not, according to whether the prince knew how to maintain his reputation with the soldiers.

For the reasons listed above, it came about that, of Marcus, Pertinax, and Alexander, all of whom lived modest lives, were lovers of justice, enemies of cruelty, humane, and kindly, all except Marcus came to an unhappy end. Marcus alone lived and died with the greatest of honor, for he succeeded to the empire by birthright, and he did not have to recognize any obligation for it either to the soldiers or to the people; then, being endowed with many characteristics which made him revered, he always held, while he was alive, both the one party and the other within their limits, and he was never either hated or despised. But Pertinax was made emperor against the will of the soldiers, who, being used to living licentiously under Commodus, could not tolerate the righteous manner of life to which Pertinax wished to return them; whereupon, having made himself hated, and since to this hatred was added contempt for his old age, he came to ruin at the initial stage of his rule.

And here one must note that hatred is acquired just as much by means of good actions as by bad ones; and so, as I said above, if a prince wishes to maintain the state, he is often obliged not to be good; because whenever that group which you believe you need to support you is corrupted, whether it be the common people, the soldiers, or the nobles, it is to your advantage to follow their inclinations in order to satisfy them; and then good actions are your enemy. But let us come to Alexander. He was of such goodness that among the other laudable deeds attributed to him is this: in the fourteen years that he ruled the empire he never put anyone to death without a trial; nevertheless, since he was considered effeminate and a man who let himself be ruled by his mother, because of this he was despised, and the army plotted against him and murdered him.

Considering now, in contrast, the characteristics of Commodus, Severus, Antoninus Caracalla, and Maximinus, you will find them extremely cruel and greedy: in order to satisfy their troops, they did not hesitate to inflict all kinds of injuries upon the people; and all except Severus came to a sorry end. For in Severus there was so much ability that, keeping the soldiers as his friends even though the people were oppressed by him, he was always able to rule happily; for those qualities of his made him so esteemed in the eyes of both the soldiers and the common people that the former were awestruck and stupefied and the latter were respectful and satisfied.

And since the actions of this man were great and noteworthy for a new prince, I wish to demonstrate briefly how well he knew how to use the masks of the fox and the lion, whose natures, as I say above, a prince must imitate. As soon as Severus learned of the indecisiveness of the emperor Julian, he convinced the army of which he was in command in Slavonia that it would be a good idea to march to Rome to avenge the death of Pertinax, who had been murdered by the Praetorian Guards. And under this pretext, without showing his desire to rule the empire, he moved his army to Rome, and he was in Italy before his departure was known. When he arrived in Rome, the senate, out of fear, elected him emperor, and Julian was killed. After this beginning, there remained two obstacles for Severus if he wanted to make himself master of the whole state: the first in Asia, where Pescennius Niger, commander of the Asiatic armies, had himself named emperor; and the other in the West, where Albinus was, who also aspired to the empire. And since he judged it dangerous to reveal himself as an enemy to both of them, he decided to attack Niger and to deceive Albinus. He wrote to the latter that, having been elected emperor by the senate, he wanted to share that honor with him; and he sent him the title of Caesar and, by decree of the senate, he made him his coequal: these things were accepted by Albinus as the truth. But after Severus had conquered and executed Niger and had pacified affairs in the East, upon returning to Rome, he complained to the senate that Albinus, ungrateful for the benefits received from him, had treacherously sought to kill him, and for this he was obliged to go and punish his ingratitude. Then he went to find him in France and took both his state and his life.

Anyone, therefore, who will carefully examine the actions of this man will find him a very ferocious lion and a very shrewd fox; and he will see him feared and respected by everyone and not hated by his armies; and one should not be amazed that he, a new man, was able to hold so great an empire; for his outstanding reputation always defended him from that hatred which the common people could have had for him on account of his plundering. But Antoninus, his son, was also a man who had excellent abilities which made him greatly admired in the eyes of the people and pleasing to the soldiers, for he was a military man, most able to support any kind of hardship, a despiser of all delicate foods and soft living; this made him loved by all the armies; nevertheless, his ferocity and cruelty were so great and so unusual—since he had, after countless individual killings, put to death a large part of the populace of Rome and all that of Alexandria—that he became most despised all over the world. And he aroused the fears even of those whom he had around him, so that he was murdered by a centurion in the midst of his army. From this it is to be noted that such deaths as these, which result from the deliberation of a determined individual, are unavoidable for princes, since anyone who does not fear death can harm them; but the prince must not be too afraid of such men, for they are very rare. He must only guard against inflicting serious injury on anyone who serves him and anyone he has about him in the administration of the principality: Antoninus had done this, for he had shamefully put to death a brother of that centurion, and he threatened the man every day; yet he kept him as a bodyguard. This was a rash decision and, as it happened, one which would bring about his downfall.

But let us come to Commodus, who held the empire with great ease, having inherited it by birth, being the son of Marcus; and it would have been enough for him to follow in the footsteps of his father in order to satisfy the soldiers and the common people. But being a cruel and bestial person by nature, in order to practice his greed upon the common people, he turned to pleasing the armies and to making them undisciplined; on the other hand, by not maintaining his dignity, frequently descending into the arenas to fight with the gladiators and doing other degrading things unworthy of the imperial majesty, he became contemptible in the sight of the soldiers. And being hated on the one hand, and despised on the other, he was plotted against and murdered.

The qualities of Maximinus remain to be described. He was a very warlike man; and because the armies were angered by Alexander's softness, which I explained above, after Alexander's death they elected him to the empire. He did not retain it very long, for two things made him hated and despised: the first was his base origin, having herded sheep once in Thrace (this fact was well known everywhere and it caused him to lose considerable dignity in everyone's eyes); the second was that at the beginning of his reign he deferred going to Rome to take possession of the imperial throne, and he had acquired the reputation of being very cruel, having through his prefects, in Rome and in all other parts of the empire, committed many cruelties. As a result, the entire world was moved by disgust for his ignoble birth and by the hatred brought about by fear of his cruelty; first Africa revolted, then the senate with the entire populace of Rome, and finally all of Italy conspired against him. To this was added even his own army; for, while besieging Aquileia and finding the capture difficult, angered by his cruelty and fearing him less, seeing that he had many enemies, they murdered him.

I do not wish to discuss Heliogabalus or Macrinus or Julian, who, since they were universally despised, were immediately disposed of; but I shall come to the conclusion of this discourse. And I say that the princes of our times in their affairs suffer less from this problem of satisfying their soldiers by extraordinary means, for, although they have to consider them to some extent, yet they resolve the question quickly, for none of these princes has standing armies which have evolved along with the government and the administration of the provinces as did the armies of the Roman empire. And therefore, if it was then necessary to satisfy the soldiers more than the common people, it was because the soldiers could do more than the common people; now it is more necessary for all princes, except the Turk and the Sultan,[29] to satisfy the common people more than the soldiers, since the people can do more than the soldiers. I make an exception of the Turk, for he always maintains near him twelve thousand infantrymen and fifteen thousand cavalrymen, upon whom depend the safety and the strength of his kingdom, and, setting aside all other concerns, it is necessary for that ruler to maintain them as his friends. Likewise, the kingdom of the Sultan being entirely in the hands of the soldiers, it is fitting that he, too, should maintain them as his friends without respect to the people. And you must note that this state of the Sultan is unlike all the other principalities, since it is similar to the Christian pontificate, which cannot be called either a hereditary principality or a new principality; for it is not the sons of the old prince that are the heirs and that remain as lords, but instead the one who is elected to that rank by those who have the authority to do so. And because this system is an ancient one, it cannot be called a new principality, for in it are none of these difficulties that are to be found in new ones, since, although the prince is new, the institutions of that state are old and are organized to receive him as if he were their hereditary ruler.

But let us return to our subject. Let me say that anyone who considers the discourse written above will see how either hatred or contempt has been the cause of the ruin of these previously mentioned emperors; and he will also recognize how it comes to pass that, although some acted in one way and others in a contrary manner, in each of these groups one man had a happy end and the others an unhappy one.

Because for Pertinax and Alexander, being new princes, it was useless and damaging to wish to imitate Marcus, who was installed in the principality by hereditary right; and likewise for Caracalla, Commodus, and Maximinus, it was disastrous to imitate Severus, since they did not have enough ability to follow in his footsteps. Therefore, a new prince in a new principality cannot imitate the deeds of Marcus, nor yet does he need to follow those of Severus; instead, he should take from Severus those attributes which are necessary to found his state and from Marcus those which are suitable and glorious in order to conserve a state which is already established and stable.

* * *

[In Chapter XX, Machiavelli asserts that the best fortress a prince can possess is the love and affection of his people. Chapter XXI advises the prince to avoid policies of neutrality and to be either a true friend or a true enemy. In Chapter XXII, Machiavelli explains how a prince may be judged by the quality of his advisers. He should, Machiavelli warns in Chapter XXIII, avoid flatterers and not punish advisers who speak the truth to him. In Chapter XXIV, Machiavelli argues that Italian princes have lost their states because of their lack of preparation and ability—not their bad fortune.]

· ❧ ·

CHAPTER XXV

On Fortune's Role in Human Affairs and How She Can Be Dealt With

It is not unknown to me that many have held, and still hold, the opinion that the things of this world are, in a manner, controlled by fortune and by God, that men with their wisdom cannot control them, and, on the contrary, that men can have no remedy whatsoever for them; and for this reason they might judge that they need not sweat much over such matters but let them be governed by fate. This opinion has been more strongly held in our own times because of the great variation of affairs that has been observed and that is being observed every day which is beyond human conjecture. Sometimes, as I think about these things, I am inclined to their opinion to a certain extent. Nevertheless, in order that our free will be not extinguished, I judge it to be true that fortune is the arbiter of one half of our actions,[30] but that she still leaves the control of the other half, or almost that, to us. And I compare her to one of those ruinous rivers that, when they become enraged, flood the plains, tear down the trees and buildings, taking up earth from one spot and placing it upon another; everyone flees from them, everyone yields to their onslaught, unable to oppose them in any way. But although they are of such a nature, it does not follow that when the weather is calm we cannot take precautions with embankments and dikes, so that when they rise up again either the waters will be channeled off or their impetus will not be either so unchecked or so damaging. The same things happen where fortune is concerned: she shows her force where there is no organized strength to resist her; and she directs her impact there where she knows that dikes and embankments are not constructed to hold her. And if you consider Italy, the seat of these changes and the nation which has set them in motion, you will see a country without embankments and without a single bastion: for if she were defended by the necessary forces, like Germany, Spain, and France, either this flood would not have produced the great changes that it has or it would not have come upon us at all. And this I consider enough to say about fortune in general terms.

But, limiting myself more to particulars, I say that one sees a prince prosper today and come to ruin tomorrow without having seen him change his character or any of the reasons that have been discussed at length earlier; that is, that a prince who relies completely upon fortune will come to ruin as soon as she changes; I also believe that the man who adapts his course of action to the nature of the times will succeed and, likewise, that the man who sets his course of action out of tune with the times will come to grief. For one can observe that men, in the affairs which lead them to the end that they seek—that is, glory and wealth—proceed in different ways; one by caution, another with impetuousness; one through violence, another with guile; one with patience, another with its opposite; and each one by these various means can attain his goals. And we also see, in the case of two cautious men, that one reaches his goal while the other does not; and, likewise, two men equally succeed using two different means, one being cautious and the other impetuous: this arises from nothing else than the nature of the times that either suit or do not suit their course of action. From this results that which I have said, that two men, working in opposite ways, can produce the same outcome; and of two men working in the same fashion one achieves his goal and the other does not. On this also depends the variation of what is good; for, if a man governs himself with caution and patience, and the times and conditions are turning in such a way that his policy is a good one, he will prosper; but if the times and conditions change, he will be ruined because he does not change his method of procedure. Nor is there to be found a man so prudent that he knows how to adapt himself to this, both because he cannot deviate from that to which he is by nature inclined and also because he cannot be persuaded to depart from a path, having always prospered by following it. And therefore the cautious man, when it is time to act impetuously, does not know how to do so, and he is ruined; but if he had changed his conduct with the times, fortune would not have changed.

Pope Julius II acted impetuously in all his affairs, and he found the times and conditions so apt to this course of action that he always achieved successful results. Consider the first campaign he waged against Bologna while Messer Giovanni Bentivogli was still alive. The Venetians were unhappy about it; so was the King of Spain; Julius still had negotiations going on about it with France; and nevertheless, he started personally on this expedition with his usual ferocity and lack of caution. Such a move kept Spain and the Venetians at bay, the latter out of fear and the former out of a desire to regain the entire Kingdom of Naples; and at the same time it drew the King of France into the affair, for when the King saw that the Pope had already made this move, he judged that he could not deny him the use of his troops without obviously harming him, since he wanted his friendship in order to defeat the Venetians. And therefore Julius achieved with his impetuous action what no other pontiff would ever have achieved with the greatest of human wisdom; for, if he had waited to leave Rome with agreements settled and things in order, as any other pontiff might have done, he would never have succeeded, because the King of France would have found a thousand excuses and the others would have aroused in him a thousand fears. I wish to leave unmentioned his other deeds, which were all similar and which were all successful. And the brevity of his life[31] did not let him experience the opposite, since if times which necessitated caution had come his ruin would have followed from it: for never would he have deviated from those methods to which his nature inclined him.

I conclude, therefore, that since fortune changes and men remain set in their ways, men will succeed when the two are in harmony and fail when they are not in accord. I am certainly convinced of this: that it is better to be impetuous than cautious, because fortune is a woman,[32] and it is necessary, in order to keep her down, to beat her and to struggle with her. And it is seen that she more often allows herself to be taken over by men who are impetuous than by those who make cold advances; and then, being a woman, she is always the friend of young men, for they are less cautious, more aggressive, and they command her with more audacity.

· ❦ ·

CHAPTER XXVI

An Exhortation to Liberate Italy from the Barbarians

Considering, therefore, all of the things mentioned above, and reflecting as to whether the times are suitable, at present, to honor a new prince in Italy, and if there is the material that might give a skillful and prudent prince the opportunity to introduce a form of government that would bring him honor and good to the people of Italy, it seems to me that so many circumstances are favorable to such a new prince that I know of no other time more appropriate. And if, as I said, it was necessary that the people of Israel be slaves in Egypt in order to recognize Moses' ability, and it was necessary that the Persians be oppressed by the Medes to recognize the greatness of spirit in Cyrus, and it was necessary that the Athenians be dispersed to realize the excellence of Theseus, then, likewise, at the present time, in order to recognize the ability of an Italian spirit, it was necessary that Italy be reduced to her present condition and that she be more enslaved than the Hebrews, more servile than the Persians, more scattered than the Athenians; without a leader, without organization, beaten, despoiled, ripped apart, overrun, and prey to every sort of catastrophe.

And even though before now some glimmer of light may have shown itself in a single individual,[33] so that it was possible to believe that God had ordained him for Italy's redemption, nevertheless it was witnessed afterwards how at the height of his career he was rejected by fortune. So now Italy remains without life and awaits the man who can heal her wounds and put an end to the plundering of Lombardy, the ransoms in the Kingdom of Naples and in Tuscany, and who can cure her of those sores which have been festering for so long. Look how she now prays to God to send someone to redeem her from these barbaric cruelties and insolence; see her still ready and willing to follow a banner, provided that there be someone to raise it up. Nor is there anyone in sight, at present, in whom she can have more hope than in your illustrious house,[34] which, with its fortune and ability, favored by God and by the Church, of which it is now prince, could make itself the head of this redemption. This will not be very difficult if you keep before you the deeds and the lives of those named above. And although those men were out of the ordinary and marvelous, they were nevertheless men; and each of them had less opportunity than the present one; for their enterprises were no more just, nor easier, nor was God more a friend to them than to you. Here justice is great: "Only those wars that are necessary are just, and arms are sacred when there is no hope except through arms."[35] Here there is a great willingness; and where there is a great willingness there cannot be great difficulty, if only you will use the institutions of those men I have proposed as your target. Besides this, we now see extraordinary, unprecedented signs brought about by God: the sea has opened up; a cloud has shown you the path; the rock pours forth water; it has rained manna here; everything has converged for your greatness. The rest you must do yourself. God does not wish to do everything, in order not to take from us our free will and that part of the glory which is ours.

And it is no surprise if some of the Italians mentioned previously were not capable of doing what it is hoped may be done by your illustrious house, and if, during the many revolutions in Italy and the many campaigns of war, it always seems that her military ability is spent. This results from the fact that her ancient institutions were not good and that there was no one who knew how to discover new ones; and no other thing brings a new man on the rise such honor as the new laws and the new institutions discovered by him. These things, when they are well founded and have in themselves a certain greatness, make him revered and admirable. And in Italy there is no lack of material to be given a form: here there is great ability in her members, were it not for the lack of it in her leaders. Consider how in duels and skirmishes involving just a few men the Italians are superior in strength, dexterity, and cunning; but when it comes to armies they do not match others. And all this comes from the weakness of her leaders; for those who know are not followed; and with each one seeming to know, there has not been to the present day anyone who has known how to set himself above the others, either because of ingenuity or fortune, so that others might yield to him. As a consequence, during so much time, during the many wars fought over the past twenty years, whenever there has been an army made up completely of Italians it has always made a poor showing. As proof of this, there is first Taro, then Alexandria, Capua, Genoa, Vailà, Bologna, and Mestri.[36]

Therefore, if your illustrious house desires to follow these excellent men who redeemed their lands, it is necessary before all else, as a true basis for every undertaking, to provide yourself with your own native troops, for one cannot have either more faithful, more loyal, or better troops. And although each one separately may be brave, all of them united will become even braver when they find themselves commanded, honored, and well treated by their own prince. It is necessary, therefore, to prepare yourself with such troops as these, so that with Italian strength you will be able to defend yourself from foreigners. And although Swiss and Spanish infantry may be reputed terrifying, nevertheless both have defects, so that a third army could not only oppose them but be confident of defeating them. For the Spanish cannot withstand cavalry and the Swiss have a fear of foot soldiers they meet in combat who are as brave as they are. Therefore, it has been witnessed and experience will demonstrate that the Spanish cannot withstand French cavalry and the Swiss are ruined by Spanish infantrymen. And although this last point has not been completely confirmed by experience, there was nevertheless a hint of it at the battle of Ravenna,[37] when the Spanish infantry met the German battalions, who follow the same order as the Swiss; and the Spanish, with their agile bodies, aided by their spiked shields, entered between and underneath the Germans' long pikes and were safe, without the Germans having any recourse against them; and had it not been for the cavalry charge that broke them, the Spaniards would have slaughtered them all. Therefore, as the defects of both these kinds of troops are recognized, a new type can be instituted which can stand up to cavalry and will have no fear of foot soldiers: this will come about by creating new armies and changing battle formations. And these are among those matters that, when newly organized, give reputation and greatness to a new prince.

This opportunity, therefore, must not be permitted to pass by so that Italy, after so long a time, may behold its redeemer. Nor can I express with what love he will be received in all those provinces that have suffered through these foreign floods; with what thirst for revenge, with what obstinate loyalty, with what compassion, with what tears! What doors will be closed to him? Which people will deny him obedience? What jealousy could oppose him? What Italian would deny him homage? For everyone, this barbarian dominion stinks! Therefore, may your illustrious house take up this mission with that spirit and with that hope in which just undertakings are begun; so that under your banner this country may be ennobled and, under your guidance, those words of Petrarch may come true:

> Ingenuity over rage
> Will take up arms; and the battle will be short.
> For ancient valor
> In Italian hearts is not yet dead.[38]

NOTES

1. Lorenzo de' Medici, the Magnificent, the Duke of Urbino (1492–1519), should not be confused with his more illustrious grandfather, Lorenzo il Magnifico (1449–92). Lorenzo received Machiavelli's dedication after an earlier preface to *The Prince*, originally intended for Giuliano de' Medici, Duke of Nemours (1479–1516), had to be changed when Giuliano suddenly died. Neither of these Medici princelings ever measured up to Machiavelli's estimation of their potential, and it is ironic that they are remembered today by Michelangelo's magnificent sculptures of them for the Medici Chapel at San Lorenzo in Florence. While the bulk of *The Prince* was completed in 1513, this dedication was probably composed between 1516 and 1519 after Lorenzo was named Duke of Urbino by Pope Leo X (1516) but before his subsequent death (1519).

2. It is interesting that Baldesar Castiglione, author of the *Book of the Courtier* (1528), the only other Italian book to rival Machiavelli's *Prince* in popularity during the European Renaissance, also employs the metaphor of the archer to describe his concept of imitation.

3. Chapter VI contains numerous references to the special Machiavellian quality of *virtù*, translated variously in this edition according to the context of Machiavelli's argument as "skill," "ingenuity," "ability," but rarely "virtue" in the moral sense of the English word. It is impossible to render this complex term by any single English word, for Machiavelli himself did not employ the Italian word in a strictly technical sense with only a single, well-defined meaning.

4. Only Cyrus, founder of the Persian Empire (599–529 B.C.), is a purely political figure, although Machiavelli's knowledge of his life probably came from Xenophon's idealized view in his *Cyropaedia*. According to Biblical narrative, Moses instituted the laws of the Israelites (although they were given to him by God); Romulus was the mythical founder of Rome in 753 B.C., just as Theseus was the legendary King of Athens. It is noteworthy that Machiavelli, supposedly a hard-boiled realist, employs literary or mythical figures as his ideal model for the new prince.

5. A dominican preacher born in Ferrara in 1452, Savonarola became Prior of San Marco in Florence in 1491, and was a major force in Florentine politics after the expulsion of the Medici in 1494. A fierce republican, Savonarola lost favor in the city after Pope Alexander VI excommunicated him, and in 1498 he was executed in the Piazza della Signoria. He was the author of an important

political work, *Treatise on the Organization and Government of Florence* (1498), which proposed a republican government for the city and an enlarged grand council based on his interpretation of that branch of the Venetian government.

6. Commander of the army of Syracuse, Hiero II (c. 306–215 B.C.) seized power and ruled the city as its tyrant; after an initial alliance with Carthage during the early days of the First Punic War, he made peace with Rome and remained her ally.

7. The sudden death of Cesare Borgia's father, Alexander VI, occurred in August 1503.

8. The Orsini and Colonna families, both powerful Roman clans, were traditional enemies, but neither group could be trusted by Cesare Borgia or Pope Alexander in their quest for power.

9. Borgia's treachery at Sinigaglia (December 31, 1502) led to the strangulation of his adversaries—Oliverotto Euffreducci (ruler of Fermo) and Vitellozzo Vitelli were killed immediately; Paulo Francesco Orsini died a few days later.

10. Named governor of the Romagna in 1501, Cesare Borgia's lieutenant was removed in order to win favor from the fickle populace of the area.

11. Here Machiavelli refers to the comparative brevity of Alexander's pontificate (eleven years), not to his age when he died. In Chapter XI, Machiavelli remarks that the average length of a pontificate was about ten years.

12. These four cardinals are Giuliano della Rovere (later Pope Julius II), called "St. Peter's in Chains" by Machiavelli, who follows the common practice of designating a cardinal by the church to which his office was attached; Giovanni Colonna (d. 1508); Raffaello Riario, Cardinal of San Giorgio (d. 1521); and Ascanio Sforza, son of Francesco Sforza.

13. Georges d'Amboise, Cardinal of Rouen, whom Machiavelli believes Cesare Borgia should have supported for the papacy through pressure upon Spanish and French prelates.

14. Tyrant of Syracuse (361–289 B.C.).

15. Readers of *The Prince* who insist upon interpreting Machiavelli as an immoral or amoral counselor of evil should not overlook this passage, in which Machiavellian *virtù* (skill, ability, ingenuity) is clearly distinguished from naked power. In other words, only a few very specific ends could ever justify such drastic means for Machiavelli.

16. Machiavelli has in mind here not only Plato but also the many abstract portraits of idealized rulers or Christian princes composed by the Latin humanists.

17. When violent squabbles broke out between the Cancellieri and the Panciatichi factions of this Florentine subject-city in 1501–02, Machiavelli was sent there several times in an attempt to restore order.

18. Machiavelli cites the original Latin from Virgil's *Aeneid* (I, 563–64).

19. It was said in Chapter IX.

20. Commander of the Carthaginian army (249–183 B.C.) who was defeated by Scipio at the Battle of Zama in 202 B.C., ending the Second Punic War.

21. Roman consul and dictator in 217 B.C. (d. 203 B.C.), whose delaying

tactics against Hannibal while his army was ravaging Italy were opposed by Scipio, who wished to wage a more aggressive offensive campaign.

22. Machiavelli takes this argument from Cicero, De officiis (I, xi), but changes it quite drastically.

23. Machiavelli's strange allegorical interpretation of Chiron's dual nature has no apparent classical source and was probably a product of his own fantasy.

24. Machiavelli found this soon-to-become-famous idea in Cicero's De officiis (I, xiii), but he changes Cicero's argument completely. Cicero had maintained that both force and treachery were inhuman and, therefore, contemptible policies.

25. The Italian original, si guarda al fine, has often been misconstrued to imply that Machiavelli meant "the end justifies the means," something he never said in The Prince. For another important statement concerning ends and means, see Machiavelli's discussion of Romulus in The Discourses (I, ix).

26. Probably Ferdinand II of Aragon.

27. Annibale Bentivogli was murdered by rivals in 1445; his son Giovanni took power in Bologna in 1462, and after his death in 1508 Giovanni was succeeded by his son, "the present Messer Annibale" (1469–1540).

28. Machiavelli refers to the succession of Roman rulers between 161 and 238 A.D.: the philosopher-soldier Marcus Aurelius (121–80); his son Commodus (180–93); Pertinax (193); Julian (193); Severus (193–211); his son Caracalla (211–17); Macrinus (217–18); Heliogabalus (218–22); Alexander (222–35); and Maximinus (235–38). Machiavelli's source for his discussion of these men is most likely the Latin translation of Herodian's Greek history done by Angelo Poliziano and first published in 1493.

29. The ruler of Turkey at this time was the Ottoman Selim I; the Sultan is that of Mamluk Egypt, who was selected from among the commanders of the slave army. Selim I overthrew the Mamluks' power in 1517.

30. Machiavelli's conception of the "new prince," his virtù, and the important opportunities chance might provide him to achieve power all presuppose a certain amount of human freedom. His discussion of fortune, however, owes more to his poetic inclinations than to a dispassionate philosophical discussion of the weighty issues involved in the conflict between human free will and determinism.

31. Once again, as he had earlier done in discussing Pope Alexander VI (Chapter VII), Machiavelli is referring to the brevity of the pontificate of Julius II, not to the brevity of the man's life itself.

32. Here, Machiavelli clearly draws a parallel between the energy required for a violent sexual encounter and that which determines the drive for political power.

33. This is probably a reference to Cesare Borgia, but Machiavelli may also be referring to Giuliano de' Medici, Duke of Nemours, whose sudden death in 1516 forced Machiavelli to change the dedication of The Prince.

34. By 1516, the probable date of the dedication of The Prince, Medici family members occupied the papacy (Leo X), and Lorenzo de' Medici, appointed

Duke of Urbino by Leo in that year, was obviously intended to be the future ruler of Florence. When Machiavelli wrote *The Prince* in 1513, he first envisioned a convergence of Medici power in Giuliano de' Medici, Duke of Nemours, and Pope Leo; after Giuliano's death in 1516, this possibility was kept alive with the brief appearance of Lorenzo de' Medici. This opportunity paralleled the opportunity that existed with a Borgia Pope, Alexander VI, and his son Cesare, until the Pope died suddenly in 1503. With the deaths of both Giuliano and Lorenzo by 1519, Medici hopes faded away, and this probably explains why Machiavelli never bothered to publish *The Prince* before his death, since the practical purpose of the little book no longer existed after 1519.

35. Cited by Machiavelli from the original Latin of Livy (IX,i).

36. A list of Italian military defeats in chronological order for rhetorical effect: Charles VIII was victorious over Italian forces at Fornovo (1495) near the Taro River; Louis XII took Alexandria (1499), Capua (1501), Genoa (1507), Valià (1509), and Bologna (1511); the Venetians were defeated near Vicenza in 1513 by foreign troops, resulting in the sack of Mestri (modern Mestre).

37. On April 11, 1512, the French cavalry under Gaston de Foix routed Spanish infantrymen.

38. Lines from Petrarch's *canzone* "Italia mia" (93–96). In citing from Petrarch's patriotic poem, Machiavelli focuses our attention on Petrarch's opposition of *virtù* and *furore* and asserts that his own *virtù* (ingenuity, a disciplined strength) will eventually triumph over undisciplined anger in the creation of an Italian state by the Medici prince.

FRANCESCO GUICCIARDINI
1483–1540

A FLORENTINE STATESMAN, POLITICAL THINKER, AND HISTORIAN, GUICCIARDINI was a member of one of the city's most illustrious patrician families and one of Machiavelli's closest friends in spite of their differences of opinion on matters of state. His some 222 maxims, collected as the *Ricordi*, were written between 1513 and 1530 but were never published during his lifetime. They constitute one of the first coherent responses to Machiavelli's political theory and remain one of the most interesting critiques of Machiavelli's central ideas about the imitation of the ancients and the use of classical models for current political behavior. Guicciardini is best remembered for his monumental *History of Italy* (1561–64), a book of European scope which deals with the momentous events occurring in Italy and Europe between 1490 and 1534. It was clearly the most popular and widely translated vernacular history during the entire Renaissance period, and its influence upon Western European thought was profound.

BIBLIOGRAPHY

Francesco Guicciardini, *The History of Italy*, trans. Sidney Alexander (Princeton: Princeton University Press, 1984), and *Maxims and Reflections [The Ricordi]*, trans. Mario Domandi (Philadelphia: University of Pennsylvania Press, 1972); Peter Bondanella, *Francesco Guicciardini* (Boston: Twayne, 1976); Felix Gilbert, *Machiavelli and Guicciardini: Politics and History in Sixteenth-Century Florence* (Princeton: Princeton University Press, 1965); Roberto Ridolfi, *The Life of Francesco Guicciardini* (New York: Knopf, 1968).

SELECTIONS FROM
THE *RICORDI*

· ❦ ·

6. It is a great mistake to speak of worldly affairs indiscriminately and absolutely, and to deal with them—so to speak—by the rule; for almost all of them are different and exceptional because of the variety of circumstances which cannot be grasped by one single measure; and such differences and exceptions are not to be found written in books but must be taught by discretion.[1]

10. No one should place so much trust in natural intelligence as to persuade himself that this is sufficient without the assistance of experience, for anyone who has managed affairs, even though he be most intelligent indeed, has been able to recognize that with experience, one succeeds in many things, the attainment of which is impossible with natural intelligence alone.

15. Like all men, I have desired honor and profit; and often I obtained more of both than I had desired or hoped; nevertheless, I never found in them the satisfaction which I had imagined; a very powerful reason, if one considers this carefully, for curbing the vain cupidity of men.

28. I do not know if there is anyone who hates the ambition, the avarice, and the soft living of the priests more than I do—both because each of these vices in itself is odious and because all of them are unsuitable for those who profess to lead a life dependent upon God, and furthermore, because they are such contradictory vices that they cannot exist together except within a very strange individual. Nevertheless, the position I have held under several Popes has forced me, in my own self-interest, to serve their greatness;[2] and if it were not for this consideration, I should have esteemed Martin Luther as much as myself: not in order to free myself from the laws of the Christian religion in the manner in which they are commonly interpreted and understood, but, rather, in order to see this bunch of scoundrels reduced to their proper position—that is, to be either without vices or without power.

32. Ambition is not to be condemned, nor are ambitious men to be vituperated who seek glory through honest and honorable means: on the contrary, it is such men who undertake great and excellent deeds, and men who lack this desire are cold-spirited and inclined more to laziness than to activity. Pernicious and detestable ambition is the kind which has grandeur for its sole goal, as is usually the case with princes, and when princes make grandeur their idol, they will level conscience, honor, humanity, and everything else in order to reach it.

35. How different theory is from practice! How many people there are who understand things well but who either do not remember them or do not know how to put them into practice! The intelligence of such men is useless, for it is like having a treasure stored in a strongbox without ever being able to take it out.

48. One cannot wield political power according to the dictates of one's conscience, since if one considers its origin, all governments are violent, except for republics within their own territories but not beyond: and I do not except the Emperor from this rule, and even less the priests, for their power is doubly violent, since they assault us with both temporal and spiritual arms.

60. An above-average intellect is bestowed upon men for their unhappiness and torment, since it serves only to keep them in a greater state of turmoil and anxiety than those men whose intellects are more limited.

66. Do not believe those who preach liberty so fervently, for almost all of them—no, probably all of them—have their own private interests as their goal. And experience often shows beyond a shadow of a doubt that if such people believed they would be better off under an absolute government, they would race in that direction as fast as they could.

76. Everything which has existed in the past and exists in the present will also exist in the future; but both the names and the appearances of things change in such a way that anyone lacking a discerning eye will not recognize them, nor will he know how to draw conclusions or form a judgment from such observations.

101. There is no rule or prescription which counts in saving oneself from a bestial or cruel tyrant except that which applies to the plague: run from him as far and as fast as you can.

110. How those who cite the Romans in their every word deceive themselves! One would have to have a city with conditions exactly like

theirs and then to govern it according to their example. That model is as unsuitable for a city lacking the proper qualities as it would be unsuitable to hope for a jackass to race like a horse.[3]

117. It is completely erroneous to judge by examples, since if they are not exactly alike in each and every detail, they serve no purpose, as each small variation in the case can be the cause of the greatest variation in the results. And to discern these variations, when they are small, requires a good and perspicacious eye.

125. Philosophers, theologians, and all the others who scrutinize supernatural affairs or invisible things all speak a lot of nonsense; for men are, in fact, in the dark about such affairs, and their investigation has served and still serves more to exercise their wits than to discover the truth.

134. All men are inclined by nature more to good than to evil, and there are none who, all other things being equal, would not more gladly do good than evil; but the nature of man is so weak and the occasions which invite him to do evil are so numerous in the world that men easily allow themselves to deviate from the good.[4] And therefore, wise legislators invented rewards and punishments, and this was for no other reason than to hold men firm in their natural inclination by the use of hope and fear.

141. Do not be amazed if you find that we are ignorant of things that happened in past ages, not to mention those which occur in the provinces or far-away places. If you think about it carefully, we do not possess accurate information about present affairs, not to mention the daily events which occur in the same city; and there is often a fog so dense or a wall so thick between the palace and the piazza that being impenetrable to the eye of man, the people know as much about what those who govern are doing or about their reasons for doing it as they do about the things which people are doing in India. And so, the world is easily filled with erroneous and vain opinions.

161. When I think of the infinite number of ways the life of man is subjected to accidents, dangers of infirmity, or chance, or violence, and how many things must coincide during a year in order to produce a good harvest, there is nothing which amazes me more than seeing an old man or a fertile year.

164. A man's good fortune is often the worst enemy he has, since it causes him to become mean, irresponsible, and insolent; therefore, a

man's ability to resist good fortune is a far better test of his character than his ability to handle adversity.

174. Do everything you can to have good relations with princes and with the states that they rule; for even though you may be innocent and live quietly and in an orderly fashion, and you are disposed not to cause trouble, events can nevertheless occur which of necessity will deliver you into the hands of those who govern. And then, the mere belief that you are not acceptable will hurt you in infinite ways.

176. Pray to God always to find yourself on the winning side, because in that way you will be praised for things which you did nothing to bring about, just as, on the contrary, anyone who finds himself on the losing side is accused of countless things for which he is completely innocent.

179. As a young man, I made fun of knowing how to play, to dance, to sing, and similar frivolities. I even made fun of writing well, of knowing how to ride, of knowing how to dress properly, and of all those matters which seem to be more decorative than substantial in a man. But later I wished I had done the opposite, for though it might not be wise to lose too much time in training young people in these matters, nevertheless I have observed through experience that such ornaments and knowing how to do everything well bestow dignity and reputation upon men who are *also* well qualified, and it may even be said that men who lack such attributes lack something of importance. Not to mention the fact that being well endowed with such talents opens the way to the favor of princes, and is sometimes the beginning or the reason for their great profit and exaltation, since princes are no longer made in the world as they should be but as they are.

186. One cannot in effect proceed according to a single general and fixed rule. If it is often unwise to speak too freely even with your friends—I am referring to matters which deserve to be kept secret—on the other hand, acting with your friends in a manner which makes them realize that you are being reserved with them is the way to guarantee that they also do the same with you, for nothing makes another person confide in you so much as the assumption that you are confiding in them; thus, if you do not speak to others, you lose the capacity to learn from others. So, in this and in many other matters, it is necessary to be able to distinguish the character of people, of circumstances, and of the times, and to do this discretion is required, but if nature has not

given discretion to you, experience can teach you enough discretion only very rarely; and books never can.

187. Know that anyone who governs himself by chance will eventually be at the mercy of chance. The proper way is to think, to examine, to consider everything, even the tiniest detail; and even living in this manner, affairs are managed with the greatest of difficulty. Imagine how things go for people who allow themselves to be carried along by the current.

189. All cities, all states, all kingdoms are mortal; everything by nature or by accident ends and finishes sometime. And so a citizen who finds himself living at the final stage of his country's existence should not so much lament the misfortune of his fatherland and call it unlucky as he should lament his own misfortune, for what happened to his country was what had to happen, but his misfortune was to have been born in that period during which the disaster had to occur.

210. "Little and good," as the proverb says. It is impossible for anyone who says or writes many things not to include in all this a great deal of nonsense; but a few things can be well digested and concise. And so it would perhaps have been better to select the best of these maxims (ricordi) rather than to have accumulated so much material.[5]

216. In this world, no one can choose the rank into which one is born, nor the circumstances or the fate with which one must live; therefore, in praising or criticizing men, it is necessary not to examine the fortune they enjoy but how they manage with it; for praise or blame of men has to arise from their comportment, not from the condition in which they find themselves. Just as in a comedy or a tragedy, the actor who plays the role of the master or the king is not more laudable than the actor who plays the role of the servant, since we pay attention only to who is the best actor.

218. In this world, the men who handle their affairs well are those who always have their self-interest[6] in mind and measure all their actions with this goal in mind. But the mistake lies in those men who do not realize clearly where their interests lie, that is to say, in those men who believe that their self-interest always lies in some monetary advantage more than in honor, in knowing how to maintain their reputation and their good name.

NOTES

—— · 🦋 · ——

1. The contrast between Machiavelli's reliance upon classical examples taken from his beloved Latin masters, on the one hand, and Guicciardini's suspicion of any political advice not grounded in practical experience and common sense, on the other, is quite marked. "Discretion" is a key quality for Guicciardini, one learned only through long trial and error in the real world.

2. Guicciardini was named Governor of Modena by Pope Leo X in 1516, a post to which the governorship of Reggio was added in 1517. When Leo died in 1522, Guicciardini defended Parma, and in 1523, he was named President of Romagna by another Medici Pope, Clement VII. He became lieutenant general of papal forces in the ill-fated League of Cognac, which ended in the sack of Rome in 1527 and Pope Clement VII's defeat by the troops of Emperor Charles V. Later, after the Medici family returned to Florence in 1530, Guicciardini was given the task by Clement VII of removing all republican opposition. In 1533, Guicciardini presided, as Governor of Bologna, over the meeting between Pope Clement VII and the Emperor Charles V. All his life, Guicciardini was involved with ruling the papal state territories for his Medici patrons.

3. This maxim, and the one which follows, aims directly at the cornerstone of Machiavelli's view of history—the belief that useful examples can be learned by a study of the classical past or our own times.

4. While Machiavelli believes man is essentially evil, he also expects that men can be persuaded or forced to achieve good and even great deeds. Guicciardini, on the other hand, defines man as naturally good but weak.

5. Guicciardini was quite conscious that the choice of the maxim form implied entirely different assumptions from those of a political theorist such as Machiavelli, who chose the treatise form. In a sense, Guicciardini's use of the pithy maxim underlines his cynical distrust of the abstract, bookish learning of Machiavelli. Rather than present a theory, incorporated in a polished literary form, Guicciardini offers us his practical wisdom in the unconnected pattern of commonsense rules that he collected over a period of several decades.

6. Guicciardini has often been attacked as a cynic for his reliance upon self-interest in his maxims. While Machiavelli viewed human nature as evil and

fallen, he could nevertheless conceive of selfless actions in the service of some higher goal. Guicciardini more often saw behind the supposedly pure and idealistic motives of the master politicians, kings, and princes of his times, and what he saw was frequently pure self-interest.

BENVENUTO CELLINI
1500–1571

A FLORENTINE SCULPTOR AND GOLDSMITH, CELLINI IS TODAY REMEMBERED as much for the history of his life as for his many artistic works. After spending the first nineteen years of his life in his native Florence, Cellini went to Rome in 1519, where he served Popes Clement VII and Paul III from 1523 until 1540. During this same period, he visited his native city on many occasions and also took a disappointing trip to France, where he worked for King Francis I from 1540 until 1545. At the age of fifty-eight, he began to compose his *Autobiography*. He died in Florence in 1571 and was buried there in the Church of the Annunziata.

Cellini's autobiography was written by a man who never considered himself "learned," and his attitude was, in many respects, not dissimilar to that of Leonardo da Vinci. However, the history of his life nevertheless draws upon a long and venerable literary tradition, employing models as diverse as Plutarch's *Lives*, St. Augustine's *Confessions*, the lives of the saints, pilgrimage stories, journey narratives such as Homer's *Odyssey* and Dante's *Comedy*, and the ribald *novella* tradition of Boccaccio's *Decameron*. Cellini adds another dimension to the traditional literary hero, transforming him into an artist of whom Cellini himself becomes the preeminent example.

The *Autobiography* is divided into two parts, recalling St. Augustine. The first section deals with Cellini's life before his imprisonment by Pope Paul III (his miraculous birth, his education, and the siege of the Castel Sant'Angelo by Protestant troops during which Cellini displays heroic prowess). It then treats the trials of his imprisonment, his attempted escape, and his religious conversion. The second section of the book leads from Cellini's conversion to his greatest artistic triumphs, the casting of the bronze statue *Perseus* in particular (1557), and reflects the successful culmination of his artistic vocation. The book ends abruptly in 1562.

Cellini's autobiography did not appear during the Renaissance. The manuscript, which was published only in 1728, had circulated earlier, but with its publication, it became one of the most popular of all Italian literary works: Goethe translated it in 1796 and Berlioz used it for the basis of an opera on Cellini's life in 1838. Renaissance historians such as Jacob Burckhardt were to see in Cellini's egocentrism and genius both the secret for the greatness and the seeds of the destruction of the brilliant civilization of Cinquecento Italy. Contemporary critics now view Cellini's writings (as well as those of Vasari—the other great biographer of artists' lives who did so much to make heroes out of artists) as representative of the same Mannerist tendencies in literature that his important works of sculpture or goldsmithery reflect in art.

BIBLIOGRAPHY

Benvenuto Cellini, *Autobiography*, trans. George Bull (New York: Penguin, 1956); Dino S. Cervigni, *The "Vita" of Benvenuto Cellini: Literary Tradition and Genre* (Ravenna: Longo, 1979); James V. Mirollo, *Mannerism and Renaissance Poetry: Concept, Mode, Inner Design* (New Haven: Yale University Press, 1984); Sir John Pope-Hennessy, *Cellini* (New York: Abbeville, 1985).

SELECTIONS FROM
THE LIFE OF BENVENUTO,
THE SON OF GIOVANNI CELLINI,
WRITTEN BY HIMSELF IN FLORENCE

──────────── • ❦ • ────────────

I first began to write this story of my life in my own hand, as can be seen from some of the odd pages attached here, but it took up too much of my time and seemed utterly pointless. So when I came across a son of Michele Goro from Pieve a Groppine, a young boy of about fourteen who was in a poor state of health, I gave the task to him. And as I worked, I dictated my story to him with the result that since I really enjoyed doing this, I worked much more diligently and produced much more. So I left the burden of writing to him, and I hope to carry on with the story to the extent that my memory permits.

Whatever kind of man one is, everyone who is of whatever quality, who has done anything of excellence, or which may truly resemble excellence, ought, if he is a person of truth and honesty, to write about his life in his own hand; but he ought not to attempt such a splendid enterprise until he has passed the age of forty. This duty occurs to me, now that I am beyond the age of fifty-eight years, and find myself in Florence, the city of my birth. I can remember many unseemly things, such as happen to all who live upon our earth, and I am now more free from those adversities than at any previous period of my life; indeed, it seems to me that I enjoy greater happiness of soul and health of body than I ever did in earlier years. I can also remember some delightful things and some incredible evils, which, when I think back upon them, strike terror in my heart, and I am astonished that I have reached the age of fifty-eight and give thanks to God I am still prosperously growing older.

It is true that men who have achieved some excellence in their work have already made themselves known to the world; and this alone ought to suffice for them, that is, the fact that they have proved their excellence and achieved renown. Still, I must do as others do, and in a work such as this, there is always occasion for natural bragging of various kinds, but the chief one is to let others know that one's ancestors are persons of worth and ancient origin.

[308]

My name is Benvenuto Cellini, son of Maestro Giovanni, son of Andrea, son of Cristofano Cellini; my mother was Madonna Elisabetta, daughter to Stefano Granacci; both my parents were Florentine citizens. It is written in the chronicles of our Florentine ancestors, men of former times and of some credibility, even as Giovanni Villani writes, that the city of Florence was evidently built in imitation of the fair city of Rome, and certain remnants of the Colosseum and Baths can still be seen. These ruins are located near Santa Croce. The Capitol was where the Old Market now stands. The Rotunda which was made for the Temple of Mars is complete and is now dedicated to our St. John. That it was so can easily be seen and cannot be denied, but these buildings are much smaller than those of Rome. The one who had them built, they say, was Julius Caesar, in company with some noble Romans, who, when : iesole had been stormed and taken, raised a city in this place, and each of them took the responsibility of erecting one of these notable edifices.

Julius Caesar had among his captains a man of the highest rank and courage with the name Fiorino of Cellino, which is a village about two miles from Monte Fiesole. Now this Fiorino took up his quarters under the hills of Fiesole, on the area where Florence now stands, in order to be near the Arno River, and for the convenience of his troops. All the soldiers and those who had anything to do with this captain used to say: "Let us go to Fiorenze," as much because this captain was called Fiorino as because there was an abundant growth of flowers in the place he had chosen to make his camp. Upon the foundation of the city, therefore, this name struck Julius Caesar as being fair and appropriate to the circumstances, and, seeing that flowers themselves bring good fortune, he gave the name of Florence to the town. He wanted, also, to pay such a compliment to his valiant captain, whom he loved all the more since he had raised him from a very humble rank himself and was responsible for his excellence. The claim of those learned and clever etymologists who infer that the name Florence goes back to the fact that Florence is located near the flowing Arno cannot hold, seeing that Rome is near the flowing Tiber, Ferrara is near the flowing Po, Lyons near the flowing Saone, Paris near the flowing Seine, and yet the names of all these towns are different, and have come to them by other ways.

Thus, you have my reasons, and I believe that we are descended from a very worthy man. Furthermore, there are Cellinis of our stock in Ravenna, an even more ancient town, where there are many aristocratic families. There are also Cellinis in Pisa, and I have discovered them in many parts of Christendom, and in this state (Tuscany), there are some excellent men devoted to the profession of arms who are Cellinis, for not

long ago, a beardless young man named Luca Cellini fought with a
soldier of experience and a most valorous man, named Francesco da
Vicorati, who had often fought before in single combat. This Luca, by
his own courage and with his sword in hand, overcame and killed that
man with such bravery and skill that everyone, expecting the opposite
outcome, was amazed; and so I take enormous pride in tracing my origin
back to men of valor.

As for the small honors I have gained for my house, under the
well-known conditions of our present ways of living, and by means of my
art (although it does not amount to much), I shall discuss these at the
proper time and place. I take far more pride in having been born humble
and having laid down an honorable foundation for my family than if I
had been born into an old, noble family and had stained or sullied it by
base qualities. I will begin, then, by telling how, as it pleased God, I was
born into the world.

My ancestors used to live in Val d'Ambra, where they sought refuge
on account of the strife among the political factions, and where they
owned much property and lived like little lords; and they were all
devoted to soldiering and all very brave. At that time, their younger son,
who was called Cristofano, started a great feud with some of their friends
and neighbors. The heads of both families took part in it, and the fire
that Cristofano had kindled burned so hot that it seemed both families
were likely to perish. Considering this prospect, the older family mem-
bers agreed that my ancestors would send Cristofano away and the other
family would banish the other young man who had started the quarrel
with him. The latter was sent to Siena, while Cristofano was sent to
Florence, where they bought him a little house in Via Chiara close to
the convent of Santa Orsola, as well as some very good property near the
Ponte a Rifredi. This Cristofano found a wife in Florence and had a
family of sons and daughters, and the daughters were all provided for;
then, after their father's death, the sons divided what remained of his
property.

* * *

[Cellini then describes how his family came to live in Florence and
how his parents were married.]

They enjoyed their youth and their married bliss for eighteen years,
always longing to be blessed with children. At the end of eighteen years,
Giovanni's wife had a miscarriage because of the doctors' incompetence,
and she lost twin sons. Then she became pregnant again and gave birth
to a daughter whom they called Cosa, after my father's mother. Two

years later she was once again pregnant, and as those longings which are common to pregnant women were exactly the same as the ones she had during her second pregnancy, they were certain that she would give birth to a girl as before, and they agreed to call her Reparata, after my mother's mother. The child was born the night before All Saints' Day at precisely half past four in the year 1500. The midwife, who knew that they were expecting a girl, having washed the baby and wrapped it in some fine white linen, came very, very softly to my father Giovanni and said: "I have brought you a fine present, one you did not expect." My father, who was a true philosopher, had been pacing in the room, and when the midwife came to him, he said: "Whatever God gives me will always be dear to me," and when he pulled back the swaddling clothes, he saw with his own eyes the son no one had expected. He joined his hands in prayer and with his eyes raised to heaven, he said: "Lord, I thank You with all my heart; this gift is most dear to me; he is most welcome." Everyone present began talking joyfully and asking him what he was going to name the child. Giovanni kept on repeating: "He is welcome [benvenuto]," and so they decided on this name, and I was baptized with it, and by the grace of God, I am still living with it today.

* * *

[Cellini describes some of the miraculous signs that augur his future greatness, including the appearance of a scorpion, which does not injure the infant Cellini, and a salamander. His early education, he relates, consisted of music lessons and watching his father build organs and harpsichords as well as other stringed instruments. The elder Cellini was an engineer who wanted his son to be a musician. However, the young Cellini was also learning the art of goldsmithing, and his father was unable to fight against his natural inclinations and artistic talents. Thus the young Cellini set out on a career that brought him into contact with many of the great political and religious figures of the age, who served as his not always reliable patrons. Whenever he was commissioned to produce a medal, a statue, or some other work, he could never be sure of being reimbursed, and as a result his life was filled with constant turmoil. Furthermore, he refused to consider himself as less than the equal of kings, Popes, and noblemen by virtue of his artistic vocation. He also proved himself both an able soldier and a strategist during the sack of Rome in 1527. Cellini thus challenged the codes of behavior of his age, hinting that artists of his caliber were different from other men and are, as such, above the law.

Cellini's outspoken behavior and his assumption of equality eventually brought upon him the jealousy and dislike of powerful men, and he wound up in prison. But for Cellini, even imprisonment provided an additional opportunity to demonstrate his absolute superiority. After a miraculous escape from the Castel Sant'Angelo, the first successful one, Cellini was hindered from getting out of the city of Rome by a broken leg suffered in the descent. Seeking refuge with the Cardinal Cornaro, he was sold back to the Pope, his captor, for a bishopric and returned once more to the Castel Sant'Angelo as a prisoner. He remained there, he tells us, in "misery and despair. This was on the feast of Corpus Christi, 1539."]

. . . As I said, it was the night after Corpus Christi, and about four hours after nightfall. They took me well concealed and covered by four men who walked in front of us to make the few men who were still in the streets move out of the way. In this fashion, they bore me to a place called the Torre di Nona, where they put me in the condemned cell, setting me down on a scrap of mattress and leaving me in the care of one of the guards, who, all night long, kept sympathizing with my bad fortune and saying to me: "Alas! Poor Benvenuto! What have you done to them?"

Partly from the place in which I found myself and partly from what the guard had told me, I now had a good idea of what was going to happen to me. During part of that night, I kept racking my brains over some possible reason why God had found it fit to punish me in this way, and since I could not discover why, I became terribly agitated. The guard did his best to comfort me, but I begged him for the love of God to keep quiet and stop talking to me, since I felt I could set my mind to rest better and more quickly if I was left alone. He promised to do as I asked, and then I turned my whole heart to God, devoutly praying that He would in His mercy take me into His kingdom; I prayed that although I had complained about my lot, because I thought that as far as human laws were concerned, such an end would be too unjust, and although it is true that I had committed murders, His own Vicar had called me from my native city and pardoned me by the authority he had from human laws and from His own. What I had done had all been done in defense of the body which His Divine Majesty had lent to me, so I could not admit that, under the laws by which man lives in the world, I deserved such a death. It seemed to me that I was like an unfortunate man walking along the street who is killed by a stone falling from some great height upon his head—this is clearly the influence of the stars. Not that the stars conspire to do us good or evil, but we are all subject to the results of their conjunctions. At the same time, I know that I have free will, and I am certain that if I could show my faith like a saint, the angels of Heaven would transport me from this dungeon and protect me against all my afflictions; but seeing that God does not seem to have made me worthy of such miracles, it must be that the celestial influences are working their malignity against me. For a while, I struggled in my soul this way, then I calmed myself and soon fell asleep.

When the day dawned, the guard woke me up and said: "Unfortunate but worthy man, there's no more time to go on sleeping now—there's a man waiting here with bad news for you."

I answered: "The sooner I escape from this earthly prison, the happier I shall be, especially since I am certain my soul is saved and that I am dying unjustly. The glorious and divine Christ elects me to the company of His disciples and friends, who, like Himself, were condemned to die unjustly. It is my turn to die an unjust death, and I humbly thank God for this sign of grace. Why doesn't the man who has to sentence me come forward?"

"He's too upset about you and he is crying."

Then I called him by name—Benedetto da Cagli—and I cried: "Come forward, Messer Benedetto, my friend, for now I am resolved and in a calm state of mind; it's far greater glory for me to die unjustly than it would be if I deserved this death. Come forward, I beg you, and bring me a priest, so that I may have a few words with him—not that I need to, since I've already made my holy confession to my Lord God. But I want to observe the rules of our Holy Mother Church, for although she is doing me this abominable wrong, I pardon her gladly. So come along, dear friend Benedetto, and get along with it quickly before my other feelings get the best of me."

After I had said all this, the worthy man told the guard to lock the door behind him, since the execution could not be carried out unless he was present. He then went to the house of Signor Pier Luigi's wife, who happened to be in the company of the Duchess I mentioned before.[1] When he presented himself before both of them, he spoke as follows: "My Most Noble Lady, I beg you for the love of God to ask the Pope to send someone else to pass sentence upon Benvenuto and perform my office, because I renounce the task, and I shall never carry it through."

Then he departed, sighing and feeling sick at heart.

The Duchess, who was present, frowned and said: "So this is the fine justice dealt out here in the city of Rome by God's Vicar! The Duke, my late husband, particularly esteemed this man because of his good qualities and his talents; he was glad to have him close by his side and was unwilling to let him return to Rome."

Then, muttering with anger and displeasure, she left the house.

Then Signor Pier Luigi's wife, who was called Signora Jerolima, went to the Pope, and throwing herself upon her knees in front of several cardinals who were present, pleaded my cause so passionately that she made His Holiness blush with shame, and he replied: "For your sake, we shall leave him alone, although we never really bore him any ill will."

But he only added these words because of the cardinals who were standing around him and who had heard everything that splendid, brave-hearted lady had said.

Meanwhile, I was waiting in great fear; I could feel my heart beating rapidly as all the men appointed to the task of carrying out my wretched execution were waiting in equal discomfort. Then, after suppertime had passed, they went off to attend to their own affairs, and I was brought some food. I was astonished at this, and I said: "For once truth has prevailed against the malignity of the stars! I pray to God, if it is His will, to save me from this storm."

Then I started eating, and as I had earlier resigned myself to my evil fate, I now began to hope for better fortune. I ate with a good appetite, and then waited without seeing or hearing anyone until an hour before nightfall, when the chief constable arrived with a goodly number of his guards and put me back in the chair in which they had brought me on the previous evening to that place. Then, after repeating several times in a very kind voice that I was not to worry, he ordered his men to take care not to jolt my broken leg, and to treat me as carefully as they would their own eyes. They did what he said, carrying me into the castle from which I had escaped; then after we had climbed to the top of the keep, they shut me up for a while in a small courtyard.

Meanwhile, the castellan had himself carried to where I lay; and ill and afflicted as he was, he said: "You see how I've recaptured you again!"

"Yes," I replied, "but do you see that I escaped as I said I would? And if I had not been sold by a papal guarantee for a bishopric by a Venetian cardinal and a Roman Farnese, both of whom have scratched with impious hands the face of God's law, you would never have recaptured me. But since they have behaved in such a vile way, you go ahead and do your worst as well: I haven't a care left in the world!"

The poor man began to shout at the top of his voice: "Ah, it's all the same to this fellow whether he lives or dies, and he is bolder and more fierce now than when he was well. Put him down there below the garden, and never speak to me about him again: he'll be the death of me."

I was carried down below the level of the garden into a very gloomy dungeon which was full of water, huge spiders, and noxious worms. They threw a wretched mattress of coarse hemp on the ground, and that evening I was left without food, locked up behind four doors. I remained in that condition until five hours before nightfall the following day. Only then did I receive food to eat. I asked them to give me some of my books to read. None of them said anything, but they reported what I had requested to that wretched castellan, who had asked them to tell him. Next morning, I was given my Italian Bible and a book containing Giovanni Villani's Chronicles.[2] I asked for some of my other books, but I was told that I could have no more and that I had too many anyway. So, I continued to pass the time miserably on that damp piece of mattress, which in three days was soaking up water like a sponge. I could hardly move because of my broken leg, and when I wanted to get out of bed to obey the calls of nature, I had to go on hands and knees, crawling, suffering considerable pain to avoid fouling the place I slept in.

For an hour and a half a day, I got a little glimmer of light which filtered into that squalid cell through a tiny chink. Only for that short space of time could I read; otherwise, the rest of the night and day, I waited patiently in the darkness, thinking constantly about God and our human frailty. I was certain that in a few more days, in such conditions and in such a place, my unlucky life would come to an end. Nevertheless, I consoled myself by calling to mind how much more painful it would have been to have passed from this life under the unimaginable agony of the executioner's blade, but as it was, I was meeting death half drugged with sleep, which was a much more agreeable way to die. Little by little, I felt my vital forces waning, until my strong constitution had become accustomed to that purgatory I was suffering. Then, when this occurred, and I was inured to it all, I resolved to put up with this tremendous suffering for as long as my strength could hold out.

I began the Bible from the beginning, reading and reflecting upon it devoutly and finding it so fascinating that if it had been possible, I would have spent all my time reading it. But when the light waned, the thought of all my sufferings immediately flooded my mind, and kept gnawing at me in the darkness until more than once I made up my mind to take my life with my own hand. They had left me without a knife, however, and so it was no easy matter to commit suicide. Nonetheless, once I took a solid beam that was lying there and propped it up in such a way that it would fall like a trap. I wanted to make it crash down upon my head, which would have been smashed at the first blow. But when I had set up the whole contraption and was resolutely preparing to knock it down, at the moment I put my hand to it, I was seized by an invisible power and hurled a distance of some four cubits from the spot. I was so terrified that I lay there half dead from shock, and I remained like that from dawn until five hours before nightfall, when they brought me my dinner. They must have come in several times without my noticing them, for when I did notice them, Captain Sandrino Monaldi had entered and I overheard him saying: "Ah, the poor, unhappy man! He was such a rare genius, and now look at the end he came to!"

I opened my eyes when I heard these words and caught sight of some priests standing there in their vestments, who were saying: "Oh, you told us he was dead!"

Bozza[3] replied: "I found him dead and that's why I said so."

Without delay, they lifted me up and took hold of the mattress, which was as soggy as a dish of macaroni, and threw it out of the cell. When the castellan was told about it, he had me given another one. Afterward, I searched my memory to discover what it was that had frustrated my attempt, and I concluded that it must have been some divine power or guardian angel.

The following night, a wonderful vision in the form of a lovely young man appeared to me in my dreams and began to rebuke me. "Do you know who lent you that body which you were ready to destroy before its appointed time?" he said.

I seemed to answer that I recognized everything about me as having come from the God of nature.

"So then," he replied, "you scorn His handiwork, and you want to destroy it? Allow Him to guide you, and do not abandon hope in His great goodness."

And he added much more in the most marvelous and effective words, the thousandth part of which I cannot remember. . . .

* * *

[Cellini was thus called back to life, and regaining his hope, he wrote a dialogue. Having restored some of his strength through meditating upon God's power and goodness, Cellini suffered terribly from the uncontrollable growth of his nails, and his teeth began to decay. But he endured his pain with prayers, song, and writing.]

The good castellan frequently used to send someone secretly to find out what I was doing, and as it happened on the last day of July, I was full of great rejoicing, thinking to myself that it was the day of the great holiday customarily celebrated in Rome on that first day of August, and I said to myself: "All these past years, I have celebrated this holiday among the frailties of the world; this year, I shall celebrate it in the divine company of God." And I added: "Oh, how much happier am I now than I was then!" Those who heard me speak these words reported them to the castellan, who said with wondrous displeasure: "Oh God! There he is thriving on such distress, and while he triumphs, I lie here in so much comfort and suffer. He leads me to my grave! Go quickly and put him in the deepest dungeon, where the preacher Foiano was starved to death; perhaps when he sees himself in such wretched conditions, he'll lose his cheerfulness."

Captain Sandrino Monaldi immediately came to my prison with about twenty of the castellan's servants; and they found me on my knees. I did not turn around to face them but continued praying to God the Father surrounded by angels and a victorious Christ arisen from the dead that I had sketched on the wall with a little piece of charcoal I had found covered up with earth after I had been in bed on my back for four months with a broken leg; I had dreamed so many times that the angels came to heal me, that after four months my leg had become as strong as if it had never been broken. They came to me heavily armed, as if they feared me to be a vicious dragon of sorts.

The above-mentioned captain declared: "You see how many of us there are and that we are making a great deal of noise, yet you do not turn around." At these words, I was very well able to imagine what harm they could do to me, but since I was by now accustomed and hardened to misfortune, I replied: "To this God who supports me, to the God in Heaven, I have turned my soul and my heart, and all my vital spirits; and to you I have turned exactly what belongs to you, for whatever there is of good in me you are not worthy of looking at it, nor can you touch it: so do to what belongs to you all that you can do."

The captain, fearful and not knowing what I might wish to do, said to four of his most powerful guards: "Put aside your weapons." When they had done this, he said: "Quickly, leap on him and seize him. Is he the devil himself that we should be so afraid of him? Hold him tight now so that he doesn't escape!"

Coerced and bullied by them, imagining much worse than what happened to me afterward, lifting my eyes to Christ, I exclaimed: "Oh, just God, You paid all of our debts on that high cross; why, therefore, must my innocence pay the debts of someone I do not know? Oh! But let Your will be done!"

Meanwhile, they carried me off by the light of a huge torch. I thought they intended to throw me into the Sammalò trap: this was the name for a frightful place which had swallowed many a man alive who had been thrown into this well shaft in the foundations of the castle. But this did not happen to me, and so I felt I had made a very good bargain when they put me in that foul cavern I mentioned above in which Fra Foiano died of hunger, and left me there to stay without doing me further harm.

When they had left me, I began to sing the *De profondo clamavi*, a *Misere*, and the *In te Domine speravi*. The whole of that first day of August, I observed the holiday with God, my heart rejoicing with hope and faith. The second day, they dragged me from that hole and took me back to where I had made my first sketches of that image of God. When I arrived there and found myself back with those drawings, I wept profusely with happiness. Afterward, the castellan wanted to know day by day everything I did and said. The Pope, who had heard the entire story (the doctors, by the way, had already given the castellan up for dead), said: "Before my castellan dies, I want him to put that Benvenuto to death in any way he wishes, for he is the cause of his death, and in this way he will not die unavenged." Upon hearing these words from the mouth of Duke Pier Luigi, the castellan said to him: "So, the Pope gives me Benvenuto, and wants me to take my revenge? Don't give it another thought, then, and leave me to take care of it."

If the heart of the Pope was ill disposed toward me, the castellan, it seemed to me, hated me with even more malice. And, at this point, the invisible being who had prevented me when I intended to kill myself came to me, and still invisible but with a clear voice, he shook me and made me get up as he said: "Alas! My Benvenuto, quickly turn to God and say your prayers; hurry and shout them out as loudly as you can." At once, I fell to my knees terrified and I said many of my prayers aloud, and after these, a *Qui habitat in adiutori*; after that, I spoke with God awhile and in an instant, the same clear and open voice said to me: "Go and rest now: fear no more."

And what happened was that the castellan, having given the most vile orders for my death, suddenly rescinded them and declared: "Is not this Benvenuto the one whom I have so eagerly defended and the one whom I know for certain is innocent and to whom all this harm has been wrongly done? Oh, how will God ever have mercy on me for my sins, if I do not pardon those who have done great injury? Oh, why must I harm him, a worthy man, innocent, who has served and honored me? Go tell him that instead of having him killed, I give him life and liberty, and I leave in my testament that no one is to ask of him to pay any of the great sum that he would have to pay for his expenses here." This the Pope heard about, and he took it very badly.

In the meantime, I continued with my usual prayers and with

writing my *capitolo* poem, and every night, I began to have the most joyous and pleasant dreams that could ever be imagined; and it always seemed to me that near me stood the invisible being I had so often heard and still heard. From him I asked no other favor except that he would take me to where I could see the sun. I told him that this was the only desire I had, and that if I could see it only one more time, I would then die content.

All the disagreeable things I had experienced in this prison, all of them had become friends and companions to me, and nothing bothered me. But those devoted to the castellan, who were waiting for him to hang me from the battlement from which I had descended, as he had declared he would, could not bear it now that they saw that the castellan had changed his mind, and they tried by various other means to frighten the life out of me. But as I said, I had gotten so used to all these things that I was no longer bothered by anything except this desire: I wanted to have the dream in which I would see the sphere of the sun. So persisting in my lengthy prayers, always directed fervently to Christ, I never left off saying: "Oh, true Son of God, I beg of You by Your birth, by Your death on the cross, and by Your glorious resurrection, make me worthy of seeing the sun, even if only in a dream; but if You make me worthy of seeing it with these, my mortal eyes, I promise to come and visit You in Your holy sepulcher."

This vow and these my greatest prayers of God I made on the second of October in 1539. When the following morning had dawned, which was the third of October, I got up at daybreak, about an hour before the rising of the sun, and rising from that wretched corner, I put on the few tattered clothes I possessed, since it had begun to get cold; and having gotten up, I prayed more devoutly than I had ever prayed in the past. In these prayers I beseeched Christ to grant me at least the grace to know through divine inspiration what sin was costing me such great penitence; and since His Divine Majesty had not wished to make me worthy of seeing the sun even in a dream, I beseeched Him in all His power and virtue to make me worthy of knowing the cause of that punishment.

Having uttered these words, that invisible being, like a whirlwind, took me and carried me away to a room where he now revealed himself to me in a visible human form, like a young man with his first growth of beard. He had a most wondrously handsome face, but austere rather than sensuous, and as he showed me into that room, he was saying: "These men that you see are all those that up to now have ever been born and then died." I asked him the reason why he had brought me there. He said to me: "Come along with me and you will soon see."

I found myself with a small dagger in my hand and on my back a coat of mail; and he led me this way through that great hall, showing me those people who in countless thousands were wandering in all directions. He led me forward, and then went out in front of me through a little door into a place which looked like a narrow street; and when he drew me before him into that street, at the moment of leaving that hall, I found myself disarmed, and I was dressed in a white shirt without anything on my head, standing at the right hand of my companion. Seeing myself in that condition, I was amazed; I was unable to recognize that street, and raising my eyes, I saw that the light of the sun was striking on a wall, like the facade of a house, just above my head.

Then I said: "Oh, my friend, what must I do for you to make it possible for me to ascend high enough to see the sphere of the sun itself?" He showed me some huge stairs that were there on my right and said to me: "Go there by yourself." Leaving his side, I ascended those huge stairs backward on my heels, and little by little, I began to feel the nearness of the sun. I hurried upward; and I went so far that I was able to see the entire sphere of the sun. The power of its rays made me instinctively close my eyes, and when I perceived my error, I opened my eyes, and gazing steadily at the sun, I said: "Oh, my sun, whom I have so greatly desired, I never again want to see anything else, even if your rays blind me." I stood with my eyes fixed on the sun, and remaining this way for a while, I saw in an instant all the power of those great rays hurl itself toward the left side of the sun; and with great delight I saw the sun, clear-cut, without its rays, and I was amazed at the way those rays had been taken away. I was pondering on the divine grace I had received that morning from God, when I exclaimed aloud: "Oh, how wondrous Your power is! Oh, how glorious is Your virtue! How much greater is the grace You granted me than what I expected!" This sun without its rays appeared to me just like a bath of the purest molten gold. While I contemplated this great sight, I saw the middle of the sun begin to swell and the form of this swelling grow, and in an instant a Christ upon the cross was created out of the same stuff as the sun was made of; and He was of such exquisite grace in His most gracious appearance that human ingenuity could not imagine a thousandth part of it. And contemplating this thing, I said aloud: "Miracle, a miracle! Oh, God! Oh merciful God! Oh, Infinite Power! What You have made me worthy of beholding this day!"

And while I was contemplating and saying these words, this Christ moved toward that part of the sun where the rays had gone, and the middle of the sun once again swelled, as it had before; and as the swelling grew larger, it suddenly took the shape of a most beautiful Madonna, who seemed to be seated on high with her son in her arms, with a most delightful expression on her face, almost smiling. She was flanked on either side by two angels of such great beauty that it was beyond imagination. I also saw on the right side of the sun a figure dressed like a priest; he turned his back to me, and kept his face turned toward that Madonna and Christ. All these things I truly saw, clearly and vividly, and continually I praised God's glory with a loud voice. This marvelous vision remained before my eyes little more than one eighth of an hour, and then it left me; and I was carried back to my pit. Immediately I began to shout out aloud: "The goodness of God made me worthy to behold all His glory, which perhaps no other mortal eye has even seen; and, for this reason, I know myself to be free and happy and in the grace of God; and you scoundrels will remain scoundrels, wretched and in disgrace with God. Know this: I am certain that on the day of All Saints, the day on which I was born in 1500, exactly on the first of November, four hours after midnight, on that day which will come, you will be forced to take me from this gloomy prison; and you will not be able to do otherwise, because I have seen it with my own eyes and on the throne of God. That priest, who was turned toward God and who kept his back toward me, that priest was St. Peter, who was pleading my cause, feeling ashamed that in his house such horrible wrongs were done to Christians. And so you may tell anyone you please that no one has the power to do me any further harm; and tell that lord who keeps me here that if he will give me some wax or paper and the means of expressing this glory of God which was shown to me, I shall most certainly make clear to him what he perhaps now doubts. . . ."

[Cellini relates how the castellan, being given no hope of recovery by his doctor, appeared to suffer bouts of conscience about what he had done to Cellini and how the Pope responded to the castellan that Cellini was mad. The castellan sent Cellini wax and writing materials, and Cellini composed a sonnet on his vision addressed to the castellan. When the castellan received it, he sent it to the Pope and asked for Cellini's release. The castellan made Cellini's lot more comfortable. Pier Luigi, the Pope's son, prevented Cellini's release. Cellini predicted his release and was taken to the comfortable rooms he had previously occupied in 1538. After the castellan's death, Messer Durante of Brescia decided to poison Cellini's food with ground diamonds, but an accomplice replaced the deadly diamond dust with a less harmful powder, and Cellini escaped death. He then arranged to receive other food and continued writing his poem on his imprisonment. During a banquet, the Cardinal of Ferrara informed the Pope that the King of France wanted Cellini released, and the Pope agreed, releasing Cellini into the Cardinal's custody.]

. . . Again, while I was in prison, I had a terrible dream and words of great importance were inscribed on my forehead as if with a pen; and the one who wrote them told me three times that I should remain silent and not tell anyone about them. When I awoke, I felt that my forehead had been touched. In any case, in my poem about my imprisonment, many such things occur. Also, it was told to me, without then knowing the significance, all that would happen afterward to Signor Pier Luigi, so clearly and so precisely that I am convinced that it was an angel from heaven who actually told it to me. There is another thing I do not wish to leave out, the greatest that has ever happened to any man, which testifies to the divinity of God and His mysteries, which He deigned to make me worthy of: from the time I first had that vision until now, a brightness, a wondrous thing, has rested above my head, and can be clearly seen only by those few men whom I wish to see it. It can be seen above my shadow in the morning during the rising of the sun for about two hours; and it can be seen much better when the grass is covered with a soft dew; it can also be seen in the evening at sunset. I became aware of it in France while in Paris, since the air in those parts is so much clearer of mists that one could see it appear much better there than in Italy where mists are much more frequent. But I am able to see it under any circumstances, and I can show it to other people, but not as well as in the region I have mentioned. . . .

[The poem on Cellini's imprisonment concludes the "first book" of his life.]

* * *

[In August 1545, the Duke of Florence, Cosimo de' Medici, was residing at his villa in Poggio a Caiano, where Cellini went to pay his respects. After the Duke and Duchess inquired about the work he had completed for the King of France, Duke Cosimo offered Cellini greater rewards than those he had received from the King.]

"If you were to do some work for me, I will treat you so generously that you will, I imagine, be astonished, provided that your works please me, and of this I have no doubt."

I, poor unfortunate one, desirous of showing that splendid Florentine School that since I had been away from Florence I had been engaged in professions other than the branch of art which that school valued, said in reply to my Duke that I would willingly make him a great statue either in marble or bronze for that beautiful piazza of his. To this, he answered that all he wanted as my first work was a Perseus; this he had been wanting for a long time, and he begged me to make him a little model of it. I willingly set myself to making it, and in a few weeks I finished this model, which was about a cubit high, in yellow wax and rather well finished, done with the greatest care and skill.

The Duke came to Florence, and several days passed before I could show him this model, and he acted as if he had never met or known me, which caused me to form a bad opinion of my business relations with His Excellency. Later, however, one day in the afternoon, I had it taken to his wardrobe and he came to see it together with the Duchess and a few other gentlemen. As soon as he saw it, he liked it and praised it lavishly; this gave me some small hope that he had some understanding of the matter. After having studied the model, his pleasure in it increased considerably, and he spoke these words: "If you could turn this small model, my Benvenuto, into a full-size work, it would be the most beautiful piece in the piazza!"

Then I answered: "My Most Excellent Lord, in the piazza there stand the works of the great Donatello and the wondrous Michelangelo, who are the two greatest sculptors since ancient times. But, since Your Illustrious Excellency is most enthusiastic about my model, let me say that I have it in me to make the statue three times better than the model."

At this, there was no small disagreement, because the Duke kept saying that he understood it perfectly and that he knew exactly what could be done. At this, I informed him that my works would decide that question and his doubt, and that most certainly I would achieve for His Excellency more than I had promised him, and that he must, however, give me the assistance I needed to be able to accomplish such a task, because without that assistance, I could not accomplish the great feat I had promised him. At this, His Excellency said to me that if I made a proposal of what I was asking from him, and included in it all my needs, he would see to it that generous arrangements would be made.

Certainly, if I had been astute enough to include in a contract all that I required for my work, I would not have experienced the great difficulties that through my own fault befell me, for he was very insistent on having the work done and on making good arrangements. Therefore, knowing that this lord had a great desire to embark on grandiose undertakings, I dealt freely with His Excellency more as a duke than as a merchant. I made my proposals, to which His Excellency responded most generously. In them, I said: "My most singular patron, true petitions and our true contracts do not consist of these words or those documents, but they actually consist in how far I succeed in doing the work I have promised; and if I succeed, then I promise that Your Most Illustrious Excellency will remember very well all that which you have promised me." His Excellency was so charmed by these words and with the way I acted and spoke that he and the Duchess heaped upon me the most immense favors that can be imagined in the world.

Having the greatest desire to begin working, I told His Excellency that I needed a house where I could accommodate myself and my furnaces for working pieces in both clay and bronze and, separately, gold and silver. I told him that I knew he understood how eager I was to serve him in these particular arts, and that I required rooms appropriate to doing such things. And so that His Excellency would see how much I wanted to serve him, I had already found the house which met my needs, located in a place which pleased me a great deal. And because I did not want to cost His Excellency either money or anything else before he had seen my works, I had brought from France two jewels, and I begged the Duke to buy me this house with my two jewels or to save them until I had earned the house with my works and my labors. These jewels had been beautifully set by the hands of my workmen according to my own designs. Having examined them carefully, the Duke spoke these spirited words which gave me false hope: "Take back your jewels, Benvenuto: I want you and not your jewels, and you shall have your house for nothing!"

Then he signed a rescript below my proposal, which I have always retained. This rescript read as follows: "Let the above-named house be seen, and let it be noted whose it is to sell and the price that is asked for it; for we wish to please Benvenuto." It seemed to me that I was certain to get the house with this rescript, for I was convinced that my work would be much more pleasing than what I had promised. After that, His Excellency had given express orders to his majordomo, who was named Ser Pier Francesco Riccio.[4] He came from Prato and had been the Duke's tutor. I spoke to this beast and told him all the things I needed to make a workshop. Immediately, this man gave the order to a certain wizened and lean contractor, who was named Lattanzio Gorini.[5] This puny man with those spidery little hands of his and his tiny mosquitolike voice moved at a snail's pace, and, as the devil would have it, he had sent to me at my house an amount of stones and sand and lime which was hardly sufficient to build an enclosure for pigeons. Seeing things going so horribly slowly, I began to become discouraged; and yet I said to myself, "Small beginnings sometimes have great endings," and seeing how many thousands of ducats the Duke had squandered on certain ugly and inferior works of sculpture made by that stupid Baccio Bandinelli[6] gave me a little hope. Taking heart, I set a fire under that Lattanzio Gorini to make him get moving; it was like screaming at a team of lame donkeys led by a blind boy; and under such difficult conditions and with my own money, I marked out the site for the workshop and pulled out the trees and bushes; indeed, I went boldly working on my own with a certain amount of real enthusiasm.

In other matters, I was in the hands of Tasso the carpenter,[7] a great friend of mine, and I had him make some wooden scaffolding in order to begin my work on the great Perseus. This Tasso was a most excellent and skillful man, the best, I believe, who ever practiced his profession. Moreover, he was agreeable and happy by nature, and whenever I went to see him, he met me smiling and singing a little song in falsetto. And I was already more than half the way down the road of despair, since I began to hear that things in France were going badly for me and since I expected little from my affairs in Florence, which seemed to be cooling off; but he always forced me into listening to at least half of his little song, and in the end, I grew more cheerful in his company and I forced myself, insofar as I was able, to forget some of my worries.

When I had put all the things I mentioned above into order and had begun to make some progress with the preparations for that aforesaid undertaking (I had already used up part of the lime), I was suddenly sent for by that majordomo; and I went to him, finding him, after His Excellency's midday meal, in the room called the "clock room"; I approached him with the greatest respect, but he received me with the greatest coldness, asked me who had installed me in that house, and by what authority I had begun building there. And he said that he was greatly astounded to find that I was such a bold, presumptuous fellow. To this, I replied that I had been installed in that house by His Excellency and that His Lordship, in His Excellency's name, had given the orders to Lattanzio Gorini; and this Lattanzio had brought the stone, the sand, and the lime, and had attended to the things I had requested, saying that he had received his orders from His Lordship to do so. After I had said this, that brute turned to me with greater anger than before, and said that neither I nor any of those whom I had mentioned spoke the truth.

Then I became offended and I told him: "Oh, Majordomo, as long as Your Lordship speaks in a way which is in accord with your noble rank, I shall respect you and speak to you with the same obedience as I do to the Duke, but if you do otherwise, I shall speak to you as I would to Ser Pier Francesco Riccio." The man then flew into such a rage that I thought he would go mad before Heaven had decided he should, and he said to me, along with a number of other abusive words, that he wondered why he thought me worthy of speaking to a man such as himself. At these words, I bestirred myself and replied: "Now, listen to me, Ser Pier Francesco Riccio, and I'll tell you who my equals are and who are your equals—masters who teach their children how to read." When I spoke these words, this man, with his face all contorted, raised his voice, repeating those same words more insolently than before. To which I again put on a fierce expression, assumed an arrogant stance like his, and said that men like me were worthy of speaking to Popes and emperors and to a great king, and that there was, perhaps, only one man like me in the world, but that there were a dozen like him in any street doorway. When he heard these words, he jumped up on a window seat in that hall and then told me to repeat once again what I had said to him. I did so a bit more heatedly, and I added that I no longer cared to serve the Duke and that I would return to France, where I had the freedom to go. The brute remained there stupefied with his face the color of clay, and in great agitation I left, determined to clear out of there, and would to God I had done so.

Thus, His Excellency the Duke could not have learned of this diabolical happening right away, because I waited several days without anything happening. I had dismissed all thoughts of Florence except those regarding my sister and nieces, for whose care I made arrangements with the little money I had brought with me. I wanted to leave them settled as best I could, and then as soon as possible after that, I wanted to return to France, and I never cared whether I saw Italy again. I had resolved to be on my way as quickly as possible and to go without taking leave of the Duke or anyone else, and then one morning that majordomo of his own accord sent for me very humbly and embarked on making a kind of pedantic oration in which I could find no style, no grace, no wit, nor any beginning or ending. I could only grasp that he claimed to be a good Christian and that he did not want to bear hatred toward anyone, and he asked me on behalf of the Duke what salary I wanted for my upkeep.

At this, I stood there lost in thought and did not respond, since I had no intention of remaining there. When he saw me standing there without an answer, he still had the wit to say: "Oh, Benvenuto, dukes expect an answer, and what I am saying to you, I say on behalf of His Excellency." Then I replied that since he was speaking on behalf of His Excellency, I would most willingly respond, and I told him that he should tell His Excellency that I would not be put second to anyone who served him in my profession. The majordomo said: "Bandinelli is paid two hundred *scudi* for his upkeep, so if you are content with that, your salary is settled." I answered that I was content, and that whatever more I deserved should be given to me when my work was seen and that I would leave everything to the good judgment of His Most Illustrious Excellency. So, against my will, I picked up the thread and set to work, with the Duke constantly doing me the greatest favors imaginable.

I had very often received letters from France, from that very loyal friend of mine, Messer Guido Guidi:[8] as yet, those letters brought me nothing but good news. That Ascanio of mine[9] also sent me advice, saying that I should concentrate on having a good time for myself and that if anything happened, he would warn me. The King was informed that I had begun to work for the Duke of Florence, and because this man was the best in the world, he often said: "Why doesn't Benvenuto return to us?" And he in turn questioned my two young men, both of whom told him that I had written to tell them that I was doing as well as I was and that they thought I no longer wished to return and serve His Majesty. The King was furious over this, and in answer to those presumptuous words, which never came from me, he said: "Since he left us without any cause whatsoever, I shall never call for him again: let him stay where he is!" These criminals arranged matters exactly as they wished, since every time I returned to France, they would have to return to being workmen under me, as they were before; whereas if I did not return, they remained free as they were and in my place. For that reason, they made every effort to keep me from coming back.

While I was having the workshop built in order to begin the *Perseus*, I worked in a room on the first floor in which I had modeled a plaster cast of the *Perseus* in the same dimensions as the finished bronze would be, with the intention of casting it from this mold. When I saw that to do so in this way would take somewhat more time, I decided on an alternative method, since a worthless little workshop had been put up brick by brick, built so wretchedly that just remembering it outrages me. I began with the figure of the Medusa, and I made an iron skeleton, which I covered with clay, and when I finished that, I baked it.

I worked with only two young apprentices, one of whom was very handsome; he was the son of a whore named La Gambetta. I used this boy to make a sketch, for no books teach this art better than the human body. I tried to get some workmen to hurry along my work, but I could not find any, and I could not do everything by myself. There were some in Florence who would willingly have come, but Bandinelli quickly prevented them from doing so, and then, after making me do without them for a time, he told the Duke that I was going about trying to steal his workmen, since it was impossible for me to construct such a great statue without the help of others. I complained to the Duke about what a great nuisance this beast was, and I begged him to get me some of the workmen from the Opera del Duomo.[10] My words only made the Duke believe what Bandinello was saying. When I became aware of this, I resolved to do what I could on my own. I set myself to doing it with the utmost effort imaginable, and then, while I was exhausting myself day and night on this, my sister's husband fell ill and in a few days died. He left behind my sister, still young and with six children of all ages; this was the first great trial I had in Florence—to be left the father and guardian of those poor things.

I was, however, anxious that nothing should go wrong, and since my garden was full of a lot of rubbish, I sent for two workers, who were brought from the Ponte Vecchio: one of these was a sixty-year-old man, and the other a young man of eighteen. When they had been with me for about three days, the young one told me that the old man did not want to work and that I would do better to send him away, because not only was he unwilling to work but he prevented the younger one from working; and he told me that what little there was to be done, he could do himself, and that there was no need to throw away money on other people: this young man's name was Bernardino Manellini di Mugello. Seeing his willingness to work hard, I asked him if he would like to remain in my service; immediately, we came to an agreement. This young man used to groom my horse, work in the garden, and then he learned to help me in the workshop, so that little by little, he began to learn the art with so much grace that I never had a better assistant. I decided to do everything with his help only, and I began to show the Duke that Bandinelli was a liar and that I could very well do without his workmen.

At this time, I had a slight kidney ailment, and since I could not work, I willingly stayed in the Duke's dressing room along with some young goldsmiths named Gianpagolo and Domenico Poggini; I got them to make a little gold pot, adorned in bas-relief with figures and other beautiful decorations. This was for the Duchess, and Her Excellency had ordered it made for drinking water out of. In addition to this, I was asked to make her a golden girdle, and this work was also to be richly worked with jewels and many pleasing inventions such as little masks and other things; and this I did. The Duke used to come to the dressing room every so often, and he took the greatest pleasure in watching us work and talking with me.

As my kidneys began to get a little better, I had some clay brought to me, and while the Duke passed away the time with us there, I sketched him, making a model of his head, considerably larger than life-size. His Excellency took the greatest of pleasure in this work, and he grew so fond of me that he told me it would give him immense delight if I would make arrangements to work in the palace; he would find some spacious rooms for me, and I should furnish them with furnaces and whatever else I needed, because he was very much amused by such things. At this, I told His Excellency it was not possible, because under such circumstances I could not have finished my work in a hundred years.

The Duchess was doing inestimable favors for me, and she would have liked me to give my full attention to working for her and not to worry about the *Perseus* or anything else. But when I thought about these meaningless favors, I knew that my perverse and biting fortune would not delay long in doing me some new harm, for always present in my mind was the harm that I had done in seeking to do a great good: I am referring to what happened in France. The King could not swallow the great displeasure he felt over my departure, and yet he would have liked me to return, but with his honor intact. I thought I was wholly in the right and did not want to humble myself, because I thought if I had condescended to write humbly, those men, like the Frenchmen they were, would have said that this proved I was at fault and that certain hateful acts that were wrongly attributed to me were true. For that reason, I stood on my dignity, and, like a man who is in the right, I wrote very properly, and this pleased those two treacherous students of mine very much. When I wrote them, I used to boast of the great kindness shown me in my homeland by a lord and lady who were absolute rulers in the city of Florence, my native city; whenever they received one of these letters, they would go to the King with it and press His Majesty to give them my castle in the same way he had given it to me. The King, who was a good and admirable person, never wished to consent to the reckless demands of these great thieves, because he had begun to realize their evil intentions; and in order to give them a little hope and me the excuse to return immediately, he had a rather angry letter written by one of his treasurers, named Giuliano Buonaccorsi, a Florentine citizen. The letter contained the following: that if I wanted to keep my good name as an honest man, in view of the fact that I had left without any cause, I was certainly obligated to render an account of all that I had administered and done for His Majesty.

When I received this letter, it gave me so much pleasure that to tell the truth, I couldn't have asked for more. I sat down and began to write, filling up nine sheets of ordinary paper; and on those, I related in minute detail all the work I had done and everything that had happened while I was working, and how much money I had spent on that work, and how I received it from the hands of two of his notaries and one of his treasurers, and how I obtained receipts from all those men who were paid with it, some of whom had given me goods and others their labor; and that I had not kept a single coin of that money for myself, and that for my finished works I had not been given anything at all; the only things I had taken to Italy were a few favors and royal promises, truly worthy of His Majesty.

And I could truly not claim to have gained anything else from my work other than certain wages arranged for me by His Majesty for my upkeep, and of these I still owed more than seven hundred gold *scudi*, which I had deliberately left behind, so that they could be sent to me for my safe return; yet, I know that some malicious men did me an evil turn out of envy, but, I said, the truth always prevails and that I glory in His Most Christian Majesty, and I am not moved by avarice. Although I knew that I obtained much more from His Majesty than what I offered to do, and although the exchange promised me did not come to me, I had no other concern than remaining in His Majesty's opinion the good and honest man that I had always been. And if there was any doubt about this in His Majesty's mind, I would come flying back at the slightest sign to give an account of my own life: but seeing myself to be held of so little account, I did not wish to return and offer myself, knowing that bread will always be given to me wherever I go; and if I am sent for, I will always respond.

There were in this letter many other details worthy of that marvelous King and in salvation of my honor. This letter, before I sent it, I carried to the Duke, who was very pleased to see it; then I immediately sent it to France directly to the Cardinal of Ferrara.

At this time, Bernardone Baldini,[11] His Excellency's jeweler, had brought a great diamond weighing more than thirty-five carats from Venice (Antonio di Vittorio Landi[12] was also interested in getting the Duke to buy it). This diamond had already been cut to a point, but since it did not have the sparkling clarity that is to be desired from such a jewel, the owners of this diamond cut off its point, which was truly no good either for table-cutting or for cutting points. Our Duke, who although he took the greatest of pleasure in precious stones did not know anything about them, gave certain hope to that great rascal "il Bernardaccio" that he wanted to buy this diamond. And because this Bernardo alone sought to have the honor of swindling the Duke of Florence, he never conferred with his partner Antonio Landi. This Antonio was a great friend of mine since boyhood, and since he saw that I was on such familiar terms with my Duke, he called me aside one day. It was nearly noon, and in a corner of the New Market, he spoke to me in this manner: "Benvenuto, I am certain that the Duke will show you a diamond which he appeared to wish to buy. You will see a large diamond: assist in the sale, and I assure you that I can give it for 17,000 scudi. I'm certain that the Duke will want your advice: if you see he is really inclined to want it, things will be arranged so that he can have it."

This Antonio appeared to be very sure of being able to profit from this jewel. I promised him that if it was shown to me and if I was asked for my opinion, I would say all that I thought without prejudice to the jewel. As I said above, the Duke came to that goldsmith's workshop for a few hours every day, and more than eight days after Antonio Landi had spoken to me, the Duke one day after lunch showed me this diamond, which I recognized from the indications Antonio Landi had given me and from both its shape and its weight. And since the diamond was of a rather cloudy, watery quality, as I said above, upon seeing it to be of that quality (they had for that reason cut off the point), I would have certainly dissuaded him from making such a purchase; still, when he showed it to me, I asked His Excellency what he wanted me to say, because it was a very different matter for a jeweler to appraise a stone once a lord had bought it and quite another matter to give it an appraisal because he would like to buy it. Then His Excellency told me that he had bought it and that I should only give him my opinion. I did not want to fail to give some indication of how little I thought of that stone. He told me that I should consider the beauty of its great facets. At that, I said that this was not the great beauty His Excellency imagined and that the only reason it appeared so was that the point had been cut off. At these words, my lord, who realized I was speaking the truth, put on a long face and told me to attend to giving an estimate of its value and deciding what I thought it was worth. Seeing that, since Antonio Landi had offered it to me for 17,000 scudi, I said that I believed the Duke must have gotten it for 15,000 scudi at the most, and for that reason, seeing he took it badly when I told the truth, I thought I should confirm the Duke in his false opinion. Giving him back the diamond, I said: "You must have spent 18,000 *scudi!*"

Hearing these words, the Duke cried out, making an "Oh" with his face greater than the mouth of a well, and said: "Now I am convinced you know nothing about this matter." I replied to him: "Certainly, My Lord, you are wrong. You attend to maintaining the reputation of your diamond, and I shall attend to understanding these matters. Tell me at least what you spent on it, so that I may learn to understand these matters in the same manner as Your Excellency does." The Duke arose with a slightly scornful smile and said: "Twenty-five thousand *scudi* and more it cost me, Benvenuto!" And he went away.

Present during this conversation were the goldsmiths Giampagolo and Domenico Poggini[13] and the embroiderer Bachiacca,[14] who was also working in a room next to ours and who came running in when he heard the noise. At this point, I said: "I would never have advised him to buy it, but if he had still wanted it, Antonio Landi offered it to me a week ago for 17,000 *scudi*. I believe I could have had it for 15,000 or less. But the Duke wants to maintain the stone's reputation. When Antonio Landi offered it to me for such a price, how the devil can Bernardone work such a shameful swindle against the Duke?" And never believing that such a thing could be as true as it was, we laughingly passed off the Duke's naiveté.

Having already executed the figure of the large Medusa, as I have said, I had its iron skeleton built; then I did it in clay, with its anatomy, and thinner by a half a finger, and I baked it thoroughly; then I put on the wax and finished it in the way I wanted it to be. The Duke, who had come to see it many times, was so worried that I might not succeed with the bronze that he wanted me to call in some expert to cast it for me.

And because His Excellency continually spoke of my expertise with great approval, his majordomo constantly tried to find some snare to make me break my neck. Now how could such a man have the authority to give orders to the police officers and all the officials of the poor unfortunate city of Florence, a man who was from Prato and our enemy, the son of a cooper, a very ignorant man? Just for having been the rotten tutor of Cosimo de' Medici, before he became Duke, he rose to such a position of authority. As I have said, since he was always on the lookout for some way of harming me, and seeing that he could find no way of getting at me, he then thought up a way of accomplishing his goal. Having gone to find the mother of my shopboy, whose name was Cencio (hers was La Gambetta), that rascally pedant and that dishonest whore together thought up a way to give me such a scare that I would go with

God. La Gambetta, drawing upon her own talent, went out on the orders of that crazy, wicked tutor, the majordomo, and they had also come to an understanding with the sheriff, who was a certain Bolognese whom the Duke later on banished for doing these kinds of things.

On one Saturday evening around three hours after sunset, this Gambetta came to find me with her son, and she told me that she had kept him locked up several days for my benefit. To this I answered that she should not keep him locked up on my account; and laughing at her whorish cunning, I turned to the boy and in her presence told him: "You know, Cencio, if I have done you any wrong." Crying, he said no. Then his mother, shaking her head, said to her son: "Ah, you little rascal, is it possible I don't know what's going on?" Then she turned to me, telling me that I must keep him hidden in my house, because the sheriff was looking for him and would seize him, at any rate, outside my house, but they would not touch him inside my home. At this, I told her that my widowed sister and her six angelic little girls were living in my home and that I did not want anyone else there. Then she said that the majordomo had given the sheriff orders and that I would be imprisoned at any rate, but since I did not want to take her son into my house, if I gave her 100 *scudi*, I would have nothing to worry about, because the majordomo was such a great friend of hers, and I could rest assured that she would make him do everything she wished, provided I gave her the 100 *scudi*.

This had already put me in such a rage that I said to her angrily: "Get out of here, you contemptible whore! If it weren't for my good reputation and the innocence of this unfortunate son you have here, I would have already cut your throat with this dagger; I've put my hands on it two or three times already." And with these words, and much pushing and shoving, I drove her and her son out of the house.

Then, after I had thought about the wickedness and power of that evil tutor, I judged it best for me to try to avoid this devilish business, and early in the morning, having consigned to my sister jewels and things worth about 2,000 *scudi*, I mounted my horse and went off in the direction of Venice, and I took with me my man Bernardino di Mugello. And when I arrived at Ferrara, I wrote to His Excellency the Duke that although I had gone away without being sent, I would return without being sent for. Then, after arriving in Venice, I thought about the many different ways my cruel fortune wounded me, but finding myself nonetheless healthy and strong, I resolved to defend myself against her as usual. And so, I went along thus, thinking about my affairs, passing the time in that beautiful and rich city, having paid my respects to that marvelous painter Titian and to Jacopo Sansovino, the worthy sculptor and architect and our fellow Florentine citizen, who was very well treated by the Signoria of Venice. We had known each other in our youth in Rome and in Florence, where we both came from. These two great artists showed me much kindness.

The day after that, I ran into Messer Lorenzo de' Medici,[15] who quickly took me by the hand with the warmest welcome imaginable, because we had known each other in Florence when I was making Duke Alessandro's coins and then in Paris when I was in the King's service. He was staying with Giuliano Buonaccorsi,[16] and since there was nowhere to go and pass the time without very great risk to himself, he used to spend most of his time in my house, watching me work on those great works of mine. And as I said, because of our past acquaintance, he took me by the hand and led me to his house, where I found the Lord Prior degli Strozzi.[17] And while they were expressing their pleasure, they asked me how long I desired to remain in Venice, believing that I wanted to return to France. To these noblemen, I replied that I had left Florence for the reasons I have mentioned, and that in two or three days I wanted to return to Florence to serve the Grand Duke. When I had spoken, both Strozzi and Messer Lorenzo turned to me with so much severity that I became very afraid, and they said to me: "You would do far better to return to France, where you are rich and famous; if you go back to Florence, you will lose all you've gained in France, and from Florence you will get nothing but trouble."

I did not respond to their words, and, leaving the day after as secretly as I could, I turned in the direction of Florence, and in the meantime the devilish business had come to a head, since I had written the Grand Duke all about the circumstances that had taken me to Venice. And with his usual caution and severity, he received me without any fuss. Remaining stern for a time, he then turned to me pleasantly and asked me where I had been. At this, I replied that my heart had never withdrawn a finger's length from His Most Illustrious Excellency, although a necessity had forced me to let my body wander here and there for very legitimate reasons. Then, making himself even more pleasant, he began to ask me about Venice, and so we talked a bit; then, at last, he told me I should attend to my work and finish his *Perseus*. So I happily returned home with a light heart and cheered up my family— that is, my sister and her six daughters. And I took up my work again, pushing it forward with as much diligence as I could.

And the first work I cast in bronze was that large bust of His Excellency, which I made in clay in the goldsmith's shop while I was having those back pains. This was pleasing work, and I did it only to gain experience in working with the clays for casting in bronze. And although I saw how the admirable Donatello had done his bronzes which were cast with the clay from Florence, it seemed to me that he had succeeded only with great difficulty; and thinking that this must have been because of a defect in the clay, before casting my *Perseus*, I wanted to take these first precautions; in doing so, I found the clay to be good, although it had not been well understood by that admirable Donatello, and I saw his works were completed with great difficulty. Thus, as I said above, by virtue of technique, I mixed the clay, which served me very well; and as I said, I cast the bust with it, but since I had not yet made my own furnace, I used the furnace of Maestro Zanobi di Pagno, a bell founder.

And seeing that my bust had come out very sharp and clean, I immediately set out to build a little furnace in the shop the Duke had made for me, according to my own arrangement and design in the very house the Duke had presented to me as a gift; and as quickly as the furnace was finished, I set things in order with as much diligence as possible to cast the statue of the Medusa, the woman all contorted under the feet of Perseus. And since this casting was a most difficult thing, I did not want to be lacking in any of the skills and care I had acquired so that I would not commit some error; and thus the first casting I did in my little furnace came out surprisingly well and was so sharp and clean that it did not seem to my friends I otherwise needed to retouch it. Certain Germans and Frenchmen have discovered how to do this very thing, and they boast of some fine secrets for casting bronzes without retouching: truly a crazy thing, because once bronze is cast it is necessary to work it with hammers and chisels, just as the wondrous ancients would do, and the moderns as well—I mean those moderns who had possessed any knowledge of how to work in bronze.

This casting pleased his Most Illustrious Excellency well, and he came to see it a number of times at my house, giving me great encouragement to do well, but the rabid envy of Bandinello, who with such eagerness whispered in His Illustrious Excellency's ears, was so effective that he made him think that although I cast a few of these statues, I would never put them together, because it was a new craft for me, and that His Excellency should take good care not to throw his money away. These words had such an impact upon those glorious ears that some of the allowance for my workmen was taken away from me; as a result, I was compelled boldly to show my resentment to His Excellency. Hence, one morning I waited for him in the Via dei Servi and I said to him: "My Lord, my needs are not being met, so that I fear Your Excellency lacks confidence in me; thus, I say again to you that I am satisfied with the prospect of executing this work three times better than the model I showed you."

Having spoken these words to His Excellency and realizing that they had borne no fruit since they elicited no response, anger immediately rose up in me along with an unbearable passion, and again I began to speak to the Duke, saying to him: "My Lord, this city has truly always been the school of the greatest talents; but however well known a person is, when he has learned something and he wants to increase the glory of his city and his glorious prince, he would do well to go and work elsewhere. And that this is true, My Lord, I know that Your Excellency remembers Donatello, the great Leonardo da Vinci, and now the miraculous Michelangelo Buonarroti: these men through their genius increase Your Excellency's glory. To this end, I also hope to do my part; so, My Lord, allow me to leave. But may Your Excellency take care not to allow Bandinello to go; rather always give him more than he asks for, because if he goes somewhere else, he is so ignorant and presumptuous that he is apt to bring shame upon this noble school. Now give me leave, My Lord; I won't ask anything more for my labors up to now except for Your Most Illustrious Excellency's favor."

Then I thanked him and said I had no other desire but to show these envious people that the prospect of bringing the promised work to completion was enough for me. Thus, after taking leave of His Excellency, I was given a little assistance; for this I was compelled to put my hand in my own pocket because I wished my work to go forward at more than one step at a time.

And in the evenings I always used to go to pass the time in His Excellency's wardrobe, where I found Domenico and his brother Giampagolo Poggini, who were working on a gold vase for the Duchess that I mentioned before, and a golden girdle. Also His Excellency had had me make a little model of a pendant, in which was to be set the large diamond that Bernardone and Antonio Landi had made him buy. And although I tried to avoid doing something I did not want to do, the Duke with great charm and courtesy had me working there every evening until four hours after sunset. Also, he pressed me in the most agreeable ways to work there in the daytime as well, something I would never wish to agree to, and I believed that because of this, His Excellency was certainly angry with me. And one evening, when I arrived somewhat later than usual, the Duke said to me: "You are *malvenuto*." To these words, I replied: "My Lord, that is not my name, because my name is

Benvenuto; and since I think Your Excellency is joking with me, I will not pursue the matter."

At this, the Duke said that he was speaking in earnest and was not joking, and that I should be prudent in what I was doing, because it had come to his ears that, taking advantage of his favor, I was deceiving one man or another. At these words, I begged His Most Illustrious Excellency to do me the honor of telling me the name of just one man I had ever tricked. He immediately turned to me in anger and exclaimed: "Go and give back what you have of Bernardone's: there's one man for you!" At this, I said: "My Lord, I thank you and beg you to do me the honor of listening to me say a few words. It is quite true that he lent me a pair of old scales and two anvils and three small hammers; I told his Giorgio da Cortona to send for these implements fifteen days ago; and so this Giorgio came for them himself. And if ever Your Excellency finds that since the day I was born, I have ever kept anything of anyone's in this way in either Rome or France—let it be understood, from those who have reported these things or from others—then punish me severely if you discover it to be true."

When the Duke saw that I was in a great passion, he turned and said to me, like a discreet and loving lord: "These things are not meant for those who are not guilty; so, if it is as you say, I will always see you willingly as I have in the past."

At this I said: "Know, Your Excellency, that Bernardone's dirty tricks compel me to ask you and beg you to tell me what you paid for that large diamond with the point cut off, because I hope to show you why that wicked, ill-bred man is trying to bring about my disgrace." Then His Excellency said to me: "The diamond cost me 25,000 ducats.[18] Why do you ask?" "Because, My Lord, on such and such a day at such and such an hour at the corner of the New Market, Antonio di Vettorio Landi told me to try to sell it to Your Excellency, and, at first, he asked me for 16,000 ducats. Now Your Excellency knows what you paid for it. And to know if this is true, ask Ser Domenico Poggini and his brother Giampagolo, who are here; for I told them immediately, and since then I have never said a word because Your Excellency said I did not understand the matter, which made me think that you wished to maintain the stone's reputation. Know, My Lord, that I do understand these matters and, as for the rest, I try to be as good a man as any ever born, no matter who he may be: I do not seek to rob you of 8 or 10,000 ducats at a time; rather, I would strive to earn them through my labor; and I entered Your Excellency's service as a sculptor, goldsmith, and coinmaker, but to report on the affairs of others, never! And what I am saying to you now,

I am saying in my own defense, and I do not wish any reward; and I am saying all this in the presence of so many good men who are here, so that Your Illustrious Excellency will not believe what Bernardone says."

The Duke immediately arose in anger and sent for Bernardone, who was forced to flee to Venice along with Antonio Landi; Antonio told me that he had not meant to sell *that* diamond. They went to Venice and returned, and I sought out the Duke and said: "My Lord, what I told you is true, and what Bernardone told you about the tools was not true; and you would do well to prove it, and I will go find the sheriff." At these words, the Duke turned to me, saying: "Benvenuto, concern yourself with being a good man as you have done in the past and never worry about anything else."

The whole affair dissolved in a puff of smoke, and I never heard any more said about it. I attended to finishing his jewel, and when I took the finished piece to the Duchess, she herself told me that she valued my craftsmanship as much as the diamond that Bernardaccio had made them buy, and she wanted me to fasten it on her bosom with my own hand; and she handed me a big pin, and with it I fastened it on, and I left with many indications of her favor. Later, I heard that they had had it reset by a German or some other foreigner, if it is true, because Bernardone said that this diamond would be better displayed in a less ornate setting.

Domenico and Giampagolo Poggini, goldsmiths and brothers, as I believe I have said before, used to work in His Illustrious Excellency's wardrobe with my designs on certain little gold vases engraved with representations of little figures in bas-relief and on other very important objects. And I thus often remarked to the Duke: "My Lord, if Your Most Illustrious Excellency would pay some workmen, I would make you coins for your mint and medals engraved with Your Illustrious Excellency's head, and I would compete with the ancients and would hope to surpass them, because since the time I made the medals for Pope Clement, I have learned so much that I will make them much better than those; and thus, I shall make better coins than I made for Duke Alessandro, which are still considered very beautiful; and I shall also make you large vases in gold and silver, like those I made so many of for that wonderful King Francis of France because of the great assistance he gave me—nor did I ever lose time working on the great giants or the other statues."

At my words, the Duke said to me: "Do so and I shall see about it." But he never gave me any assistance or aid of any kind. Then, one day His Illustrious Excellency had me given several pounds of silver and he said to me: "This comes from the silver in my mines; make me a beautiful vase."

I did not want to neglect my *Perseus*, but since I was also anxious to serve him, I gave the work, along with my designs and wax models, to a certain villain named Piero di Martino, a goldsmith, to do. He began it badly, and he also made so little progress that I lost more time on it than if I had done it all with my own hands. Thus, after wasting several months and seeing that Piero was not working on it nor having anyone else work on it, I made him give it back to me; and I experienced great trouble in getting it back, along with the body of the vase which he had begun so slowly, as I said, and the rest of the silver that I had given him. The Duke, who had heard something of the uproar, sent for the vase and the models and never even told me why or how; suffice it to say that he had them made on my designs by various persons both in Venice and in other places and was quite badly served.

The Duchess often told me to do some work in goldsmithing for her; and in response I told her more than once that everyone knew quite well all over Italy that I was a good goldsmith, but Italy had never seen works of sculpture by my hand. And in the arts, certain rabid sculptors, laughing at me, call me the "new" sculptor. I hope to show them I am an experienced sculptor, if God will give me enough grace to be able to exhibit my finished *Perseus* in His Illustrious Excellency's noble piazza.

And going back home, I applied myself to my work day and night and never made an appearance at the palace. And still thinking of maintaining myself in the good graces of the Duchess, I had made certain little vases for her which were as big as a cheap pot and done in silver with beautiful masks in a very rare style, after the antique. And when I took these little vases to her, she gave me the kindest welcome imaginable, and paid me the silver and gold that I had put into them: and I also recommended myself to her Most Illustrious Excellency, begging her to tell the Duke that I had little help for such a great work and that she should tell the Duke not to give such credence to the evil tongue of Bandinello, with which the latter was impeding me from finishing my *Perseus*. At these tearful words, the Duchess shrugged her shoulders and only said to me: "Certainly the Duke ought to know that this Bandinello of his amounts to nothing."

I stayed at home and rarely presented myself at the palace, working as I did with great diligence to finish my project. Then it became necessary for me to pay my workmen, since after the Duke had certain workmen paid by Lattanzio Gorini for eighteen months, he came to find it a nuisance and took the subsidy away from me. For this reason, I asked Lattanzio why he was not paying me. And he answered, shaking his spidery little hands, with a shrill little mosquito's voice: "Why don't you finish your statue? It's thought you'll never finish it."

I immediately replied to him angrily: "Damn you and all those who think I won't finish it!"

And so, in despair, I returned home to my unlucky *Perseus*—not without tears, since it all came back to me how I had left a fine situation in Paris in the service of the marvelous King Francis, who gave me everything, while here I had nothing. And several times I resolved to give myself over to despair, and once feeling this way, I mounted my handsome little horse and put 100 *scudi* in my pockets and went to Fiesole to see a natural son of mine whom I put out to nurse with a close friend, the wife of one of my workmen. And having joined my little son, I found him very well, and I, full of discontent, kissed him; and when I wanted to leave, he would not let me go, holding me fast with his little hands and with a storm of crying and screaming, which was absolutely incredible, given that he was only about two years old.

And since I had resolved in my desperation that if I found Bandinello, who used to go every evening to his farm above San Domenico, I would throw him on the ground, I detached myself from my little boy and left him crying desperately. And proceeding toward Florence, I arrived at the piazza of San Domenico, and Bandinello entered just at that moment from the other side of the piazza. Immediately I resolved to carry out my bloody plan; I approached him, and raising my eyes, I saw he was unarmed, mounted on a sorry little mule, or rather a donkey, and with him he had a little boy of about ten years; and as soon as he saw me, he turned white as death and trembled from his head to his toes. Recognizing what a vile thing it would be to attack him, I said: "Don't be afraid, you contemptible coward, I won't do you the honor of hitting you!"

He looked at me meekly and said nothing. Then I recovered my faculties and thanked God that His true power and goodness had prevented me from committing such an intemperate act. Thus, liberated from that diabolical rage, my spirits rose, and I said to myself: "If God gives me the grace to finish my work, I hope in that way to overwhelm all my knavish enemies, and in this fashion I shall make my revenge far greater and more glorious than if I had showed only one of them what I think of them." And with this good resolution, I returned home. Three days later, I learned that this wetnurse of mine had smothered my only son, which caused me greater grief than I had ever felt before. However, I knelt down and, not without tears, I thanked God in my usual fashion, saying: "My Lord, You gave him to me and now You have taken him away, and for everything I thank You with my whole heart." And although my great grief had nearly destroyed me, in my normal fashion I made a virtue out of necessity and as best I could, I went about adjusting to it.

At this time, a young man named Francesco, son of Matteo the blacksmith, had left Bandinello. This young man asked me if I would give him work; and I was agreeable and put him to work cleaning the figure of the Medusa, which had already been cast. A fortnight later, this young man told me that he had spoken with his master—that is, Bandinello—and that Bandinello had told him to tell me that if I wished to do a marble statue, he sent me the offer of donating a fine piece of marble to me. I immediately replied: "Tell him I accept: and it may be an ill-fated marble for him, since he is always provoking me, and doesn't remember the great risk he ran with me in the piazza of San Domenico. Now tell him that I want it in any case: I never speak of him and the beast is always annoying me; and I believe that you came to work for me, sent by him to spy on my affairs. So go and tell him that I will have the marble in spite of him, and return here with it."

After many days had gone by, during which time I did not put in an appearance at the palace, I went there one morning when the fancy took me, and the Duke had almost finished dining, and, from what I heard, His Excellency had been talking and saying many good things about me, and among other things, he had greatly praised my skill in setting jewels; and for that reason, when the Duchess saw me, she had me called to her by Messer Sforza. When I presented myself to Her Most Illustrious Excellency, she asked me to set a small pointed diamond in a ring for her, and she said she would always wear it on her finger, and gave me the measurements and the diamond, which was worth about one hundred *scudi*, and asked me to do it quickly. Immediately, the Duke began to argue with the Duchess: "Certainly, Benvenuto used to be unequaled in this craft, but now that he has given it up, I think that making a little ring like the one you would like will be too much trouble for him; so I beg you not to tire him out in this small matter, which would be a great bother for him since he is out of practice."

At these words, I thanked the Duke and then asked him to let me do this small favor for the Duchess; and once I had put my hands to it, I finished it in a few days. The ring was for her little finger: thus I fashioned four cherubs in relief with four little masks which made up the ring. And I also adorned it with some enameled fruits and ligatures in such a way that the jewel and ring looked very good together, and I immediately took it to the Duchess, who with gracious words told me I had made her something very lovely and that she would remember me.

She sent this little ring as a gift to King Philip,[19] and from then on was always ordering something from me, but so kindly, that I always forced myself to serve her, although I saw little money from it, and God knows I had great need of it, because I wanted to finish my *Perseus* and had found some young men to help me, whom I was paying myself; and again, I began to put in an appearance more often than I had in the past.

One feast day, I went to the palace after dinner, and arriving in the clock room, I saw the door of the wardrobe standing open, and as I drew a bit nearer, the Duke called me and with a pleasant greeting, he said to me: "You are welcome! Look at that little chest that my Lord Stefano di Pilestina[20] sent me as a gift; open it and see what's inside it." I opened it at once and said to the Duke: "My Lord, it's a statue in Greek marble, and it is a splendid thing! I must say I don't remember ever having seen such a beautiful statue of a little boy among the antique monuments, especially one so beautifully styled; I would like to make an offer to Your Most Illustrious Excellency to restore the head, arms, and feet for you. And I will make an eagle, so that it can be baptized as a Ganymede. And although it is not advantageous for me to repair statues—because this is the craft of certain bunglers who do truly wretched work—the excellence of this great master beckons me to serve him."

The Duke was very pleased that the statue was so beautiful and asked me many things, saying to me: "Tell me, my Benvenuto, in what exactly consists the skill of this master, which makes you so full of admiration?" Then I showed His Most Illustrious Excellency in the best way I knew how to appreciate such beauty, such intelligence, and such rare style; I gave a lengthy discourse on such things and did so most willingly, knowing that His Excellency took very great pleasure in it.

While I was entertaining the Duke in this pleasant fashion, a page happened to leave the wardrobe, and, as he left, Bandinello came in. When he saw him, the Duke, being somewhat disturbed, said to him with a harsh look: "What are you doing here?" Bandinello, without any other response, immediately stared at that little chest where the statue was uncovered, and with his malicious sneer, shaking his head, he said, turning toward the Duke: "My Lord, here you have one of those things I have mentioned many times to Your Most Illustrious Excellency. You see that the ancients understood nothing about anatomy, and, as a result, their works are all full of errors."

I remained silent, and paid no attention to anything he was saying; in fact, I had turned my back on him. As soon as this beast had finished his disagreeable, empty speech, the Duke said: "Oh, Benvenuto, this is completely the contrary of what you have just now been arguing with many fine explanations; so now defend the statue a bit." To these ducal words, delivered to me with such graciousness, I quickly responded and declared: "My Lord, Your Most Illustrious Excellency has to realize that Baccio Bandinelli is thoroughly wretched, and he has always been this way, so that whatever he looks at, as quickly as his disagreeable eyes see it, although it is of superlative quality, it is immediately converted into an absolute evil. But being only drawn to what is good, I see things in a more holy fashion, so that what I have said about this most beautiful statue to Your Most Illustrious Excellency is the whole truth, and what Bandinello has said of it only reflects the evil of which he is composed." The Duke was listening to me with great pleasure; and while I was saying these things, Bandinello grimaced and made the ugliest faces imaginable, and his face was already the ugliest face you could ever imagine!

Suddenly, the Duke moved off, making his way through some lower rooms, and Bandinello followed him. The Duke's manservants took me by the cape and guided me after him, and thus we followed the Duke, until His Most Illustrious Excellency reached an apartment and sat down with Bandinello and me standing on either side of him. I remained silent, and those who were around us—some of His Excellency's servants— were all staring intently at Bandinello, snickering a bit among them- selves over what I had said in the room above. Then Bandinello began to speak and said: "My Lord, when I uncovered my *Hercules and Cacus*,[21] I am certain that more than a hundred bad sonnets were written about me, which said the worst that one could imagine coming from that rabble." I then responded and said: "My Lord, when our Michelangelo Buonarroti revealed his Sacristy,[22] where there are so many beautiful statues to be seen, this admirable and virtuous Florentine School, friend of truth and goodness, wrote him more than one hundred sonnets, all of them competing to see who could give him the greatest praise: and thus, just as the statue of Bandinello deserved all the bad things that he says were said about it, so Buonarroti's deserved all the good that was said."

At the sound of my remarks, Bandinello became so enraged that he almost burst, and turning to me, he said: "And what faults are you able to add?"

"I will tell you, if you have the patience to bear listening to me." Bandinello replied: "Go ahead then."

The Duke and the others who were present there all waited atten- tively, and I began, saying first of all: "You must realize that I regret having to say what the defects of your work are, but I shall not tell you such things—rather I shall inform you as to what that virtuous school of Florentine artists says about it."

And because this wretched man was either muttering something unpleasant or moving his hands and feet here and there, he made me so angry that I began in a much more unpleasant manner than I would have, had he behaved differently.

"This virtuous school says that if Hercules' hair were shorn, there wouldn't remain enough of his skull to hold his brain in; and that one cannot tell if his face is the face of a man or a cross between a lion and an ox, and that it does not pay attention to what he is doing, and that it is poorly joined at the neck, so unskillfully and so ungracefully that nothing quite as bad has ever been seen; and that his ugly shoulders resemble the two pommels of an ass's pack saddle; and that his breasts and the rest of those muscles are not drawn from a man but from a great, huge sack of melons that has been set straight up against the side of a wall. Moreover, the thighs seem to be drawn from a sack full of long gourds; as for the two legs, it is impossible to know how they are joined to that ugly torso, because it is impossible to see on which leg he is standing or on which he is giving a show of strength; nor does it seem that he is resting upon them both, as is customary in the works of masters who know something about such things. It is easy to see that the body is leaning forward more than a third of an arm's length, and that this alone is the greatest and the most intolerable error that common, mediocre so-called craftsmen could make. Of the arms, they say that both are extended without any grace, and there is no art in them, as if you have never seen live nude models; and that the right leg of Hercules and that of Cacus share equally the calves of their legs, so that if one of the two were separated from the other, not only one of them but rather both would remain without calves at that point where they are touching. And they say one of the feet of Hercules is buried and that the other looks as if a fire were lit underneath it!"

This man just could not wait patiently while I was still talking about the great defects of Cacus; one reason was that I was telling the truth and the other was that I was making it clearly known to the Duke and the others in our presence, who were giving signs and making gestures of amazement and understanding that I was telling the precise truth. All at once, this stupid man said: "Oh, you vicious slanderer, what about my design?"

I replied that anyone who was good at making designs would never make a bad statue, and I therefore believed that his design was like his work. Now, seeing the Duke's expression and the others, and insulted by their looks and gestures, he let his insolence get the better of him and turned his mean, ugly head toward me and cried out suddenly: "Oh, be quiet, you filthy sodomite!"

At the sound of that word, the Duke frowned angrily at him, and the others closed their mouths and narrowed their eyes at him; I, who felt myself so wickedly insulted and driven to fury, immediately found a retort: "Oh, you madman, you are going too far, but I wish by God that I knew how to practice such a noble art; after all, we read that Jove enjoyed it with Ganymede in Paradise, and here on earth, the greatest emperors and kings in the world practice it: I am a lowly and humble human creature, who would not be able to even know how to get involved in such a wondrous thing."

At this, no one could restrain himself, and the Duke and the others broke out into the loudest peals of laughter imaginable. And although I gave the appearance of being so gracious, I would have you know, kind readers, that my heart was bursting inside me at the thought of how this man, the most filthy villain ever born, was daring enough in the presence of such a great prince to insult me in such a fashion. But, you know, it was the Duke he insulted and not me, for if I had not been in the company of such a great presence, I would have struck him dead.

Seeing that the laughter of these noblemen did not cease, this filthy, wicked moron began, in order to distract them from making fun of him, to change the subject, saying: "This Benvenuto goes around bragging that I have promised him a piece of marble!" At these words, I quickly said: "What! Didn't you send Francesco, the son of Matteo the blacksmith, your apprentice, to say that if I wanted to work in marble, you wanted to give me a piece? And I accepted it and now I want it!"

Then he replied: "Oh, you can count on never having it!"

Then, still full of anger for the unjust lies he told about me at first, out of control and blinded to the Duke's presence, I said in great fury: "I tell you directly that if you do not send the marble to my house, you'd better look for another world, because in this one, I shall surely flatten you!"

Immediately remembering that I was in the presence of such a great duke, I humbly turned to His Excellency and said: "My Lord, one madman makes a hundred; this man's madness has blinded me to your Most Illustrious Excellency's honor and to my own; may you pardon me." Then the Duke said to Bandinello: "Is it true that you promised him the marble?" Bandinello admitted that it was true. The Duke then said to me: "Go to the Opera and take a piece that suits you." I said that he had promised to send it to me at my house. The words that we exchanged were terrible, and I did not want it in any other way. The following morning, a block of marble was brought to my house; I asked who had sent it to me; and they said that Bandinello had sent it to me and that this was the marble he had promised me.

I had it carried immediately into my workshop, and I began to chisel it; and while I was working, I made the model; and I had such a strong desire to work in marble that I could not muster the patience to decide on a model with the care that is expected in such an art. And because it sounded as if it were cracked, I often repented ever having begun to work on it: still, I got what I could out of it—that is, the *Apollo and Hyacinth* which is still to be seen in all its imperfection in my workshop. And while I was working on it, the Duke would come to my house and often remark: "Leave the bronze alone for a while and let me see you work a bit on the marble." At once I took the tools for carving marble and worked on boldly.

The Duke asked me about the model I had made for the marble, to which I said: "My Lord, this marble is all cracked, but in spite of that I will get something out of it; I have not, therefore, been able to decide on a model, but I will go ahead this way, doing the best I can."

The Duke very promptly had a block of Greek marble brought to me from Rome, so that I could restore his antique *Ganymede*, which was the cause of the dispute with Bandinello. Once the Greek marble came, I considered it a sin to make pieces to redo the head and arms and other things for the *Ganymede*; and I provided myself with another piece of marble, and for the piece of Greek marble I made a little wax model, to which I gave the name of *Narcissus*. And because this marble had two the holes of the depth of a quarter of an arm's length and the width of two large fingers, I gave my statue the attitude that is now seen, avoiding holes in such a way that I removed them from my statue. But it had rained on the marble for scores and scores of years, so that these holes were always full of rainwater, which had penetrated into it so much that it had been weakened; and how rotten the top hole had become was proved later on when the flood came to the Arno and the water rose more than one and a half arm's lengths in my workshop. And since the *Narcissus* was placed on a block of wood, the water turned it over, causing it to break across the breasts. I patched it together, and so that the crack would not be visible, I made that garland of flowers which is now seen across its chest; I brought it to completion by working at the hours before sunrise and even on feast days, only to avoid losing time from my work on the *Perseus*.

And then one morning as I was preparing some little chisels to work on it, a very fine splinter of steel flew into my right eye, and went so far into the pupil that I could not find a way to extract it. I thought for certain that I would lose my sight in that eye. After several hours, I called for Maestro Raffaello de' Pilli, a surgeon, who took two live nesting pigeons and with a little knife cut a hole in a vein on their wings so that the blood flowed into my eye; I quickly felt relief from the blood, and in the space of two days, the steel splinter came out and my sight was fine and improved. And since the feast of St. Lucy was coming and we were only three days from it, I made a golden eye out of a French *scudo*, and had it presented to her by one of my six nieces (daughters of my sister Liperata) who was about ten years old, and with her I gave thanks to God and St. Lucy. And for a time, I did not want to work on the *Narcissus*, but went forward with the *Perseus* under all the difficulties I mentioned above, and I was ready to finish it and to leave Florence (God willing).

Since the cast of the Medusa turned out so well, I brought my *Perseus* toward completion. I had done it in wax and promised myself that it would turn out equally well in bronze, just as the Medusa had. The model was done extremely well in wax, and the Duke thought it looked very beautiful. Either because someone may have given him to believe that it could never turn out properly in bronze, or because the Duke himself thought this, he came more often to my house than he used to, and on one occasion, he said to me: "Benvenuto, this figure can't be done in bronze, because the rules of your craft do not permit it." I strongly resented these words from His Excellency and replied: "My Lord, I know that Your Most Illustrious Excellency has very little faith in me, and I believe this comes from the fact that Your Most Illustrious Excellency puts too much faith in those who say so much evil of me, or perhaps you truly do not understand the matter." He hardly let me finish my words before saying: "I profess that I do understand it, and that I understand it very well."

I quickly responded and said: "Yes, you do, but as a prince and not as an artist; for if Your Most Illustrious Excellency understood it in the way you believe you understand it, you would believe in me on account of the fine bronze that I made, the great portrait bust of Your Most Illustrious Excellency that has been sent to Elba, and because of my restoration of the beautiful marble *Ganymede* where, despite extreme difficulties, I endured greater labors than if I had done it anew; and again through the casting of the Medusa, which you now see here in Your Excellency's presence, an extremely difficult casting in which I achieved what no other man has achieved before me in this devilish art. You see, My Lord, I built the furnace with a design different from the others, because, besides the many other variations and skillful technical devices that are evident in it, I have made two outlets for the bronze, because this difficult and contorted figure could not have come out in any other way; and only through my intelligence did it come out so well. None of those practicing this craft would ever have believed it possible. And I would have you know for certain, My Lord, that all the great and extremely difficult works I created in France under that most admirable King Francis succeeded so well only because of the great courage which that good King inspired in me with his generous provisions and the manner in which he granted me as many workmen as I requested. There were some times that I used more than forty workmen, all of my own choosing; and for this reason, I created such a quantity of works there in such a brief time. Now, My Lord, believe in me and give me the assistance I absolutely require, because I hope to finish a work that will please you. Whereas if Your Most Illustrious Excellency disheartens me and refuses to give me the assistance I absolutely need, I can produce nothing truly good and neither can any other man in the world."

It was so difficult for the Duke to remain and hear my arguments that he kept turning now in one direction and now in another, and as for me, I was in despair, a poor wretch grieving at the remembrance of my fine situation in France. Quickly the Duke said: "Now, tell me, Benvenuto, how is it possible that the fine head of Medusa, which is high up there in the hand of Perseus, can ever come out all right?" I replied at once: "Now you see, My Lord, that if Your Most Illustrious Excellency had such knowledge of the craft as you imply you have, you would have no fear that the fine head you speak of would not come out; but instead you would justly be fearful about the right foot, which is so far below."

At my words, the Duke suddenly turned, half in anger, to certain noblemen who were with His Most Illustrious Excellency, and declared: "I believe this Benvenuto does this out of arrogance, setting himself in opposition to everything." And he quickly turned around to me, half mockingly, and as all those in his presence did the same, he began to say: "I will be sufficiently patient with you to listen to the arguments you can think up to make me believe it." Then I declared: "I will give you such a convincing argument that Your Excellency will understand perfectly."

And I began. "You know, My Lord, that the nature of fire is to go upward, and for this reason I promise you that the head of the Medusa will turn out very well. But because the nature of fire is not to go downward, in order to get it there, I will have to force it down six arm's lengths by artificial means; and for that precise reason, I say to Your

Most Illustrious Excellency that this foot cannot possibly turn out; but it will be easy for me to restore it."

The Duke said: "Well, why didn't you think of how to make that foot come out in the same way you said the head came out?" I replied: "It would have been necessary to make a much bigger furnace, in which I could have built a drainpipe for the wax as big as my leg, and with the weight of the hot metal, I could by necessity make it go there. Now my drain, which goes down those six arm's lengths to the feet, is only about two fingers wide. However, it isn't worth the expense of changing it, because it can easily be repaired. But when my mold is more than half full, as I hope, from this middle point onward, the fire will climb according to its nature, and the head of Perseus and that of the Medusa will come out perfectly: you may be very certain of it."

Once I had presented my solid arguments along with endless other explanations, which are too lengthy to write down here, the Duke took his leave, shaking his head.

Left to myself in this way, I happily regained my confidence and drove away all those melancholy thoughts which used to come to me from time to time and which often made me cry bitterly over my regret at having left France in order to come to Florence, my dear homeland, and only out of charity toward my six nieces. I now realized that having done this good deed was obviously the source of so much evil; still, despite all this, I promised myself that when I had finished the *Perseus* I had already begun, all my labors would turn into great happiness and glorious good.

And with renewed strength and all my resources of body and purse (the rest of the little money I had left), I began to procure a few piles of firewood, which I got from the pine woods at Serristori near Monte Lupo; and while I was waiting I covered my *Perseus* with the clay I had prepared several months earlier, so that it would be properly seasoned. And once I had made its clay tunic (as it is called in this craft), and armed it well and enclosed it in an iron framework with the greatest of care, I began with a slow fire to draw out the wax, which issued forth through the many vents I had made, for the more of these one makes, the better the mold will fill. And when I had finished extracting the wax, I built a furnace around my *Perseus*—that is, in its shape around the mold—out of bricks, piled one on top of the other, and left many spaces where the fire could be vented. Then I began to put in wood very slowly, and I made the fire burn continuously for two days and two nights so that when once the wax had been extracted and the mold was well baked, I immediately began to dig the pit in which to bury my mold, with all the fine techniques that this fine craft demands.

When I had finished digging the pit, then I took my mold, and by means of winches and strong ropes, I set it upright and, having suspended it an arm's length above my furnace and hoisted it perfectly so that it was hanging right in the middle of the pit, I very slowly lowered it into the bottom of the furnace, and set it down with all the care that one could possibly imagine. And when I had finished this delicate task, I began to bank it with the same dirt I had excavated; and as I gradually piled up the earth, I put in the vents, which were little conduits of terracotta used for sinks and other similar things. When I saw that I had set it up well and that this method of banking it and putting these drainpipes carefully in their places was done, and that my workmen had well understood my method, which was very different from those used by all the other masters of this profession, and when I had made sure that I could trust them, I turned my attention to the furnace, which I had filled with many blocks of copper and other pieces of bronze. And having placed them one on top of the other according to the rules of the craft—that is, having piled them up so that they would give way to the flames of the fire and so the metal would heat up more quickly and thereby melt down and be reduced to molten metal—I told them boldly to fire up the furnace. And I put in the pine wood, which, because of the pine's greasy resin and the fine workmanship of my furnace, worked so well that I had to attend to one side and then the other with such effort that it was intolerable, and still I forced myself to continue.

To add to all this, the workshop caught fire and we were afraid that the roof would fall in on us, and at the same time from where the garden was the heavens drove so much water and wind inside that my furnace began to cool down. I fought these perverse misfortunes for a number of hours, but this labor was a greater strain than even my strong constitution could withstand, and as a result I was seized by a day-long fever, the worst you can possibly imagine. For that reason, I was forced to throw myself upon my bed; and thus, very upset, having by necessity to suffer through it all, I turned to those who were assisting me, numbering about ten or more, among whom were masters of casting bronze, unskilled laborers, farm workers, and the particular workers from my own shop, including a certain Bernardino Manelli from Mugello, whom I had trained for a number of years. To him I said: "I now commend myself to you: make sure, Bernardino, that you follow the instructions I gave you, and do it as quickly as possible, because the metal will soon be ready. You can't make any mistakes, and these other good fellows will quickly make the channels. You will surely be able to do the job with these two herdsmen, and I am certain that my mold will fill nicely. I feel sicker than I have ever felt since the day I was born, and I truly believe that this terrible illness will have killed me in a few hours." Then, very unhappily, I left them and went to bed.

Once I had put myself to bed, I ordered my servant woman to take food and drink to all those in the workshop, and I said to them: "I certainly will never be alive by tomorrow morning." They encouraged me, saying that my great illness would pass and that it was the result of overtiring myself. And so I spent two hours fighting hard against the fever as I continually felt it rise, and I kept repeating: "I feel myself dying." My servant, who ran the whole house, was named Mona Fiore di Castel del Rio; this woman was the worthiest woman in the world and also the kindest; continually scolding me for being discouraged, she nevertheless served me with the greatest kindliness in the world. However, when she saw how terribly ill and dejected I was, for all her bravery of heart, she could not prevent a few tears from falling from her eyes, and even then, insofar as she could, she did her best to prevent me from noticing them.

In the midst of this torment, I caught sight of someone coming into my room, whose body appeared to be contorted like the letter S, and he began to speak in a mournful and tormented tone, like those who commend the souls of people who are going to be executed, and he said: "Oh, Benvenuto! Your work is spoiled, and there is no way at all to avoid it!" When I heard the words of that wretched fellow, I quickly let out a scream so piercing that it could have been heard from the moon; and dragging myself from my bed, I seized my clothes and began to get dressed; and I dealt out kicks and blows to my servants and my boy and to everyone else who attempted to help me, and I complained, declaring: "Oh, the jealous traitors! This is a cunning betrayal; but I swear by God that I'll get to the bottom of it, and before I die, I'll leave such proof of my worth that more than one person will be amazed."

Having finished dressing, I set out in a foul mood toward the workshop, where I saw all those people whom I had left in good spirits standing around astonished and terrified. I began saying: "Come on, now, listen to me; and since you either didn't know how or want to do as you were told, listen to me now that I am with you in the presence of my work, and let no one oppose me, because now work is needed—not advice!" At my words, a certain Maestro Alessandro Lastricati answered me, saying: "Look, Benvenuto, you want to do something that art does not allow and that cannot possibly be accomplished." At his words, I turned with such fury and violence that he and all the others cried out in a single voice: "Go on, give orders, and all of us will help you in whatever you command, as long as there is life in us." And I think that they spoke these loving words because they were expecting me to drop dead at any moment.

I went at once to look at the furnace, and I saw the metal had coagulated, a thing which is called a "cake." I told two of the workers to go over to the home of Capretta, a butcher, for a load of young oak wood that had been dried out for more than a year, which Ginevra, Capretta's wife, had offered me; and when they came with the first armloads, I began to fill the grate in the furnace. The oak that I used, incidentally, burns more fiercely than all the other kinds of wood, so alder and pinewood, which are slower to burn, are used to cast artillery. So when that terrible fire started to reach the cake, it began to light up and glow. At the same time, I continued working on the channels and also sent some men up to the roof to tend the fire, which had spread quickly from the greater strength of the flame; and I had boards and other mats and hangings set up on the side facing the garden, which sheltered me from the water.

As soon as I had provided a remedy for all those disasters, I said in a very loud voice to one and then another: "Bring it here! Take it there!" And then, seeing that the cake was beginning to liquefy, the whole group obeyed me so willingly that each of them did the work of three. Next, I had someone get half an ingot of tin, which weighed about sixty pounds, and I threw it on the cake inside the furnace, which, with the help of the wood and stirring now with iron rods and now with poles, became liquefied in a short time. Then seeing that I had brought a corpse back to life, despite the doubts of all those ignorant fellows, I felt so reinvigorated that I did not notice whether or not I had the fever any longer or if I was afraid of dying.

Suddenly, we heard a noise and saw an enormous flash of fire, which actually seemed as if a thunderbolt had been created in our presence; everyone was overwhelmed by an extraordinarily horrible fear of this flash—I more than the others. Once this huge noise and brightness had passed, we were again able to see each other; and seeing that the cover of the furnace had burst and come off in such a manner that the bronze was spilling out, I quickly had the mouths of my mold opened, and at the same time, had the two plugs put in. And noticing that the metal did not flow as fast as it should, I realized the cause was perhaps that the base-metal part of it had been consumed by such a terrible heat, so I sent for my pewter plates, soup plates, and trays, which numbered around two hundred, and one by one I put them in front of my channels, throwing the rest straight into the furnace. When they saw how my bronze had liquefied nicely and that my mold was filling up, everyone bravely and happily assisted me and followed my orders, while I was now here and now there, giving orders, helping, and declaring: "Oh, God, who with Your immense power arose from the dead and ascended into heaven in glory . . ." And then, in an instant, my mold filled. Because of this, I fell to my knees and thanked God with all my heart; then I turned to a plate of salad that was there on a little old bench, and ate and drank with a hearty appetite along with the entire crew. Afterward, I went to bed, healthy and happy, because it was two hours before daybreak, and I slept so sweetly that it was as if I had never had anything wrong with me.

That good servant woman of mine, without my saying a word, had prepared a fat capon for me, and when I got out of bed around lunchtime, she came to me happily, saying: "Oh, is this the man who thought he was dying? I think that the kicks and blows you gave us last night when you were so infuriated and that devilish rage you seemed to have inside you may have made your terrible fever so frightened of being beaten that it ran away in order to escape!"

And so all my poor little family, relieved of so much fear and such hard labor, quickly went out to purchase earthenware dishes in the place of those pewter plates and soup bowls, and all ate lunch together so happily that I could not remember ever dining with greater joy or better appetite. After lunch, all those who had helped me came to see me; they were rejoicing happily, thanking God for all that had happened, and they were saying they had learned and witnessed things done that other masters held to be impossible. Thinking myself rather knowledgeable and feeling a bit haughty, I felt proud of myself; and putting my hands inside my purse, I paid them all to their satisfaction.

That evil man, my mortal enemy Messer Pier Francesco Riccio, the Duke's majordomo, most diligently sought to discover how everything had turned out: those two men whom I suspected of having caused the caking of the metal reported to him that I was not a man but rather some great devil, because I had accomplished what art was not capable of achieving, along with a number of other incredible things, some of which would have been too much even for a demon to accomplish. They exaggerated what had happened, perhaps to excuse themselves, and at once the majordomo wrote it all down for the Duke, who was in Pisa, in a way which was still more dramatic and filled with marvels than they had recounted to him.

Letting my statue cool for two days, I began to uncover it bit by bit; and the first thing I discovered was that the head of the Medusa had come out very well because of the vents, just as I had explained to the Duke that the nature of fire was to ascend; then I continued to uncover the rest, and I found that the other head—that is, that of Perseus—had come out equally well; and this amazed me even more, because, as can be seen, it is quite a bit lower than that of the Medusa. And because the mouths of the work were placed above the head of Perseus and by the shoulders, I found that all the bronze in my furnace had been used up in completing the head of Perseus. It was amazing to discover that none of the metal was left in the channels, and nothing at all was wrong; and this astonished me so that it seemed likely it was a miraculous occurrence, guided and managed by God Himself.

I proceeded happily to finish uncovering it, and I kept finding everything to be perfect, until I came to the foot on the right leg upon which the statue rests, where I discovered that the heel had turned out perfectly, and continuing further I found it was all complete: on one hand, I was very delighted, and on the other, I was rather displeased, but only because I had told the Duke it could not turn out. But then, on finishing the uncovering of the statue, I realized that the toes of this foot had not come out, and not only the toes but a little above the toes, so that about half was missing, and although this cost me a bit of labor, I was glad of it, if only to demonstrate to the Duke that I understood what I was doing. And although more of the foot had come out than I had expected, the reason for this was that—with all the various accidents— the metal had been hotter than the laws of the art should permit, and also for the reason that I had had to help it out with the alloy in the way I have described, and with those pewter plates—a method which had never been employed by anyone before.

Now seeing that my work had come out so well, I immediately went to Pisa to find my Duke, who received me as kindly as anyone could imagine, and the Duchess did the same. And although that majordomo of theirs had informed them about everything, it seemed even more stupendous and amazing to Their Excellencies to hear me tell it myself; and when I came to the foot of Perseus that had not come out as I had earlier warned His Most Illustrious Excellency, I saw him filled with astonishment, and he told the Duchess how I had predicted this to him beforehand. Now, seeing those two lords so well pleased with me, I then begged the Duke to allow me to go to Rome. He graciously gave me leave, and told me to return soon to finish his *Perseus*, and he wrote me a letter of recommendation to his ambassador, who was Averardo Serristori;[23] these were the first years of Pope Giulio de' Monti.

Before departing, I gave orders to my workmen to continue according to the method that I had shown them. And my reason for going was that I had in exact proportions made a bronze bust of Bindo d'Antonio Altoviti,[24] and when I had sent it to him in Rome, he had put this bust of himself in his study, which was very richly adorned with antiquities and other beautiful things. But this study was not designed for sculpture or paintings, since the light coming from below did not show them as well as if they had received the proper illumination.

One day this Bindo happened to be at his door when Michelangelo Buonarroti, the sculptor, passed by, and he begged Michelangelo to do him the honor of coming inside to see his study. He then led him there, and once Michelangelo had entered and seen the room, he declared: "Who is the master who has made such a fine bust of you in such a splendid manner? You know, this bust pleases me as much as and even somewhat more than the ancient ones; and there are indeed some excellent ones among them. And if these windows were above instead of underneath, they would look so much better and your bust would stand out among so many fine works."

As soon as Michelangelo had visited Bindo's house, he wrote me a very kind letter, which read as follows: "My Benvenuto, I have known you for many years as the greatest goldsmith we know of; and now I recognize you to be a sculptor of like talent. You know that Messer Bindo Altoviti took me to see a bust of himself in bronze and told me it came from your hand. I was very pleased with it, but I thought it very unfortunate that it was placed in poor light, for if it had good light, it would show itself to be the fine work it is."

This letter was full of the most kind and propitious words about me; and before I left to go to Rome, I showed it to the Duke, who read it with much interest, saying to me: "Benvenuto, if you write him and can persuade him to return to Florence, I will make him one of the forty-eight."[25] I therefore wrote him a most affectionate letter in which I offered him on the Duke's behalf more than a hundred times what I had been authorized to tell him; and not wanting to make any mistake, I showed it to the Duke before I sealed it, and I told His Most Illustrious Excellency: "My Lord, I have perhaps promised him too much." He replied, saying: "He deserves more than what you have promised him, and I will please him even more." Michelangelo never answered my letter, and as a result, the Duke was very angry with him.

Now, after having reached Rome, I went to stay at Bindo Altoviti's home. He immediately told me how he had shown his bust in bronze to Michelangelo, and how he had praised it greatly; and we discussed this at great length. Now, I had gone ahead with this bust because Bindo had in his hands twelve hundred gold *scudi* of mine, which were part of the 5,000 *scudi* he had lent to the Duke, of which 4,000 were his; and mine were lent in his name, and he gave me the interest on my part which was due me. When Bindo saw the wax model, he sent fifty golden *scudi* for me through his notary Ser Giuliano Paccalli, which I did not want to take and sent back to him through the same messenger; later I said to Bindo: "It is enough for me that you hold that money of mine for me in investments, and that it earns me something." I noticed that he bore some ill will over the matter, because instead of treating me kindly, he was very cold with me; and although he took me into his home, he never seemed very open with me, but, rather, he was always sulking. However, we settled the matter with a few words. I lost my fee for his bust and also for the bronze in it; and we agreed that he would keep the money at fifteen percent for the rest of my life.

I had gone first thing to kiss the Pope's feet, and while I was discussing matters with the Pope, Messer Averardo Serristori, our Duke's ambassador, arrived. And I had also made some proposals to the Pope, on which I believe we could have come to an agreement, and I would have willingly returned to Rome because of the great difficulties that I was experiencing in Florence; but I learned that the ambassador had acted against my interests.

I went to Michelangelo Buonarroti, and repeated what I had written to him from Florence on the Duke's behalf. He replied that he was employed on the construction of St. Peter's, and that for this reason he could not leave. Then I said to him that since he had decided on the model for its construction, he could leave his Urbino,[26] who would do exactly what he instructed; and I added many other promises on the Duke's behalf. All at once, he stared at me and said with a sneer: "And how are you satisfied with him?" Although I said I was very content and that I was very well treated, he showed that he was aware of most of my troubles, and then he said that it would be difficult for him to find a way to leave. Then I added that he would do better to return to his native city, which was governed by a very just lord who was a greater admirer of talent than any other prince ever born.

As I said above, he had with him his apprentice from Urbino, who had been with him for many years and had served him more as a shopboy and servant than anything else, and the cause was obviously that he had learned nothing about art. And because I had pressured Michelangelo with so many good arguments that he did not know what to say, he quickly turned to his Urbino as if to ask him his opinion. This Urbino, in his coarse way, suddenly said in a very loud voice: "I will never leave my master Michelangelo, until I skin him or he skins me." At these foolish words, I was forced to laugh; and without saying goodbye, I turned with slumping shoulders and left.

Since I had conducted my business with Bindo Altoviti so badly, what with the loss of my bronze bust and giving him my money for life, I was now well aware of how much the word of a merchant was worth; and dissatisfied, I returned to Florence. I immediately went to the palace to pay a visit to the Duke, but His Most Illustrious Excellency was at Castello, beyond Ponte a Rifredi. I found Pier Francesco Riccio, the majordomo, at the Palace, and as I approached him to pay him the usual compliments, he immediately said with enormous astonishment: "Oh, you've returned!" And with the same astonishment, clapping his hands, he continued: "The Duke is at Castello." And turning his back on me, he left. I could not understand or even imagine why that beast had acted that way.

I immediately went to Castello, and having entered the garden where the Duke was, I saw him at a distance, and when he saw me he showed some signs of surprise, and gave me to understand that I should leave. I, who had promised myself that His Excellency would show me the same kindness as he had when I left, and even more, now seeing such a sudden change of behavior, left and returned to Florence very unhappy. And taking up my work again, I hastened to complete my statue, but I could not imagine what it was that had caused this change. However, observing how Messer Sforza and certain others among those closest to the Duke were behaving, I was seized by the desire to ask Messer Sforza what the meaning of all this was. Smiling, he said: "Benvenuto, apply yourself to being a good man and don't pay attention to anything else."

A few days later, I was given the opportunity of speaking to the Duke, and he greeted me with a kind of gloomy affection and asked me what I had done in Rome. And so I started conversing as best I could and told him of the bronze bust I had made for Bindo Altoviti and all that had followed. I realized that he was listening to me most attentively, and so I told him all that had happened with Michelangelo Buonarroti. He seemed rather offended; and hearing the words of Urbino about the "skinning," he laughed. Then he said: "So much the worse for him." And I left.

Undoubtedly the majordomo, Ser Pier Francesco, must have done me a bad turn with the Duke which did not succeed, because God—the lover of truth—defended me as He has always saved me up to this moment from so many immense dangers, and I trust he will always save me until the end of my life, no matter how troubled it may be. However, I make my way forward, only through His strength, with courage, fearing neither any rage of fortune nor the perversity of the stars. May God only sustain me in His grace!

Now, kind reader, you will hear of a terrible misfortune. With as much care as it is possible to take, I applied myself to finishing my work, and I went to spend the evening in the Duke's wardrobe, assisting those goldsmiths who were working there for His Most Illustrious Excellency. Because the greater part of the works they were undertaking were based upon my designs, and also because I saw that the Duke took as great a pleasure in watching me work as in chatting with me, it seemed to me a good idea to go there sometime during the day.

One day I was in the wardrobe and the Duke came in as usual, and all the more willingly, since His Illustrious Excellency knew that I was present; and as soon as he arrived, he began discussing many different and pleasing things with me, and I responded most aptly, charming him to such an extent that he treated me more graciously than he had ever done in the past. Then all at once, one of his secretaries appeared, who whispered in His Excellency's ear, and as if it was something very important, the Duke quickly arose and went off to another room with his secretary.

And since the Duchess had sent her page to see what His Most Illustrious Excellency was doing, the page informed her: "The Duke is talking and laughing with Benvenuto and is in good humor." Hearing this, the Duchess immediately came to the wardrobe and, not finding the Duke there, sat down next to us; after she had watched us work for a while, she turned to me most charmingly and showed me a string of large and truly exceptional pearls, and when she asked me what I thought of it, I told her that it was something very beautiful indeed. Then Her Most Illustrious Excellency said to me: "I want the Duke to buy it for me; so, my Benvenuto, praise it to him as highly as you can." At this request, I disclosed my thoughts to the Duchess with as much respect as I could and I replied: "My Lady, I thought that this string of pearls already belonged to Your Most Illustrious Excellency; and so reason would never permit me to say any of the things that, knowing the necklace not to belong to Your Most Illustrious Excellency, I must say, or rather that I am compelled to say. You know, Your Most Illustrious Excellency, that since I am very qualified in my profession, I recognize many, many defects in these pearls, and for that reason, I would never advise Your Excellency to purchase them."

The Duchess responded to my reply: "The merchant is giving them to me for six thousand *scudi*, and if they didn't have any of those little defects, they would be worth more than twelve thousand." Then I said that even if the necklace were of perfect quality, I would never advise anyone to go to five thousand *scudi*, because pearls were not jewels: pearls were fishes' bones, and in time they become defective; but diamonds, rubies, and emeralds did not grow old, nor did sapphires—these four were jewels, and these one should purchase. To my explanation, the Duchess replied a bit indignantly: "I want these pearls, and I do beg you to take them to the Duke and praise them as highly as you can, and although it seems you will have to tell some little white lies, tell them to serve me, and it will be to your advantage."

I, who have always been a friend of truth and the enemy of lies, being compelled to avoid losing the favor of so great a princess by my desire, took those damned pearls, with great discontent, and went with them into the other room, where the Duke had withdrawn. As soon as he saw me, he said: "Oh, Benvenuto, what are you up to?" Uncovering the pearls, I replied: "My Lord, I come to show you a very beautiful string of pearls, one most exceptional and truly worthy of Your Excellency; and for eighty pearls, I don't believe that anyone could ever put together so many that would look better in a necklace; so buy them, My Lord, for they are marvelous." At once the Duke remarked: "I do not wish to buy them, because they are not pearls of the quality you describe, and I have seen them and they do not please me."

Then I said: "Pardon me, My Lord, but these pearls exceed in rare beauty all the pearls that were ever put into a necklace." The Duchess had gotten up and was standing behind a door and heard everything I said. So after I had said a million things more than I have told, the Duke turned to me with a kind look and said to me: "Oh, my Benvenuto, I realize you know all too well about such matters; and if these pearls were of as rare a quality as you attribute to them, I would not hesitate to buy them, either to please the Duchess or merely to have them, since I need such things not as much for the Duchess as for the arrangements for my sons and daughters." And responding to his words, since I had already begun to tell lies, I continued to tell even more audacious ones, giving them the semblance of truth, so that the Duke would believe me, and trusting in the Duchess to help me when I needed it. Though two hundred *scudi* were promised to me if the deal were made (the Duchess had suggested this to me), I was nevertheless determined and resolved not to touch a single *scudo*, if only for my own safety, so that the Duke would never think that I had done it out of greed.

Again the Duke began to speak to me in the kindest words: "I know that you understand all about these things. Therefore, if you are the honest man I have always thought you to be, now tell me the truth." Then turning a bit red and with tears in my eyes, I replied: "My Lord, if I tell the truth to Your Most Illustrious Excellency, the Duchess will become my mortal enemy, and I will be forced to leave, and my enemies will immediately attack me and the honor of my *Perseus*, which I have promised to Your Most Illustrious Excellency's noble school; so I ask for Your Most Illustrious Excellency's protection."

Having realized that what I had said had been forced out of me, the Duke declared: "If you have faith in me, you need not fear for anything in the world." Again, I replied: "Alas, My Lord, how can the Duchess be kept from finding out?" At my words, the Duke raised his hand as a pledge of faith and affirmed: "You may rely on its being buried in a little diamond chest." After hearing these honorable words, I immediately told the truth about my opinion of those pearls and that they were not worth much more than two thousand *scudi*.

Having heard us grow quiet again, since we were speaking as softly as possible, the Duchess came forward and asked: "My Lord, will Your Excellency please buy me this string of pearls, because I would really like to have them, and your Benvenuto has said that he has never seen any more beautiful." Then the Duke answered: "I do not wish to buy them."

"Why, My Lord, does Your Excellency not wish to please me by buying this string of pearls?"

"Because it does not please me to throw money away!"

Again the Duchess asked: "Oh, how would you be throwing money away, since your own Benvenuto, in whom you place such well-deserved faith, has told me that it would be cheap even at three thousand *scudi*?"

Then the Duke declared: "My lady, my Benvenuto has said that if I buy it, I shall be throwing my money away, because these pearls are neither round nor even, and that many of them are old; and to see that this is true, look at this one and at that other one there, see here and here: these pearls are not something I need." Upon hearing these words, the Duchess looked at me with great animosity, and threatening me with a nod of her head, she left; and I was quite tempted to go away and disappear from Italy, but since my *Perseus* was almost finished, I did not want to miss putting it on display—but you can understand what a serious bit of trouble I found myself in. The Duke had ordered his porters in my presence always to allow me to enter the rooms where he was; and the Duchess ordered the same men that whenever I arrived at the palace, they should chase me away; as a result of this, whenever they saw me, they immediately left their doorways and chased me away, but they took care not to be seen by the Duke, because if the Duke saw me before these wretches did, either he called to me or made a sign that I should come forward.

The Duchess called that broker Bernardone, the man of whose laziness and contemptible worthlessness she had so often complained to me, and she begged for his help as she had done with me, and he replied: "My Lady, let me take care of it." This great scoundrel went before the Duke with this necklace in hand. As soon as he saw him, the Duke told him to get out of the room. Then this great scoundrel with that nasty voice of his that resonated through his ugly donkey's nose said: "Wait! My Lord, buy this necklace for that poor lady who is dying to have it and can't live without it." And adding many other stupid and coarse words, he managed to annoy the Duke to the extent that he said to him: "Either you will get away from me, or I'll slap your cheeks."

This dirty scoundrel, who knew perfectly well what he was doing—since by either having his cheeks slapped or by singing "La Bella Franceschina" he could get the Duke to make this purchase and thereby gain the favor of the Duchess and his commission, amounting to several hundred scudi—therefore puffed up his cheeks.

The Duke gave him several slaps on his ugly cheeks, and to get him out of there, he gave him a few even harder than usual. At these hard blows, not only did his cheeks redden but the tears began flowing. And for all that he began to speak: "Oh, My Lord, as one of your faithful servants who is trying to do the right thing, I am willing to put up with every sort of mistreatment, if only that poor lady is happy."

Growing very annoyed with this nasty man, the Duke—either because of the blows he had dealt him or because of his love for the Duchess (whom His Most Illustrious Excellency always wanted to satisfy) —suddenly said: "Get out of here, and may God bring you misfortune: go and purchase them—I am delighted to do all that My Lady the Duchess wishes."

Now, here one can see how ill-fortune rages against a poor man and how shameful fortune favors an evil man: I completely lost all the Duchess' favor, which was sufficient cause for losing the Duke's as well, while he gained a fat commission and their favor. So it is not enough to be a good and virtuous man.

At this time, the war with Siena broke out;[27] and wishing to fortify Florence, the Duke distributed the duty of seeing to the gates among his sculptors and architects. Hence, I was consigned the gate to Prato and the little gate on the Arno, which gives out onto the meadow on the way to the mills. To Cavaliere Bandinello went the gate of San Friano; to Pasqualino d'Ancona, the gate of San Pier Gattolini; to Giulian di Baggio d'Agnolo, the cabinetmaker, the gate of San Giorgio; to Particino, the cabinetmaker, the gate of Santo Niccolò; to Francesco da Sangallo, the sculptor, called Il Margolla, the gate of Santa Croce; and to Giovambattista, called Il Tasso, the gate of Pinti; and besides this, certain other ramparts and gates were given to various engineers, whom I do not remember and who add nothing to my subject.

The Duke, who had always been a man of some ability, went around the city himself; and when His Most Illustrious Excellency had made a thorough examination of it and had made up his mind, he called for Lattanzio Gorini, who was one of his paymasters; and because this Lattanzio also rather enjoyed this kind of work, His Most Illustrious Excellency had him make designs of all the ways in which these gates could be fortified, and he sent to each of us the design for his gate. When I saw the one for my gate, it seemed to me that the best way was not according to his thinking; that it was, in fact, entirely incorrect. I immediately went off to find my Duke with this design in hand, and when I tried to show His Excellency the defects of the design which had been given to me, no sooner had I begun to speak than the Duke turned to me in a rage and declared: "Benvenuto, in the matter of making fine statues, I yield to you, but in this profession, I want you to yield to me; so follow the design I have given you."

At these strong words, I answered as mildly as I knew how and said: "Still, My Lord, I learned something about making statues from Your Excellency, as we have always discussed it a bit together; hence, in the matter of fortifying your city, which is a much more important matter than making statues, I beg Your Most Illustrious Excellency to be so kind as to listen to me; and thus, by discussing it with Your Excellency, you will be better able to show me how I must serve you."

Upon hearing these gracious words, the Duke kindly began to discuss it with me, and when I showed His Excellency with sharp and clear explanations how what he had designed for me would not have been suitable, His Excellency said: "Then go and make your own design, and I will see if it pleases me."

And so I made two designs according to the rules of the proper method for fortifying those two gates, and I took them to him; being able to distinguish the true from the false, His Excellency very graciously said to me: "Go and do it in your own way, and I will be satisfied." And with great diligence, I began.

There was a Lombard captain on duty at the gate of Prato. He had a terribly sturdy build and spoke in a very coarse way; he was also arrogant and utterly ignorant. This man immediately began to ask me what I was doing; I kindly showed him my designs, and with great pains I gave him to understand how I planned to defend the gate. But this crude beast kept shaking his head and turning now one way and now another, shifting his weight from one leg to another, twisting his enormous mustache, and he often pulled the fold of his cap down over his eyes, saying over and over: "What in hell is this all about?"

Then, when this brute started to become wearisome, I said: "Well, then, let me get on with it, since I know what it's about!" And when I turned my back on him to go back to my work, this fellow began shaking his head in an angry manner, and putting his left hand on the pommel of his sword, he raised the point a little bit, saying: "Look here, Maestro, are you trying to start a bloody fight with me?"

I turned toward him in great anger, because by this time he had exasperated me, and I replied: "It seems to be less trouble to quarrel with you over this than to make the rampart for the gate."

In an instant, both of us put our hands on our swords, and we had hardly drawn them before a number of honest folk, some of our Florentines and others who were courtiers, started to surround us; and most of them railed at him, telling him that he was in the wrong and that I was the type of man who could give a good accounting for myself, and that if the Duke found out, he would be in trouble. And so he went off to tend to his own business and I began my rampart.

And after making the arrangements for this rampart, I went to the other little gate on the Arno, where I found a captain from Cesena, the most courteous man of honor I have ever known in that profession. He had the manner of a polite young woman, but when necessary, he was one of the bravest and most deadly men imaginable. This gentleman was watching me so closely that he often made me self-conscious; he wanted to understand what I was doing, and I courteously showed him. Suffice it to say that we vied to see who could be the most courteous, so that I built this rampart even better than the other one.

I had very nearly finished my ramparts when some of Piero Strozzi's men carried out a raid which so frightened the district of Prato that the people all abandoned their homes, and for that reason, they loaded up all the carts from that district and carried their belongings into the city. And because the carts were lined up one after another in endless numbers and great confusion, I told the guards at the gate to take care that a disturbance like the one that had happened at the gates of Turin did not take place here, for if it had been necessary to use the portcullis, it could not have performed its function because it would have remained suspended, stuck on one of these carts.

When that great brute of a captain heard my words, he turned on me with offensive remarks, and I responded to him in the same fashion, so that we might have had an even worse quarrel than the first time. However, we were kept apart, and when I finished my ramparts, I unexpectedly got my hands on a number of *scudi* which I made use of, and I willingly returned to my *Perseus*.

In those days, certain antiquities had been found in the countryside near Arezzo, among which was the *Chimera*, which is that bronze lion seen in the rooms next to the great hall of the Palace; and together with the *Chimera* was found a quantity of small statuettes, also made of bronze, which were covered with earth and rust, and all missing the head or the hands or the feet. The Duke took pleasure in cleaning them himself with some small goldsmith's chisels. It happened that I had to speak to His Most Illustrious Excellency, and while I was discussing things with him, he handed me a little hammer with which I struck the small chisels that the Duke was holding, and in that way, we cleaned off the dirt and rust from the figurines. After passing several evenings together this way, the Duke put me to work, and I began to restore the parts of the little statues that were missing. His Excellency took so much pleasure in these little trifles that he made me work during the day as well, and if I was late in getting there, His Most Illustrious Excellency would send for me.

Many times I tried to make His Excellency understand that if I kept going astray from the *Perseus* every day, several problems would result; and the first of these, which scared me the most, was that the great length of time that I saw myself taking to finish my work would cause His Most Illustrious Excellency to become annoyed with me—as later happened. The other was that I had several workmen, and when I was not with them, they created two notable problems. The first was that they were ruining my work, and the second was that they worked as little as possible. And so the Duke allowed me to go there only after nightfall. And because I had made His Most Illustrious Excellency so wonderfully compliant, in the evening when I arrived his kindness toward me always increased.

At this time, they were building those new rooms where the lions were, and so His Excellency, wishing to retire to a more private part of the palace, had a certain little room in these newly built quarters put in order, and he told me that I was to go there through his wardrobe, and so I would pass secretly above the gallery of the great hall and through some little nooks and crannies and go to this little room in great privacy. But in the space of a few days, the Duchess deprived me of it, having all my secret passageways locked up, so that every evening when I arrived at the palace, I had to wait a long time, as the Duchess was engaged in her personal affairs in the anterooms I had to pass through. And since she was not well, my arrival there always upset her.

Now, for this reason or another, she became so sick and tired of me that she could not bear the sight of me; but despite all this great embarrassment and my infinite displeasure, I patiently continued to go there. And the Duke had given express orders that as soon as I knocked at those doors, they were to be opened to me, and without a word being said, I was allowed to go anywhere I liked. Thus it sometimes happened that when I entered quietly and unexpectedly through those private rooms, I would discover the Duchess engaged in her personal affairs. She would immediately begin croaking with such rage and fury that I became terrified, and she would always say to me: "When will you ever finish restoring those little statues? Your coming and going has now become rather quite annoying."

To her remarks, I would respond mildly: "My Lady, my only patroness, I desire nothing else but to serve you with fidelity and absolute obedience, and since this work which the Duke has prescribed for me will last many months, please tell me, Your Most Illustrious Excellency, if you don't want me to come here anymore, and I shall never come again. Let anyone call for me who will, even if the Duke summons me—I shall say that I feel ill, and there is no way that I shall ever come again."

She answered: "I do not say that you are not to come, and I do not say that you should not obey the Duke, but it does seem to me that your work will never come to an end."

Whether the Duke had heard a rumor about this, or whether it was for some other reason, His Excellency began sending for me again, and would send someone for me near nightfall. And the person who came to call me always told me: "Take care that you don't fail to come, because the Duke is waiting for you." And thus I carried on under the same difficulties for several evenings. And one evening, as I was entering as usual, the Duke, who must have been discussing things that were probably private matters, turned to me with the greatest fury imaginable; I was rather terrified, wishing to retire right away, when he quickly said to me:

"Enter, my Benvenuto, and go right to your work, and I shall be with you shortly." While I was passing through, Don Grazia, then a little boy, grabbed me by the cape and told me the cutest little jokes that a child can tell. As a result the Duke was amazed and declared: "Oh, what a nice friendship my children have with you."

Every evening while I was working on these silly things, the Prince, Don Giovanni, Don Arnando, and Don Grazia used to stand near me, and without the Duke's knowledge, they would tease me playfully, and I asked them kindly to stop.[28] They answered me by saying: "We can't." And I said to them: "What can't be done shouldn't be done; so go ahead." All at once, the Duke and the Duchess burst into laughter. Another evening, after I had finished those four little figurines in bronze which are set into the *Perseus'* base—the Jupiter, the Mercury, the Minerva, and the Danae, mother of Perseus with her little Perseus sitting at her feet—and had them carried into the room where I would work in the evenings, I put them in a line, elevated a little above eye level so that they were a very beautiful sight. When the Duke heard about it, he came in a little before he usually did, and because the person who told His Most Illustrious Excellency about them must have made them seem better than they really were, telling him that they were better than the ancients and other such things, my Duke came together with the Duchess, still discussing my work. I immediately sprang up to meet them.

With his fine and princely welcome, he raised his right hand, in which he held as large and as fine a pear branch as one could hope to see, and he said: "Here, my Benvenuto, plant this pear tree in the garden of your house." To these words, I responded graciously: "Oh, My Lord, is Your Most Illustrious Excellency really saying that I may plant it in the garden at my house?" Again the Duke said: "In the garden of the house that belongs to you. Have you understood me?" Then I thanked His Excellency and likewise the Duchess with as much ceremony as I could muster.

Then they both sat down opposite those little figures, and for more than two hours, they talked of nothing but how beautiful those statues were. As a result, the Duchess was taken by a strong desire which she then explained to me: "I don't want these beautiful little figures to be lost on that base down in the piazza where they run the risk of being ruined; rather, I want you to arrange them for me in one of my rooms, where they will be given the kind of respect their rare qualities deserve." To her words, I answered in opposition with countless arguments, but seeing she had resolved that I should not put them on my base, where they are now, I waited until the following day, went to the palace at nightfall, and found that the Duke and Duchess were out riding. Having already prepared my base, I had the little figures brought down, and I immediately soldered them with lead just where they are meant to be. Oh! When the Duchess found out about it, she became so angry that if it had not been for the Duke, who skillfully helped me out, I should have had the worst of it. And because of her anger over that string of pearls as well as this business, she managed things so that the Duke gave up that little amusement. This was the reason why I no longer had the chance to go there, and all at once I found myself once again in the same difficulty as before with respect to gaining access to the palace.

I returned to the Loggia where I had already brought the *Perseus*, and there I tried to finish it with the same difficulties I had before—that is, without money and with so many other misfortunes that only half of them would have demolished a man of stone. However, I went on as usual, and one morning, after hearing Mass at San Pietro Scheraggio, Bernardone—a broker and a horrible goldsmith, and through the Duke's kindness, the purveyor to the mint—stepped in front of me, and he was hardly outside the door of the church when the dirty pig let loose four farts which could have been heard from San Miniato! I said to him: "Well, you shiftless, lazy pig, you ass, is this what your filthy talents sound like?" And I ran for a stick. He quickly withdrew into the mint, and I stood just inside my door; and I kept one of my young boys outside to signal me when the pig left the mint. Now, after I waited for quite a while, I grew weary of it, and once my anger had subsided, I considered the fact that anything can happen in a fight and that it could lead to certain drawbacks, so I decided to take my revenge in another way. And since this incident took place one or two days before the feast of St. John, I composed these verses for him and stuck them up in the corner outside the church where one goes for a piss or a shit, and they read as follows:

> Here lies Bernardone, pig and ass,
> A thievish broker and a spy,
> In whom Pandora put
> Her worst of evils, transplanting them
> From him into that blockhead, Maestro Buaccio.

The incident and the verses circulated through the palace, and the Duke and Duchess laughed about them; and before Bernardone became aware of it all, a lot of people stopped and got the biggest laugh imaginable out of them; then they would look over toward the mint and stare at Bernardone. When his son noticed this, he tore the verses down in a rage. And Bernardone bit his finger and made threats with that ugly, nasal voice of his, putting on a big show.

When the Duke heard that my work on the *Perseus* was ready to be exhibited in its finished form, he came one day to see it and gave many clear signs of being very satisfied with it. Turning to several gentlemen who were with His Most Illustrious Excellency, he said: "For all that this work strikes us as being very beautiful, it must also please the people; so, my Benvenuto, before you put on the finishing touches, I would like you, for my sake, to open up the screen a little for half a day, so that it can be seen from my piazza, and we will see what the people say about it. For no doubt when it is displayed in this restricted manner, it will seem very different than when it is displayed in open space." At these words, I said most humbly to His Most Illustrious Excellency: "You know, My Lord, that it will look twice as good. Oh, does Your Most Illustrious Excellency not remember having seen it in my garden, where it was so well displayed in such a broad space that Bandinello came to see it through the garden of the Innocenti, and for all his foul and wicked nature, he was forced to say something good about it—he who has never said anything good about anyone in his life? I know Your Most Illustrious Excellency lends only too much credence to him." At my words, smiling rather contemptuously but using the most agreeable phrases, the Duke said: "Do it, my Benvenuto, just to give me a little satisfaction."

Once he had left, I began to give orders to uncover it. And because a bit of gold, some polishing, and other similar things that are part of completing such a work were missing, I grumbled indignantly under my breath, lamenting and cursing the wretched day that brought me to Florence, for I realized the great and certain loss that I had incurred by leaving France, and I could no longer see any good I might hope for from this prince of mine in Florence. From the beginning, through the middle, and down to the end, everything that I had done always turned out to be to my great disadvantage. And discontent as I was, I uncovered the statue the following day.

Then, as it pleased God, as soon as it was shown, an enormous outcry of praise for my work came from the people, which brought me some consolation. The people did not stop tacking up verses on the doorposts, which were hung with some curtains while I was putting on the finishing touches. Let me tell you that on the same day I displayed the statue for a few hours, more than twenty sonnets in boundless praise of my work were tacked up. After I had covered it up again, every day a quantity of sonnets or verses in Latin and Greek were tacked up there for me, because the University of Pisa was on vacation, and all the most excellent professors and scholars vied with each other in writing them.

But what gave me the most satisfaction, along with the hope of better feelings on the part of my Duke, was that those in the arts—that is, sculptors and painters—also vied to say the best things about it. And among all of them, the opinion I especially appreciated was that of the splendid painter Jacopo Pontormo,[29] and even more than his, that of his excellent pupil, the painter Bronzino.[30] It was not enough to tack up several sonnets there, for he sent some more to me at my home through his boy, Sandrino;[31] they were so well written and in such an exceptionally beautiful style that they helped to console me. And I covered up the statue again and hastened to finish it.

My Duke, for all that His Excellency had heard of the approval that had been lavished upon me by the excellent Florentine School on the basis of that glimpse of my work, declared: "I am very pleased that Benvenuto has had this bit of satisfaction; it will make him bring it to a finish with greater diligence and speed, but he shouldn't think that later, when it is seen from every side completely uncovered, people will receive it in the same manner; rather, they will discover all the defects that are in it and try to find many that are not even there; so he must be prepared to arm himself with patience."

Now, these were the words that Bandinello had spoken to the Duke in referring to the works of Andrea del Verrocchio,[32] who did that fine bronze of Christ and St. Thomas which is displayed on the facade of Orsanmichele; and he referred to many other works, even the marvelous *David* of the divine Michelangelo Buonarroti, saying that it only looked good when seen from the front. Then he mentioned the infinite number of defamatory sonnets tacked up about his *Hercules and Cacus* and began to speak ill of the Florentines.

My Duke, who put too much belief in his words, had been moved by him to say such things, and he was convinced that things would happen in large part just in this way, because that envious Bandinello, once in the presence of the Duke, never ceased speaking evil. And once that rascal Bernardone, the broker, in order to make good Bandinello's remarks, said to him: "You know, My Lord, that making large statues is a very different kettle of fish than making the small ones; I don't want to say he hasn't done a good job with the little figures, but you will see that he hasn't succeeded with the others." And he mixed many other nasty comments with these, telling his stories and combining them with a mountain of lies.

Now, as it pleased my glorious Lord and immortal God, I finished the whole thing, and one Thursday morning, I completely uncovered it. Immediately, before it was even midday, so vast a number of people that could not be counted assembled there, and in one voice, they all competed to praise my work. The Duke was at one of the lower windows above the door of the palace, and in a half-hidden position inside the window, he heard all that was said about my work; and after he had listened to the comments for several hours, he rose with so much confidence and satisfaction that, turning to Messer Sforza, he said: "Sforza, go and find Benvenuto and tell him that insofar as I am concerned, he has made me happier than I ever expected, and tell him that I will make him happy in a way that will astonish him. So tell him to be of good humor."

Thus, this Messer Sforza brought me his glorious message, which comforted me; and that day as a result of this good news, people would point me out to each other as something marvelous and unusual. Among others, there were two gentlemen who had been sent by the Viceroy of Sicily to our Duke on business. Now these two agreeable men greeted me in the piazza (I was pointed out to them as I was passing by, so that they had to catch up with me), and quickly, with their caps in hand, they made me a speech so ceremonious that it would have been too much even for a Pope. Nonetheless, I was as humble as I could be, but they so overwhelmed me that I began to beg them kindly to agree to leave the piazza, because people were stopping to stare at me more than at the *Perseus*. And in the midst of their compliments, they were so enthusiastic that they asked me to go to Sicily and said that they would make terms to my satisfaction, and they told me how Friar Giovanagnolo de' Servi[33] had made them a perfect fountain adorned with a number of statues, and that they had made him a rich man, though these statues were not of the same high quality they saw in the *Perseus*.

I did not allow them to finish saying all that they had wanted to say before I replied to them: "I am most astonished that you would try to make me leave such a lord, a greater lover of the arts than any other prince ever born, and even more, since I am in my own native city, the school of all the greatest arts. Oh, if I had an appetite for great profit, I would have remained in France in the service of that great King Francis, who gave me one thousand gold *scudi* for my allowance and also paid the bills for all my work, so that every year I managed to save more than four thousand gold *scudi*. And I left in Paris the fruits of my labors for the past four years."

With these and other words, I cut their compliments short and thanked them for the great praise they had given me, which was the greatest reward that could be given anyone who worked hard; and I said that they had so greatly increased my desire to do well that I hoped in a few years to display another work which I hoped would please the admirable Florentine School even more than the *Perseus*. The two gentlemen would have liked to renew their stream of compliments, but I tipped my hat, and with a bow I said goodbye to them.

After I had let two days pass, with the great praise of my statue continuing to increase all the while, I decided to go and show myself to My Lord the Duke. With great courtesy, he said to me: "My Benvenuto, you have satisfied and pleased me; but I promise that I shall satisfy you in a way that is going to astonish you, and I assure you that I don't intend to wait later than tomorrow."

At these splendid promises, I immediately turned all my strength of body and soul for a moment toward God, truly thanking Him; and at the same instant, I approached my Duke and half weeping with joy kissed his robe. Then I said: "Oh, my glorious Lord, true and most generous patron of the arts and the men who work in them, I beg Your illustrious Excellency to do me the favor of allowing me to go off first of all for eight days so that I may have time to thank God. I know full well the immensity of my labor and I realize that my great faith has moved God to assist me, and in return for that and for every other miracle of His assistance, I want to go on a pilgrimage for eight days, spending my time thanking my immortal God who always helps all those who call on Him with true devotion."

Then the Duke inquired as to where I wanted to go. At this, I answered: "Tomorrow morning I shall leave and go to Vallombrosa, then to Camaldoli and to the Eremo; and then I shall go to the Baths of Santa Maria and perhaps as far as Sestile, because I understand that there are some beautiful antiquities there; then I will return to San Francesco della Vernia, and thanking God all the while, I shall return content to serve you." The Duke quickly said with a happy voice: "Go and return, for you have truly pleased me, but leave me a couple of verses as a reminder, and I'll see to the rest. . . ."

[The remainder of the autobiography—a few pages—relates some of Cellini's business dealings as well as some additional work he performs for the Duke. Contrary to his great expectations, Cellini never received satisfaction or adequate payment from the Duke for his *Perseus*. The narrative of his life ends abruptly in the year 1562, as Cellini is preparing to go to Pisa. Thus the last nine years of his life are not covered by the autobiography.]

NOTES

· ❦ ·

1. Pier Luigi Farnese, the natural son of Alesandro Farnese, Pope Paul III. Pier Luigi was Cellini's bitter enemy for a variety of reasons and died in 1547. He is immortalized by a famous Titian portrait (1546) in the Capodimonte Museum of Naples.

2. Giovanni Villani (d. 1348) wrote an important history of the city of Florence entitled the *Chronicles*.

3. Little is known of Captain Sandrino Monaldi or Bozza except that they served in the Castel Sant'Angelo.

4. Riccio (c. 1490–1564) served first as Duke Cosimo's tutor, then as provost of the Cathedral of Prato.

5. Gorini is mentioned in the account books of the Duke's court between 1543 and 1545.

6. Bartolomeo or Baccio Bandinelli, sometimes spelled by Cellini Bandinello (1488–1560), was one of the most important sculptors in Florence during the time Cellini worked there. As a rival and archenemy of Cellini, Bandinelli is vituperated throughout the autobiography.

7. Giovambattista Tasso (1500–55), one of the great woodcarvers of the time, executed the ceiling designed by Michelangelo for the Laurentian Library in Florence.

8. Guido Guidi (d. 1569) became the court physician for King Francis I of France in 1542 and was later appointed to a chair of medicine by Duke Cosimo in Pisa.

9. Ascanio de' Mari, Cellini's assistant, traveled with Cellini to France, where he remained.

10. The Opera del Duomo (still in existence today) was charged with the construction and maintenance of Florence's major cathedral, Santa Maria del Fiore.

11. Bernardo Baldini (d. 1573) worked for Duke Cosimo in the Mint and was one of his favorite goldsmiths—and therefore was one of Cellini's archrivals for patronage.

12. Landi was probably a merchant in precious stones; he also lectured to the Florentine Academy and wrote a comedy to celebrate the marriage of Duke Cosimo to Eleanora of Toledo in 1539.

13. Giampagolo or Giampaolo (1518–c. 1582) and Domenico (1520–90) Poggini were sons of the jewel engraver Michele Poggini.

14. Antonio Ubertini, called Bachiacca (1499–1572), designed cartoons for tapestries and was a master embroiderer.

15. Lorenzino de' Medici (1513–48) assassinated his cousin Alessandro de' Medici in 1537; afterward, he fled to Venice, where Cosimo's agents eventually murdered him. He became the symbol of anti-Medici sentiment among the Florentine exiles, who considered his act of tyrannicide equal to that of Brutus in murdering Julius Caesar.

16. Buonaccorsi (d. 1563) was a Florentine who served France's King Francis I in paying debts owed to Italian merchants.

17. Leone Strozzi (1515–54), Prior of Capua, served two French kings—Francis I and Henry II.

18. Earlier, Cellini had discussed the stone's value in scudi, not ducats. He apparently never corrected his manuscript for accuracy on this point.

19. Philip became King of Spain in 1556.

20. Stefano Colonna (d. 1548) was named lieutenant general of Cosimo's army in 1542.

21. The marble that eventually was employed by Bandinelli to produce this work was originally intended for Michelangelo, who was to have done a Hercules to accompany his David. Bandinelli completed his work in 1530–34.

22. The New Sacristy of San Lorenzo Church in Florence was left unfinished by Michelangelo in 1534; the tombs for the Medici family were completed following Michelangelo's designs by his pupils and the Sacristy was opened in 1545.

23. Serristori was Duke Cosimo's ambassador to Rome until 1564. Pope Giulio de' Monti (1487–1555) took the title of Pope Julius III and was one of Cosimo's allies. He built the Villa Giulia in Rome.

24. Altoviti (1491–1557), one of the era's richest bankers, was a patron of the arts and an enemy of the Medici family. His Roman palace was destroyed by fire in 1888. Cellini's bust was purchased by Bernard Berenson for the Isabella Stewart Gardner Museum of Boston in 1898.

25. One of several institutions created by Pope Clement VII in 1532 to govern Florence, which had recently been recaptured by the Medici family from republican forces in 1530.

26. Francesco di Bernardino d'Amadore (d. 1555), Michelangelo's assistant for years, came from a small town near Urbino—hence his nickname.

27. The war broke out in 1553 and ended in 1555 with the annexation of Siena to Cosimo's Grand Duchy of Tuscany.

28. The Prince was Francesco de' Medici (1541–87), who became a cardinal in 1560. Don Arnando or Ferdinando (1549–1609) eventually became Grand Duke in 1587. Grazia died in 1562.

29. Iacopo Carucci from Pontormo (1494–1557), the great Mannerist painter, was a student of Andrea del Sarto.

30. Agnolo di Cosimo, called Bronzino (1503–72), was Pontormo's student and worked for the Medici family between 1538 and 1565.

31. Alesandro Allori (1535–1607) was a follower of Bronzino who worked for the Medici family.

32. Andrea del Verrocchio (1453–88) was Leonardo da Vinci's master.

33. Giovanni Angelo Montorsoli (1507–63) worked in Sicily on various sculptures between 1547 and 1557.

MICHELANGELO BUONARROTI
1475–1564

APPRENTICED AS A YOUTH TO THE FLORENTINE PAINTER GHIRLANDAIO, Michelangelo enjoyed the patronage of Lorenzo de' Medici in Florence from 1490 to 1492, living in the Medici family household, where he met the leading intellectuals of the time. What is perhaps his best-known work of sculpture, the *David*, was placed outside the Palazzo Vecchio of Florence in 1504, and while the artist worked in Florence, he completed a number of equally important paintings, sculptures, and architectural designs. One worthy of mention included the modifications in San Lorenzo Church in Florence, which was the Medici family's place of worship. Here Michelangelo worked upon a number of projects—a new facade (never completed); the famous Medici Tombs in the New Sacristy of the church (eventually completed by Michelangelo's followers after his original designs); and the famous staircase to the Laurenziana Library.

In 1534, Michelangelo left Florence for Rome, where he would serve a succession of papal patrons. Never again would he return to his native city. Michelangelo's long lifespan permitted him an incredibly productive career; he produced masterpieces in every art form and became one of the Renaissance's greatest architects. Although far more famous for his work as an artist, Michelangelo was an excellent poet. Even though he thought very little of his lyrics, he wrote poetry almost throughout his life and his work consists of more than three hundred poems. While indebted to the models of both Dante and Petrarch, Michelangelo's verse is typical of late-Renaissance lyrical style with its difficult but clever conceits and sometimes rather awkward syntactical patterns. The few selections reprinted here concentrate upon several major poems that deal with Michelangelo's consistent preoccupations—the nature of beauty, the definition of love, the process of artistic creation, and the realization that death eventually triumphs over art.

MICHELANGELO BUONARROTI

BIBLIOGRAPHY

Michelangelo Buonarroti, *Complete Poems and Selected Letters of Michelangelo*, trans. Creighton Gilbert (New York: Vintage, 1965); Glauco Cambon, *Michelangelo's Poetry: Fury of Form* (Princeton: Princeton University Press, 1985); Robert J. Clements, *The Poetry of Michelangelo* (New York: New York University Press, 1965); David Summers, *Michelangelo and the Language of Art* (Princeton: Princeton University Press, 1981).

· ❦ ·

Sonnet[1]

Even the best of artists can conceive no idea
That a single block of marble will not contain
In its excess, and such a goal is achieved
Only by the hand that obeys the intellect.[2]

The evil which I flee and the good I promise myself
Hides in you, my fair, proud, and divine lady;[3]
And working against my very life,
My skill is contrary to my purpose.

My ill cannot be blamed upon your beauty,
Your harshness, bad fortune, or your disdain,
Nor upon my destiny or my fate,

If in your heart you bear both death and mercy
At the same time, and if my lowly talent
Ardently burning, can draw forth only death.

· ❦ ·

Madrigal

Just as by carving,[4] my lady, we set
Into hard mountain rock
A living figure
Which grows most where the stone is most removed;
In like manner, some good works
For the sake of my trembling soul
Are concealed by the excess of my very flesh

With its rough, crude, and crusty shell.[5]
You alone can raise me up
Away from my outer parts,
For in me there is no will or power over myself.

Sonnet[6]

With your lovely eyes I see a sweet light
That I could never see with my blind ones;
With your feet I bear a burden too heavy
For my lame ones ever to bear.

I fly, featherless, with your wings;
With your intellect I am thrust toward the sky;
At your will I am both pale and flushed,
Cold in the sun, hot in the coldest mists.[7]

In your will alone resides my own,
My thoughts are molded only in your heart,
And my very words are in your breath.

When alone, I seem to be like the moon,
For our eyes can only see in the sky
As far as the sun illuminates it for us.

The Poetic Exchange Between Giovanni Strozzi and Michelangelo over *Night*[8]

Strozzi's Epigram

Night, that you see in such sweet repose
Sleeping, was sculpted by an angel
In this stone, and since she sleeps, she lives;
Wake her, if you don't believe me, and she will speak to you.

Michelangelo's Reply[9]

Sleep is dear to me and even more so being made of stone,
As long as injury and shamefulness endure;
Not to see, not to hear is my great good fortune;
Therefore do not wake me, lower your voice.[10]

———————— · ❦ · ————————

Sonnet[11]

The course of my life has already reached,
Across a stormy sea and in a fragile ship,
The common port,[12] where we must give
An account of our every evil act or good deed.

The impassioned fantasy, which made
Art an idol and lord over me,
Was, I now realize, full of error,
Like all else that men desire against their will.

What will become of my amorous thoughts, once so vain and gay,
Now that I draw near to my double death?
Of one death I am certain, and the other threatens me.[13]

There is no painting nor sculpture now which quiets
The soul turned toward that divine love
Which on the cross opened to take us in Its arms.[14]

NOTES

·❦·

1. This is Michelangelo's most famous poetic work, probably addressed to Vittoria Colonna (1490–1547), a noblewoman and talented poetess. Like Michelangelo, Colonna employed Neoplatonic ideas and metaphors in her poetry. So popular was this poem among Michelangelo's contemporaries that Benedetto Varchi (1503–65) read a learned explication of it to the members of the Florentine Academy in 1546.

2. The opening quatrain of the sonnet provides us with a perfect expression of Michelangelo's definition of artistic creation: the "idea" of the artist is already potential in the uncarved block of marble; the skill of the artist only releases the form held captive in the "excess" marble that is removed to reveal the work of art inside.

3. The poet now compares Vittoria Colonna to the block of marble to be carved for the good she hides within her, but the artist fails to meet the challenge and only manages to extract death.

4. In the sonnet above, Michelangelo implicitly compares the sculptor to the male lover. Now reversing this concept, he makes the man who speaks in the poem the object of the lady's handicraft. She must extract from his rough outer shell the best of which she is capable. The woman Michelangelo refers to is probably Vittoria Colonna.

5. Seeing the body as a material shell with the soul as the purer essence of humanity was characteristic of Renaissance Neoplatonists, including Castiglione and Michelangelo.

6. This sonnet was inspired by Michelangelo's affection for Tommaso Cavalieri, an aristocratic young Roman. Whether Michelangelo's attraction to Cavalieri was completely platonic in nature is difficult to determine.

7. In these lines, among others, Michelangelo reveals his debt to the Petrarchan tradition of love poetry, which employed antitheses and paradoxes to define the nature and effects of human love.

8. Between 1519 and 1533, Michelangelo worked on the Medici Chapel (the so-called New Sacristy) in San Lorenzo Church in Florence. The chapel contains the tombs of important members of the Medici family. One of the statues is of Giuliano de' Medici, Duke of Nemours, who had just died in 1516 and to whom Machiavelli had originally dedicated The Prince. Facing Giuliano is another similar statue of Lorenzo de' Medici, Duke of Urbino, who had died in 1519 and

to whom Machiavelli changed his final dedication. Below the statue of Giuliano, reclining on a tomb, are the famous statues *Night* and *Day*. Michelangelo was already working in Rome when the completed statues were finally installed in the Florentine chapel. A young Florentine, Giovanni di Carlo Strozzi (1517–70), was so struck by the emotional power of *Night* that he composed this epigram.

9. Michelangelo's reply was probably written around 1545, some years after the Medici family had crushed the republic for which Michelangelo had struggled between 1527 and 1530. While he often worked for the Medici family and owed the family a great debt for support during his beginning years as an apprentice in Florence, he himself favored a republican form of government for his native city and even designed the fortifications for the republican defenses which yielded to superior forces in 1530. Michelangelo was eventually forgiven by the Medici rulers of Florence for his republican misdeeds, but in spite of this, when Michelangelo had the opportunity, he left Florence for Rome and never returned again during his lifetime.

10. Here, Michelangelo assumes the voice of the statue, *Night*, and in four brief lines expresses the torment and shame he feels over being a citizen in a town which has lost its liberty.

11. Michelangelo wrote this poem in 1554. Its note of Christian renunciation of the world's follies and faith in Christ's redemptive powers make it an interesting contrast to the more passionate lyrics of his earlier years.

12. Death is the "common port" of the human race, all of whom must travel the allegorical journey symbolized by a dangerous voyage across a tempestuous ocean.

13. The death of the body is certain, but Michelangelo also fears that of the soul, if condemned to eternal punishment.

14. The satisfactions of art pale in the face of death and the chance to obtain eternal salvation through Christ's sacrifice on the cross for the human race.

GIORGIO VASARI
1511–74

BORN IN AREZZO, A TOWN IN CENTRAL ITALY, VASARI WAS APPRENTICED TO Michelangelo in Florence and became an ardent follower and admirer of his master's style. His first version of a collection of artists' lives appeared in 1549–50; the second and enlarged edition was printed in 1558. Vasari was an excellent artist and architect in his own right, enjoying the patronage of the Medici Grand Dukes of Tuscany. He was named architect of the Palazzo Vecchio, where he painted a number of important frescoes; he started the construction of the building now known as the Uffizi Museum; and he founded the Academy of Design in 1563. Most of his work, including Michelangelo's tomb in the Cathedral of Santa Croce in Florence, reflects the Florentine Mannerist style of his times.

Vasari's collection of artists' biographies constitutes his most lasting contribution to Renaissance culture. It ranges from Cimabue to his own day, includes most of the artists we continue to remember, and contains a wide range of fascinating stories, anecdotes, and artistic judgments. To Vasari we owe the general view of Renaissance painting still held today— the view of a progressive development from the early infancy of art (the late thirteenth and fourteenth centuries, represented by Cimabue and Giotto) to a period of youthful vigor (the fifteenth century of Donatello, Brunelleschi, Ghiberti, and Masaccio), followed by the mature period of perfection, dominated by Leonardo, Raphael, and, most of all, Vasari's teacher, Michelangelo. The grand design of the work—the progress of the arts leading inexorably from the revolutionary new discoveries of Giotto through the rise of perspective to the perfection of Michelangelo— constituted a perspective upon Italian Renaissance art that has not lost its appeal after four centuries. Perhaps more than any other writer, Vasari, who lived in the twilight age of that period, was supremely aware that a renaissance had occurred in Italy. In fact, his work popularized the concept of artistic rebirth, and when the term "Renaissance" was eventually adopted by modern scholars as a label for the centuries Vasari studied, this choice was, in large measure, a tribute to Vasari's enduring influence.

BIBLIOGRAPHY

Giorgio Vasari, *The Lives of the Most Famous Artists*, trans. A. B. Hinds, 4 vols. (London: Dent, 1927; rev. ed., 1963), and *Vasari on Technique*, trans. G. B. Brown (London: Dent, 1907); Anthony Blunt, *Artistic Theory in Italy 1450–1600* (New York: Oxford University Press, 1940); T.S.R. Boase, *Giorgio Vasari: The Man and the Book* (Princeton: Princeton University Press, 1978).

SELECTIONS FROM
LIVES OF THE MOST FAMOUS ARTISTS

— · ❦ · —

Preface to Part One

I realize it is a commonly accepted opinion among most writers that sculpture, as well as painting, was first discovered from Nature by the peoples of Egypt; and that others attribute to the Chaldeans the first rough carvings in marble and the first reliefs in statuary; and still others assign to the Greeks the invention of the brush and the use of colors. But I believe that design, which is the basis of both arts, or rather the very soul which conceives and nourishes within itself all the aspects of the intellect, existed in absolute perfection at the origin of all other things when Almighty God, having created the great body of the world and having decorated the heavens with its brightest lights, descended with His intellect further down into the clarity of the atmosphere and the solidity of the earth, and by shaping man, discovered in this pleasing invention of things the first form of sculpture and painting. For who will deny that from man, as from a true model, statues and sculptures were carved out along with the difficulties of various poses and their surroundings or that from the first paintings, whatever they might have been, came the ideas of grace, unity, and the discordant harmonies which are produced by lights and shadows? Thus, the first model from which issued the first image of man was a mass of earth; and not without reason, for the Divine Architect of time and Nature, being all perfect, wished to demonstrate in the imperfection of His materials the means to subtract or add to them, just as good sculptors and painters are accustomed to do when by adding or subtracting from their models, they bring their imperfect drafts to the state of refinement and perfection they seek. . . .

I am convinced that anyone who will discreetly ponder this question will agree with me, as I have said above, that the origin of these arts was Nature itself, that the inspiration or model was the beautiful fabric of the world, and that the master who taught us was that divine intelligence infused in us by a special act of grace which has made us superior not only to other animals but even similar, if I may be permitted to say so, to God Himself. And if in our own times (as I hope to demonstrate further on with numerous examples), simple children, crudely brought up in the wilderness, have begun to draw by themselves, using as their models only those beautiful pictures and sculptures from Nature, is it not much more probable and believable that the first men—being much less far away from the moment of their divine creation, more perfect, and of greater intellect, taking Nature as their guide, with the purest of intellects as their master, and the world as their beautiful model—originated these most noble arts, and improving them little by little finally brought them from such humble beginnings to perfection? . . .

But since Fortune, when she has carried men to the top of her wheel, either for amusement or out of regret for what she has done, usually returns them to the bottom, it came to pass after these developments that almost all of the barbarian nations in various parts of the world rose up against the Romans, and, as a result, in a brief time not only did they bring down so great an empire but they ruined everything, especially in Rome itself. With Rome's fall the most excellent craftsmen, sculptors, painters, and architects were likewise destroyed, leaving their crafts and their very persons buried and submerged under the miserable ruins and the disasters that befell that most illustrious city. Painting and sculpture were the first to go to ruin, since they are arts that serve to delight us more than anything else; and the other one, that is architecture, since it was necessary and useful to the welfare of the body, continued, but now without its former perfection and goodness. Had it not been for the fact that painting and sculpture represented before the eyes of the newly born those men who had in that way been immortalized, the very memory of one or the other of these arts would soon have been erased. Some men were commemorated by images and by inscriptions placed upon private or public buildings, such as amphitheaters, theaters, baths, aqueducts, temples, obelisks, coliseums, pyramids, arches, reservoirs, and treasuries, and finally upon tombs themselves, but the majority of these were destroyed by savage barbarians, who had nothing human about them save their appearance and their name. . . .

But what was the most infinitely harmful and damaging to the above-mentioned professions, even more so than the things noted earlier, was the fervent zeal of the new Christian religion, which, after a lengthy and bloody struggle, had finally beaten down and annihilated the ancient religion of the pagans by means of a multiplicity of miracles and the sincerity of its actions. Then with great fervor and diligence it strove to remove and completely to destroy on every side the slightest little thing from which sin might arise; and not only did it destroy or pull to the ground all the marvelous statues, sculptures, paintings, mosaics, and ornaments of the false pagan gods, but it also did away with the memorials and the testimonials to an infinite number of illustrious persons, in honor of whom statues and other memorials had been constructed in public places by the genius of antiquity. Besides this, in order to build churches for Christian worship, not only did the Christians destroy the most honored temples of the pagan idols, but, in order to ennoble and adorn St. Peter's[1] with more ornaments than it originally possessed, they plundered the columns of stone on the Tomb of Hadrian, now called the Castel Sant'Angelo, as well as many other monuments which we today see in ruins. And although the Christian religion did not do such things out of any hatred for genius but only to condemn and cast down the gods of the pagans, the complete destruction of these honorable professions, which entirely lost their ways of doing things, was nevertheless the result of this ardent zeal. . . .

Up to now, I have discussed the beginnings of sculpture and painting, perhaps at greater length than was necessary at this point; I have done so not because I was carried away by my love for the arts but rather because I was moved by the desire to be of some good use to our own artists. By showing them how the arts had reached the summit of perfection after such humble beginnings, and how they had fallen into complete ruin from such a noble height (and consequently how the nature of these arts resembles that of the others, which like our human bodies are born, grow up, become old, and die), they will now more easily be able to recognize the progress of art's rebirth[2] and the state of perfection to which it has again ascended in our own times. . . .

* * *

[In the first book of his *Lives*, Vasari offers biographical sketches, descriptions of various works, and aesthetic judgments on some thirty-four painters, sculptors, and architects who lived and worked in Italy between the mid-thirteenth century and the first decades of the fifteenth century. These include Cimabue, Giotto, Simone Martini, Orcagna, Niccola and Giovanni Pisano, and Duccio. Towering over them all in importance, however, is the figure of Giotto (1266–1337), who Vasari believes was almost personally responsible for the rebirth of painting. About Giotto, Vasari says: "That same debt which painters owe to Nature, which continuously serves as a model to those who, selecting its best and most beautiful parts in order to reproduce and imitate them, strive always to do their best, is also owed, in my opinion, to Giotto, the Florentine painter: for when the methods and outlines of good painting had been buried for so many years by the destruction of wars, he alone, although born among inept artists, through God's grace, revived what had fallen into an evil state and brought it back to such a form that it could be called good. And it was certainly an extraordinary miracle that in such a gross and incompetent age, Giotto could have been inspired to work with such skill so that design, of which men during those times had little or no knowledge, was through his efforts completely brought back to life."]

———————————— · ❦ · ————————————

Preface to Part Two

. . . At the beginning of these *Lives,* I spoke of the nobility and the antiquity of these arts insofar as it was necessary to do so at that time, leaving aside many things which I might have cited from Pliny and many other ancient writers, had I not desired (perhaps against the opinion of many) to leave each reader free to observe for himself the fantasies of others at their proper source. It seems to me it is now time to do what was not proper for me to do then, if I wished to avoid tediousness and excessive length—mortal enemies of close attention—that is, to reveal more carefully my purpose and my intention and to demonstrate my purpose in dividing this body of lives into three sections.

It is certainly true that although greatness in the arts is born in some artists through hard work, in others through study, in others through imitation, and in still others through a knowledge of the sciences which all assist these arts, there are some artists who possess either most or all of the above mentioned qualities. . . . I shall discuss this matter in a general way, considering instead the quality of the times when the persons grouped and divided by me—in order to avoid examining the matter in too great detail—into three periods—or ages, if you wish— from the rebirth of these arts down to the century in which we are living, according to the obvious differences between them. Consequently, in the first and most ancient period, the three arts are seen to be very far from their state of perfection; and although they possess some good qualities, they are accompanied by such imperfections that they certainly do not deserve lavish praise. But since they provided a point of departure and paved the way for the style of the better art which followed afterwards, if nothing else, it is impossible not to speak well of them and to attribute to them a bit of glory which, if they are to be judged according to the perfect rules of art, the works themselves have not deserved. In the second period there is a clear improvement in invention and execution, with a better design and style and more careful completion; and so artists cleaned off the rust from the old style, along with the stiffness and lack of proportion typical of the coarseness of that time which had brought it on. But who would dare to say that in this second period there existed a single artist perfect in everything and who had brought things up to the standards of today in invention, design, and coloring? And who has observed in their works the soft shading away of figures with the darkness of coloring, the light being left to shine only on the parts in relief, and likewise who has observed in their works the perforations and certain exceptional finishes on the marble statues which are produced today? This kind of praise clearly belongs to the third period, and I may safely declare that its art has achieved everything which could possibly be permitted to an imitator of Nature, and that it has risen so high that there is no more reason to fear its decline than to expect further improvements. Considering these matters carefully in my own mind, I consider this to be a property and a peculiarity of these arts that from humble beginnings they finally reach perfection. . . .

Now that we have, in a manner of speaking, taken these three arts away from their nursemaid and they have survived their infancy, there follows the second period, during which everything is seen to improve enormously. Inventions are more elaborately filled with figures and are richer in ornamentation; and design is more often firmly grounded and more natural and lifelike, and besides the finishing touches even in works executed with less expertise but more thoughtful diligence, the style is lighter, and the colors are more charming, and very little remains to bring all things to complete perfection, so that they imitate exactly the truth of Nature. For in the first place, by the study and diligence of the great master Filippo Brunelleschi,[3] architecture rediscovered the measurements and proportions of the ancients, as much in round columns as in square pilasters and the rough and smooth exterior corners; then it distinguished between the different architectural orders, and made obvious the difference between them; it required everything to be done according to rules, to follow them with greater orderliness, and to be partitioned by measurements; the power and the method of design grew, and bestowing upon these works a pleasing grace, the excellence of this art was made manifest. Architecture rediscovered the beauty and the variety of capitals and cornices in such a way that the plans of churches and other edifices were well conceived and the buildings themselves more ornate, magnificent, and most beautifully proportioned. This is evident in the stupendous structure of the dome of Santa Maria del Fiore in Florence, in the beauty and grace of its lantern, in the ornate, varied, and graceful church of Santo Spirito, in the no less beautiful edifice of San Lorenzo Church; and in the most extraordinary invention of the octagonal church of the Angioli, the airy church and convent of the Badia at Fiesole, and the magnificent and grandiose beginnings of the Pitti Palace. . . .

I would say the same about painting and sculpture as well, where we still may see today some most exceptional works by the masters of this second period, such as the works of Masaccio in the Carmine,[4] who painted a naked man shivering from the cold and other lively and spirited works, but as a general rule, such artists did not reach the perfection of the third period, which we shall discuss at the proper moment, since we must now speak of artists of the second period, first of all the sculptors. These men departed a great distance from the style of the first period, and they improved upon it so greatly that they left little for the third age to accomplish. And their style contained so much more grace, so much more life, so much more order, design, and proportion that their statues soon began to seem as if they were living beings and not mere statues like those of the first period. . . .

And painting made the same improvement in these times as sculpture, and here the most excellent Masaccio freed himself completely from the style of Giotto and invented a new manner for his heads, draperies, buildings, nudes, colorings, and foreshortenings, and he gave birth to that modern style which was from those times to our own day followed by all our artists and which has been enriched and embellished from time to time with more gracefulness, invention, and decoration. This will be seen in detail in the lives of the artists, where we shall recognize a new style of coloring, foreshortening, and natural poses; a more highly expressive depiction of emotions and physical gestures combined with a continuous search to approach closer to the truth of natural phenomenon in design; and facial expressions which completely imitate the men as they were known by the artists who created them. In this manner these artists sought to produce what they saw in Nature and no more; and in this manner their works came to be more highly regarded and better understood; and this gave them encouragement to set up rules for perspective and to make their foreshortenings exactly like natural reliefs, while proceeding to observe shadows, lights, shadings, and other difficult matters, and to compose their pictures with greater verisimilitude; and they attempted to make their landscapes more similar to reality, as well as trees, meadows, flowers, breezes, clouds, and other natural phenomena. They did this so well that it can be boldly declared that these arts were not only improved but were brought to the flower of their youth, giving promise of bearing that fruit which would come later and which in a short while would have attained its perfection.

* * *

[Part Two of Vasari's *Lives* offers biographical sketches of over sixty artists, including Paolo Uccello, Masaccio, Ghiberti, Donatello, Brunelleschi, Piero della Francesca, Botticelli, Mantegna, and Fra Angelico.]

----------------- · ❧ · -----------------

Preface to Part Three

Those most excellent masters we have described to this point in Part Two of these *Lives* truly made enormous improvements in the arts of architecture, painting, and sculpture, adding to the accomplishments of the first period rule, order, proportion, design, and style; and if they were not perfect in everything, they were at least so close to the truth that the artists in the third group, whom we shall discuss from here on, were able, with the help of their illumination, to rise up and to reach the highest perfection, the proof of which we have in the finest and most celebrated modern works. But to clarify the quality of the improvements that these artists made, it will not be out of place to explain in a few words the five qualities I named above and to treat succinctly the origins of that true goodness which, after surpassing the ancient world, has made the modern age so glorious.

Rule, then, in architecture is the means of measuring the antique monuments, following the plans of ancient edifices in modern works. Order is the distinction between one kind of style and another, so that each body has the members appropriate to it and there is no confusion between Doric, Ionic, Corinthian, and Tuscan Orders. Proportion in architecture as well as sculpture is universally considered to be the making of bodies with erect, upright figures with properly arranged members; and the same is true in painting. Design is the imitation of the most beautiful things in Nature in all figures, whether sculpted or painted; and this quality depends upon a steady hand and skill which reproduces everything the eye sees with great accuracy and precision on the same plane or design or on a sheet of paper, a panel, or another flat surface; and the same is true for relief in sculpture. Then style comes to be the most beautiful when the artist makes it a habit to copy beautiful things and combines the most beautiful hands, heads, bodies, or legs together, and makes of all these beautiful qualities the most perfect figure possible, using it for all the figures in each of his works; and because of this it is said to be excellent.

Neither Giotto nor any of the artists of the first period did this, even though they had discovered the principles of all such artistic problems and had superficially resolved them, as in the case of design, which became truer than it had been before and more similar to Nature; thus the blending of colors and the composition of figures in narratives, and many other things, about which enough has already been said. But although the artists of the second period greatly improved the arts in the areas listed above, they nevertheless were not so thorough that they reached complete perfection, for they still lacked, within the boundaries of the rules, a freedom which—not being part of the rules—was nevertheless prescribed by them and which could coexist with order without causing confusion or spoiling it; and this required a copious invention in everything and a certain beauty down to the smallest detail which demonstrated all of this order with more decoration. In proportion, they lacked good judgment, which, without measuring the figures, bestows upon them a grace which goes beyond measurement. In design they did not reach the potential of its goal, for even when they made a rounded arm or a straight leg, there was no real understanding of the muscles and that charming and graceful facility which is partly seen and partially concealed in the flesh and in living things; and their figures were crude and stunted, which made them difficult to see and harsh in style. Moreover, they lacked a lightness in touch in making all their figures slender and graceful, especially those of women and children, which should have members as natural as those of men but with a plumpness and fleshiness that are not awkward like real bodies but created by design and judgment. They were also deficient in the abundance of beautiful costumes, the variety of imaginative details, the charm of their colors, the diversity of their dwellings, and the distance and variety in their landscapes. . . .

But their error was later clearly demonstrated by the works of Leonardo da Vinci, who introduced the third style, which we call modern; besides his bold and courageous design and his most subtle imitation of all the details of Nature, just exactly as they really are, his work possessed good rule, the best order, correct proportion, perfect design, and divine grace. Prolific in his work and profoundly knowledge-able in the arts, Leonardo may be said to have made his figures move and breathe. Somewhat later followed Giorgione of Castel Franco,[5] who shaded his pictures and gave everything in them an amazing sense of movement because of his use of depth of shadow, which he well understood. Fra Bartolommeo of San Marco[6] was by no means less skillful in giving to his own paintings a strength, relief, sweetness, and grace in color. But the most graceful of all was Raffaello of Urbino,[7] who studied the accomplishments of both the ancient and the modern masters, taking the best from them all; and after doing so, he enriched the art of painting with that complete perfection reflected by the ancient works of Apelles and Zeuxis. . . . But the man who wins the palm among both dead and living artists, who transcends and surpasses them all, is the divine Michelangelo Buonarroti, who holds first place not only in one art but in all three at once. This man surpasses and overcomes not only all those artists who have almost surpassed Nature but even these same most celebrated ancient artists, who beyond all doubt surpassed Nature in so praiseworthy a fashion; and he alone has triumphed over ancient artists, modern artists, and over Nature itself.

* * *

[The third part of the *Lives* treats another large group of artists, including Leonardo, Raphael, Correggio, Piero di Cosimo, Bramante, Andrea del Sarto, Giulio Romano, Domenico Beccafumi, Pontormo, Titian, and Vasari's own works. Interestingly, Cellini is only mentioned in the life of his archenemy Baccio Bandinelli and in the life of Michelangelo. The entire last section of the collection is dominated both in length and in importance by the towering figure of Michelangelo.]

NOTES

·❦·

1. Vasari should have referred not to St. Peter's but to St. Paul's Outside the Walls, a major basilica in Rome.

2. Here Vasari presents his influential thesis on artistic "rebirth," the concept which has provided the period name for the epoch we remember as the Renaissance.

3. Florentine sculptor and architect (1377–1446), most famous for the design of the dome of Santa Maria del Fiore (the cathedral of Florence), the Pazzi Chapel at Florence's Santa Croce Church, and a number of important churches in the same city (Santo Spirito, San Lorenzo). His architectural style can be said to reflect both the principles of Italian humanism and a new awareness of the styles from classical antiquity.

4. The painter Masaccio (1401–c.28) completed the famous Brancacci Chapel in the church of Santa Maria del Carmine in Florence, which became a model for all subsequent painters, just as Giotto's frescoes were imitated by artists of that earlier generation.

5. A Venetian painter (c. 1476–1510), perhaps most famous for the painting called *The Tempest*, now in the Accademia Museum of Venice.

6. Florentine painter (1472–1517).

7. Raphael, painter and architect from Urbino (1483–1520), best known for his decoration of the papal apartments at the Vatican (*The School of Athens, The Disputation*, and others), as well as his numerous portraits, altarpieces, and paintings.

THE ITALIAN RENAISSANCE:
FURTHER READINGS

· ❧ ·

The critical literature on all aspects of the Italian Renaissance is vast. The most important book ever written on the subject, even after a century of critiques, still remains Jacob Burckhardt's classic *The Civilization of the Renaissance in Italy*, 2 vols. (New York: Harper, 1975). Other general books which are most useful include Agnes Heller, *Renaissance Man* (London: Routledge and Kegan Paul, 1978); E. F. Jacob, ed., *Italian Renaissance Studies* (London: Faber, 1960); Lauro Martines, *Power and Imagination: City-States in Renaissance Italy* (New York: Vintage, 1980); Eugenio Garin, *Science and Civil Life in the Italian Renaissance* (New York: Doubleday, 1969) and *Portraits from the Quattrocento* (New York: Harper, 1972); Robert S. Lopez, *The Three Ages of the Italian Renaissance* (Boston: Little, Brown, 1970); Joseph A. Mazzeo, *Renaissance and Revolution* (New York: Pantheon, 1967); and Peter Burke, *Tradition and Innovation in Renaissance Italy: A Sociological Approach* (London: Fontana, 1972).

The standard introduction to Italian Renaissance art is Frederick Hartt's *History of Renaissance Art: Painting, Sculpture, Architecture* (New York: Abrams, 1969). Also very useful as a guide to the period are James Hall's *A History of Ideas and Images in Italian Art* (New York: Harper, 1983), and Adelheid M. Gealt's *Looking at Art: A Visitor's Guide to Museum Collections* (New York: Bowker, 1983). For discussions of the techniques and materials of Renaissance art, see Bruce Cole's *The Renaissance Artist at Work* (New York: Harper, 1984). The integral link between Renaissance art and Renaissance society is perceptively analyzed by Bruce Cole's *Italian Art 1250–1550: The Relation of Renaissance Art to Life and Society* (New York: Harper, 1987). Paul Barolsky's *Infinite Jest: Wit and Humor in Italian Renaissance Art* (Columbia, Mo.: University of Missouri Press, 1978) contains an excellent discussion of the comic vein in both art and literature.

Collections of writings by the Italian humanists may be found in Benjamin G. Kohl and Ronald G. Witt, eds., *The Earthy Republic: Italian Humanists on Government and Society* (Philadelphia: University of Penn-

sylvania Press, 1978) and in Renée Neu Watkins, ed., *Humanism &*
Liberty: Writings on Freedom from Fifteenth-Century Florence (Columbia:
University of South Carolina Press, 1978). Documents pertaining to
Italian Renaissance art are collected in Creighton E. Gilbert, ed., *Italian*
Art 1400–1500 (Englewood Cliffs, N.J.: Prentice-Hall, 1980). Interesting
information about all aspects of social life in the Renaissance may be
found in Robert J. Clements and Lorna Levant, eds., *Renaissance Letters*
(New York: New York University Press, 1976); David Herlihy and
Christiane Klapisch-Zuber, *Tuscans and Their Families: A Study of the*
Florentine Catasto of 1427 (New Haven: Yale University Press, 1985);
Gene Brucker, ed., *The Society of Renaissance Florence: A Documentary*
Study (New York: Harper, 1971), *Giovanni and Lusanna: Love and Mar-*
riage in Renaissance Florence (Berkeley: University of California Press,
1986), and *Two Memoirs of Renaissance Florence: The Diaries of Buonaccorso*
Pitti & Gregorio Dati (New York: Harper, 1967). War in Renaissance
society is studied by J. R. Hale, *War and Society in Renaissance Europe,*
1450–1620 (Baltimore: Johns Hopkins University Press, 1985).

Florence dominates the critical literature on the Italian Renais-
sance. For specific studies of this city and its contribution to Renaissance
culture, see Gene Brucker, *Renaissance Florence* (Berkeley: University of
California Press, 1983); Nicolai Rubinstein, ed., *Florentine Studies: Poli-*
tics and Society in Renaissance Florence (Evanston: Northwestern Univer-
sity Press, 1968); Richard Goldthwaite, *Private Wealth in Renaissance*
Florence: A Study of Four Families (Princeton: Princeton University Press,
1968), and *The Building of Renaissance Florence: An Economic and Social*
History (Baltimore: Johns Hopkins University Press, 1980); and J. R.
Hale, *Florence and the Medici: The Pattern of Control* (New York: Thames
and Hudson, 1978).

For an introduction to other centers of culture during the Renais-
sance (Rome, Venice, Ferrara), see Peter Partner, *Renaissance Rome*
1500–1559: A Portrait of a Society (Berkeley: University of California
Press, 1976); Charles L. Stinger, *The Renaissance in Rome* (Bloomington:
Indiana University Press, 1985); Frederic L. Lane, *Venice: A Maritime*
Republic (Baltimore: Johns Hopkins University Press, 1973) J. R. Hale,
ed., *Renaissance Venice* (London: Faber and Faber, 1974); and Werner L.
Gundersheimer, *Ferrara: The Style of a Renaissance Despotism* (Princeton:
Princeton University Press, 1973).

For the history of Italian literature, see Ernest H. Wilkins, *A History*
of Italian Literature, 2nd ed. (Cambridge: Harvard University Press, 1974);
and Peter Bondanella and Julia Conaway Bondanella, eds., *The Macmil-*
lan Dictionary of Italian Literature (London: Macmillan, 1979). or *Dictio-*

nary of Italian Literature (Westport, Conn.: Greenwood Press, 1979). Two useful reference encyclopedias to the entire Italian Renaissance may be consulted for information on all fields: Catherine Avery, ed., *The New Century Italian Renaissance Encyclopedia* (New York: Appleton-Century-Crofts, 1972); and J. R. Hale, ed., *A Concise Encyclopedia of the Italian Renaissance* (New York: Oxford University Press, 1981).